It was as if Cridhe called her, promised the magic in her strings if Christy would learn it. Mairi had never chided Christy for touching the harp, had only insisted that Christy's fingers be absolutely clean. But while Mairi, bit by bit, taught Christy how to tune the harp and play it, Christy was painfully sure that this legacy, Fearchar's songs and Mairi's, others that went back to the misted glory of Norse and Celtic kings and heroes of Ireland, should have belonged to Mairi's dead daughter. Christy adored the harp that had sung for a thousand years, outwearing many lives and many strings, but she had been filled with joy when the captain brought her the small harp.

It was hers, truly hers. She could play it without feeling like — like a changeling, stealing the rights of the true heiress. When Mairi looked at her in a certain way, a tight knot twisted in Christy's depths.

She's wondering why David fell and I didn't, Christy thought. She's never forgiven me because I lived when her baby died.

Jeanne Williams has written more than fifty novels including *The Island Harp*, which also features Mairi MacDonald. She lives in Portal, Arizona.

BY THE SAME AUTHOR

The Longest Road
The Island Harp
Home Mountain
No Roof but Heaven
Lady of No Man's Land
Texas Pride
So Many Kingdoms
The Heaven Sword
The Cave Dreamers
Mating of Hawks
Harvest of Fury
The Valiant Women
Daughter of the Sword
Bride of Thunder
A Woman Clothed in Sun
A Lady Bought with Rifles

DAUGHTER

of the

STORM

Jeanne Williams

KNIGHT

First published in Great Britain
by Chapmans in 1994
Published in 1996
by Orion Books Ltd,
Orion House, 5 Upper St Martin's Lane,
London WC2H 9EA

A CIP catalogue record for this book
is available from the British Library.

ISBN 1 84429 079 4

Printed and bound in Great Britain

This edition published 2004 by Knight,
an imprint of The Caxton Publishing Group

This one's for Judy Alter,
a true MacBean and true friend

PROLOGUE

Truncheons ready, the constables formed two lines down the single street of the village. Benches, chairs, chests, cooking pots, huddles of bedding and garments were piled outside several houses. Small children wailed and hid in their mothers' skirts. A dazed old woman wandered among the houses as if searching for something she had lost.

Officers tossed furnishings from a door, including a web cut from a loom. Others pried at the roofing with pickaxes. A woman ran out, clutching a baby. She screamed, "They are murdering my children!"

In spite of being heavy with the child she would bear in two months, Mairi ran down the slope. "I have a letter from the laird," she cried but no one heard her in the uproar.

Scores of women and a few men and boys ran up from the shore, arms heaped with pointed rocks. They let these fly at the men tearing down the roof who ducked and retreated behind the constables.

More villagers scooped up rocks from a streambed and hurled them at the evicters. Most fell short of the police. Mairi, gasping, plunged between them and the women.

"Stop!" she cried. "Stop! I have word from Lord Mac-Donald—"

Her shout was lost in the howling of the crowd and an order from MacBean, the superintendent of police. The constables charged. A truncheon struck the side of her head. As she crumpled into fireshot darkness, a boot struck her side.

A long whistle pierced bloody mists that thickened, parted, and thickened again as Mairi tried to see. "Och, ochone!" came a woman's voice. "MacBean be calling off his hounds! Brave ones, the lot of them, clubbing women!"

Giant thumbs dug and ripped at Mairi's entrails. It was as if her baby, furious at the way she'd exposed it, wanted to punish her, hurt her as much as it could. Was she losing it? Oh Brigid and Mary, what would Iain do? He had made her vow, before he left to sell horses in America, that she would take great care of herself and this baby.

But she had the letter of Lord MacDonald for Patrick Cooper, his agent. She carried the laird's promise, little as it was, for the people of Sollas. As she heard the tread of the police moving back to the street, she raised herself against the restraining hands of several women, one of whom was smeared with blood from a gash on her forehead.

"Help—help me walk to Mr. Cooper," she panted. "Tell your friends that—that I've a letter here from Lord MacDonald." At the flare of hope in their faces, she shook her head. "I'm sorry. You must leave Sollas. But if you promise to go next year, the laird will let you stay the winter—" Savaged by pain, she bit her lips to keep from screaming.

"Och, lass, that you would do this for us!" said a yellow-haired woman whose face was still pretty in spite of its lines. "I'm Elizabeth MacRae. Here, I'll go with you to the commissioner. Then you must lie down and let us help you." She swept a commanding gaze at the other women. "Go tell everyone what the laird offers!"

" 'Tis not so wonderful," grimaced the one with the bloody head.

"Better than wandering the shores," retorted Elizabeth. "We'll have a hearth and roof, our 'taties, oats, and barley." She raised Mairi on one side and another woman helped on the other, getting her gently to her feet.

Mairi swayed, contracting with white-hot pain. "Lass," began Elizabeth. "You should come away—lay yourself down . . ."

With all her will, Mairi commanded her body, took one step forward, and then another, aided by the women. "Mr. Cooper!" called Elizabeth to a stocky young man with a florid face. "Here's a message for you from Lord MacDonald!"

He probably didn't understand Gaelic but he recognized the names. It didn't take much wisdom to see that the little group was not threatening. Drawing herself up against the rending pangs, Mairi held out the letter. "Sir," she said in careful English, "his lordship sends you this."

Cooper's lip curled. Mairi suspected that his flushed complexion came more from angry excitement than natural coloring. " 'Tis a poor time for reading."

"I have just come from the laird at his castle of Armadale on Skye. I can go again."

He gave her and her arisaid a curious glance. "I doubt you'll go anywhere till after your lying-in, my good woman," he said with brutal good humor, but he took the envelope, broke the wax seal, and scanned the words. "Mr. MacBean!" he called to the superintendent. "Hold your men in ranks. Here's word from his lordship that may help the parson talk sense into these people."

The news spread among the women battered by the police's charge, some bathing their bloodied heads in the burn, some, half-stunned, beginning to rise from sand and heather.

"Mairi of the Isles!" one woman cried. And like gathering echoes came the words from others. "Mairi! Mairi of the Isles!"

Cooper, flanked by MacBean, strode to the black-garbed minister who spoke earnestly with the people. A crofter nodded slowly, then another, then most of the folk.

The searing fingers inside Mairi clutched at her baby and

clenched into fists. Women almost carried her to a house. The white-haired eldest ordered water put on to boil, clean sheets spread under Mairi, and sent for the same remedies Gran would have used, nettle, centaury, bramble leaf, tormentil, and lavender.

Gentle hands unpinned Mairi's arisaid and helped her off with her clothing, bathed her thighs and perspiring face. She fought back a shriek as the giant hands crushed and wrenched her.

"Scream, lass," urged the old woman. "We already know you're brave. Here, take my hands. Don't fight the pain, breathe with it if you can."

Mairi tried but she couldn't breathe except in short gasping pants. It was as if the babe, rudely jarred from its peaceful life within, tried now to rip loose its roots. Mairi screamed till her throat was raw. There was no relief in it.

Elizabeth gave her a whittled stick to bite on. "Och, ochone, lassie, push hard! There, rest. Now—*now!*"

Drenched in cold sweat, Mairi screamed at a rending, tearing peak of anguish that cleaved her body. The giant hand loosed its grip though the fingers still clawed within her. There was another contraction. She felt as if her bruised insides flowed out of her, but now she could breathe.

There was a flurry at the end of the bed, then hushed murmuring. "My bairn?" Mairi tried to raise herself.

Elizabeth MacRae pressed her back. "Don't fash yourself, love. You must rest—"

"My baby!"

The old woman smoothed her hair. "Och, child, 'tis a bitter thing. Your wee lass is already playing with the angels."

"Let me have her!"

Within a few heartbeats, a small swaddled form lay in Mairi's arms. Elizabeth folded back the towel from the little face with its flat eyelids and nose, the black damp curls, fine as silk. Perfect tiny fingers and nails, dark eyelashes, the miniature chin cleft like Iain's.

Iain's daughter. Mairi's heir to the harp and songs of the island. "She never breathed the air of this world," said the white-haired woman. "I cleaned out her nose and mouth, tried to blow life into her wee lungs, but God called her to his heaven."

The blood in Mairi's mouth was thick and salty. She started to say, *God had naught to do with it—I killed my bairn by faring on this journey*. But that would reproach these women, who had done all they could.

She caressed the fingers that would never strum the harp, kissed the mouth that would never sing, the closed eyes that would never gaze, delighted, on island or sea. Then she covered the infant's face. "I must take her home. We will make her a grave above the highest cliffs where the sea birds will sing to her and the sun shines longest."

"I'll wrap her with lavender and thyme." Elizabeth's eyes glistened with tears. "But you should rest a few days. Your folk can ill have the burying of you as well."

Mairi had a flash of wishing she *could* die—not have to face Iain or live haunted—but it was only a flash. There was wee David. And Gran and Tam and Clanna. Iain, if he could forgive her. They were young. Surely, surely, they would have other bairns.

But not this one. Never this little fragrant one. "I must go tomorrow." Mairi looked at the women around her. "Sorry I am that you must leave." Even above her own anguish, her heart cried, *It is not right! It should not be!*

Elizabeth smoothed her cheek and smiled shakily. "You won us our crops for our use. We'll have shelter for the winter instead of being set down freezing and penniless on some Canadian shore."

She laved Mairi's swollen, torn parts, thighs, and legs with lavender water and astringent tormentil and bathed Mairi's face and arms while her helpers took away the stained sheets and brought fresh ones.

"You did bravely, lass," said Elizabeth. "That is balm to our woes. It will strengthen us to endure whatever comes so that you will not have lost your babe for nothing. Now drink this primrose brew. It will let you sleep.''

She started to take the small bundle. Mairi tightened her arm around her daughter. ''Let me keep her by me.'' She drew the wee body to the breast it would never suckle.

When Mairi roused or tossed fitfully, the women gave her herbal brews or frothed milk to drink. Once, as she drifted into consciousness, she became aware of warmth against her, a small body snuggled close.

Her baby! Then the rest was a bad dream. *My bairn's alive! She's alive!* Quivering with joyful relief, Mairi turned back the covers.

The child was a year at least with pale brown hair and golden eyes, wide and wondering, that gazed into hers. Mairi recoiled. ''What's this?'' she asked Elizabeth. She felt the pitiful huddle of her own child at her back and could not keep the tremble of anger from her voice. If this was someone's notion of how to solace her—

'' 'Tis wee Christy,'' Elizabeth said apologetically. ''Last summer my Rob found her mother on the coast, out of her head with fever. The babe lived, as you see, but the poor lass . . .'' Elizabeth shook her head. ''She was not from Lochmaddy or this part of the island, but Gordon of Cluny is clearing his tenants from South Uist. We reckoned she came from there.''

The old woman had come to relieve Elizabeth. Her bony hand stroked the little girl's tangled hair. ''Poor lassie, we've passed her among us and kept breath in her body, but most families already have more bairns than they can feed.''

''Usually she bides with me,'' said Elizabeth. ''But when I flit next year—'' She flushed and met Mairi's eyes. ''I thought since you had lost your babe and all—''

When Mairi didn't soften, Elizabeth sighed and reached to take the child. ''I see I did wrong. Forgive me.''

At least they didn't flay my baby and wrap her skin on this one as we do with orphaned lambs. Mairi looked at the little girl, who stared back, neither smiling nor frowning. Those tawny eyes, in the shadowy gloom, caught all the light from the peats, shone like a wild creature's drawn by cold and hunger to a human hearth. A chill shot down Mairi's spine. Her scalp prickled.

She knew songs of changelings, of mortal babies stolen away and a fairy child left in their stead. To this day, women were uneasy for their bairns and never left them alone till they were baptized. Gran herself had seen the Fairy Washerwoman washing the bloody shirt of her son who was killed at Waterloo. It was weeks before they had the news, but Gran already knew. Mairi thrust such eeriness from her mind. Her wee daughter lay beside her, her life stolen not by some fairy but by what Mairi had felt her duty. She had placed the woes of strangers above the claim of her unborn child, her promise to her husband.

This other child, this Christy, had been fetched from the dying body of a homeless lass. The bairn was the fruit of the Clearances.

If she bides here, Mairi thought with pitiless lucidity, the folk will somehow carry her with them. But many die on the ships. What chance has a tiny creature with no mother, no one to whom she is more than a burden? And should she survive, it will be across the ocean.

Mairi could not shelter all the people of Sollas but she could take home the waif. She placed her arm over the girl, not embracing her, but fending off Elizabeth. "You did no wrong. I will take her with me."

The child shivered. She was clad in a scrap of plaid and a clout. Mairi brought her under her own shawl. She found it strange that she could warm the child with her body when her heart was so cold it seemed it must freeze her blood.

Book I

THE WAIF

I

Christy sighed contentedly and gave a little stretch as she snuggled against Gran's knee. Gran had worked the tangles out of Christy's hair so now it was soothing, like being caressed, to feel the gentle tug of the comb. Through drowsy eyes, she looked around the hearth room, so often crowded with neighbors, singing or telling stories as the women knitted or carded wool and the men twisted heather rope or mended nets, as Tam MacLeod was doing now. With his sea green eyes and pale hair, Tam looked like a kelpie or water horse in the handsome mortal guise that lured many a maiden to death beneath the waves. Tam, Gran's real grandchild, was much too kind for such tricks, of course, though he kept evading Molly MacAskill's hints that it was time they wed.

Ceilidhs, gathering for stories, songs, and riddles, passed many a long winter evening. Christy loved them and often played her own small harp, but it was delicious now and then for just the family to gather near the peat fire, especially when Mairi Mór, Tam's sister and also Gran's true grandchild, put aside her work to play Cridhe, the harp cherished by the family for countless generations.

A single glossy russet braid hung over Mairi's shoulder while truant wisps curled at ears and forehead. She rarely wore the fluted white cap that brides put on the day after their weddings and wore the rest of their lives. Dark lashes shadowing her gray-green eyes, Mairi seemed to listen to some inner music as she played the song of a mother searching for her baby who had been stolen away by the fairies.

Was Mairi thinking of the baby on the hill, the wee lost daughter who had never breathed the air of this world? Gran had explained that Mairi felt to blame for that death and that was why she was sometimes curt with Christy, whom she had brought home to Clanna along with the dead body of her child.

Christy didn't want to think about that, not now when she was blissful. She turned her gaze toward the two heads of wavy black hair bent over the chessboard, much alike except that the captain's had streaks of gray at the temples. Mairi's husband, Iain MacDonald, had resigned from the English queen's forces as a major, but since he had been a captain when Clanna folk first knew him, that was what they still called him. Chul, David's black-and-white border collie, slumbered with his muzzle on David's foot. David's face was losing its boyish roundness and taking on the lean, long angles of the captain's.

"Christy love," Gran scolded fondly. "When will you be patient enough to get the tangles out of your hair? You comb the top and leave a bramble bush underneath, which is a shame, for you have pretty hair, just the shade of fine ripe barley."

Mairi set Cridhe in the corner and draped a MacLeod plaid around her to keep out smoke and damp. "Why should Christy bother with tangles when she knows you will, Gran, ever so tenderly? I was combing my hair and Eileen's and Tam's, too, long before I was Christy's age." Mairi smiled but her tone had a slight edge.

"Eleven is no great age," Gran said. "When you were young, Mairi, it was all we could do to scrape a living. Christy is doubtless the last bairn whose hair I'll comb."

"Oh Gran—" Mairi began contritely.

Gran's blue eyes danced. Her snowy white cap with its carefully fluted ruffle framed her face, weathered by eighty years of island storms and sea winds. "Wheesht, after getting out the snarls I need a sip of whisky!"

"Any excuse will do, Rosanna." The captain grinned cheekily and pushed back from the chessboard. "I need comfort myself with my thirteen-year-old son checkmating me three games running. Tam, you'll have a sip?"

"Have I ever said no?" laughed Tam.

The captain, with just the slightest limp from an old wound, crossed to the dresser with its plate rack and poured a small glass of whisky for Gran. "Will you have wine?" he asked Mairi in the courteous but formal way he used with her.

"Thank you, no." Her tone was equally polite and cool. "I'll have a cup of tea. Christy, David, will you have tea or milk?"

They chose milk. Christy fetched it and Gran gave them each a raisin scone. Looking around at these people who had taken her in as an orphaned baby, Christy thought, I'm so lucky to be here, so lucky Mairi Mór brought me, even if she can't love me because I lived when her baby died. Gran loves me! And David—oh, how terrible it would be to live anywhere there was not David!

Tam went off to his bed in the passage leading to the captain's study, which also served as his bedroom and the village school. Mairi had the bedroom next to that and Gran and Christy had a box bed in the storeroom. David's box bed served as one wall of the hearth room.

Even though Mairi was the mistress of this house, it was Gran who smoored or banked the fire each night and blessed the home. Kneeling by the hearthstone that had come from her burned home in Aosda, Gran put the larger peats to one side for use next day. Then she raked the coals into a circle with a raised heap in the center.

"In the Name of the God of Life," Gran said as she set the edge of the first peat against the small mound. "In the Name of the God of Peace," she prayed over the second. The third peat finished dividing the embers in three equal parts. "In the Name of the

God of Grace.'' She covered the glowing bits with ash and raised her hand above them.

> "Thou Holy Three, Mary, Christ, and Brigid,
>   Save, shield, surround this hearth,
>   This house, this household, this night
>   And every night. Each single night. Amen."

"Amen," breathed Christy, along with Mairi, David, and the captain. Her heart swelled with thankfulness. Surely this was the best house and best hearth and best family in all the world. If one day Mairi Mór could be glad Christy shared them, there would be nothing left to wish for.

Silently, Christy prayed for this and followed Gran to bed.

The cattle fed on channeled wrack, a yellow-brown that grew on rocks along the high-water mark, and so did most of the sheep except for wilful little Cailan. That dainty four-horned throwback to the ancient Highland sheep frolicked along the cliff high above, sending shags and cormorants scolding from their ledges. David came in sight as Chul circled the errant sheep.

Christy wished David wouldn't get so near the edge though he was the nimblest and swiftest of all the children of Clanna—not that he cared to be considered a child since turning thirteen that March. He and Chul would soon have Cailan back with the other sheep. Christy bent to her task of gathering beard-of-the-rock for Gran's dyeing kettle.

An oyster catcher stalked along the muddy inlet on his pink legs and speared his bright orange bill down for a limpet or mussel. *Ghille-Brighde,* he was called, servant of Brigid. Gran said that for hiding the infant Jesus in seaweed to save him from Herod, the bird was granted a white cross to his back that showed when he spread his wings. Ringed plovers searched along the shore for smaller shellfish and crustaceans.

This east shore of the island of Lewis was a haven for birds but not for man. South of Stornoway, the island's only town, peat stretched almost to the cliffs that towered above the sea, and those who won a living here got more of it from the waters than from the stony, boggy land. Even the animals depended on seaweed now they had pastured on the stubble left from harvesting barley and oats.

There was an especially good patch of beard-of-the-rock if she could just clamber up to it. Christy's legs were growing fast but often they still weren't quite long enough to get her where she wanted to climb, places David scaled with ease. She found a foothold for her bare toes and gripped the huge rock. There was a cry. She looked up.

David was flying! For a heart-stopped second, that was how it looked, as if he had joined the eddying seabirds, as if his outspread arms might turn to wings and soar, lift him to the heights. The ledge that had given way beneath him crumbled into bits of rock and turf as it struck outcroppings on its plunge to the shore.

Then David fell. Fell so swiftly. Fell among the rocks. A scream clogged Christy's throat, would not come out. This couldn't be real! It must be a nightmare. But she couldn't wake up and so she ran toward him.

He lay still, still, like a crushed gull. He needed Mairi or Gran. Quickly! Even in her terror, Christy knew that. She hated to leave him alone but she had to get help. At least Chul was scrambling down a narrow defile and would soon be with David if he didn't fall, too.

Christy sped up the sand and rocks, leaped the stream, zigzagged through lazybeds and kaleyards, and pelted, gasping, into the largest house in the village.

"Davie!" she cried, bursting into the hearthroom. "Hurry! He—he's fallen from the cliff!"

Mairi Mór turned white, cried out, and ran. The wind whipped her long auburn braid to one side. The captain couldn't outrun her because of his old wound but he wasn't far behind. Gran caught up her skirts and came fast as she could. Christy skimmed past her foster parents.

Oh, Davie! Are you killed then? Oh, Davie, Davie—

Chul, whimpering, licked a motionless outstretched hand. Facedown, David lay utterly still. Blood trickled from a gash in his forehead. Christy dropped down beside him, whispering his name, beseeching him to be alive.

"Don't move him!" the captain warned as he panted up. He caught his wife's arm. "Wait! If his spine's hurt, we mustn't make it worse. Don't move him or let him move till I bring a door."

He would know. He'd seen plenty of wounded men. "He's breathing!" Christy said.

Mairi knelt by her son, calling his name. A contused bump was swelling on the right side of his skull but there seemed to be no bleeding. His legs weren't doubled beneath him and his arms didn't look broken.

"He—he flew like a bird," sobbed Christy, overcome. "Just for a minute, he flew! Then he fell—"

"Hush!" Mairi cried. "Run up to Sheila! You're in the way!"

Christy didn't go but shrank among the rocks where she could see David. The men were out fishing but the rest of the village streamed down to the shore, several of the women helping Iain bring the door from a winnowing space in a barn. Gran bent over David, running skilled fingers over his head, down his neck and back, arms and legs.

"No bones seem broken," she said. "But there's that great lump on his head and to fall so far—och, let's move him slow and careful. Mairi, hold his head still as you can so his back stays straight. Iain, lift him easy while I hold his legs. Katie, Sheila, push the door under him. Barbara, Rose, help Katie and Sheila carry him. Mairi, keep his head from moving. Captain, you and I and Christy will walk along and hold him steady."

Bless Gran! Even in a moment like this, she had a thought for Christy, not like Mairi Mór who wanted her out of her sight.

"David," Mairi pleaded as they made their way through the rocks. "Davie, can't you hear me?"

His eyelids never flickered. The breath fluttered in his chest like a captive bird. He made no sound at all. In the house, Gran examined him more carefully, moving his fingers, pressing the nails and nodding approvingly when they pinkened as the blood flowed quickly back. She felt along his ribs and abdomen, pressed the soft parts of his body. When she pressed the nails of his big toes, they stayed white.

"The blood is not running as it ought." Her eyes met the captain's. He was already whirling toward the door, moving past the sympathetic neighbors.

"I'll bring the doctor from Stornoway." The captain whistled for Chieftain. Christy heard him get his saddle and bridle from the barn. In a few minutes, hoofbeats drummed the turf.

It was fourteen long miles of bogs and moors to Stornoway. David was so pale. Only the rise and fall of his chest, a pulsing in his throat, showed that he lived.

"Can't we do *something*, Gran?" Christy entreated.

Mairi rounded on her. "Do get out from underfoot! If you—"

"Wheesht, Mairi," soothed Gran. "Sit here and hold your laddie's hand and talk to him."

"What good will that do?"

"Sometimes folk hear even when it seems they don't. You tell Davie we love him and his father's gone for the doctor. Just keep talking soft and strong. Christy, you know where my herbs are. Steep some plantain and groundsel and make a poultice to bring down the swelling of this great lump."

"I'll bring in your supper," said golden-haired Sheila Nicolson, who was wedded to Mairi's cousin. "Seana will milk your cows. What else can we do?"

"Bless you, nothing at the moment," Gran said. "Go home to your bairns. I'll send Christy if we need help."

"We'll pray," said Morag Nicolson, Sheila's dour mother-in-law and the most pious soul in the village. "But God's ways are beyond a mortal's ken and—"

"We will be glad of your prayers, Morag." Gran's tone indicated that they were not glad of her presence.

As soon as the women had gone, Gran went to the cupboard and got out the silver flask the captain had given her. He kept it filled with the best whisky, of which Gran was a connoisseur. As a young widow, she supported her family through distilling and she claimed there was nothing like a nip to oil up creaky old bones.

She whipped milk and a handful of oatmeal into a froth, added a dollop from the flask, and gave it to Mairi. "Drink up," Gran commanded when her granddaughter refused. Mairi could never be less than beautiful in Christy's eyes but her clear skin was white as David's and her gray-green eyes looked almost black with none of the light that usually shone in their depths.

Christy's heart swelled with pity for this woman she loved and feared and to whom she owed her life. Oh, if she could have fallen instead of David! Gladly she would throw down her life to give him safe footing. There was more to her grief than that even. If David died or was badly hurt, how could Mairi Mór keep from wishing that the ledge had crumbled beneath the cuckoo waif in place of her son?

For a cuckoo, a changeling in her tiny dead daughter's place, was how Mairi thought of Christy. Christy had always felt a queer, cold bruising inside when Mairi looked at her in a certain way, especially since the time several years ago when she'd overheard Mairi confess her feelings to Gran. Christy felt weak with guilt and worry but she ground the herbs in Gran's mortar and set them to steep in a little water at the edge of the peat fire.

"I doubt you'll sleep this night," said Gran, urging the cup on the younger woman. "You must keep up your strength for Davie's sake."

That reached Mairi. She sipped as she held David's limp hand and went on talking to him. Apparently she said whatever came into her thoughts. When the groundsel and plantain were a thickened mass, Christy spooned them onto a doubled snowy linen towel, folded it carefully as Gran had taught her, and placed it on the raised contusion, smoothing David's wavy black hair out of the way. Sometimes, Gran said, the brain swelled from such an injury. If it swelled a lot, it could be better if the skull had fractured, since that reduced the pressure.

"Thank you, Christy," Mairi said. "You're a good lass. I'm sorry I scolded you."

What Christy would give to hug her foster mother and comfort her! But she knew Mairi was only being fair. She was always that, when she'd had a chance to master her irritation. Christy, with Gran's help, believed that Mairi didn't want to resent her but simply could not help it.

If David, too, were laid to rest by the baby on the hill, Christy hoped she could follow him. Not only because she couldn't imagine life without him, but because she couldn't bear to be the one child left at Mairi's hearth with the true ones dead.

Yellow-haired Seana, at sixteen the oldest of Clanna's children, brought the milk into the *fasgalan* or entry space. She poured it into pans where cream would form and came in to stand beside David. Tears glinted in her hazel eyes as she bent to stroke Chul, who lay guarding the box bed.

"Och, Mairi . . ." The girl fumbled for consoling words. "Surely the doctor will set him right. Caitlyn and I will bring your broth and bannocks as soon as I scour out the milk pails." Caitlyn was her sister, a sweet flaxen-haired girl six months younger than David.

Black houses, so-called because they were stones laid up without mortar, were always scantily lit. Many had no windows, though every house of Clanna boasted at least one paned window and Mairi's house had three. When she, a crofter lass, had unbelievably married her captain and been off visiting his gentry kin in Inverness, the villagers had built this home for them in the style of the old chieftains' houses, with space for guests and storage and a room of his own for Iain.

With what high hopes the newlyweds must have entered this very room, welcomed by friends and Mairi's family, though not by David, who had roundly told his father to go back to Afghanistan! Born while his father was fighting the queen's distant wars, David had been lovingly nurtured by the folk of Clanna and had neither known nor cared that his parents were not married. At two and a half, he'd had no use for the tall stranger who took his mother away for what had seemed a very long time.

Now, as the last dim light faded from the windows, Gran lit a rush lamp and set tea to brew. She pressed steaming cups on Mairi and Christy and had one herself. As they ate their supper, Mairi kept talking to David though he had not moved or given any sign of hearing. It was, Christy realized, as much for Mairi's sake as David's that Gran had persuaded her to speak to him.

"I expected a splotched, wrinkled little red tyke like most," Mairi told her son with a faint smile. "But when Gran put you in my arms, David, you were fair and smooth and perfect. You were christened at the Stones of Callanish, you know. Gran carried you as the sun moves three times around the great stone in the center. She gave you your name, since the parson would not. 'Twas not my fault, darling. To win your christening, I stood as the parson told me, bareheaded outside the church while everyone passed in—and, oh, how good it was when all the Clanna folk, even Morag, came to stand with me! But then the parson said I must burn Cridhe. She was your great-grandfather's, laddie. Fearchar— that means 'dear man'—Gran always called him so—caught fire and died going back into the house to save her when the constables burned our roofs at Aosda. You understand, don't you, that the harp was not mine to burn? Though later I thought she would blaze in the great fireplace of Stornoway Castle when I played Fearchar's song to all the lairds and ladies.

"Oh, Davie! If you could have seen your father march into the hall in his officer's coat and MacDonald plaid! He skirled his pipes in 'The MacLeod Salute' and there in front of the laird of Lewis, Sir James Matheson, and his friends, your father said he wanted to wed me! So Cridhe did not burn and Sir James came to our wedding.

"Do you remember why your father brought you Chul? When we came home from Inverness, we fetched you from Gran's and moved into this new house. There was a feast that night to welcome us and you had a grand time, but in the middle of the night, there you were tugging at my pillow and saying that you didn't like your bed and you heard a giant, a fearsome ugly *gruagach*.

"I lit a cruisie and we looked. Your father waked, none too pleased, but he helped hunt for the giant, too, in every cranny and nook and shadow. Never a giant nor ghostie could we find. Your father told you he'd shoot any bad things with his pistol. He tucked you in and expected that to be the end of it but you were used to sleeping in a room with Gran and Eileen and me and your Uncle Tom in his wall bed.

"Your father thought you badly spoiled but I sat up and told you stories till you went to sleep. When I came in next morning to light the fire, there was no laddie in your bed. Such a fright I had, but then I was sure you'd run to Gran's. Sure enough, there you were!

"I hoped to slip you into your bed before your father roused, but he had tea and porridge waiting for us. You gave him a little side glance and said, 'The gruagach wasn't scared of your pistol, Da. She showed her long sharp teeth—said pistol not have powder and balls!'

"Your father said next time you must come to us—that the

three of us could handle any monster. He rode to the Lodge that day and brought you home your puppy. You knew Cuchulain's story. You said your dog would be a hero, too, and so you called him Chul."

The aging border collie whined softly at his name. Mairi scratched behind his ears and went on reflectively. "That was before Red Donald Munro became Sir James's factor and made his passel of burdensome rules and regulations. It never occurred to your father that crofters can be forbidden to keep dogs. Even when it is allowed, gamekeepers and sheep masters may kill dogs that run deer or sheep out of a crofter's fields. Ewan Fraser was gamekeeper then, a good man who wouldn't shoot a dog without warning, but he's gone to America and I hear the new gamekeeper, Dugald Craigie, is mean as Mr. Munro. It's lucky for us that your father's Uncle Roderick is a crony of Sir James's. They both made their fortunes as traders in China.

"Sir Roderick, Davie, came to see you while you were in your cradle. Your father, his heir, was believed killed in Afghanistan. Your great-uncle wanted to take you home to raise. Be sure I sent him off with a flea in his ear! He's married since and sired his own heirs, so he bothers us no more. His wife, Beatrice, is my age, and very kind she was while we were in Inverness.

"So Chul kept giants and all such scarrity things out of your box bed, Davie. We had peace at night, but a few days later, didn't Seana come calling us to see you perched on Chieftain, your father's big cavalry horse? There you were, bold as brass, legs curled behind you to fit the horse's back while all the children watched and wished they could be there, too. Rascallion! You'd climbed up the stone steps in the outer wall of the house that lead to the *tobhta*, or ledge where people sit in the sun or work on the thatch.

"Your father tried to act stern but I could see he was proud of you. He asked how you got on the horse and you grinned and said you climbed up to the ledge and offered Chieftain your bannock. You wanted to go for a gallop but your father set you on the

ledge—how you scowled at him, your eyes and his just that same
smoky gray-blue! So he told you that if you'd fallen under Chieftain's hoofs, you could have got him in trouble, and that Alai Gunn
and Seana might try to ride and get hurt.

"You promised not to go near the horse unless your father
was with you. Then he let you help him brush Chieftain, saddled
him, and took each of you children for a ride."

The captain's clock showed eleven. Every hour or so, Gran
examined David's head. "The swelling's going down," she said as
Christy changed the poultice. "He feels a mite fevered, though."

"Why doesn't Iain come with the doctor?" Mairi fretted.

No one said that the doctor might be a day's ride from Stornoway at Port of Ness, at Callanish on the west coast, or indeed
anywhere on the island.

"Mairi love," ventured Gran. "Would you just lie down for
a bit on the settle here?"

Wordlessly, Mairi shook her head. Gran sighed. She put
down her knitting, went into the fasgalan and returned with fresh
milk. Again, she frothed this with oatmeal and added whisky.
"We'll all have some," she decreed, and handed cups to the
others.

Mairi swallowed obediently and resumed her one-sided conversation with David. Christy had heard these stories before, but
she never tired of them. How after Aosda was burned, the captain
had taken the survivors to the Lodge, which he was leasing—how
Mairi's cradle-mate cousin, Catriona, had taken his offer to pay
passage to America for any who wanted to go. How Mairi found
the ruined *broch,* the ancient tower by the sea, and moved her kinfolk there, how the captain, before he rejoined his regiment,
helped roof the broch and prepare for the winter, known now in
Clanna as the legendary Winter of the Broch when Katie and Donald Gunn had been found dying in the snow with little Alai sheltered between them.

That same winter, Murdo MacKinnon with his son, Gavin,

and old Meggie Ross, staggered to the broch more dead than alive. Since then, bright-haired Gavin had been swept overboard in a storm and Meggie slumbered near the baby on the hill, but they'd had happy years at Clanna. That was how Clanna grew in sixteen years from eight MacLeods and Nicolsons to a thriving community of almost fifty souls—oh, it was a saga as grand to Christy as David's favorite Cuchulain tales!

Mairi found a good market in Stornoway for the women's weaving. They earned enough for Donald Gunn, a former ship-builder, to oversee the construction of *Brighde,* their first boat. What a difference that made! With a boat, the men brought in cod and ling to be dried and sold as well as plenty to supply the village. Next came the building of *The North Star,* designed to follow the profitable herring into the North Sea, and then a curing shed so the women could gut and salt the fish and Clanna could be independent of the avaricious curers of Stornoway who kept most fisher-men deep in debt.

In spite of three terrible years when the potatoes failed all over the Highlands and islands as well as in Ireland and Europe, the women knitted and wove and Clanna shared with starving villages. Mairi pledged her harp to James Matheson as surety for loans she persuaded him to make to various communities so they could build fishing boats and sheep to supply wool. The score of villages had all repaid their debts—a good thing! Red Donald Munro, who had managed Sir James's affairs these past six years, would never have allowed crofters grace on their rents.

For the first time, David stirred, throwing up his hand. "Chu-u-ul!"

That was the intonation of the dog's name that commanded him to go left after a sheep or cow. When the puppy had started herding chickens to Mairi or rounding up the cows from peaceful grazing, Malcolm Ferguson, once a shepherd, had taught small David, who was too young to whistle, how to control his dog through calling his name in various ways.

"Chu-lah!" In the chase of his fevered dream, David ordered the dog to stop.

Bewildered but in a frenzy of joy at hearing his master's voice, Chul rose on his hind legs, leaning forepaws on the bed to lick David's hand and try vainly to reach his cheek.

"Bad Calain!" David scolded. "Come down from there, you daftie!"

He was reliving the fateful moments before the cliff edge gave way beneath him. Mairi smoothed back the tangles of black hair. "It's all right, Davie. Yon silly little sheep is with the others though goodness knows I feel like skinning her."

He moved restlessly and winced, murmured something, and was still again. Chul whimpered. Mairi sat down, sighing, and grasped David's hand. Christy got more herbs and set them to steep.

It was midnight. Would the doctor never come?

II

Autumn nights were long but gray light showed at the windows when the captain fetched Doctor Miller. They had come through bogs and brambles from Breasclete on the west coast where the doctor had been called to a young woman who had been sent home ill from her employment on the mainland as a housemaid. She had typhoid, and the thin, weary-eyed doctor said he could only hope she would not infect her family and friends. Isolated as islanders were, they built up little immunity to contagions.

David was still unconscious. Doctor Miller examined him from head to foot and nodded approvingly at the way the poultice had reduced the swollen bruise. At last the doctor straightened.

"The lad has a concussion. We can hope it will have no lasting ill effects. I fear, though, that he has injured his spine. His legs and feet do not respond to stimulus."

Mairi went even whiter. The captain steadied her. "Is—is there anything you can do?" he asked huskily.

The doctor shook his head. "He's a strong, healthy child. In time, he may get back some function in his lower body. Of course you will encourage him to exercise as much as possible—"

"He's crippled?" Mairi whispered.

"To some extent, I'm afraid." The doctor met the captain's grim stare. "You may want to call in a doctor from the mainland, Major MacDonald. I won't be offended. Indeed, I would be more than happy if another physician could help your son."

"You must stay the night, sir," said the captain. "Tomorrow I'll ride back with you and catch the mail steamer. It's not that we lack confidence in you but I could not forgive myself if I did not do everything in my power to help our son walk again."

The doctor nodded. "I understand."

In a daze, Christy helped Mairi and Gran bring the men food and drink and slipped off to make up the captain's bed for the doctor. Crippled! Davie crippled! The fleetest runner of them all, the best at scaling cliffs, the foremost at shinty, that game played long ago by his favorite hero, Cuchulain.

Doctor Miller's a good man, she told herself. But he's only from Stornoway. Belike he doesn't know the latest cures. A doctor from Inverness or Edinburgh or even London—ah, they'll know some way to help. Passing the doctor in the passage, Christy went back to the hearth room.

"If you're riding soon, you must rest a while," Mairi told her husband. "I'll watch by David." When he started to protest, she said, "I cannot sleep anyway."

"Go to bed, laddie." Gran patted his cheek and gave him a gentle but determined push. "I'll stay with Mairi."

Gazing at Mairi, the captain hesitated. Then, for the first time that Christy could remember, he took Mairi in his arms. Her hands locked behind his neck, her face was buried against his chest. They stood that way a long time, as if the bodies that had created David strove to comfort each other.

"If the best doctor in Inverness can't help, I'll get the best from Edinburgh," the captain promised. "If any care or operation will heal Davie, he shall have it."

He kissed her forehead and went down the passage. For the first time, Christy pondered the fact that he and Mairi slept apart, he in his study. She had supposed it was because of his old injuries, but seeing him embrace Mairi shocked her into realizing that for people who had gone through so much to be married, they seemed to have little joy of it.

"You should go to bed, child," Gran told Christy.

Christy shook her head. "I want to stay with David." *Why didn't he wake up? Could a concussion make him sleep forever?* Her eyes felt scratchy and raw but she picked up her knitting.

After a time, Gran drowsed off in her wicker chair. Mairi's voice was frayed. Every now and then, she whispered David's name or crooned to him but mostly she sat there with her face bent to his hand.

The doctor and Iain slept till midmorning. Christy brewed tea for them and made bannocks and porridge. The doctor found no change in David and warned Mairi not to try to feed him until he was conscious. After the men rode off, Sheila and Seana came in, shaking their golden heads as Gran gave them the doleful news.

"Och, one of those fancy mainland doctors will fix Davie good as new," declared Seana.

Her mother quickly nodded. "To be sure he will! And now you must get some rest Mairi, love, and you, too, Gran and Christy."

Mairi refused but Gran caught her wrist and tugged. "Come, lass. You'll be no use to David when he rouses if you're so fagged you stumble over your own feet."

"We'll call you the second Davie wakes up," Sheila promised. She hugged Mairi and kissed her cheek. Gran urged Mairi down the passage through Iain's study to her bedroom.

"Oh Gran!" Christy heard Mairi sob. "If Davie can never run again—Or even walk! Gran, I can't bear it!"

"You can and will." Gran's voice was stern. "Wheesht, the laddie has a fine brain and he has his hands. There's much a man can do in this world without the use of his legs."

"And more that he can't!"

"The captain and his uncle will do all they can for Davie, all money can buy."

"Money can't buy a new spine."

"No, and a good thing, too, or the rich would buy them out

of us poor folk and we'd crawl about like worms. Now go to sleep, m'eudail. You'll need your strength for your laddie.''

What they said next was so hushed that Christy couldn't hear. Entering the room where woolens and other supplies were stored and where she and Gran shared the boxbed that formed a wall of the passage, Christy prayed harder than she ever had in her life. She didn't think she could go to sleep, but she never knew when Gran joined her.

David lay unconscious for three days. Once he whimpered, ''Mama?'' but made no response when Mairi caught his hands and called his name. Chul could not be coaxed from his vigil at his master's feet, nor would he eat though he drank when Christy brought him a pan of water or milk. Now and then he whined and licked David's hand.

Christy and Gran sat with David when Mairi could be persuaded to rest. When Mairi wasn't in the room, Christy talked or sang to David or played the small harp the captain had brought her long ago from Inverness because Christy, for as long as she remembered, had been powerfully drawn to Mairi's treasured ancient harp.

It was as if Cridhe called her, promised the magic in her strings if Christy would learn it. Mairi had never chided Christy for touching the harp, had only insisted that Christy's fingers be absolutely clean. But while Mairi, bit by bit, taught Christy how to tune the harp and play it, Christy was painfully sure that this legacy, Fearchar's songs and Mairi's, others that went back to the misted glory of Norse and Celtic kings and heroes of Ireland, should have belonged to Mairi's dead daughter. Christy adored the harp that had sung for a thousand years, outwearing many lives and many strings, but she had been filled with joy when the captain brought her the small harp.

It was hers, truly hers. She could play it without feeling

like—like a changeling, stealing the rights of the true heiress. When Mairi looked at her in a certain way, a tight knot twisted in Christy's depths.

She's wondering why David fell and I didn't, Christy thought. She's never forgiven me because I lived when her baby died. I wish it had been me that fell. I wish I could give my spine to Davie.

On the fourth day, David grew restless, turning his head, fretting with his hands, though he still didn't open his eyes and his body from the hips down lay inert.

"Why don't you play Cridhe for him?" Gran asked Mairi. "It might help him rest sweeter."

Gran probably wanted Mairi to play for her own easing but she brought the harp closer to the bed and tuned it. She played "My Little Fragrant One" and the old lullabies. At first, her deep, sweet voice trembled and sometimes broke, but after several songs, David seemed to relax.

His eyelids fluttered, then stayed open. He raised up on one arm and cast a startled glance at Gran and Christy before his gaze reached his mother. "Mama! Why—why can't I move my legs?"

Even in the dim glow from the peats, his eyes shone the blue of a summer twilight. Air filled Christy's lungs in a rush of thankfulness. He had his wits! He was awake! Those were grand things by themselves.

Mairi embraced her son in relieved joy, careful not to jostle his lower parts. "You fell, laddie, and hurt yourself. But you'll get better now."

"My legs—"

"Wheesht, darling, your father's gone to fetch the best doctor from the mainland. He may know how to set you right."

David's mouth quivered. "Can he fix my legs? I can't make my toes move, Mama. I can't make my feet do anything!"

How Mairi must have longed to promise the boy and herself that all would be well! Christy ached for them both and marveled the way that Mairi kept her tone steady and reassuring. "The doctor will do all he can, darling. So will we. So must you."

"I want to walk! I want to run!"

"Of course you do! Your father and I and Gran want you to more than anything." Mairi's eyes brimmed and it was a moment before she could go on briskly. "You have to get strong again. I'll warm you some broth."

Chul had leaped up on the bed, whimpering ecstatically at his master's being awake again. "Oh, Chul!" David sobbed. He hugged his faithful companion and buried his face against the dog's neck. Christy, blind with tears, knew that from then on, David would tell Chul many things he would never tell anyone else, not even her.

The grand doctors could not help David: not the gruff, kindly one from Inverness; the jolly red-faced one from Edinburgh, or the lank specialist from London. They prodded, manipulated, questioned, and in the end, shook their heads.

A wild hope stirred in Christy. The surgeon from London had performed some miraculous operations. She caught him alone for a moment and swallowed hard, summoning her courage. "Sir—is there any way you could give David the bottom part of my spine?"

His long jaw dropped. "Are you mad, child? Of course not!"

"But—"

He shook his head. "Such butchery would kill you and cannot help him. The spine is delicate and attached to many nerves. There's no way to replace it." More kindly, he added, "After such a fall, your brother's fortunate to be alive. He'll soon learn to get around on crutches."

Small crutches now, then bigger ones, all the way to his man's growth. An endless line of crutches loomed in Christy's mind. That his spine could not be mended by any amount of will, love, work or money, overwhelmed her.

It must have been even worse for Mairi. The captain had seen soldiers without arms or legs. To him a crutch must be a useful device that allowed a crippled person to get around. It was that, of course. God be thanked for anything that helped. Gran had seen so much woe that she braced herself to bear this, too, and hearten Mairi as much as she could.

Donald Gunn carved a pair of crutches from two rowan saplings, snugly fitting underarm bars at the top. Gran showed Christy and Mairi how to pad these with cotton grass and wool.

"Oh Gran!" wept Mairi. "I can't bear to think how many times we'll do this—how many crutches Davie will heed in his life."

"Our lad has the use of his body except for his legs," said Gran. "We'll let him do everything he can for himself—keep busy and not fall into self-pity."

David, in truth, managed better than his mother. His crutches stuck in rocks or boggy spots. He took many a tumble. But Christy was there to reach his crutch to him or let him steady himself on her shoulder except for the times when he angrily told her to leave him alone, to go play with the others.

Christy never did this but went about her work, always keeping David in sight. He was tending the sheep again. No need for him to run, with Chul ready to follow his commands. More than once, she saw them on the moor, David with his arms around Chul, face buried on his neck.

Gran stirred spearwort into the sour milk, using it as rennet to form cheese, and instructed Christy in brewing a sleep-inducing potion for Morag, who was having one of her nervous spells. "Powder a half-handful of hart's-tongue fern and the same amount of crushed chamomile. Steep them and a few pinches of coltsfoot and meadow rue in four cups of boiling water. Strain it and tell Morag to heat a cup and have it at bedtime. I've tried to teach her to make it but she doesn't have the knack.''

Glowing at the implied compliment, Christy poured the fragrant tea into a pitcher. ''While you're out,'' said Gran, ''make a bogbean infusion for the Gunn's wee bairn who has worms. And the pony has a swelling on his hock. What will you do for that?''

Christy searched her memory. ''Pound groundsel with stonecrop and mix it with fish oil to make an ointment.''

Gran nodded. ''A poultice would be better but it's the devil to keep one on a pony. I'm glad you take an interest in the herbs, lass. Mairi has skill but not the true gift.''

Christy felt a thrill of pride and a wave of guilt for it, as if it were disloyal to rejoice that there was something she did better than her awe-inspiring foster mother. As she stepped out into the morning mists, she saw the younger children playing among the rocks. They looked ethereal. For a moment, she caught a flash of them grown, young men and women all born at Clanna, who would rear their children here. The sun glimmered through the overcast, gilding Caitlyn Nicolson's hair as she swooped to pick up an object. Her high, sweet voice floated to Christy.

''You can't kill me! I've got something magic!''

It was one of their favorite games, pursuing the child who was ''it'' till he or she was caught or found the certain kinds of shells or rocks that were agreed to make the finder invulnerable.

You all have something magic, Christy thought. *You were born here and belong to this place as it belongs to you. But no one knows who my parents were or where they came from.*

Nearing Morag's door, Christy heard Morag telling Sheila that David's crippling might be a sign of God's displeasure that the boy had never been christened in a church. Christy froze and couldn't keep from listening.

''Rosanna MacLeod got those heathenish ways from her mother and her mother before her, all the way back, they claim, to when those Stones were raised," Morag said. "Till Rosanna got too old, she went there with Mairi every Midsummer's morn to hail the sunrise. It's the custom to present the girls of that family at the first Midsummer after their first bleeding."

"Will they take Christy?"

"Rosanna would, I'm bound, if she could still tramp so far, all the way across the island. She dotes on the lass." A tiny bit of malice sounded in Morag's tone. Her husband, Andrew, had always deferred to his older cousin, Michael MacLeod, Gran's husband, but Morag deplored Gran's taste for whisky, dancing, and merry songs. "Christy's a bright child and Rosanna pours into her all she knows about herbs and cures and making dyes. But we don't know a thing about the girl's family, only that her poor mother died birthing her along the coast of North Uist."

Sheila, always kind, said quickly, "Then that makes her more than ever a daughter of the Stones—a child of the islands, since she has no blood kin."

"What a notion!" Morag scoffed. "Better the peat had covered those heathen stones entirely! Animals used to be sacrificed there, and humans, too, most likely! But Sir James would have the peat cleared away and gentlemen with more money and time than sense are busy arguing who built Callanish and why."

She grumbled on. Christy retreated a few steps. When she had controlled her hurt resentment, she called, "Morag! I've brought your sleepy tea from Gran." If Christy said she'd brewed it herself, Morag would think it wasn't effective.

As Christy walked home, a desperate hope kindled and blazed in her. Could the Stones help David? He had been presented to them, given his name there. Since the wisest doctors could not help, nor prayers, perhaps the age-old Powers could.

She would go. She would ask them.

After that resolve, fears crowded in. Since she was not of Gran and Mairi's blood, the Stones might punish her for coming. What if they demanded her life? Unknown terrors loomed and threatened but she gazed out to where David watched the sheep on the winter hill——the cows had been brought last week into the byres at the end of the houses——and she thought if David could walk again, she would be happy even if she were dead.

That night she lay awake planning. She wanted to tell Gran but a superstitious feeling made her believe that this pilgrimage must be undertaken in secret. Along the track to Stornoway, a fainter path turned west toward a few coastal villages around Loch Roag, including the hamlet of Callanish which was not very far from the Stones.

The days were so short that she couldn't go and return before night, but she knew stone shieling huts had been built where there had once been summer pastures for the crofters' beasts. She could shelter in one of them, wrapped in the lovely warm shawl Gran had woven for her in the MacLeod plaid.

It wouldn't do, though, to worry folk. She'd leave a note on top of David's clothes so he'd be bound to see it when he woke, tell him there was something she had to do——something private—— and she'd be away the night, so would he, around midday, say she'd gone on an errand and would be home the next afternoon?

The sooner she went the better, or she'd grow too much afraid.

It was a good thing Gran slept sound for Christy kept rousing and creeping into the hearth room to see if the night was lifting. As soon as she thought she could travel without stumbling over rocks, she put on wool stockings, the buskins Andrew made for all the villagers for days so bitter they couldn't go barefoot, a petticoat of dark blue *drogad* with a cotton warp and wool weft, and a voluminous skirt of wool so tightly woven that it shed rain. She pinned her shoulder plaid over her linen blouse and then gathered the larger, heavier shawl over her head and shoulders.

Her skirt had a large pocket. She stuffed it with several bannocks rolled around a small smoked herring. Yesterday she had made crowdie, a soft white cheese. She spread some of this on another bannock and made her breakfast on it as she trudged along in the murky cold.

The curtains to David's bed had been pulled so she hadn't got to look at him before she left, but she left the note on his clothes folded neatly on the settle. As she walked along, her mood shifted from wild hope, picturing him fleet and light-footed as he once had been, to dread of the spirits of the Stones. They could take her if they wished; she had made up her mind and will to that. But what if they struck her down for her temerity and didn't help David, either?

What would be, would be, but she prayed to the protectors of the hearth as Gran did every night when she smoored the fire. *Thou Holy Three, Mary, Christ, and Brigid, bless David and help him to get well. Lend my thy grace and help me not to fear the terrors and dangers of this night . . .*

The dark was fading, enough to see the glimmer of shallow bogs and the wider sheen of a loch with a small islet in its center. The bit of land was dense with slender silver-gray trunks of naked rowans, none more than twenty feet high. Moorhens swam jerkily and coots bobbed along the shore, white foreheads and bills contrasting starkly with glistening black bodies. A flock of teal drifted among the reeds and sedges and from the other side of the loch, Christy caught the dazzling green flash of a mallard drake's head.

As the sun rose, lochs, lochans, and bogs lit like a shout, mirroring sun and sky. A mixed flock of peewits and golden plovers burst upwards, trilling as they spiraled, looped, and plunged dizzily in rollicking somersaults, the sharply pointed wings of the golden plover making them easy to tell from the broader, blunter-winged peewit.

All of these were seeking food, but the birds, soaring and plunging in their sky dances, surely flew and sang their joy in life and their wings and the shining day. Christy hummed snatches to echo notes of theirs. A song formed in her mind, some parts bold and vibrant as lark plover, others shy as the water rail, or melodious as the silvery bubbling of the curlew.

The twisted gray rocks thrusting from peat and bog were no longer softened by tussocks of grass but goldfinches garnered the last thistles protected by a curious beehive-shaped stone hut. Christy peeked in and saw bed niches built into the wall and ledges for the milking things. She could almost imagine she heard young women laughing and teasing each other about their sweethearts, singing as they milked the cows, churned the butter, made the cheese, and enjoyed freedom from their elders. Lads got away from fishing when they could and came to see their lassies and many a marriage followed courting at the shielings.

Late in summer, lassies brought the fattened sheep and cattle to the village. That was what Mairi and Catriona had been doing, creels laden with cheese and butter, when they saw the flames of Aosda and ran to find their homes burned and Fearchar stumbling from his house with Cridhe, his white hair ablaze . . .

Christy shivered and hurried away from the abandoned little hut. What had happened to the girls who used to stay there? Had they been driven from their homes? Had they gone across the ocean to America or Canada or Australia? Or had they been blown like flotsam to the stinking alleys of Glasgow or Liverpool?

These onetime common grazings for the people had been taken from them by Red Donald Munro and added to deer parks leased by rich gentlemen from the mainland. Queen Victoria's husband, Prince Albert, had made deer stalking highly fashionable. Lairds got more money from renting to hunters than could be got from the sheep farmers for whom the crofters had first been dispossessed. A cruel wicked business that was doubtless behind why Christy's poor young mother had been found wandering the shore.

Who was she? Christy wondered as she did every time she remembered her origin. Why was she alone? Was my father dead or torn away from her and thrown bound into a ship as many were?

Is he alive somewhere, maybe far across the waters? She refused to think it possible that her father had trifled with a lass and then deserted her.

Rob MacRae, who found her mother on the beach and brought her home, had lived in Clanna since his village of Sollas was cleared. Especially in these last years, Christy had begged him to repeat the story and pestered him with questions, but all he could tell her was that her mother was in rags and near-starved though she was a bonnie lass with tawny hair she had passed to Christy and the same golden eyes.

"Had you hugged to her breast, she did, but she had no milk, poor lassie." Even eleven years later, Rob's blue eyes clouded at the memory. "We did the best we could. The mercy was that as my mother held her at the end, the lass thought she was safe with her own mother. Smiling, she was. Just remember that, child, and don't fash yourself about the rest of it."

But Christy did. How could she help it when she knew that kind as Mairi tried to be, her foster mother could never really love her because of what had happened at Sollas? The last time Christy had questioned Rob, she summoned up her courage and said, "Rob, please. Tell me more about Sollas."

Never before had she dared to ask that, though she had often wondered. Rob didn't answer for so long that Christy feared she had done wrong to call up those memories but when he spoke, it was as if it were a relief to share them.

"The folk of Uist are called the Children of Colla after the Irish prince who once ruled in the isles, lass. We are descended from Conn of the Hundred Battles, High King of Ireland. You've heard Mairi Mór sing the old song about them. 'With their full-laden, white-sailed fleet, they sail upon the oceans . . .' But that was long ago.

"Six hundred souls lived in the District of Sollas at the Atlantic edge of North Uist. A fortune in kelp was garnered several generations ago by the MacDonald laird, second baron of the Isles and uncle of the present laird who was deep into debt from feeding his tenants through the potato famine. His creditors pressed him hard to evict his people and make their land into sheep runs.

"Mairi had met him at Stornoway Castle and when I begged her to help us, we took her first to Armadale Castle on Skye." Rob sighed and shook his head. "Big with child she was, not able for such a journey . . . It weighs on me that I asked her to go, though I swear I didn't know she had promised her husband not to do anything that might bring harm to her or the babe.

"Any road, the laird finally agreed to let the Sollas folk bide that winter in our homes if we would promise to leave next summer. With that, we crossed the roiling Minch to Uist and walked overland to Sollas, but the police were there ahead of us. And you know the rest. Mairi lost her babe but we of Sollas had that winter and the eating of our 'taties, oats, and barley," Rob went on. "The Perth Destitution Committee bought land for us next year but it was far from the sea and so barren nothing grew. In the end, the Government Emigration Commission sent most of the people to Australia—but smallpox broke out below decks and only God knows how many lived."

"But you came to Clanna. And old Jock MacDonald, and the MacPhails——"

Angus and Peggy MacPhail were in their thirties, and their children, twenty-year-old Geordie and eighteen-year-old Janet had grown up at Clanna. "Aye," said Rob. "But when I see Mairi go up the slope to her baby's grave, my heart aches. And the love that shone between her and her captain—It must still be there, but he has never forgiven her nor can she forgive herself."

Lost in these somber thoughts, Christy didn't realize how near she was to the western coast till she came to the top of a gentle slope. In one marveling glance, she beheld the Stones on a promontory thrusting into what must be Loch Roag, which opened into the boundless ocean. A small island lay between the Stones of Callanish and the larger mass that was surely Great Bernera to the west. Christy held her breath, entranced by the lustrous sweep of earth, sky, and water.

All her fears melted. She felt she had come here hundreds of times in other bodies, other lives, that she had seen the great stones raised, had brought her cattle for purification and carried home a torch lit at the sacred fire to start a new flame on her hearth.

The pillars resembled cloaked figures frozen to silence by the coming of a mortal. Peat had been cleared away from the stones of the aisle and two other rows radiating from the circle. It was partially cut away from the five stones of the south row and the thirteen forming the circle with the great megalith in the center. The top of the squared pillar had a graceful slant, as if shaped and polished by the eternal winds.

The world had changed but the Stones had not. Christy felt as if she had come home and closed her eyes. *You have seen Picts and Scots and Northmen, watched them blend into a people, the folk of this Island. You have endured. Help us, all of us, to do the same in spite of evil men like Red Donald Munro.*

And then she knelt and breathed her special prayer, that David's back would grow strong and sound again, that he would walk and climb and run.

She felt no answering.

At least, let him walk.

The Stones were mute. Mists swirled in. Dark clouds pressed against the earth. She felt as if they crushed her. The safety she had felt vanished. Were the Stones angry? Did they sense she had no right to be here?

Still, she persisted. *Ancient Ones, do what you will with me, but help David. He was conceived among you. Here he had his christening. If you can help him and won't, you're cruel! Cruel as Donald Munro!*

"What a moil, lass!" A white-haired man stepped out of the mists, taking a clay pipe from his mouth. His blue eyes twinkled and his voice held an echo of the roaring sea. " 'Twill all run straight in the end. Davie will be a great man of his people.''

"What can that mean to a lad who can run no more, or climb, or frolic? What is that kind of havey-cavey promise beside two good legs?'' Christy stared at the man. Oddly, she wasn't afraid of him at all, only exasperated. "Who are you? And what do you know about David?''

The stranger ignored both rudeness and question. "Och, ochone! What good are sound legs except to carry one off when the laird says to flit? Davie must use his brain now. That's what our folk need.''

"He could use his brain and still have his legs.''

"But how many do?''

Before she could think of an answer, a girl perhaps a year or so younger than she peered around the central stone and then ran forward, laughing, to catch the old man's hand. "I told you she'd come someday, Fearchar! She's the one who brings me shells and driftwood.''

A chill prickled Christy's neck but the two before her looked so solid and real and their talk was so everyday that she couldn't be afraid. "Shells are all very well for babies,'' the girl told Christy in a tolerant way. "But now I'm older, maybe you could bring me some ribbons.''

"Ribbons?'' Christy echoed.

"I'd dearly love a blue one.''

"But if you're—'' Christy hesitated. "Don't you have everything you want?''

"Well . . .'' The girl furrowed eyebrows that arched just like Mairi's. She had curling russet hair, a pointed chin, and sparkling gray eyes. "When we're in heaven, we don't want anything, but when we come back here, we get little cravings. Fearchar wants tobacco—and I want ribbons!''

"I'll bring you one.'' Christy summoned up her courage. "Do you know my mother?''

"Och, lass!" Fearchar spread his hands. "All the souls there are in heaven! I had a rare hard time finding this one."

"And you're sure, really sure, nothing can be done for David?"

"David will do for himself."

Christy blinked. When she looked again, the pair of them were gone. Had she dreamed? Were they tricksters from the village? No, that couldn't be. Strangers wouldn't know the things that they had.

The mist thickened into rain. Night was beginning to settle. It was an hour's walk to the nearest shieling. "I can't thank you," she said to the Stones. "But perhaps your magic doesn't work these days. Maybe all you can do now is stand here and remind us that our folk were here long before the lairds, long before Red Donald." She hesitated. "Still, that is quite a lot. I guess I do thank you."

She wrapped the shawl tighter against the rain and hurried away.

III

Exhausted from hours of tramping and the dream or vision or whatever it had been at the Stones, Christy was glad to enter the shieling and devour the rest of the fish and half of her last bannock. It was so dark she could barely make out the bed niche, but oddly enough, what she had seen made her feel protected rather than threatened. She made a pillow of her shoulder plaid, wrapped up snugly in her shawl, and slept sound till the faintest hint of dawn.

Dream or not, she was going to get a blue ribbon for Mairi's daughter. In spite of Fearchar's prophecies, Christy was bitterly disappointed. To start with, she had probably conjured up the child and old man. She'd often heard Fearchar described, with his voice that had a bit of the roar of the sea, and it was easy enough for an overwrought imagination to produce a girl who was a miniature of Mairi. Christy wanted to talk the experience over with Gran but she was afraid to tell Mairi, who doubtless would think her a liar, an interfering intruder, and most of all, be angered that Christy dare pretend to have seen the child who was buried on the cliff.

A heavy mist settled into rain, the kind that lasts for days. Mercifully it didn't lash Christy with the gale force more common than not on the island but by the time she reached Clanna, the relentless downpour had penetrated even the tight-woven shawl and outer skirt.

David and Chul weren't on the hill. Except on fine days that sent them scampering across the moor, it wasn't necessary to herd the sheep closely in the winter. They huddled out of the wind in the hollow, seeking each other's warmth.

Mairi was so preoccupied with David that she seemed in another world most of the time. Christy hoped to slip unobtrusively into the household routine and escape questioning about her absence. She entered the fasgalan, took off her dripping outer garments, and gave them a shake. Her heart sank at the worried irritability of Mairi's voice. "Where can the girl have got to? Jauntering off without a word to anyone except that note to David, and now here's this rain! It'll be a mercy if she doesn't drown in a bog or catch her death of cold."

"I'm home, Mairi Mór." Christy took a deep breath and stepped into the hearth room. From down the passage came the murmur of the classroom. David would be there with Chul. Hanging her shawl and skirt over the heather rope that ran along one side of the wall for just such uses gave her an excuse not to face her foster mother immediately. "Indeed, I'm sorry to have fretted you."

"Where did you go?" Mairi demanded. "Sneaking off before dawn, dragging in soaked, as if you'd stayed the night in a bog! What in heaven's name possessed you?"

Christy found she couldn't tell an outright lie. Besides, what would it serve? "I—I went to the Stones."

"There!" Gran nodded triumphantly. "Didn't I say it?"

Mairi ignored that, fixing her whole attention on Christy, an attention that was hard to endure though Christy forced herself to meet those gray-green eyes that changed like the sea.

"Why?" asked Mairi.

Christy's mouth was dry. Mairi had never struck her, in truth had never berated her as Morag and a few of the other women often did their children and grandchildren. Christy could not have dreaded her foster mother more, though, had she habitually whipped her raw with alder switches.

That dread was rooted in awe and worship of the woman who had preserved her. Great Mairi was a nickname often given to a large woman to distinguish her from smaller women of the same popular name. In Mairi MacLeod MacDonald's case, the Mór was a tribute. Christy could sooner argue with God than with her—attempt to lie, either.

"I hoped the Stones could help David," she whispered guiltily.

A startled look shot across Mairi's face. Was hope mixed with it? Christy said in a shamed, small voice, "The Stones told me nothing."

Mairi's shoulders drooped. "Indeed, how should they?" she said in a harsh tone. "You are not of the blood line that belongs to the Stones."

"How do you know that?" Gran took her granddaughter up sharply. "For all we know, Christy's forebears helped raise Callanish as much as ours did."

"She comes from nowhere!"

"That means from everywhere."

The two women Christy revered and loved scowled at each other before they burst out laughing. "Run change your clothes," Gran said. "Then you must have a bowl of barley broth and get to your lessons."

The captain gave her a curious glance when she took her place on a bench behind one of the two plank desks. Rona Nicolson, Seana's cousin, scooted over to make room. She had her father Lucas's rusty hair. Beside her was green-eyed Brigid Gunn and then came Colin Nicolson, brown of hair and eyes, who was cousin both to Rona and Seana. These three were Christy's age-mates but they tended to play with one another and slightly younger children than tag after David as Christy had. David, though two years younger than Seana and Alai Gunn, had always been the leader of the older group, and Caitlyn, David's age, usually ranged with them since her big sister, Seana, was charged with looking after her.

MacLeods and Nicolsons weren't the only cousins. The children, and now the young grandchildren, of the black-haired, green-eyed twin MacAskill brothers, were related, and what with marriages over a span of sixteen years, the original founders of the village had mixed with those who came later to truly form a clan, a family.

The "babies," the two- and three- and four-year-olds, snuggled with Chul beside the fire, were allowed to listen to their elders so long as they were quiet, just as Christy used to do.

"The lassie knows sums as well as David," Christy had heard Gran boast one night after tucking her in. "She can even spell some words in Gaelic and English!"

"She's just memorized what she hears," Mairi said derisively. "She doesn't really *know* it anymore than a—a cuckoo."

Huddled in the box bed, a three-year-old Christy had wept herself to sleep with the hateful name sounding in her head. She jumped now as the captain called her name, evidently repeating a question. "Christy, will you please explain Mr. Charles Darwin's theory of evolution?" He smiled reassuringly at her confusion. "You wrote an excellent paper on it. Now see if you can put it into words the primer class can understand."

That helped even though, with his back turned to the captain, nine-year-old Hamish MacAskill was twisting his freckled face into droll grimaces, trying to make her laugh. Christy fixed her gaze on his elfin-faced six-year-old sister, Anne, and began to explain. She loved to learn but she equally enjoyed getting the younger children interested in things that seemed wonderful and exciting to her.

"You're a good teacher, Christy." The captain's smile eased the stern lines of his face. "Perhaps that's what you'll do when you grow up."

The captain was gone so much on his trips to America that Christy had to make an effort to think of him as her foster father.

At least he had never seemed to blame her for being alive. She flushed at his praise.

"It would be grand to be a teacher, sir." *But it depends on Davie. No one knows him the way I do or can keep him company without him thinking it's from pity, which he cannot endure. If he stays here, I'll never leave him. If he goes, I'll follow.*

Tired out from her journey and all her hopes and fears, Christy couldn't hold her eyes open to knit and went to bed early. When she told David good night, he said so softly no one else could hear, "It was brave of you to tramp across the island, Christy. Don't feel bad that it couldn't get my legs back."

She glanced around. The captain was reading. Mairi and Gran, knitting, were deep in conversation about Morag's headaches and what might help them. Leaning close to the box bed, Christy kept her voice low. "I saw your grandfather, Davie. He looked as real as anyone—even blew smoke from his pipe. He—he said you must use your brain instead of your legs." She drew a deep breath. "He said you will be a great man."

David's eyes had widened. Then dark brows drew together and he gave a brusque laugh and turned away from her. "I'm not a baby, lass. No need to spin me fairy tales."

"But, Davie—"

"A great man!" His voice jerked and he kept his face hidden. "No doubt I'll be a rare hand at mending fishing nets! Don't say such foolishness, Christy! I know you mean it well but—"

Crushed at the hurt she had caused him, she feared that persisting would distress him more. She whispered a good night and crept off to bed like a criminal.

Gran joined her before Christy could sleep. "Now, my dear, what is all this about the Stones?" Gran asked, lying down and taking Christy's hand.

Christy told her, gulped, and said, "Do you believe me?"

"Every bit. Why, child, did I not see my dear man at Mairi's wedding? That was the first time I could let myself know that he was dead. For years I insisted that he was off on a long voyage."

"Has—has Mairi Mór seen him? Or her daughter?"

Gran shook her head. "Mairi doesn't see spirits, though she told me Fearchar helped her compose the song she sang at Stornoway Castle."

"Davie thought I was making up what I saw."

"Davie is having a cruel war of it. He can't allow himself to accept sympathy because he's terrified of falling into self-pity." Gran put an arm around Christy and smoothed her hair. "Be sure, though, that you sparked a gleam of hope even though David can't admit it."

Christy sighed and nestled closer to Gran though she was really too old for that. After a moment, Gran mused, "My great granddaughter wanted a blue ribbon? The captain brought me a lovely one for a cap. You shall have that to take her."

It was dusk by the time Christy finished scrubbing out the milk pail with a heather brush, scalded it, and set it upsidedown to dry on the bench in the fasgalan. Potatoes and fish were cooking in the same pot for supper. Gran winked at Christy, pressed something into her hand, and said she'd make the bannocks.

Flinging her shawl around her, Christy hurried toward the cliff. She felt a mite daft, taking a ribbon to a grave, but Gran thought it reasonable. Reaching the mound which over the years had become covered with Christy's offerings of shells, ocean-polished pebbles, driftwood, and brilliant-colored seaweed, Christy gazed at the small oval protected by the larger one of old Meggie.

It couldn't hold the girl Christy had seen with Fearchar, the girl who was almost as tall as she, but probably that didn't matter. "I don't know if I saw you or not," she said. "Maybe I dreamed it because I want to believe you're happy where you are—that you don't really mind never being alive. Any road, here's your ribbon with Gran's love.''

Kneeling, Christy tucked it beneath the shells. Then, from the corner of her eye, she saw someone coming up the slope. Her heart lurched before she saw it was Mairi Mór, and then it lurched again.

She and Mairi had never met on their pilgrimages to the cliff. Vexed as Mairi still was with her for going to the Stones, Christy didn't wish to aggravate her further. The only way down the slope led past Mairi. Ducking low, Christy fled to lie flat among some tall heather a stone's throw from the graves. She scarce dared breathe. To be caught hiding—spying—would be worse, much worse, than meeting her foster mother on the path. If she'd only had time to think—

Mairi settled by the grave. She touched a few shells and rearranged some driftwood. Then she began a song in her sweet resonant voice and Christy caught in her breath, for she knew the tune though she hadn't known there were words.

> "I have told gulls and dolphins, I have told young seals in their
> white coats, I have told lark and lapwing and called to swans
> and graylags—I have told rowans and orchids and butter-
> cups, bees in the heather and butterflies over the ling. I have
> told moor and sea and the stars in heaven, the sun on your
> grave, and the gentle moonlight. I have told them you will not
> see them, with them you will never play. But they answer,
> 'She is with us. She is the breath of flowers, the soaring of
> wings, bright cloud at dawning, sheen of the Merry Dancers,
> the light that glimmers in the deep sea caves. She sees with all
> our eyes and breathes the honeyed air. She pulses with our
> life. She is everywhere . . .' "

Christy's eyes stung at the poignant lament. Mairi often played it on her harp, and when the captain was there, he joined in with the pipes, nimbly fingering the chanter as the music wove in and out, creating variations, lilting grace notes, building to the end which fell, like the sparkling flow of a fountain into the beginning.

Had he known it was their daughter's song, did he join in to mourn and salute her? Using the language of the pipes, if his life with Mairi had begun with love as the Ground or *Urlar,* moved through countless variations, quickenings and doublings to the crowning movement, would it not surely at the end return to its being, the Ground of love?

Christy prayed it might. If the captain forgave Mairi, it might be possible for Mairi to forgive her. A shape loomed as it reached the hollow of the cliff. As if the thought had called him, there was the captain. Christy squirmed.

She shouldn't be here—shouldn't hear what might be said. But it was far too late, after Mairi's song, to rise up out of the heather.

"Mairi."

She started and rose to her feet. "Oh, Iain!" Her arms reached to him but fell to her sides as he halted.

"I've delayed leaving for America because of David, but I must be going soon." The captain hesitated. "Mairi, I know it will be hard for you, but I'm convinced it will be for the best to take David with me as far as Inverness and place him in an academy."

"No! He's still a bairn! And with his legs useless—"

"You must see that an education is the only road now for our son."

"But you *are* educating him!"

"Not to the level he must reach to enter a profession." The captain raised a silencing hand. "I won't force him against his will. As usual, I'm hiring a teacher for the children while I'm gone. It will be no great harm if David studies here for another year or so, but I wish to put the matter to him. So I have come to ask you, Mairi, not to cling to the lad and hold him if he is willing to go."

She didn't speak. Her husband said impatiently, "If you

worry about favoring him over the other Clanna lads, remember that I have offered to pay the expenses of any boy who wants to go on to a university. And there are scholarships for clever poor lads—I'll say that for Scotland.''

Mairi's tone brightened. ''Maybe that's where we'll get our lawyer!''

''Lawyer?''

''Aye.'' Mairi hesitated. Then the words poured out. Evidently she had brooded over this for years. ''At Sollas, here was the county superintendent of police, the procurator fiscal of Inverness-shire—the one, I am told, who makes criminal charges—sheriff-substitutes, Lord MacDonald's commissioner, and that boiling of constables. They dragged old women and cripples out of their houses and tore down the roofs and walls. This is the law!''

''Mairi—''

''Since the lairds' hearts will not change, the laws must—and that will take a canny lawyer.''

The captain gave a short, exasperated laugh. ''Canny lawyers don't plead for the powerless and destitute.''

''Ours will. He will be one of us. A crofter can't rise to Parliament but one might become a lawyer and attack the present laws. Men aren't hung, drawn, and quartered these days as Highlanders were after Culloden little over a hundred years ago. A child's no longer hanged for stealing a few pence worth of food. The slave trade was done away with when Gran was a young woman—''

''You should have been an advocate yourself.'' Unwilling admiration mixed with irony in the captain's tone.

''If I could reach the people—those with kind hearts who contributed to the Destitution Fund in the famine years! But they can vote and they do read newspaper articles like those Mr. Mulock wrote about Sollas. They'd support a change in the laws that give a laird the power of God over his tenants.''

The captain didn't respond for a moment. When he did, his

voice was expressionless. "Since you've learned it's futile to struggle against the present law, does that mean you'll not interfere
with other evictions?"

"It's not futile when articles like Mr. Mulock's tell what the
evictions are like. So long as folk pack up quietly and go over the
sea, it's easy for the landlords to say they were glad to leave—and
comfortable for people to believe it."

"Who will be a mother to David if your skull is split by a
constable's truncheon or you are sent to prison?"

It was too dark for Christy to see Mairi flinch but she was
sure that she did, though she answered her husband in a level tone.
"David has a mother in every woman of Clanna."

"And a father in every man?"

"Indeed, before you knew he existed, even before he was
born, they all vowed to help rear him."

Dear heaven! thought Christy. *Don't let such things be said!* The
quiet of the captain's was more terrible than rage. "Are you saying
David is more the son of Clanna than he is mine?"

"How can *you* ask that?"

Christy could see his shadow turn away from the smaller
shadow that was Mairi. When he turned again, he spoke so soft
that Christy could scarcely hear. "I cry your pardon, Mairi. It's
true I was far away when David was born, no help to you at all. But
I had told you to write my solicitor if you were in want of anything."

"Oh, Iain! There's no need for casting up accounts! When
you learned about David, you married me in the teeth of the
world."

"I married you because I'd learned you were the only
woman in the world for me." He smiled bleakly. "Except you are
not for me—are you, Mairi?"

Christy ached for them both, could not have said which one
she felt for most. Strange that her foster parents, who seemed so
capable and infallible, to whom everyone came for help and ad-

vice, should themselves be so helpless in the snare of their own cruel problems.

"I loved you for what you are," he said slowly. "I never guessed it would cost us our child. And now our lad is crippled." As Mairi's husband, the captain had close to absolute legal authority over her. He could force her to move to the mainland, or command her never to leave Clanna, or even her own house. In a history lesson on the ancient Romans, the captain had pointed out that though the Roman husband and father, the pater familias, had the right of life and death over his wife and children, modern English and Scots law was not much of an improvement.

"Indeed," said Mairi in a voice that trembled. "I am sorrier than words can say."

"But you would do it again."

"I would *have* to do it again."

Christy could almost feel the bruised, aching heartbeats between them. "I will leave after the New Year," he said.

He turned away. Mairi followed. When they were far enough ahead not to hear a dislodged pebble, Christy rose from the heather and went to stand by the smaller grave.

"Why did you not appear?" she asked, half-crying. "Why didn't you tell them you do well enough where you are and they must stop cutting each other to pieces?"

There was no answer. The wind was rising, even reaching this sheltered spot. Christy wrapped close in her shawl and hurried down the slope.

IV

The captain and David played chess that night. Christy watched the game as much as she could while mending. David beat her so easily that she wanted to learn how to be more of a challenge to him.

"Check and mate," crowed David.

His father grunted and toppled his king. "You're getting too good for me, lad. You could give your Great-uncle Roderick a tussle and he's the terror of all his friends."

David shrugged, as if that could have nothing to do with him. "Shall we have another game? You need to look further ahead, Father."

"I'm trying to, my son." The captain helped set up the board again. "I'm trying to think of your future."

So it was coming. Christy felt sick and faint. How could she bear it, what would she do, if David went away? Yet she could see clear enough that the captain was right. David's legs could not carry him so his brain must.

David sat up very straight. The muscles tightened in his cheeks as he glanced at his crutches. "My future, Father?"

"Yes. You'll be fourteen in March. I've drilled into you all the Latin and Greek and mathematics that *I* know. Business takes me to America early next year. What would you say to traveling with me to Inverness and enrolling in the academy there?"

The boy's breath drew in sharply. He looked at his mother.

She kept her face still and her eyes on her knitting. "As you know, your great-uncle married late," continued the captain. "One of his sons is only two years younger than you. I imagine you would get on famously. Uncle Roderick's wife is about your mother's age and very nice. She's asked many times if you couldn't come for a visit. It would be easier for you to spend your holidays at Uncle Roderick's than to use up the time in traveling both ways."

Especially since you're crippled. The words weren't spoken but Christy was sure everybody thought them.

"It—it's so far," David said at last.

"It is, lad. But now more than ever you surely understand that you must acquire a good education."

David gazed at Chul, who lay snuggled at his feet. "Chul wouldn't understand."

"Chul? Good heavens, son, you can't let a dog rule your fortunes!"

David ducked his head and bit his lip. Christy felt tears sting her own eyes and hoped David could keep them out of his. "I—I'd take the best care of Chul, Davie," she ventured. It would help her loneliness a little, to look after David's dog.

"I know you would," he muttered. "But Chul's not young anymore, Father. I'm afraid he'd grieve. Remember how he wouldn't eat till I was able to get out of bed and get around? What would he do if I left entirely?"

The captain started to say something but Gran spoke first. "Enough's been said tonight, my lads. You both must think on it. Now who would like some tea and a raisin scone before we go to bed?"

Will Davie go? was the question always in Christy's mind. The captain said no more, in fact no one did. It seemed to Christy that David caressed Chul more than usual and Mairi's eyes, when they rested on her son and he wasn't looking, were full of pain.

The northern lights, or Men of the Tricks, *Fir-Chlisne,* glowed in long shimmering folds, white, green, and deepest rose. As December wore on, the sun barely rose above the slope that protected the village from gales, and then not till nine by Iain's clock, to sink behind the western moors by midafternoon. Storms howled in with driving hail and sleet that sent seabirds screeching from the shore to huddle wherever they found shelter. The sheep clustered in hollows, snuggling for warmth. High tides scoured the beaches and Christy and the other children searched for driftwood that was saved for building if it was sturdy enough.

Heavy storms made the fish seek deeper waters out farther than the boats could safely go in such uncertain weather, so there were days when the men could work outside but not fish. That was when they worked sand and tangle brought by Kelpie, the stout little pony, from the west side of the island into lazybeds where seed potatoes would be planted in February or March. Men threshed grain on the clayed threshing floors at the end of the barns and winnowed it in a shallow circular sieve where the winnowing hole and open doors created a draft of air.

Donald Gunn supervised the making of new barrels, Andrew Nicolson made brogues for those who needed them most, Barry taught anyone who wished to learn how to make wicker furnishings, baskets, and creels, and always there were nets to make and mend, tools and churns and buckets to fashion or repair, and heather rope to be twisted. David worked unstintingly at all these chores, as if determined to show he could earn his keep.

This was the season when the women accomplished most of their spinning and weaving, which almost as much as the fish helped to support the village. When a web was ready to be waulked or fulled to cleanse the wool of oil, soften the texture, set the dye, and shrink the yarn, the ammonia-soaked cloth was brought to Mairi's storeroom where a table was set up. Ten or twelve women sat on opposite sides of the table and passed the web rhythmically back and forth, rubbing and thumping it in tune to some of the scores of waulking songs.

Christy wasn't yet strong enough to help with this, but she did the cooking and other household work while Gran and Mairi worked at the cloth. Gran, because of her experience and skill, was in charge of the waulking. At intervals, she inspected the web.

"Not shrunk enough yet, lasses," she might say. " 'Twill need three or four more songs." And she would lead them in her high, strained, but still sweet voice, in "Brown-haired Allan," "The Jealous Woman," or another song of the right tempo.

When Gran judged the web tight enough, it was rolled and patted to improvised verses. *"Who turns red as rowan berries when Tam goes by?"* they teased poor Molly MacAskill, who had been trying for years to coax Mairi's younger brother, Tam, into wedding. Or the women might gibe at Rose Nicolson, who was not an over-careful cook, *"Who scorches her porridge till her husband and bairns think that's the right flavor?"*

Christy could help rinse the finished cloth in the stream and stretch it to dry, outside on the heather if the weather allowed. After it was tightly rolled, Gran then blessed the fine, warm material and all the hands that had made it. Then it was stored to be made into clothing for Clanna folk, or paid as rent, or carried by Magnus Ericson to be sold to mainland merchants.

Christmas was a quiet celebration, with Morag reading from the Bible, and all of them chanting Psalms. Murdo MacKinnon acted as precentor, reading a line and waiting for the blended voices to echo him.

Hogmanay, New Year's Eve, was the time for merriment. For days, Christy helped bake black buns rich with dried fruit and spices, the crunchiest of shortbreads, and bannocks dipped in beaten eggs, crisped on a griddle.

Tam persuaded David to go around that night with the other lads and young men to visit every house of Clanna, a custom that might have been as old as the Stones of Callanish. Tam, as leader, borrowed David's old sheepskin rug to wear like a cloak. Alai Gunn carried a sack. Christy, delighted that David had agreed to go out with his former playmates, ran to open the door when they stopped at Mairi's house and lustily sang.

> This is the night of gifts.
> Mistress of the hearth, rise up and bring the Hogmanay
> bannock. We will be glad of cheese and butter, too.
> We ask it in the name of Father, Son, and Holy Spirit."

Christy let the troop inside and Mairi welcomed them, looking archaically regal in her arisaid. This had once been the attire of island women, and Mairi had been wedded in this costume designed lovingly for her by Gran and the other women. She saved it for special occasions, so it still looked new, a white plaid decorated by widely spaced, very narrow, stripes of black, red, and blue, and a red bodice with full sleeves worn under the plaid with a pleated skirt.

The captain, Christy knew, had combed the shops of Stornoway for his bride's antique silver brooch and wide leather belt ornamented with silver panels. Belt and brooch were engraved with fantastical creatures and studded with rubies and sapphires. Beautiful, Mairi looked, and almost happy for the first time since David's fall. David was laughing, too. That made Christy's heart swell with gladness.

Tam pranced around the fire wagging the sheepskin. The captain, Gran, Mairi, and Tam's followers drubbed the hide with sticks, David balancing on one crutch while he thumped away with the other. Gran thought the ritual went back to an age when an animal had been sacrificed, perhaps even a human, to secure good luck for the coming year.

"Ouch!" cried Tam at an overenthusiastic whack from David. "Have done! I'm properly buffeted and want my bannock!"

Christy put a bannock for each young man into the sack and

Mairi and Gran added cheese, black buns, and shortbread. At the end of the procession, the lads would have a feast and divide what was left.

The older ones might take the buns as gifts to their hostesses when they went "first-footing" after midnight. Iain had a bottle of whisky ready for that, and a welcome first-footer he would be, for he was dark. That was the luckiest kind of man to have first across one's threshold in the New Year.

"Mind now," Mairi said to her fair-haired brother, "don't be first at my hearth or you'll get no goodies! And you, Marcus, with that rusty red hair, you wait till last." Red hair was unlucky in a first-footer, though a woman was worse, especially one with blond hair. Women seldom went first-footing and when they did, the man accompanying them entered first.

Chuckling, the band withdrew, Tam giving a mischievous flick of the sheepskin. "Thank goodness our Davie is learning he can have fun even if he is on crutches," Gran said. "And you, Captain, you must be on your way to save some household the bad luck of being first-footed by one of our redheads or blonds. Malcolm Ferguson's hair is more gray than black and Murdo MacKinnon is all gray. That leaves just you and the MacAskill twins to bring good luck."

"Then I must be about it," he said in the teasing, tender way he had with Gran. The two had a special love for each other that had never wavered, whatever troubles he and Mairi had. He went off for his cloak and bottle. Mairi put buns in a basket for him to give each hostess to ensure that there'd be plenty of food in the home throughout the coming year.

Christy helped Gran and Mairi set out the refreshments. Gran had on her black wedding gown and her most lavishly ruffled cap. Christy wore the new red petticoat Gran had given her at Christmas. That wasn't a time for presents but when a family could afford it, everyone got some kind of clothing.

The captain's dazzling bright brass oil lamp was lit for the occasion and he had placed several bottles of wine beside the whisky decanter and crystal on the tall dresser that served as both cupboard and sideboard. The crystal had belonged to his mother as well as fine china, silver, and other grand things that were stored away. That vexed the captain but Mairi insisted that she was afraid of breaking such fragile things. It was well enough to keep out a few goblets for the captain's wine but apart from them, she preferred to keep the heirlooms safe for David's wife.

"Wheesht!" Gran clapped her hands. "I almost forgot my heather ale. Christy, lass, will you fetch a jug from the storeroom?"

Gran was renowned for this ale, made with a secret recipe that had been handed down in her family since the time of the Picts. Christy was setting the jug on the dresser when an imperious knocking sounded at the door.

"Heavens, are they going to knock it down?" said Gran. "Someone's already been at the whisky! Let them in, Christy, before they break the door."

A strange woman in a velvet cloak almost fell into Christy's arms. Her hood fell back to reveal elaborately coifed hair the color of winter moonlight. Christy stepped back, unable to check a cry of dismay. This fair-haired woman was the worst kind of omen! And the man beside her was just as pale-haired.

Who were they? Gentry, to be sure, from their clothing and rudeness. No crofters would behave like this, bursting inside a home before they were bid. Gran was right about the whisky. They both reeked.

Mairi stood as if frozen in the door to the hearth room. "We've come to wish you joy of the New Year, Mrs. MacDonald." The man put his tall-crowned hat on one end of the milk bench. "Will you not ask us in? I've brought some choice claret, the kind Major MacDonald enjoys when he calls in at the Lodge. I am Charles Forsyth and this is my sister, Chellis Forsyth Tarleton."

Of course! These were the wealthy Virginians who were leasing the Lodge, where the captain had been staying years ago when he rescued Mairi and her folk from their burned village. The woman's husband had broken his neck in a hunting accident a year ago and her brother had brought her to Scotland in an attempt to bring her out of a severe depression. He helped her now to be seated in Gran's high-backed wicker chair.

"My husband is not here." Mairi had learned English from her husband but did not speak it often.

"We'll wait." The man stared at Mairi and smiled slowly, as if he had just made an interesting discovery. "My sister and I regret that you have been—too occupied to come for dinner. Sir James has told us how beautifully you play the harp and we have often urged the major to bring you to the Lodge. We see him, of course, when he goes back and forth to Stornoway."

"Indeed," said Mairi, "he has mentioned your hospitality. Allow me to acquaint you with my grandmother, Rosanna MacLeod, and my foster daughter, Christy."

He bowed, but there was a hint of mockery in it. Gran said in Gaelic, "This is an unlucky pair for sure, Mairi, and not just because they came first-footing. Can you not send them about their business?"

"Their business is to see Iain—and have a look at his crofter wife," said Mairi. "They're Iain's friends. It's up to him to get rid of them."

Chellis Tarleton glanced about and burst into uncontrollable laughter. "So this is a real *tigh dubh!* A black house with a cozy peat fire in the middle of the floor and cows across the way! I wonder that Major MacDonald—"

"Hush, Chellis!" commanded her brother, gripping her arm in no gentle fashion. Christy thought the false graciousness of his smile more insulting than his sister's ridicule. His eyes gave back the flicker of the fire as soullessly as the mirror. "When we heard of this delightful custom of first-footing, we resolved to be the first to wish you and the major a happy and prosperous New Year."

He drew a bottle from under his cloak, pried out the cork and sloshed dark red wine into four of the crystal glasses. "Does your fosterling partake?"

"Thank you, no," said Christy.

He gave her a glance as if she had been a talking beast, and she had difficulty in not laughing. She spoke English more fluently than Mairi because she and David, at the captain's behest, often conversed in that language. The captain insisted that David must speak both tongues well and when he was off on business, he relied on Christy to keep David in practice.

Forsyth handed Gran and Mairi their glasses before giving one to his sister. He raised his own, blinked, and glanced about. "Where's the major? Can't drink his health if he's not here."

"He is first-footing." Mairi thought out the words. "He is dark. That brings good luck, so he must get to houses before the blond and red-haired men visit."

"The gamekeeper said something about that nonsense," shrugged Mrs. Tarleton. "Unlucky first-footers he said we'd be, since we're both fair. But you don't believe that?"

"Indeed," said Mairi, openly indignant at the other's scorn and drunkenness, "I could wish anyone but you, madam, had first set foot through my door this New Year."

"Why, you—" Chellis screamed a word Christy had never heard before and hurled the goblet at Mairi.

The glass crashed against the dresser, shattering into pieces that broke again with small tinklings as they dashed against the stone floor. Wine splashed dresser, floor, Mairi, and Forsyth, hissed as it struck the glowing peats.

"What a to-do!" cried Gran. "I'm going to fetch the captain! He must get this evil-boding nasty-mannered pair out of here at once!"

Gran hurried out, breathing Gaelic imprecations. "Oh,

Mairi Mór! Your beautiful arisaid!'' wailed Christy. She ran to wet a cloth while Mairi stood as if stunned.

Forsyth crossed to his sister and struck her across the face, hard, deliberately. He spoke beneath his breath. ''You'll always do it, won't you? Won't you?'' He called Chellis the name she had called Mairi.

Blood trickled from the woman's lip. Her tongue crept out to stop it. To Christy's surprise, Chellis didn't rage at her brother when he caught her wrist, but rose docilely enough.

''We cry your pardon, Mrs. MacDonald,'' he said. ''In truth, I am sorry and shamed.'' He looked from the broken crystal to Mairi's stained white plaid. In spite of Christy's desperate efforts, the wine had dyed the material and would not sponge out. ''I'll make such amends as I can,'' the American went on. ''For now we'll do you the favor of taking ourselves off.''

Chellis stared blankly, an odd little smile on her swelling lips. Forsyth pulled on her gloves and arranged her hood. ''Is—is she all right?'' Mairi asked.

''In the morning she won't remember a thing.'' He sighed heavily. ''I should have known the island would be too quiet for her, but I thought the hunting—'' He seemed so worried about his sister that Christy almost pitied him, but the way the peat glow reflected from his eyes sent a chill up her spine.

He bowed over Mairi's hand. ''I wish you a prosperous year, Mrs. Macdonald. My regards—and apologies—to the major.''

The moment they were gone, Mairi unpinned the arisaid and laid a towel beneath it. Wordlessly, Christy helped her work at the claret stains with cold water. Gradually, the spots faded.

Christy made a sound of relief. ''I think when the plaid dries you can hide any spots by the way you pleat it.''

''I'll always know the stains are there, though.'' To Christy's horror, tears glistened in Mairi's eyes. After all, the arisaid wasn't only her attire for special occasions, it was her wedding dress.

That awful woman! And she and her brother casting it up to

Mairi that they were such friends with her gentry husband! Was there ever such an unlucky first-footing?

Christy scooped up the shattered crystal and collected tiny slivers with a bit of old wool before she cleaned the stone floor while Mairi hung the arisaid over the drying rope and went off to put on another skirt. She returned with her best shoulder plaid pinned with the glittering arisaid brooch, and even managed to smile.

"Let's hope they were our bad luck for the whole year! Thank you, lass, for cleaning up so well. We're ready now for better company."

Christy flushed with pleasure at the compliment. She always tried to win Mairi's approval, but most often it was Gran who praised her efforts and encouraged her. Another knock came at the door.

It was Neil MacAskill, as dark a man as one could wish, already so tipsy from port and whisky that he swayed as he came in. At Mairi's invitation, he collapsed on the settle and regarded her blearily from light green eyes.

"Och, Mairi, a pretty woman by her hearth is one of the grand sights of this world. When you turn your face away, I could almost think you were Ellen, my poor wife." He brooded and asked suddenly, "How old are you, lass?"

"Thirty-three, Neil. Won't you have a cup of tea, dear man, and a black bun or shortbread?"

"Ellen was but two years older when she died. Not a long life, was it, Mairi? Her hair was almost the color of yours, dark brown with sparkles of red. The lad took after her."

"Neil—"

"How old is that lad of yours?"

"He'll be fourteen in March."

"The age my Jamie would be. He was only three when he starved along with his mother down in South Uist while I was off in India fighting for the English queen." The slight, muscular man's weathered skin and dejected posture put Christy in mind of a root twisted from the ground and left to wither.

"You need some tea to warm you, Neil," said Mairi in a soothing voice.

"Who warmed my blind old mother and crippled father? Did they freeze after they were driven from our home? Did they starve? What could they think of me, off fighting English wars when they needed me, their husband and father and son?"

His despair must have brought back Mairi's grief for Fearchar, wrung her heart for the island folk cast out to starve along the coasts, beg their way to hovels of Lowland cities, or be shipped across the ocean like so many cattle. Mairi sank down by Neil and grasped his calloused hands.

"Neil, your Ellen and wee lad and parents are with my grandfather. He came back for my wedding. Gran saw him. It's well with them, and very well. Why, right now they're probably having a ceilidh and singing better than the angels—"

"Do you believe that?"

She met his tormented stare. "I don't know about heaven and hell—why the innocent suffer. But I believe Gran saw Fearchar. I know he and Cridhe gave me the words for what I thought was their last song, the one I gave the lairds in Stornoway Castle."

"Aye, you've the music."

"You have it, too." Mairi undraped Cridhe's plaid, quickly tuned the harp, and settled herself to play a song of Uist, his home island. "Sing with me, Neil. And you, Christy."

> *Fragrant, fresh Uist of the handsome youths,*
> *The sun does not shine on a fairer place.*
> *The girls of Uist are pretty like the glitter of sun on*
> *gold . . ."*

Huskily, at first breaking off to weep, he sang that song and another and then asked if Mairi knew the lullaby his mother had sung to him and his Ellen had sung to their baby. Mairi did and again they sang together, sweet and soft, "Little boy, little boy of the sheep, my darling you are . . ."

That was how Neil's twin, Gerald, found them. Gerald unpuckered his brow when he saw how his brother was behaving. He poured Mairi a drink of his whisky, winked at Christy as he gave her a smaller taste, and savored port while Neil accepted the tea Christy brought him.

Singly and in pairs, the blond and brown and red-haired men came with their bottles. Mairi and Christy had a tiny sip from each visitor and served them, though by this time none of the men needed more wine or whisky. At least they hadn't far to travel.

Gran came in last of all, tugging at the captain, who frowned at Mairi's changed garb and the arisaid hung over the cord, but said nothing while company was present. "At least that precious pair is gone!" hissed Gran in Christy's ear. "Did they cause more mischief?"

"No." Christy spoke so only Gran could hear. "Mr. Forsyth begged pardon handsomely. But I hope we never see them again! Gran, do American gentlemen hit women?"

"Some do, I reckon, same as do some Scots and English gentry."

"I hated that woman, Gran! But it was awful, the way her mouth bled. And worse, the way she smiled then——"

Gran made a noise of disgust. "Put them out of your mind, love. I gave Iain a proper earful about his fine friends, you may be sure."

The company in the house must needs drink a final toast and the bottles were emptied by the time the visitors called out final New Year's wishes and walked, staggered, or reeled outside. Neil MacAskill, steadier now than his twin, had to support Gerald.

"Thank you for your songs, Mairi," Neil said quietly as he paused at the entry to the fasgalan. "I could almost think I heard my mother, young again, sing that lullaby. And my Ellen——"

Mairi nodded. "That's what I do with Fearchar. Remember the good times, the laughing and love. The way he died isn't the most important thing. The way he lived matters more."

"Aye."

Gerald went completely limp. Grunting, Neil swung his brother to his back. Bent double, he trudged off, muttering about lads who couldn't hold their whisky.

The captain shut the door and came to stand by the hearth where Mairi was smooring the fire. "Well, my dear?" he said.

"Well?"

He frowned. "Believe me, I am sorry. That Forsyth should burst drunken into your home with his sister—"

"They seemed to be great friends of yours."

"I sold them riding horses and have taken refreshment with them a few times, perhaps a meal or two."

"The lady was curious to see your wife, I think." Color burned in Mairi's cheeks.

"Sir James has told them of you. You have refused their several invitations—"

"I'm not a paid entertainer!"

"No. But doubtless Mrs. Tarleton was intrigued that you declined." The captain frowned. "Mairi, you are sure Forsyth's behavior was in no way objectionable?"

"Apart from coming in the first place, no." She smiled faintly. "There is no need at all to call him out with pistols in the way I hear is fashionable amongst gentlemen."

"All the same, it is a shame about your arisaid."

She inspected the plaid, keeping her back to him. "The spots are fading. The plaid will be all right. But Iain, one of your mother's goblets is smashed to bits!"

He shrugged. "Goblets break. 'Tis no great matter."

David came in then, flushed and full of funny stories. It was the first time since his fall that he had joined the other lads in merrymaking, and his parents were so glad about it that they seemed to push away the blighting effect of the ill-omened first-footers. Gran reminisced of other Hogmanays and Christy served tea all around. By the time Mairi knelt to smoor the fire and invoke Mary, Christ, and Brigid to protect the household, Christy could almost imagine the Forsyths' visit had been a dark but fleeting dream.

There was always a shinty match on New Year's Day. Last year, David had found an excellent piece of driftwood, perhaps the limb of an oak, and fashioned a fine shinty stick. With it, he had so many times driven the wooden ball over the other team's boundary that in spite of his youth, he was often picked first. David especially loved the game because it was the one played by his hero, Cuchulain, when as a boy of seven, he bested all the kings' and nobles' sons who were training through games to be warriors, and became leader of the Boys' Troop at the court of the king.

As time for the match drew near, heralded by shouts and laughter from the game field, the flattest stretch of land near the village, David picked up his shinty stick and went out on his crutches.

He returned without it. Christy was sure he had given it to a player, perhaps Alai. How difficult that must have been, to admit he could no longer play the game at which he had excelled.

"Would you like a game of chess?" Christy asked. The captain, Mairi, and Gran had gone to watch the match but Christy had waited to see what David wished to do.

He gave her a look that said he saw through her tactic and resented it. "I'm going to the game," he said. "Come on, Chul." He watched the game, cheering and hooting and shouting advice. Back and forth between the boundaries the players flailed the ball and often one another. The game ended when everyone was gasping and could barely jog, with Tam's side far ahead thanks to Alai Gunn's irresistible dashes with David's stick.

Alai, dark hair plastered to his forehead and violet eyes glowing, came over to David. " 'Twas your grand stick, Davie! Such a grip it has, such a swing!" His face fell. "But 'tis shame indeed you cannot—"

David reached for his crutches and swung up from the rock where he'd been sitting. "I'm glad the stick suits you, Alai. Next year I'll wager you're made captain." He managed a hardy grin before he turned abruptly and maneuvered away. He scarcely ever fell anymore.

Alai, staring after David, said, "Did I do wrong? It must be cruel hard for him."

"You did right," Christy said. In a rush of pride and worship, she added through her tears, "And so did he!"

V

A week into the new year of 1861, David looked up from the chessboard and said to the captain, "Father, by your leave, I will not go to Inverness. Not this time."

The captain raised an eyebrow and waited.

"I can't leave Chul. I cannot do it."

His father sighed and shook his head, more in compassion than anger. "Lad, this cannot serve. How will you manage to live in this world if you allow yourself to be so tenderhearted for a dog?"

"He's my dog, Father."

"And a faithful companion he has been. But, Son, people often cannot arrange their lives in order to oblige their families, much less their animals."

David's jaw had the same determined set as his father's. "It's that Chul will think I deserted him. I can't tell him why I need to go away the way I can tell Christy."

I can understand but I would mourn as much as Chul . . .

"David——" began the captain.

Mairi looked up from her work. "Iain! You said you would leave it to the lad."

Her husband tensed. He glanced from wife to son and back again. "Very well," he said at last. "For now David stays, though I trust both of you will consider his future while I'm away and grow more reasonable."

"Thank you, Father."

"You may not thank me long. I'll send a schoolmaster from the mainland and I shall tell him to ground you solidly in the subjects you should be studying at the academy."

"Oh, I don't mind studies, Father!" Laughing in relief, David bent to scratch Chul's ears. Chul, not knowing the misery he had escaped at least temporarily, yawned, nuzzled his master's hand, and settled back to doze with his head by David's feet.

Next day, a servant from the Lodge brought a parcel and a note for Mairi. "It's in English," she said, handing it to Christy. "I can read print but by no means can I make out this writing."

Christy, too, had problems with the elegant spidery hand. Puckering her brow, she slowly deciphered the words.

> "Dear Mrs. MacDonald:
>
> Accept our apologies and these glasses to replace the broken one. I could not find another white plaid so I trust the money in the envelope will pay for making a new one. My sister is still in a depressed state after her husband's death. We will seek more diversion for her on the mainland but it is my hope that you will someday allow me to hear your famous harp. Assuring you of my deep regard, and with cordial greetings to your husband, I remain your obedient servant,
>
> Charles Forsyth."

Gran blew out her cheeks. "Well, that's polite! But I'll warrant Charles Forsyth is in the same style as his sister. There's something uncanny about the pair of them."

"A five-pound note!" Mairi held it as if it might bite. "Almost enough to buy a cow! But far too much."

"Keep it," said Gran.

Mairi shook her head. "If he had sent two pounds for the arisaid, I would take it. But not by any road will I be under obligation to Charles Forsyth. I hope never to see him or his sister again, and certainly I won't play Cridhe for them." She stuffed the money back into the envelope and handed it to Christy.

"Lass, will you run after the servant and tell him to give this to Mr. Forsyth?"

"Maybe you should see what's in the parcel. You may want to send it back, too."

Mairi opened the bundle and unwrapped six goblets of gleaming crystal.

"Will you send five back?" Gran teased.

"Indeed not." Mairi gave a rueful laugh. "I'll pack away Iain's mother's goblets and keep these to be broken next time sottish gentry come calling."

The captain, who had been busy in his study, flushed to the roots of his hair when he heard about the five pounds. "Had Forsyth found the same plaid and sent it, there could be no question of affront," he growled. "But to send money is blasted insolence."

"I sent it back," Mairi reminded. "Don't be too vexed. Perhaps that's how things are done in America."

"I cannot think it."

"He's gone," Mairi shrugged. "Or soon will be."

"Aye," said Gran, chuckling. "And we've packed away your crystal so now it's his we'll break."

For eleven years now, the captain had been in partnership with Mairi's older brother, Calum, who had come home from the wars to follow his sweetheart, Catriona, to Texas. Not only love called him, but he was given a mighty push because he had escaped the Stornoway tolbooth or jail after severely beating the official responsible for Fearchar's death and the burning of the village. Mairi and a friend had managed to free him and Magnus Ericson smuggled him aboard *Selchie* for the first leg of his journey to Texas.

Prospering there, he had returned to visit his family while on a mission to locate several horses and bulls for his Texas neighbors. For some time, the captain's uncle, Sir Roderick, had been breeding Clydesdales from Flanders stallions and large local mares. The Flanders horses went back to the war chargers of the Middle Ages. Grand beasts they were, hoofs as large as platters, but no use at all on the islands.

They were well worth their hay and grain where there was much plowing and hauling to be done. Canada got its first Clydesdale stallion in 1840 and others followed. Australia imported hundreds. So it worked out that the captain helped Calum buy good animals from Sir Roderick and accompanied him to Texas to collect more orders.

This arrangement meant the captain was gone much of the time but was probably the salvation of his marriage. Though he did his share of the work when he was home, cutting and lifting peats, plowing and hauling tangle, the captain was no fisherman-crofter, nor with the best will in the world could he ever be.

Knowing that his absences meant extra work for Mairi's male relatives, he bought Kelpie to haul peats and tangle and plow, and installed a mill so that the women didn't spend hours each day in grinding meal on stone querns, which hadn't changed much since the dawn of time. When he was home, he taught school and helped do Clanna's accounts. There had been hard years during the potato famine, but since then the village sustained itself and even got a bit ahead from the sale of fish and woolens. Mairi, Christy knew, had refused to desert her people and go to live on the mainland and lead the life of the gentry.

"Life isn't all kisses and ceilidhs," Gran was fond of saying. Certainly it hadn't proved so for Mairi and Iain. But if their baby daughter hadn't been stillborn at Sollas—

The old sickening guilt churned in Christy as the captain came out of his study with his traveling bag. Mairi and her husband made no private farewells. His warm hug and kiss for Gran made a painful contrast to the formal kiss on the cheek that he gave his wife, scarcely more than the swift brush of his lips across Christy's forehead.

All Clanna turned out to wave him on his journey. David, on Kelpie, would accompany him to Stornoway to bring Chieftain back. A mercy that David could ride. Christy, waving and calling with the rest, was very grateful he would be coming back.

Toward the end of January, Bruce Urquhart, the teacher the captain had hired from the mainland, trudged over the slope with more books in his pack than clothing. Gaunt and so tall he'd acquired a stoop from entering low doors or bending to speak with shorter folk, Mr. Urquhart had flyaway brown hair and gray eyes that were beautiful when he took off steel-rimmed spectacles. An orphaned crofter lad of exceptional intelligence, he'd been reared by a Ross-shire schoolmaster who worked him hard for his keep but saw that he went to the university. At parish schools on Skye, Bruce had seen his pupils cleared along with their parents.

"When Major MacDonald's back, he'll help me find another school on Lewis in a parish not likely to be cleared," Bruce said. "It's hard to teach young ones and then see them shipped off to Canada and Australia where they'll get no more education."

"Then what you gave them was all the more important," Mairi said. "If folk can read, they can teach themselves. God grant there'll be no more villages cleared on Lewis."

She settled him in the office-schoolroom. He was delighted to live with a family. On Skye, he'd lived in a tiny room attached to the school and boiled enough porridge in the morning to last him all day. Under Gran's cosseting, he soon filled out. The children took to him at once. He excited them with worlds that had been, with far countries and peoples, and taught a good deal less from the Bible than had previous dominies.

He joined the ceilidhs those long winter nights. The men

were at first reserved with him, suspicious of a man who made his living with his mind, but he was so unassuming and good-natured that the first awkwardness quickly passed.

Although ten years older than David, he became his friend. While they played chess, they exchanged quotes in Greek and Latin, but these quiet nights were often changed into ceilidhs when neighbors dropped in to hear Mr. Urquhart's news of the great world beyond the island.

"God protect my Catriona and her family!" breathed Morag, upset at the teacher's prediction that there would soon be a war in the United States.

"And Iain and Eileen and all the rest!" said Gran. "Bruce, lad, do you think it likely there'll be fighting in Texas?"

"I doubt that many battles will be fought on the frontier, though from the Texans' reputation they like to fight and many won't be kept out of a war. The main struggle, surely, will be in the east, the most settled part of the country."

"Calum had enough fighting in the queen's wars," said Mairi. Hopefully she added, "Iain says the North and South have been squabbling for years but so far they've always compromised."

The young man shook his head. "I fear it's gone past that."

"Wars and wars!" cried Gran. "I lost two sons in the British war against Napoleon. Our island lads were hustled off to fight the czar, who was never the tyrant that some lairds are! Let's talk no more of battles this night. Mairi, tune your harp, do, and give us a song."

David couldn't help with spreading sand and seaweed in the lazybeds where potatoes would soon be planted nor could he work with a cas-chrom, a special kind of spadelike foot plow used when cultivated plots were too boggy or rocky for the horse-drawn plow. He helped take care of Kelpie, though, as Tam MacLeod plowed most of Clanna's arable land. The captain had once plowed for his own widowed, impoverished mother and had taught his brother-in-law how to take his place in following the contours of the little slopes so the furrows wouldn't turn into gullies during heavy rain and let good, scarce soil be sluiced away.

Sturdy little Kelpie seemed to take satisfaction in his work. The dun gelding pushed his weight into the collar, snorting and nodding his head, tossing his thick mane, dug his hoofs firmly into the earth and lifted them out in neat, quick fashion. His neck and sides grew sweaty and he held his tail high to cool himself, but he never stopped till Tam gave the order.

At the end of the day, Tam uncoupled the plow, looped the chains and reins to the harness, and led Kelpie slowly toward the house. After Tam unharnessed, David briskly rubbed the pony's damp hide and crooned soft Gaelic endearments. When the pony had cooled enough to drink, David led him to the stream and brought him back to graze near the house till twilight.

Christy carried fresh straw bedding to the stall so it would be ready when David led Kelpie through the fasgalan down the passage to the barn and stable built against the back side of the house. Because Kelpie was working, David fed him oats and Christy put hay in front of him. Helping David this way gave her a warm, happy feeling unless she thought about how it must eat at him not to be able to do a man's work.

In March and February, oats were sown and potatoes planted. March was the best month for cod, along the coast and David persuaded Tam to let him help row and learn to handle the fishing lines.

Brighde and *An Clanna,* the third boats to bear those names, for in these rough seas a fishing boat did well to last five years, couldn't safely venture beyond the Minch, but they were best for this winter fishing, which was done with lines instead of nets. It took an hour's smelly, slippery work to bait the eight hundred to a thousand hooks on a line with eels, mussels, or limpets. Each hook dangled from a horsehair tipping attached to the main line, which was skillfully coiled at the wider end of an oval willow basket with the baited hooks in the narrow end, placed so they wouldn't tangle as the lines were "shot" or trailed out of the boat.

Fishermen thrust a gaff into a gill or head to hoist the thirty- to forty-pound fish into the boat and cut its throat with a knife before throwing it down to bleed. If fishing was slow, the catch might be headed and gutted at sea, with the valuable livers and swimming bladders saved.

When a boat approached the quay, the women and older girls slipped into oilskin coverall aprons and got their knives, hurrying to the three-walled curing shed. Morag's and Gran's fingers were too stiff for the work. They, Christy, Caitlyn, and Rona looked after the younger children, prepared meals, tended to the milking, and took turns keeping up a fire in the shed with a simmering pot of tea so the workers could warm their icy fingers and heat their insides.

It was fascinating to see the silvery gray fish that might be five feet long be dumped on a long table with built-up sides like a trough. In a few deft motions, the heads were cut off and tossed in one creel, livers in another, and the swimming bladders in yet an- other—these brought a guinea a firkin from the owner of an isin- glass factory who was a friend of Magnus's. Guts and the elongated backbones were cast aside, and the fish dropped into brine vats. The women worked in teams, two gutting while the third packed.

Mairi's fingers, like those of the other women, were wrapped with old linen for protection, but inevitably, as the sharp knives sliced, hands smarted from cuts and nicks and fumbled with cold. Christy hated to see fingers that could bring such music from the harp put to such a use, hated to see her foster mother spattered with blood and entrails, but she had heard Mairi tell the captain that she could not, in conscience, avoid this dirtiest, most grueling task the women had.

Still, there were fresh fish aplenty and Gran made tasty

dishes, broiling a small fish stuffed with livers, wild thyme, and oatmeal or bannocks filled with chopped livers.

Christy helped Gran melt fish livers to oil that was strained and used for cruisies, and thrust scores of fish on sticks that hung from the rafters to be dried and smoked. Then, when it seemed they had worked forever with the fish, a storm howled in. The boats had to be pulled far up the beach out of the reach of the hungry sea, and there was time for visiting again, a bit of frolic and music.

The Nicolsons came by after supper and Andrew said plaintively to Tam, "We've not heard your pipes for a long while, laddie."

Gran nodded. " 'Tis a night for music that will sound over the shriek of the gale."

"You mean my pipes shriek?" chuckled Tam. "Well, if you can stand it, I can pipe it."

Lucas Nicolson's hazel eyes lit and he turned toward the door. "I'll get my fiddle."

His slightly younger brother, fair-haired Paul, handed baby Colin to his Rose. "I'll tell the others we're having a ceilidh."

By the time the Nicolson brothers were back, Tam had taken his pipes out of their tartan cover, the black and green checks intersected by narrow lines of red and yellow of the MacLeods. Tucking the bag beneath his right elbow, Tam moved the drone slides to make them harmonize with his fingering of the flutelike ebony chanter.

When he was content with the sound, he bowed to the company and began the "MacLeod Salute." He played first the opening or Ground that flowered into variations of the tune, doublings, treblings, and grace notes as he listened to some inner music and followed it into the swirling *Crunluath* or crowning movement, the theme note followed by a chain of eight grace notes that flowed back into the Ground.

"Grand piping, Tam," applauded Murdo MacKinnon, gray

eyes shining. In his early sixties, the elected skipper of *Brighde* was the oldest man of Clanna and a one-time shepherd who had helped David train Chul. "Captain MacDonald taught you well." For Iain had given Tam the pipes and rudiments of playing that Winter of the Broch.

The villagers came in, carrying milking stools, sheepskins, or mats to sit on, leaving the padded settle for mothers with babes in arms. When the hearth room filled, the younger men took places in the broad passage and Iain's office. Small children tumbled down on the sheepskin with Chul, who graciously accepted their hugging and crooning. The women knitted or carded fleece and the men twisted heather rope or mended gear.

Lucas Nicolson tossed back his rust-brown hair as he tuned his fiddle. "The best thing I can say for the army of the English queen," remarked the former soldier, "is that it's kept the pipes alive."

" 'Tis a strange thing," added his brother, Paul, with a wry grin, "for men to battle foes of the queen to the same tunes that once urged us to fight the English." The brothers, along with Mairi's brother, Calum, had taken the queen's shilling along with the promise that if they went for soldiers, their families would be secure in their tenancy. The same lying promise had been made to the MacAskill twins, Gerald and Neil. Neil's family had died of exposure but Gerald's blue-eyed Marta sat knitting him a jersey while their daughters carded wool.

It was well that carding was done more by touch than sight for Molly MacAskill watched Tam constantly except when he chanced carelessly to look her way. Molly blushed then to the roots of her dark hair and paid great attention to the fleece till it was safe to steal another glance at Tam.

He was a handsome man, resembling Mairi not at all with his long narrow face with a pointed chin, brilliant green eyes, and hair bleached silver. Not hard to imagine him rising out of the white-capped waves, taking shape and form. Met along a sea cliff or the shore, he could have been one of the seal folk in human guise or an *uisge-each* or water horse in his beguiling shape of a handsome lad who swept mortals to their death by drowning.

He piped "The Great Spree" and "The Bespeckled Bull" before urging Lucas to take his turn. The russet-haired fiddler played "Flora MacDonald's Lament" and "Come Under My Plaidie" before he launched into strathspeys, reels, and hornpipes that set feet tapping. Gran could bear it no longer.

Springing up, she tugged Paul into the fasgalan where they had room to dance. They were joined by Una and Marcus MacFarlane. Molly dragged Tam—but he didn't pull back enough to discourage her.

Alai grinned a question at Christy. Though flattered that the handsome young man had asked her, she shook her head. "Go on," said David gruffly. "No need for you to sit here because I must."

"Alai was just working up courage to ask Seana," Christy laughed. "Look, there they go!" She crowded her milking bench against the wall to make more room. "Anyway, it's more fun to watch. Look at your mother and Murdo! And there goes Mr. Urquhart with Noreen MacAskill!"

Those couples, with the Gunns and elder MacAskills, danced in the storeroom till they were out of breath. Happily gasping, the neighbors found seats and ignored Morag's dour stare. She held with the ministers that dancing and music were devil's lures, though it was her son who'd done the fiddling.

"I mind what happened to one fiddler, though he was a laird's own son," she said grumpily. "Didn't James Macpherson hang high at the Cross of Banff and didn't he first break his heathen fiddle over his knee—"

"Wheesht, Mother!" objected Lucas good-naturedly. "He broke his fiddle since no one could play it as well as he. And sure, he was hanged for his robberies, not his music."

"Whose story is this?" snapped Morag.

"A story, is it?" teased Lucas, ducking a crack of his doughty mother's knuckles. "I thought 'twas a preachment."

"Well, so it is, if you've ears to listen, rascallion! Jamie Macpherson grew up to the devil's tunes and made up more of his own—"

Lucas cut in. "Aye, 'Macpherson's Farewell' that he played on the gallows is a very fine tune—"

Morag's knuckles found their mark this time on her son's curly red-brown head. "Will you leave me tell my story?"

"When did you need anyone's leave, Mother?" Everyone laughed as Lucas dodged another rap. With the air of a saint much tried, Morag continued.

"The Macpherson had friends in high places and the sheriff got wind that a pardon was on its way. So he set the clock forward and Macpherson hanged half an hour early, just as the messenger with his pardon galloped into sight." She dipped her head in mournful satisfaction and gazed at her fiddler son. "So the devil claimed his own, and what jolly reels does Macpherson dance now on the eternal coals of hell?"

"Better dance than broil, Mother," grinned the unregenerate Lucas. "Whatever, he left the world some bonny tunes. Mairi, will we have a song from Cridhe this night?"

Christy knew that Mairi had a painful cut from her gutting knife on a finger that would have bled had she tried to play. "I'll tell a story instead." She smiled at David. "A Cuchulain story."

"No!" David's cry was so fierce that everyone stared, then looked swiftly away. He flushed and said in a husky voice, "I—I'm too old for those stories."

Mairi didn't point out that even Gran had never raised that objection. It was painfully clear that David, crippled, couldn't bear to hear tales of his former hero's exploits. Smiling, Mairi said, "Well, I can see where you might begin to have your doubts about a laddie who had seven pupils in each eye, seven toes on each foot, seven fingers on each hand, cheeks that were yellow, blue, red, and green, and long hair, dark at the roots, red in the middle, and light at the tips. That was when he was in a good mood. In battle, his hair stood on end and sparks of fire shot from it. A jet of blood spurted high from the top of his head and flames poured from his mouth. In this state he was invincible, and small wonder. Who wouldn't run?''

She told a hair-raising story then of Stronach, a murderer who had roamed the Lewis moors in her childhood, waylaying travelers and even drowning a boy. ''Gran used to scare us with him,'' Tam said, pitching his voice crankily. '' 'Hurry with your chores, children, or Stronach will get you!' ''

''You loitered anyway,'' retorted Gran. ''But after that tale, Lucas, will you not play a soft tune to make us all sleep sound and sweet?''

Lucas obliged with an old song of the seagulls on the waves. Then neighbors gathered up knitting, ropes, nets, stools, and children, pulled shawls and cloaks snug, and called their good nights. Christy stole a glance at David.

Tonight he had cleared the hurdle of watching others dance. His whole life would be like that, Christy realized with a pang, having to accept his limits. But there'd be gains, too. He could row a boat. He could rub down the horses and ride. She was increasingly afraid though that the captain was right. If David was to make the most of his life, he would have to win the kind of education that could only be got on the mainland.

The cattle were joyful at being out of their byres after the long winter and lowed with pure pleasure in their freedom as they fed on the channeled wrack. Sheep, too, fed on seaweed and so did Kelpie, frisking along the shore as he enjoyed his chance to eat the weed rather than haul it.

Below the channeled wrack grew bladder wrack with its paired air bladders about the size of peas that held up the plants as the tide rose so they wouldn't dash hard against the rocks. Yellow-green discs of thongweed about an inch or two in diameter formed mats on gently sloping rocks protected from heavy surf or grew in pools, sending out flattened straps that contrasted with the bright pinkish purple of coralline weeds.

Oarweed or tangle grew right at the bottom of the shore and was exposed only at the lowest water for a few days of the year. The stems could grow up to five feet long and Gran said quarreling kelpers had used them for clubs on occasion. Brownish sea lace grew underwater in the summer, the cordlike fronds that might be as long as twenty feet a danger to swimmers. And there were other kinds of seaweed that massed together like underwater forests, some beautifully colored as long as they stayed submerged.

At the ebbing of the tides as the spring equinox approached, Christy and the other girls and young women searched up and down the coast to gather purplish carrageen and pull red dulse loose from rocks or the "warts" on the lower stems of a seaweed that was much like tangle.

Carrageen grew on rocks at this level. Well washed, it would be dried till it was white. Then, added to milk, it made a nice pudding. Dulse was tough and had to be cooked a whole morning or afternoon, but it could also be washed, dried, and chewed on as a snack.

The sea harvest came when last year's grain and potatoes were running low. Christy was carrying a small creel of dulse to the house when a horseman came in sight over the slope.

It couldn't be the captain back so soon. Crofters didn't have big horses, only shaggy little ponies like Kelpie, and they seldom rode them, saving the animals' strength for work. The moment Christy saw the rider's arrogant posture as he and his horse appeared on the skyline, she had a premonition that grew into certainty before she could make out Charles Forsyth's face.

She thought of trying to elude him by going within but decided it was better to meet him outside and perhaps keep him from upsetting Mairi Mór. It was silly to be so fearful. Sheila and Morag were at the mill, Katie Gunn was fetching water from the stream, and the men were visible down at the shore where they were working on the boats.

Grateful that she was obviously far from alone, Christy greeted the horseman in her best English. "Good morning to you, sir."

"What?" Charles Forsyth slipped easily from the saddle and held his horse's reins. "No hundred thousand welcomes?"

"If you are hungry, sir, there's bannocks and fresh crowdie. If you're thirsty, I'll fetch you milk or *brochan*."

He lifted an amused silver eyebrow. His eyes were almost as pale as his hair, with only a hint of green. "Will you fetch out Mistress Mairi? It's she I wish to talk with."

"She—she is busy, sir."

His tone was mocking. "Well, I have a flask of good whisky so I will forego your skimmed milk and oat water. The wind nips chill, though. I should expect your hospitality to stretch to a place by the fire."

It went against all she had been taught to deny the request of a visitor, but she spoke with forced composure. "After what happened last time you were here, sir, I do not think that Mistress MacDonald can want you at her hearth."

"I must see her all the same." He moved away from his horse as Mairi came out, followed by Chul, who raised his hackles at the stranger.

Mairi said in her careful English, "It is a surprise to find you here, Mr. Forsyth. We have heard a war is like to break out in your country."

"All the more reason to be here," he said. "I have hired a substitute, a poor farmer who will be very glad to fight in my place. But it's not that I wish to discuss with you."

"We cannot have much to say to each other, sir."

"Your voice is colder than the wind." He pretended to

shiver beneath his warm cape. "No wasting words, then. A proud woman like you can scarce desire to chain a man against his will."

Christy gasped. Mairi could not have looked more surprised had he drawn a hidden knife but somehow she kept her voice steady. "What do you mean?"

"To be brief, your husband fancies my sister."

"I don't believe you!"

"I grant it makes sad hearing." His sympathy was more hateful than his jeers. "But you can hardly be surprised at the consequences of marrying out of your class. You can't be happy with your husband gone most of the time. Give him his freedom and gain your own. I've heard of that handsome Orkney sea captain."

Mairi was pale but she looked straight into the Virginian's eyes. "If my husband wishes a divorce, he must say so himself."

"He's chicken-hearted where you and the lad are concerned. Can you wish to hold a man who loves another woman?"

"I do not think he loves her. I think that you, sir, cannot rule her and you wish to pass that duty on to another."

Forsyth reddened. "I'll admit that I want to see my sister wed to a man who'll control her fidgets. Her first husband was a weakling. The next must be able to use spur and rein."

"I wish you luck in finding him."

"You don't understand. Chellis wants your husband. She'll toy with others but he's the only one she'd consider marrying."

Mairi gave a contemptuous laugh. "Is Iain a poppet that she screams for like a spoiled brat and thinks I must give him up? Such talk is gormless."

"You'll condemn him to this unlucky marriage?"

"If Iain feels condemned, he has a tongue."

Forsyth's smooth face twisted. "If Sir James would sell this island, I'd have you and your rabble out of your huts the instant rents were due!"

"You—you would buy the island?" If the terrifying thought was like a kick in Christy's stomach, what must it be to Mairi?

"I've offered more than Matheson paid," shrugged Forsyth. "But he's set on pouring his money into a place that clearly should be turned into one great deer forest. I'd leave a few fishing villages, enough to supply gillies for stalking and servants for the lodges."

Sir James had refused to sell to this man! Christy's relief was immediately engulfed by horror. Lowlander, Englishman, American, anyone with money could buy an island or large estate and do exactly as they pleased with the tenants.

Mairi said, "I count it among God's blessings that you are not our laird. You will excuse me now. I must be about my work."

"Have you no pride, to hold a man who loves elsewhere?"

"Your sister has no pride, or decency either, to flaunt herself at a married man. And you—I think there is an English word for a man who seeks out custom for a whore."

Forsyth half-raised his whip. Chul growled. David appeared in the door, steadied himself against it, and leveled his father's pistol.

"Take yourself off, sir! Do not be coming back."

Forsyth's lips pulled back from his teeth. "You wouldn't dare draw that pistol on me, boy, were you not Major MacDonald's son."

"I *am* his son. And my mother's. So you had better go."

Forsyth's eyes dilated before he shrugged and laughed. "So the crippled whelp can bark! You won't be so brave, though, when your father renounces his ill-made marriage and you're just another crofter lad, a gimpy one at that!"

The man mounted, turned his horse, and slashed down the whip. As they galloped out of sight, Mairi said, "I wonder if he'll have the face to complain of us to Sir James?"

"I hope he does!" gritted David. "I couldn't hear all he said, Mother, but—"

She touched his hand. "Put it out of your head, laddie."

"I'm sorry, Mairi Mór," said Christy. "I tried to send him on his way."

"I thank you for that, lass." Mairi drew a long breath. "Let's hope we've seen the last of him—and his sister, too. Now, if that dulse's to be ready for supper, let's set it on to boil."

VI

Sea pinks brightened pockets of shell sand along the shore. The huge spring wash was done and the barley sowed. Wild greens, mustard, spinach, and nettles brought zest to broth and shriveled potatoes. No ewe had lost her lamb, no cow her calf, and the season promised fair. Except that David could not walk, nor ever would again.

That clearly distressed Magnus Ericson who brought *Selchie* into the Clanna harbor that spring to collect the winter's store of fish. His mist-blue eyes rested intently on Mairi as Gran explained Iain's business that kept him so much on the mainland and in America.

"To be sure, it's a grand undertaking," said the big weather-burned man whose hair was so bleached by wind and sun that it shone gold only in streaks shielded by the longer strands. His gaze moved from Mairi to her son, as if he wondered how any man could leave them. "Shall we have a game of chess, lad?"

When he was leaving, in front of everyone, he took Mairi's hands in his large, powerful ones. "Mairi, lass, if—if there is aught I can do for you, vow you will let me know."

She smiled and slipped her hands away. "You already do too much for us, Magnus."

"I make a good profit from Clanna goods." In spite of the brisk words, for an instant his heart showed in his eyes for even one as young as Christy to read.

In May, the *North Star* left for the herring fishing with every male of Clanna over sixteen on board. As herring approached their first spawning season, immense shoals of them came in from the open Atlantic to feed near the coast of Southern Ireland. From there they migrated around the West Highland coasts and Northern Scotland till they reached the North Sea. Following them, the Clanna men would not return till late August or September.

With the men gone, Clanna took on some of the female gaiety of the fondly remembered summer shielings when young women went up to tend the village herds. There was much work to do, but most of it was outside where friends could banter or sing together.

With Chul bringing in recalcitrant sheep with his crouch and dominating stare, the women clipped the sheep carefully with sharp knives, not cutting too close lest a late cold rain soak in and fatally chill the animals. "Sheep are always looking for an excuse to die," Gran said. "Let's not give it to them."

Christy helped Mairi hold Cailan down, soothing her with gentle words, though Christy all too well remembered that it was this dainty, wilful little creature that had caused David's fall. Did the ewe know how lucky she was not to be a rug and some jars of pickled meat?

Gran deftly took off the last of the four-horned sheep's coat, much finer and wispier than that of the black-faced sheep, whose long, coarse fleeces hung almost to the ground like shaggy mantles. Katie Gunn brought a pail of tar mixed with old butter and rubbed this into the roots of Cailan's hair before she was allowed to scramble up, blatting indignantly, and run off to her lamb.

Sheep had to be smeared to ward off numerous insect pests, the worst being maggots, which could burrow deep in the animals' flesh and even kill them. This sticky, dirt-attracting mixture stuck to the clipped fleece, and washing the fleece free of it was one of the most tedious and difficult chores. Then it would have to be carded, combed, cleaned, and dyed before it could be spun.

Christy enjoyed gathering dyestuffs for Gran: sorrel and lady's bedstraw for beautiful reds, bramble roots for orange, heather for green, heather tops for yellow, and water lily roots for black and gray. When there was enough breeze to keep off the swarms of tiny midges that bred in the wavery line of seaweed left by the highest spring tide in March, Christy wandered along the shore, gathering lichens from the rocks for Gran's dye pots.

Whales appeared like small floating islands, dolphins played, and now and then she glimpsed the dorsal fins of a party of killer whales who all blew at the same time, their fins rearing high. Andrew said a full-grown bull's fin could be six feet long though the creatures themselves were seldom more than twenty feet long. They were the brigands of the sea, attacking dolphins, seals, and the largest whales.

The sea cliffs were alive with the black and white flutter of nesting birds, guillemots in crowded colonies on precipitous ledges with kittiwakes nearby, dark cormorants and shags thick along the top and sides of a deep chasm, and noisiest of all, the many tribes of gulls and terns.

About a mile south of the Clanna harbor was a small sea loch with a great rock that was a favorite resting place of seals. Eelgrass grew thickly along the shore, and one May morning, Christy was collecting a creel of it to dry and use with fluffy cotton grass to stuff Gran's and David's mattresses, which had worn lumpy and thin in places.

It was hard to keep her mind on eelgrass when it was such fun to watch the dozen or so young and old seals sunning companionably on the rock. Their colors ranged from black, gray-blue, and light brown to greenish cream. It especially delighted Christy when a mother slipped into the sparkling water, pup riding happily on her back, holding onto her with its tiny flippers.

A shape in the waves caught her attention. She shielded her

eyes and made out the rust-red sail of a small boat. Who could it be? Apart from Magnus Ericson with his ocean-worthy ship, *Selchie,* craft seldom called in at the harbor. Stuffing a last handful of eelgrass in her creel, she fitted it on her back and hurried to tell Mairi.

Together, they walked down to the quay where the boat was being tied by the oarsmen while one of them helped a frail man to safe footing on the quay. Beneath his oilskin, he wore a black suit and high white collar.

"Father Coll!" Mairi cried, hurrying forward with outstretched hands. "Father Coll MacDonald!"

Christy remembered the name and even, faintly, the priest, though she was only five when he last came to Mairi. He had sought help for his destitute people after the clearing of Knoydart. He had seemed old then. Now he was a wisp, but fire still burned in his eyes.

"Mairi," he said. "There is great trouble at Greenyards near where the cruel Glencalvie clearing took place nine years ago."

"Trouble?" she echoed.

"Alexander Munro, who holds the lease on Greenyards, vows before God that he has not asked for evictions but the owners of the property desire them and can drive out the people with or without his consent." Father Coll shook his head. "Whatever his part, on March seventh, a sheriff and constable came with writs. A crowd of women searched the men and burned the papers but did not hurt them. Greenyards men took the lawmen to the inn and treated them to refreshments and whisky."

"Well, then—"

Father Coll raised his hand. "Two weeks later, three drunken officers tried to serve the writs. One of them leveled a pistol at a woman. Her young son pulled out a rusty old pistol and told the officer to leave his mother alone. So the writ-servers scurried to town with a tale of being menaced by a rioting mob."

"And of course they were believed!"

"Of course."

"That means more constables, if not soldiers."

Father Coll nodded. "A friendly journalist sent word that a force of constables and officers will come down on Greenyards very soon. The people have heard of you, Mairi. So have the lawmen. The tenants have a letter signed by Alexander Munro that denies he has authorized these evictions—though Munro is keeping a distance from all this, you may be sure. The crofters pray for you to bring your harp and songs and they ask that you give Munro's letter to the sheriff or procurator fiscal."

"I did little good at Sollas."

The name stabbed Christy. Remembering the captain's reproaches to Mairi, Christy could guess at the misery her foster mother must be feeling. The captain would be furious if Mairi interfered again with writ-servers as she had done at Sollas when she miscarried.

"You won a winter's grace for the Sollas folk," reminded the priest. "I know this is much to ask. But Mairi, whatever befalls, it will mean the world to these people that you came to sing and stand with them."

Don't go! Christy wanted to plead. *Davie needs you even though he won't let on he does. Clanna needs you. And what will the captain say?* But Christy also realized that Mairi had no choice when she was called, when Cridhe was invoked. And through a dizzy swirling, Christy knew what she herself must do.

The crew of the boat waited a little distance off. Mairi beckoned to them. "You must warm yourselves and have food and drink," she said. "Then we must go."

"I will go with you," Christy said in a voice that cracked.

Mairi shook her head. "I cannot let you, child. Besides, there's nothing you could do."

"I can be where you are."

Mairi looked at her as if she had never seen her before. "Lass, it is brave of you but there is no need—"

'' 'Tis a need for me,''. said Christy. ''Let me pay back a little the luck that saved me when my mother died.''

Mairi opened her mouth to protest, met Christy's gaze, and sighed. ''As you will, then. Put on your warmest clothes.''

When his mother said where she was going, David said, ''Let me come, Mother, and bring father's pistol!''

''That would invite murder for sure,'' said Mairi.

Father Coll added kindly, ''Besides, lad, it is a long tramp from where we land to Greenyards.''

David's thin face twisted. ''It's my place to protect you, Mother, while father is away.''

''You ran off Charles Forsyth,'' she reminded him and smoothed back his hair. ''I'll be careful, Davie, and I'll worry less knowing you're safe. I wish Christy would stay home, too.''

''You're letting her go?'' cried David. He started to leap up and sank back when his legs would not support him. ''Why, she's a girl, and not yet twelve years old!''

Gran said quietly, ''The lass has that right, David. Remember, she's from Sollas where not a soul is left.''

He argued no more. Mairi changed into her arisaid and Christy put on her woolen overskirt and got her heavy shawl. As the party was leaving, David said to Christy, ''You'll have a care for mother?''

''Aye.''

''You're going in my place.''

''No, Davie! This is *my* place, sure as my poor mother died along the shore of Uist.'' She laid her hand on his arm and looked up at him. He was growing taller in spite of the damage to his legs. ''Laddie, there will be grand brave things for you to do—much greater than this.'' One of Morag's countless proverbs edged into her mind. ''Possess your soul in patience.''

''Oh, aye! Easier said than done.'' David squeezed her hand. ''Watch out for mother, then, but have a care for yourself, too,'' Warmed by his hand and wish, she hurried after the others.

They were blessed that the Minch was not in a turbulent mood. They spent the night in a fishing village on Uist and crossed next day to sail through Dornoch Firth to the mouth of the Carron, which flowed through the wide green valley beneath rounded dun hills. There was an urgent message for Father Coll in the little village of Ardgay. One of the old Knoydart women whom he had taken into his home was on her deathbed and pleading for the sacrament. He had to get back in the boat and make for Loch Nevis, but first he blessed Mairi and Christy.

"Do your best to convince the people not to resist the officers, if they will not heed the letter from Alexander Munro," he cautioned. "There's fear among the lairds that revolutionaries are inflaming tenants to violence. The greater that fear, the more cruelly the law will act to maintain order."

Mairi's eyes blazed. "The order of the poor crushed underfoot or banished across oceans! But a slaughter like that at Sollas will help nothing. Never fear, Father. I'll try to hearten the people to endure even if they must flit."

One of the Greenyards men went with Father Coll to lend a hand with the oars. The other three tramped along with Mairi and Christy. The younger two, husky blond brothers named Angus and Diarmid Ross, took turns at carrying Cridhe.

The older man, graying Donald Ross, who said he was nearing seventy and limped from rheumatism, kept telling Mairi he could scarce believe the folk of Greenyards would be forced away. "Didn't I fight nine battles for the Crown?" he demanded. "Didn't I and other Highlanders help drub old Napoleon at Waterloo? What were we fighting for if it wasn't to be safe in our homes?"

"Och, Uncle Donald," said Angus, with a shake of his yellow hair. "You know how our kindred were driven from Glencalvie nine years ago. Didn't they scratch their names and grief on the kirk windows? Only six families were given other land. God knows where the others are.''

"James Gillanders cleared Glencalvie," remembered Diarmid. "He drove four hundred people from Strathconan.''

"Aye, and now that he's married the daughter of our laird, there's no bridle on his wickedness," said Angus. "It's true what the song says about him: *'He is a poor creature, without responsibility, without honor, understanding, or shame . . .'* Och, for the old days when we could take salmon from the river, and shoot grouse or a deer if we were hungered.''

"Those rights were bought by city gentlemen," grunted Diarmid. "And now we're fined twenty pounds if we cut a tree for roof timbers or a bridge. Much Gillanders cares for a song!''

"The worse for him," shrugged Angus. "Look, here come the women to meet us! You'll be staying with Christina Ross, Mistress MacDonald. She has the letter from Alexander Munro. In it, he vows he has not asked for these evictions. He holds the lease on the glen. How can it be cleared without his approval?''

"It seems the owners can do as they will," said Mairi.

To Christy it seemed that Munro might simply assure his tenants he did not authorize their removal but at the same time allow the landlord's factor to proceed. The Greenyards women called out greetings and warmly welcomed them.

Buxom, rosy-faced Christina Ross embraced Mairi, thanked her for coming, and brought her and Christy into the hearth room of a neat turf cottage and served them bannocks, milk, and barley broth.

"Can you read English?" Christina handed the precious letter to Mairi. "Doesn't Mr. Munro tell the laird he doesn't want us evicted?''

Mairi scanned the spidery writing, shook her head, and handed it to Christy. "You read handwriting better than I can. What does it say, lass?''

The letter was addressed to the laird, Major Robertson, who

was also the father-in-law of the factor, Gillanders. "Mr. Munro says he has not asked for evictions," Christy read.

Mairi glanced around at the eager faces and warned, "That may not mean that he has refused to allow them."

"Then 'tis playing with words and truth!" flashed Christina. "If Mr. Munro will not support us, why does he not say so?"

"Pontius Pilate washed his hands," said Mairi.

In spite of what must have been her weariness from huddling in the boat all day with Cridhe and then walking so far, she sang far into the night for the folk of the glen. Her last song was the one she had played in Stornoway Castle.

> If you would be rid of us, you must break the stones,
> You must sink the Highlands below the ocean.
> One day will come justice . . .
> Folk will bide safe in their homes.
> There will be no one with power to cast them out . . ."

Before dawn next morning, a lad burst into Christina's house, waking Christy from her sleep on the settle and bringing Christina and Mairi running from the bedroom.

"There's more than two score men coming!" the boy gasped. "Thirty-five constables and police superintendents from Dingwall and Fort William. I saw them come over the hills."

"So they're coming, the devils!" gasped Christina.

The lad's eyes were wide and frightened. "They had baskets of whisky and ale and swilled it like water. Swearing, they were, that they'd take no food till they'd taught the women of Green-yards not to interfere with law officers and writs."

Christy's heart pounded. She thought of what Mairi had told her of the constables at Sollas. They hadn't been drunk when they made their brutal charge on the women. Christina got Munro's letter from the dresser and held it as if it were magic.

"Those high officials are educated men, not a gang of brawling constables. They'll have to heed Mr. Munro's letter." Hastily, she tied on her frilled cap. "I'll go to meet them. But our men must get clean away or there's no telling what a crowd of drunken bullies might do to them." She seized the boy's shoulder and pushed him toward the door. "Run round the houses, laddie, and tell the men to hide. They cannot help, and would only wind up in jail where they'd be no use at all to their families."

Mairi fastened the brooch of her arisaid. "Will you let me carry Munro's letter, Christina? It may be the officers saw their grannies wear old-style clothes like these. Perhaps it'll startle them into reading Mr. Munro's message."

Christina gave over the letter and glanced toward Cridhe. "If you could bring your harp— 'Twould show we mean no mischief."

In ages past, Christy thought, the harp had sung in battle, sung till armies grew too large to hear her. This was a very small army at Greenyards. Christy felt sick at her stomach and her legs would scarcely carry her but she put on the bravest face she could and caught up with Mairi.

Gentlemen in a carriage, a host of constables. The police carried brightly polished truncheons blazoned with the initials of the English queen, Victoria Regina. Perhaps seventy women of the glen waited with their plaids drawn over their heads. Most of the men had gone into hiding but Donald Ross, the old Waterloo veteran, stood with the women as did several other men and boys.

The officers in the carriage got out. A ruddy-faced, dark-browed one walked to the head of the constables. "I am Sheriff-Substitute Taylor from Tain," he shouted in Gaelic. "If you don't wish to bide in our tolbooth, clear the way."

Mairi stepped forward, Cridhe in her arms. "Sheriff Taylor, will you please read this letter from Alexander Munro? He says——"

The officer glowered at her. "Are you that riot maker, Mairi of the Isles?"

"I am Mairi MacLeod MacDonald. I have made no riots."

"You are here instead of at your home on Lewis. I'll waste no time with your forgeries!"

"Sir!" Mairi cried. She held out the letter.

"Read them the Riot Act, sheriff," said a florid gentleman with such an air of authority that Christy thought he must be the procurator fiscal. Sheriff Taylor pulled a paper from his pocket and began to mouth the words.

The women, seeing that he meant to ignore Munro's letter, began to call out protests. "Mr. Munro gave me this letter himself, sir!" pleaded Christina, taking it from Mairi and trying to thrust it into the sheriff's hand. "He says he does not want us to flit."

"Aye!" shouted several women. Another cried: "We pay our rents to Mr. Munro. If he's content, who can put us out?"

Others pressed forward, trying to make the sheriff listen. "Mr. Munro vowed before God that he has not asked for this clearance!" "Go ask him!" "Forbye, read his writing, sir!"

Taylor, livid, thrust the act into his pocket and stepped back. "Clear the way!" he told the police superintendents.

Christina Ross, still pleading, still holding out the letter, went down under the truncheons. They kicked her with hobnailed boots in the head, on her face and breasts and shoulders. Christy tried to shelter her but was knocked aside. Women snatched up sticks and rocks to defend themselves but went down under truncheons swung with all a strong man's force.

Christy found a stick and brought it down as hard as she could on a constable's arm as he tried to hit Mairi. The woman beside her was struck so hard that the truncheon broke in half. The part with Queen Victoria's initials came to rest by Christy's skirt.

Wild eyes in a whiskered, cursing face, the sour smell of whisky. Christy tried to get in front of Mairi, who was shielding

Cridhe with her body. Christy was felled by a glancing blow. Mairi was knocked down on top of her. Before Christy came to her senses enough to move, her foster mother was dragged away.

Through a splitting headache, Christy heard the sheriff's voice. "Don't beat that one! She's wed to a major. We don't need him angry. Just handcuff her and throw her in the wagon."

A heavy boot crashed into Christy's skull. Instinctively, as her brain seemed to burst into white-hot flame, she threw her arms across the harp and fell into spinning darkness.

As Christy's mind cleared, she tried to sit up. It looked like a battlefield except instead of wounded soldiers, the grass was strewn with women and girls, most with blood running from gashes on their heads and shoulders. There were two mangled boys, and another man besides Donald Ross, the old veteran, whose white hair was dyed with blood. He lay near Christina Ross who did not move at all. Her face was so battered and broken that Christy wouldn't have known her except for her garments and the trampled letter she still clutched in her hand.

Constables roughly manacled the injured and heaved them in the wagon where Mairi was beginning to stir. Other police pursued the fleeing women and clubbed them down. A girl about Christy's age was kicked out of a thorn bush and one constable kneeled on her small breasts to hold her wrists up for another policeman to handcuff. Women screamed along the river, but soon there was only moaning.

Christy pushed the harp into the shelter of a bush and tried to crawl to Mairi but a policeman dragged her to the carriage and chained her to a wheel. It was like a war! In spite of what Mairi had told her about Sollas and Aosda, Christy could scarcely believe what she saw.

Officers and police moved from house to house, tacking up the writs since there was no one to receive them. Women of the village across the river ventured across and warily began to tend their battered, beaten neighbors.

"Och!" groaned Donald Ross. He tried to sit up and fell back. "In nine battles, never have I seen such a slaughter! Not of wounded enemy soldiers, or of prisoners of war—"

"There, Donald man," soothed a woman, bathing his head. "I don't think your skull is cracked. It's too hard belike!"

Christina did not rouse to her friends' gentle handling. They were trying to lift her on a blanket to carry her home when the sheriff's force returned.

"That one, she's for jail." The sheriff jerked his thumb at Christina. Had he no heart at all, to see what he had done? Seemingly at random, he pointed out three other women to the constables. "We'll bring along the ringleaders. Make a litter for the old harridan and that younger woman who put up such a fight. The others can walk." He gave Mairi a jeering grin. "And so can you, Mairi of the Isles."

The massive tower of Tain's tolbooth had a spire with a bell. The building served as both town hall and jail. Christy, Mairi, and the Greenyards women were locked in a cell with a heap of old straw, a couple of stools, and a bucket that was empty but stunk of its previous contents. Christy, Mairi, and the other youngest prisoner, a lissome brown-haired lass of perhaps eighteen, hastened to spread straw for the two unconscious women or the constables would have dumped them on the stone floor.

"Och, you poor souls!" The jailer's wife, a stout kind-faced woman, stared in fascinated horror at Christina Ross, whose pallid lips moved as she breathed heavily and groaned. Blood had clotted the two head wounds of the other victim, a young woman named Margaret Ross. "I'll call the doctor to these two as soon as he's back from Greenyards," said the jailer's wife. "A lad came running before you trudged up the way. Said his mother's head was broken and a score of other women carried away on litters. But if you will mob and riot—''

''We did not,'' said Mairi. ''But we'll thank you for water and clean rags.''

While Christy helped Mairi carefully bathe the hurts of the wounded, Ann Ross, the fourth prisoner from the glen, poured a little water on her stained, torn cap and wincingly worked it loose from the cuts on her head.

''There's bits of my cap driven into my skull,'' she murmured. ''Margaret, love, will you see if you can pick them out?''

Tidying themselves and having hot broth and bannocks revived the three who could eat. The elder Margaret roused and tried to sit up. ''My head!'' she moaned and began to retch.

Christy was closest and supported her over the malodorous pail. The abused woman, pale as if every drop of blood had drained from her body, broke into icy perspiration. They covered her with frayed blankets the jailer's wife had brought along with the sheets.

There were bloody bare patches on Ann Ross's skull where hair and skin had been clubbed away. *If they live, these women will carry scars to the grave. The English queen, can she be proud that her initials on the truncheons are clotted with the blood of Highland women?*

Christina Ross did not rouse from her stupor when Dr. Gordon examined her. ''At least she is not paralyzed.'' The graying man with deep-set weary eyes had dried blood on his dark clothing. ''But from the length of time she's been out of her senses and the severity of the wounds, I fear her mind may be affected.''

''I hope she is only concussed,'' he said of the older Margaret. ''Do not feed her till she has stopped vomiting for several hours, and then allow her only sips of broth or milk.''

He sewed a gash in Ann's head, his jaw set as if he were gritting his teeth. As he turned to leave the cell, a troubled-looking young gentleman hurried up. ''Reverend Aird,'' said the doctor, ''it is wicked to jail women beat as savagely as ever serfs of the czar could be. Will you join me in interceding for them?''

"Indeed I will," promised the boyish minister. "God help us all, this is worse than Glencalvie!"

"Well, it is a sermon for your pulpit, Gustavus. How can this happen in a Christian nation?"

"Still, a proprietor can do as he will with his land."

"It is *not* his land, sir." Mairi spoke for the first time. "All these Highlands and islands belonged once to the clans. A new generation will grow out of this—one that remembers the Clearances but has no memory of lairds who deserved respect, who lived among their folk. What the lairds have done—it is as if a father cast out his children! Folk have gone meekly, men have not resisted, because they are still bound by ancient loyalties. It will not be so with their sons and daughters."

"Your accent is not that of Ross-shire," frowned the minister. "And that antique garb—you must be Mairi MacDonald."

Young Margaret looked at Mairi with pride and something near worship. "She came from Lewis to play her harp for us. She is Mairi Mór, Great Mairi, Mairi of the Isles."

"Ah," said the doctor, and almost smiled. "I was asked to tell you that your harp came out of the thorns with no hurt but scratches and is safe in the village." He turned to the minister. "Now, Gustavus, let us try to make the judge see reason."

VII

At least the straw was clean and the jailer's wife frequently emptied the bucket and rinsed it. Christy helped Mairi tend the wounded women as best they could and wished fervently for Gran, or at least some of her herbs. It seemed an eternity, but two days later, Doctor Gordon and Reverend Aird were allowed to put up bail for the prisoners.

The doctor took the two seriously hurt women home in his carriage while the others walked. Christina roused now and then but her eyes darted wildly about, one pupil dilated, the other a pinpoint. Her speech was garbled and confused. The doctor feared her brain had been so injured that she would never regain her reason.

Margaret could keep down broth and porridge and her terrible headaches were lessening. It would be a long time before the splits in her scalp healed. Excepting Mairi, the women had been ferociously kicked and their faces, shoulders, necks, and arms were purple-black and bore the dents of hobnails.

What I'd like to do, thought Christy, is raise an army! I'd like to give sheriffs and superintendents, judges, factors, lairds, and constables a draught of their own medicine. But scythes and caschroms can't win over pistols and carbines.

Young Margaret said bitterly, "We expected Mr. Munro to support us and tell the sheriff he hadn't asked for evictions. 'Twas all for naught, poor Christina's brains addled, all the wounds—and it's sure that some will be sentenced to jail."

Mairi put an arm around the younger woman and held her. "But, lass, it was for something! The law will change when enough decent people who can vote are forced to know what is going on. Lairds can't work their will these days with no one the wiser."

"That won't give us our homes back."

"No, my dear. But you can be proud of your scars." The girl looked a little brighter and Mairi pressed on. "Didn't the doctor say that the same journalist who wrote of Knoydart has come to Greenyards and is writing a great blast in the papers and asking the Lord Advocate to inquire into the behavior of the sheriff and the police? What you suffered may keep the same wickedness from befalling other folk."

Margaret, from some depth of grit and spirit, summoned a chuckle. "Since I have my hurts, as well make ornaments of them and hope some lad will wish to wed such a grand heroine!"

"Your scars are more honorable than those medals the English queen invents," said Mairi. They laughed together, almost gaily.

Christy was marveling at her foster mother when she saw a man coming. She couldn't believe her eyes, thought it a trick from the blow on her head. She blinked. He was still there, marching down the track.

The captain! He was carrying the harp, thank goodness. Mairi had seen him, too. The laughter died on her lips and she looked frightened. As for the captain, Christy had never seen him look so savage.

Mairi moved ahead to meet him. "Iain—" She was visibly trembling and her voice broke in her throat.

He strode toward her. She stopped as if paralyzed. The carriage stopped. Iain only nodded to the doctor and minister. His eyes fixed on Mairi like gray lightning and the angry lines in his face changed to concern and tenderness.

"Mairi," he said. "My love, my brave one. Our son is waiting for us on the shore." And he took her in his arms.

Because of the war that had broken out in America, the captain had returned early. Since the grown men were away, David, Colin Nicolson, and Hamish MacAskill had clamored to help sail *An Clanna* to Dornoch Firth, and there the lads were waiting. The captain thanked Dr. Gordon and Reverend Aird for their kindness and added that he would likely see them in court when whoever the sheriff decided to designate as ringleaders were brought to trial.

"I will testify," vowed the captain, "that I saw stout ash truncheons broken in two from the force of the blows they delivered. Patches of scalp and hair and skin stuck to them. I saw heaps of torn, bloody clothing—caps torn and bloodied where clubs drove them into the skulls of the women. There were strands of long hair clotted with blood, and strips of skin torn from shoulders. That Glasgow lawyer and writer swears there were pools of blood in the field, so much that dogs came to lick it up."

"I saw it," said the doctor. "The blood of Greenyards women and a few men. No policeman got more than a bruise or a dented helmet."

The minister shook his head. "I do not understand Mr. Munro's position in all this. His name was on the writs and he met early in March with James Gillanders and the laird's law agent. Munro must have agreed then to the writs even if he didn't ask for them."

"Then he's responsible!" burst out Mairi. "The women would never have protested without Mr. Munro's letter."

"That will come out at the trial," Iain assured her. "We can do nothing more now, Mairi. Folk from other villages have taken in the evicted families and are seeing to the wounded. I left money for food and clothing and Lawyer Ross says he will return with more supplies."

Mairi embraced young Margaret and whispered, "Wear your

medals proudly!'' She pressed Ann Ross's hands and touched the elder Margaret's cheek as she leaned into the carriage to bid her farewell.

"My head's better.'' Margaret smiled weakly and patted Christy's face. "You were a brave lass to come with your mother.''

"Oh, I'm not—'' began Christy.

To her amazement, Mairi said, "She is a brave lass, true enough—and so are you.''

Christina did not hear them or even seem to see. She mumbled and groaned and whimpered like a scared child. Christy's cheeks were wet as she followed Mairi and the captain away. It was worth her bruises and the nightmare of the tolbooth, though, that Mairi hadn't said she wasn't her real daughter.

"Only a few scratches!'' Mairi said as she examined Cridhe, and called over her shoulder to Christy, "That was quick thinking, to hide the harp in a bush. Otherwise I have no doubt those drunken constables would have smashed it.''

Christy stayed far enough behind to allow the couple privacy. But when the captain's voice rose, she could not help but hear. "That men should so use women, women of their own Highland blood!''

"I got off lightly. The sheriff told the constables not to kick or beat me once I was knocked down—''

The captain made an unintelligible sound. "If I had been there—''

"Well that you were not.'' Mairi tried to joke. "Would it do for a retired major to be charged with mobbing and rioting?''

"It may happen.'' The captain bit off each word. "Even after I found you and the Aosda folk in such sorry plight, roofs burning, and your grandfather dead, I still believed emigration overseas was the only answer to poverty. I still think it the best thing for those who will go—look how well your brother and Catriona have done in America. But I cannot believe it just that a laird drive away people and give their crofts over to sheep or deer parks.'' He closed his hand over Mairi's. ''When I saw what happened at Greenyards, I understood why you had to go there, why you were at Sollas.''

''Iain——''

He drew her close and kissed her. ''If you are called again, I will go with you.''

''But your uncle! Sir James——your friends——I do not ask this, laddie, that you turn your back on your own kind.''

''I am your kind. I am your kind, and our son's.''

Tears blinded Christy. It healed some deep and secret hurt in her to see her foster parents walk arm in arm, the wall between them swept away. It was as if the trials that rose from their marriage, the doublings, treblings, and variations, had all resolved to flow back into the Ground, the great love that was the beginning of their life together.

What was it Gran said? ''Whatever burden doesn't break a back only makes it stronger.'' Perhaps that was true of love.

She decided to make a wide circle around Mairi and the captain and run on ahead. After all, Davie was waiting.

His face drained of color when he saw the cuts and bruises on Christy's face and arms, and Colin began to swear. ''I look worse than I feel, lads,'' she said quickly. ''Your mother will be along directly, Davie.''

''Is she——''

''She's hurt no worse than I. But some of the poor women——'' Oddly, now that it was over, Christy began to weep.

The outrage of Gran and the other Clanna folk over what had happened at Greenyards was tempered by thankfulness that once again all was clearly well between Mairi and her captain. What a difference it made! Christy had never known them when they existed in more than remote civility. Of course it was Sollas that had raised the great barrier, Mairi's going there in spite of

Iain's charge that she must take good care of herself and their expected child.

Now their love and happiness warmed the whole village. David laughed more. So did Christy. Sometimes pure joy welled up in her and overflowed. For the first time, she felt that Mairi *liked* her, that she wasn't wishing her own daughter stood in Christy's place.

The captain had no need for his old bed in the schoolroom. He asked Mr. Urquhart to remain. The young man was bringing David along well with advanced subjects. Besides, though the captain intended to stay home a good while, he meant to take some horses to Australia that autumn and make some contacts there.

"I fear the war in the States will last a long time," he told his family. "I need to establish other markets."

"I'm glad you say Calum won't be going to fight," Gran said.

"He's nearing forty and he's had his wars. Besides, garrisons that protected settlers from the Indians—or tried to, at any rate—are being ordered east. That leaves the defense of their families and settlements up to the frontiersmen." With a glance at Mairi, he added in a casual tone, "I'm surprised that Charles Forsyth doesn't go back to fight for Virginia and his plantation but he seems content to shoot grouse and deer instead of Yankees."

"You've seen him?" Mairi asked in a strained tone.

"On my way from Stornoway I chanced on him and his sister out with that fox-faced gamekeeper, Dugald Craigie." The captain hunched a shoulder in disgust. "Their gillies led two ponies that were laden down with their prey. That pair don't hunt. They slaughter."

"I dare say they'll soon return to the mainland," Mairi said. "Mrs. Tarleton seems easily bored."

The captain smiled at his wife. "I made it very clear to both of them that I am much too busy to help relieve their boredom."

A look passed between them that brought a flush to Mairi's cheeks. They were, that evening, the first to say good night.

However happy she was, Mairi still visited the grave of her daughter. She wasn't sad now when she returned, but tranquil and at peace. Christy was milking one evening when she saw Mairi going up the slope. In summer, cows were milked in the open wherever they happened to be, and Sholma, this evening, was grazing with her fine calf on the small hill across the stream from the hollowed cliff.

Sholma readily let down her creamy milk as Christy sang her favorite songs and the calf greedily sucked his fill from the teats on the other side. Christy praised the cow and stroked her before picking up stool and bucket. As she straightened, she saw someone moving up the sloping back of the cliff—someone in skirts, too tall to be Gran, the only woman Christy could think of who might have ventured to join Mairi's visit to her daughter.

Perhaps someone had been hurt or taken violently ill—let it not be David! Gran knew more of cures than anyone, but Mairi was skillful, too. There had to be some simple explanation for the other woman but Christy felt uneasy.

No harm in following . . . She wedged the milk pail securely between some rocks, covered it with her shawl, and hurried across the stream and along the incline that led to the hollow. The last smolders of sunset outlined the crest that rose steep and sheer above the sea, the cliff where a ledge had given way and sent David flying in that heart-stopped moment before he fell.

Strange and terrifying that just a second could change a life forever. Christy shivered and hurried on. Voices reached her. The unfamiliar one was shrill and high. Christy caught a word or two of English though the wind blew most of them away.

English! Save Mairi, no woman of Clanna spoke English.

Christy cupped her hands. "Help! Help!" she shouted toward the village. Surely someone would hear.

She couldn't wait. The English voice was shrieking now, screaming vile names. Christy gathered up her skirts and ran up the slope as fast as she could.

"Crofter bitch!" Chellis shouted. "Dragging Iain down with you, trapping him by making him believe your crippled brat is his! Well, Dugald Craigie's stalked you for me, just as he would a stag I wished to kill. He said you came here almost every evening." She laughed wildly, triumphantly. "So here you are—and so am I!"

Christy gaped over the lip of the hollow just as Chellis raised a pistol with both hands, aiming it at Mairi. Christy swooped down, grasped a rock, and heaved it at Chellis, followed it with another. The second one hit the woman on the shoulder, sent her staggering.

"Run, Mairi! Run and get help!" Christy threw another rock and refuged behind a boulder.

Mairi ran for the top of the cliff. Crannies here and there led down to shallow sea caves where Chellis couldn't follow. If Chellis fired and missed, she'd have to stop and reload. With the skill of the hunter she was, she didn't panic into a wild shot though her plan had been skewed by Christy's arrival.

A hole in the skull of one person could be disguised as a fall injury but two such deaths would cause suspicion. "Where are you, you little slut?" howled Chellis. "I'll kill you if I can't blast her! Why did you have to sneak up here? If she were dead, Iain would love me!"

Had anyone heard Christy's shout? Why didn't they come? At least Mairi had disappeared from the cliff, must be making her way toward the village.

This luminous hours-long twilight was both in Christy's favor and against her. It made it harder for Chellis to aim with accuracy, but neither did it give Christy the full concealment of night. She picked up rocks in both hands, determined to kill the crazed woman if she could.

"You must be behind that rock!" Chellis cried. She started forward. Christy glanced desperately around. There was no other place to hide. She'd have to dash for the cliff and try to scramble down.

She hurled one rock and then the other, aiming for the head. Both struck the woman's chest. Chellis screeched and ran at the boulder. Christy bent over and ran.

There was a crashing sound. Something burned her arm as she pelted to the top of the cliff. Chellis wasn't used to running. Christy could hear her panting, like some frightful creature of the night.

Shags and cormorants shrieked at being disturbed in their nesting ledges along a jagged cleft that slashed the cliff from jutting overhang to giant boulders. If Christy started down, she couldn't dodge. It would be all she could do to win a perilous way to the shelter of the boulders. Chellis could take several shots as Christy clung to the slippery ledges, but there was no other hope.

Christy caught up her skirts and tucked them into her waistband. Praying that the turf at the edge wouldn't give way as it had beneath David, she set her toes on the first niche.

Deafened by the clamor of the birds, braced against the flapping of their wings, she was feeling for the next ledge when a cry of outrage pierced the uproar of the seabirds.

The captain's voice, or were her ears playing tricks? Someone *had* come. It was too soon for Mairi to have brought help. Someone must have heard Christy's call or seen Mairi outlined against the sky. Christy dragged herself back to the top, could see two shadowy figures struggling near the edge of the cliff.

"Chellis!" It was the captain. "Stop this! Give me the pistol!"

There was a snarling cry, and then a shot, an unearthly keening wail as the larger body stumbled and fell. The smaller one teetered for an instant on the ledge, then hurtled downward, twisting in the air. A wail split off as if the throat uttering it had been cut.

Christy's legs would not support her so she crawled. "Captain! Captain!"

She reached him as Mairi and Gran did, with all of Clanna behind them, running up the hill. Except for David. He couldn't run but he'd be coming fast as he could.

Mairi raised her husband. "There's blood on his back!" She ripped her petticoat to stanch the hole where the ball had gone clear through him.

"No use," he said weakly. "I—tried to take the pistol away. It went off—" He raised his hand to her face. "Mairi. Mairi, my love—You will raise our son well. Tell—him to take care of you for me."

"No, Iain! You'll be all right! Laddie, laddie—" Mairi kissed him.

A breath shook him, faded. Mairi held him long after he was quiet. She kissed him again and lifted her head dazedly. "His mouth is warm, Gran! He's warm all over. He must be alive!"

Gran sank down, felt for a pulse in Iain's throat, bent her face close to his to detect any breath. "No, lassie."

Mairi groaned. She was calling his name, rocking him, when David swung up on his crutches and dropped beside his parents. "Father! Father! Can't you hear me?"

Gran embraced them all in her frail arms. "Och, laddie, your father's left us. Come, lass, come along, Davie. Let's take the captain home."

David was sobbing bitterly. Christy brought his crutches from where he had flung them. "If I'd had my legs," he choked, "I would have got here before—before—"

"Och, Davie!" Gran soothed. "There's no use taking on so. You must help your mother—"

"A lot of help I am! When we heard Christy shout, father ran. Everybody did. Everyone but me!"

"Oh, my laddie, you were in your father's last words." Mairi put her arms around her son. "I'm sure he knew you were there." They wept together while Chul whimpered.

By placing several shawls beneath him, the women improvised a litter in which they could carry the captain home. Mairi walked with her son on one side while Gran was on the other. She stumbled and Christy took her arm.

"You're bleeding, lass!" Gran exclaimed.

"A pistol ball grazed me. It's no real harm."

Gran examined it by touch. "After we're home, I'll sprinkle it with powdered nettles. As well let it bleed a little to cleanse the scrape."

Such a long way home, yet too short. As they reached the stream, several boys carried Chellis Tarleton up from the shore. Christy could not bear to look at her, but Morag cried, "See how her head lolls about—her neck's snapped."

"Her head's crushed like an eggshell," said Colin Nicolson with a shudder. "She fell in a mass of rocks."

"Where will we be taking her?" asked Hamish MacAskill.

"If you go over the hill, you'll find Dugald Craigie with her horse," said Mairi. "He had stalked me for her as if I'd been a trophy that she wanted—learned my habits. She taunted me with this before she raised her pistol."

"Craigie should hang!" cried David.

"He could swear he didn't know her intention," said Mairi in an emotionless voice. "Perhaps he didn't. Two dead are enough, my son. Let Craigie take his mistress home."

"And give him an earful for his master," said Gran between gritted teeth. "He must tell Forsyth that his sister killed the captain when she could not kill his wife. I have the pistol in my shawl. We'll send it with her. Craigie must tell Forsyth that when his sister saw she'd killed the man she wanted, she leaped off the cliff."

"If Forsyth makes a moil—" began Morag.

"How can he, with my husband shot and all of us to swear what happened?" demanded Mairi.

"In the morning," David said in a ragged tone, "I will ride to the castle and tell Sir James if he is at home. He is Uncle Roderick's friend more than father's but he will want to attend the funeral."

The schoolmaster had gone to visit friends on Skye so it was on the narrow bed in the schoolroom that Mairi and Gran, Morag and Sheila took off Iain's bloody clothes, washed him, and dressed him. Gran closed his eyelids—those beautiful gray-blue eyes with a glow deep in them. He was smiling the slightest bit, as at some tender joke. David sat in his father's chair by his father's desk, Chul at his feet.

Gran thrust the bundle of bloodied clothes at Christy. "Sink them in a bog," she said beneath her breath. "They are fine cloth but the blood has ruined them."

At this time of year, it never grew completely dark. Christy followed the track till she reached a bog. She wrapped each garment around a heavy stone. Taking several in her arms, she kilted up her skirts and waded through bogbeans and iris till the water was over her knees.

Gran had told her to do this yet she felt like a criminal concealing evidence. She ran all the way home and then wished herself back at the bog for David sat like a statue and Mairi was caressing the wealed scars that ran from her husband's left eyebrow to right temple and from cheekbone to chin. It was as if she longed to imprint his face forever in her memory.

"Belike the laird will bring his chaplain, Robert MacMillan, the one who married you," Morag said to Mairi. "There's no time to send for Sir Roderick."

"I'll write him a letter," said Mairi. "He was Iain's only close kin."

All Clanna watched by Iain that night. Fine wax candles from Inverness burned at Iain's head and feet. The women brought food and Gran served heather ale but there was no drunkenness or boisterous talk. David had moved close beside his mother at his father's bed.

It was still, so still for a house with nearly a score of people gathered. Mothers hushed their wee ones, took them away to change their clouts, and the oldest folk nodded on the settle. It was so still, so still . . . Except for the distant hammering of old Jock MacClean of Sollas. With the help of the older boys, he was making a coffin.

"The captain loved music," Gran said. "It's not right he shouldn't have it. Mairi, love, can you play at all?"

"I cannot, Gran."

"He would wish it."

"I know." Mairi's eerie calm shattered. "I played all night for Fearchar till my fingers bled. I have played for the cleared villages and for my little daughter. But, oh Gran! I cannot play for Iain!"

Gran turned to Christy. "Lass, can you?"

Christy's heart stopped, then began to pound. Draped in the MacLeod plaid, Cridhe waited. Around the hearthstone glimmered luminous misty forms, bright and beautiful, the guardians who had followed the old stone from Aosda.

Christy whispered, "Mairi Mór. Shall I play?"

Wordlessly, Mairi nodded. Christy got up and uncovered the harp, took the ornate harp key and tuned the strings. She began with the MacDonalds' "Salute to the Chief" and moved into the captain's favorites, "The Marquis of Huntley's Farewell," "Whistle and I'll Come to You, My Lad," and many others.

Scores of harpers who had played their sorrows and triumphs through the generations seemed to strengthen her to play for Mairi. When she grew tired, the women talked. Each had some special memory of the captain, especially those who had known him since he brought them away from burning Aosda.

"What was that verse of Walter Kennedy's Iain spoke at the first ceilidh of ours he attended?" Gran asked, and Mairi answered.

> *I will nae priests for me sall sing,*
> *Nor yet nae bells for me to ring;*
> *But ae bag-pype to play a spring."*

And so the night passed. Before dawn, David, with Colin's help, saddled Kelpie and rode for Stornoway Castle. The younger women and bigger boys delved out a grave in the cliff hollow next to the small one.

It was late afternoon when Sir James rode up with the Reverend Robert MacMillan. "A tragedy," the laird said to Mairi, shaking his head. He was graying and portly, though his dark eyes were keen. "I had fondness and respect for the major even though he——"

Married one of your tenants? Christy thought. *Resigned his commission rather than evict crofters?* Mairi held herself rigid. How doubly cruel to lose her husband-lover when they were reconciled after so many years!

Sir James went on as if giving reasons would help. "Mrs. Tarleton was taking laudanum at her physician's behest. No doubt it overset her reason. The gamekeeper says she bade him wait for her while she shot some grouse."

"That's not what she said," Mairi told him. "She said Mr. Craigie watched me for her, found out when I would be alone."

The laird peered at her. "Do you believe that, Mairi? According to Mr. Forsyth his sister was prone to delusions."

"I believe it," said Mairi. "But it's Craigie's word against hearsay. No doubt he would get off, even if he were charged. He was her tool as much as the pistol. Let it go, my lord. I have no wish to journey to Inverness for his trial."

Sir James looked relieved. He was not eager for scandal. "Mr. Forsyth will take his sister back to Virginia for burial. I have told him I cannot renew his hunting lease."

"Thank you for that, Sir James."

Like a benevolent laird and friend of the dead man, he walked with Mairi and Gran at the head of the procession that followed the coffin. Iain was wrapped in the heather-hued coverlet Mairi had given him so long ago, the one that had comforted him when he lay wounded unto death. Christy followed with David and Chul.

The chaplain intoned the service as kittiwakes swirled in the sun and gulls shrieked. The wake and music had been Clanna's true farewell to the captain, though it was a pity none of the men were there to speed him. The company threw in handfuls of earth.

Sir James seemed to understand that his presence, honor though it was, constrained the mourners. He expressed his sympathy again and took his leave with great courtesy. The chaplain, gray-haired and kind-eyed, pressed Mairi's hand.

"God be with you, young woman. When I united you and Major MacDonald almost thirteen years ago, I had my fears of how such a marriage could fare, but from all I hear, you had overcome your difficulties. I have never been more sorrowful to consign a soul to the love and mercy of God, but that love and mercy will sustain you now."

The laird and minister went down the hill to where their horses were tethered, but the Clanna folk lingered, women softly weeping, children snuffling, the older boys and old Jock scrubbing away tears as they heaped the long mound beside the little one.

Christy helped Gran dig up wildflowers and plant them on the grave. The exertion after the sleepless night must have tired the old woman for she was breathing heavily, almost gasping.

Foxglove she planted in the yielding loam, buttercups, daisies, and wild thyme with purple blooms that sweetened the air. She patted the earth firmly around the roots, telling the plants how pretty they were, asking them to grow. Then, still kneeling, she gazed up at the sky, her eyes as blue as the deepest shade of the horizon.

Her face spasmed. An earth-stained hand clutched at her

heart. Christy dropped beside her, catching the frail body as it slumped. "Gran! Gran, what's the matter?"

Gran's lips were blue. She was sweating, a cold dew that beaded her forehead. "Och, ochone!" shrilled Morag. "Let's get her to the house, warm her with blankets!"

Several women hurried forward but Gran motioned them off. "Warm me with whisky," she breathed. "The good uisge-beatha——"

Christy sped off at once. Gran couldn't die! She couldn't! Not now . . .

When she returned with Gran's silver flagon, Gran was resting in Mairi's arms. Christy held the whisky to the blue lips. Gran swallowed feebly.

Faint color flowed into her cheeks. "Gran," begged Mairi. "Let us carry you home."

"You will—soon enough." Gran breathed jerkily, eyelids fluttering as if she could not hold them open. With labored effort, Gran placed her hand on Christy's.

"There's my bonnie good lass. Remember—what I've taught you. Stay Davie's friend. Help Mairi——"

Pressing the limp hand to her lips, Christy said through her tears, "I—I'll remember. I'll look after Davie. I'll help Mairi Mór." Christy clung to the fragile old hand as if it were all the faith and strength and hope in the world. "Oh, Granny, love, Granny! I'll remember you——"

She offered the flagon again. Gran sipped and looked at Mairi. Her voice was little more than a whisper.

"I'm going with your laddie, m'eudail. Mayhap I will catch up with him on that low road of the spirits—bear him company till we meet with Fearchar and your wee bairn."

"Gran, don't! Oh, Gran, darling——"

David caught his grandmother's other veined, thin hand. "Gran, it's your Davie! Gran——"

She didn't hear them. Her face was alight. "Fearchar," she

breathed. "Michael, my dear man—" She sat up, reaching, then fell back as if struck by an invisible thunderbolt. She was smiling. She seemed to feel no pain.

"Michael," she said clearly. "Do you know the captain?"

Those were all her words. Her heart stopped, and her breath, and her long, long habit of life and loving.

VIII

Before Gran's coffin was shut, Christy heaped wildflowers around Gran, and Mairi broke off a branch of pink-flowering whortleberry, the badge of the MacLeods, and placed it on Gran's breast. So peaceful she looked, so eager, almost young, as if she had run to meet her Michael, and fallen asleep in his arms.

How can Mairi bear it? Christy thought as her foster mother knelt between the two new graves with her daughter at Iain's other hand. Losing both at once! I don't know how I can manage without Gran, how any of us can . . .

David leaned on his crutches, cheeks streaked with tears. Mairi looked up at Christy, as if her bones and spine were broken along with her heart. "I should play Cridhe over Gran but I cannot. It is beyond my strength."

Christy's fingers were sore from the captain's wake but that was not why she had to shake her head. "Forgive me, Mairi Mór. I can't play either."

Ashamed to fail Mairi, head hanging, Christy at first thought she was imagining the music, but it grew louder as more joined in.

Mouth-music! It was the invention of the folk to simulate fiddle notes when parsons through threats of hellfire burned their fiddles, pipes, and harps. Morag was leading Gran's favorite strathspey, a blithe dancing melody. Those who hadn't the knack for mouth-music hummed the tune or sang the words about the wily cat who had stolen the cream and butter, the black cock, and the fat red hen.

Gran would have loved it. Christy closed her eyes, could almost see her dancing, hold out her hand to the captain. What a love she had ever had for him, and he for her. Christy joined in the song. Her voice caught, but it didn't matter. There were other voices to carry hers. Others to make music when she could not. And Mairi was singing, too.

As the music swelled, Christy knew another thing Gran would want. She hurried back to the house, lined a basket with wetted heather, and put in glowing peats. She brought them to Mairi who at first looked startled and then pleased.

"Yes, we must smoor the fire for Gran." Using the heather to place the peats, Mairi made them into a cross. Then, as Gran had through all the years, Mairi invoked the Holy Three, Mary, Christ, and Brigid. "Save, shield, protect this soul. Surround her with your light, your grace, this night and every night and every day forever."

Lammas came, the first of August, with bannocks made from the first grain, grain that had grown tall since Iain and Gran died. Heather, at its deepest purple, swarmed with bees and butterflies. Drifts of yellow iris edged the bogs and Mairi found the first sweet flowers of grass-of-Parnassus growing among the graves. Dolphins still arced from the waves, seemingly in sheer joy of play, but soon they would swim to warmer waters like whales and basking sharks.

The men returned from the fishing to stand mute and stricken beside the new graves. Gran had been mother and grandmother to everyone. As for the captain, he was mourned not only for himself but because of Mairi's and David's grief.

Tam felt the deaths especially. Gran had reared him and Mairi after their parents died, and Tam had adored the captain since he was twelve and Iain had given him the pipes. Before Tam left for the fishing, Molly had at last won his promise that they would marry that autumn.

Now the couple offered to put off their wedding but Mairi said, "Neither Gran nor Iain would want that, my dears. Besides, who knows when Molly could get you in the notion again? No, after harvest we'll have a grand feast and dancing."

After the funerals, Christy never saw Mairi weeping in the day but her eyes were often red and swollen in the morning. She must be trying to live by Gran's precept. "Night is for weeping. But at dawn, a body must put on a morning face and greet the world, not show a sour countenance to other folk who have their own troubles. It is our bounden duty to be as happy as we can."

Christy tried, too. She put on her morning face and most of the time wore it till she went to bed, the bed she had shared with Gran. How lonely it was! Too much room, no one to rest against.

Oh Gran, she sometimes wailed silently. How can I manage without you? But she knew it was much worse for David and worst of all for Mairi, who had lost not only her husband but her grandmother, the last person to whom she could be a child, to whom she could cry, be weak or silly—the last soul in all the world with whom she could be human. Unless, perhaps, it was Magnus Ericson.

The huge fair-haired sea captain had, on their first meeting, rescued both Mairi and Tam from the drunken Captain Tarbert who had kidnapped Tam off the beach. He had smuggled Calum to safety. In the way that general knowledge is absorbed in a village, Christy knew that Magnus had wanted to wed Mairi when she was big with David. Through the years, through her marriage, he had been her friend and Clanna's. The *Selchie* had not called in since spring, but usually Magnus stopped in the autumn, and that would hearten everyone.

Mr. Urquhart was a blessing, too. The deep masculine timbre of his voice was a comfort, and he was more a friend to David now than any of the boys. Besides, it was good for the captain's room to fill with Clanna's children, with their laughter and high spirits. Christy attended classes but she no longer felt she was a child—in fact she had never really felt that she was, had even wondered if she were indeed a changeling, a freak left in place of a human child.

David took over the care of Chieftain, brushing him daily, combing his mane and tail, cleaning out the frogs of his hoofs. The captain had contrived a pad with a buckled strap that David could put on a horse, and Chieftain cooperatively slipped his head into the bridle, so David could ride without asking help. Chieftain was nineteen years old, whitening around the muzzle, and of course wasn't used for farm chores. Still, for both the captain's sake and David's, no one grudged the horse his grazing, though it would have fed two cows or eight sheep.

Sir Roderick, responding to Mairi's letter about the captain's death, had offered to undertake David's further rearing in the great house at Inverness and pay his fees at the university should David qualify. At Mairi's request, David read the letter aloud.

> "I suspect, Mairi, that you are no more willing than you have ever been to give me the care of your son. I am willing, therefore, to send an annual sum for his expenses since a crippled lad cannot be of much use on a croft. I urge you, however, to keep him in school and later, if his gifts merit it, send him to the university at my charge. It may be he could become my son's man-of-business. I know the boy rides and I would like to send him a serviceable well-trained young gelding."

"Well!" Mairi said between vexation and amusement. "Would you like the horse, David? Do you want to go live with your great-uncle?"

"No to both, Mother! Clanna can't afford to graze another horse. I'd rather ride Chieftain so long as he's able, and when he isn't he must still have his oats and hay. As to the university—'' He paused, brow furrowing. "While you were at Greenyards, I thought how grand it would be if I were a lawyer, if I knew how to defend those poor women in court."

"David!" It was hard to tell whether Mairi's cry was of dismay or gladness. Perhaps it was both. "You thought that?"

"I did. And I thought how I wished I could change the laws so at last there could be justice." He sighed and bent to scratch Chul behind the ears. "Someday I suppose I'll have to go to the university if I'm to be of any real use in the world. But I can't leave you just now, Mother. Not so soon after father—And I don't know how I ever can bear to leave Chul. He would pine away without me. It—it would be like killing him."

Mairi placed her hand on her son's larger, bonier one. He was shooting up and soon would reach the captain's height though he had much filling out to do. "Don't fret about the whole future now, lad. Wheesht, you're only fourteen! I can write English better than I can read your uncle's scrawly hand, so I shall tell him your father left us enough for university fees though we appreciate his offer. And I shall tell him you do your share at Clanna and we need no extra money. That it's kind of him, too, to offer a horse, but you prefer Chieftain." Mairi chuckled. "I'll invite Sir Roderick to visit us, though I'm sure he will not. Now he has two sons, he doesn't view you as a potential heir but he'll do his duty by his nephew's son."

Both because it made her feel close to Gran and because she was determined not to forget what Gran had taught her, Christy wrote down the instructions for herbs and dyes and collected plants, roots, and lichens to replenish Gran's supply.

Christy with other girls and women sang behind the reapers as she knelt to bind the oats and barley while geese and ducks and swans winged south. Next the dried peats must be brought to the houses and stacked in neat piles and the potatoes dug up and stored in the barn between the threshed fodder and barrels of salt fish.

"Lovely potatoes!" Mairi's eyes sparkled and she sniffed the good earth smell of the potatoes, spreading them on the straw as if they were jewels. "We'll have 'tatie scones this night, and 'taties mashed with cream and butter, and 'taties boiled with kale and fish and—"

"Mairi Mór!" It was the first time Christy had laughed heartily since she went with Mairi to Greenyards. "At that rate, the 'taties will be gone in a week!"

" 'Eat your crannachan first,' Fearchar used to say. 'Life be aye uncertain.' " How good it was to hear Mairi laugh! More soberly, she added, "You don't remember the starving years, child. For three summers, the potatoes turned to stinking slime. To those of us who lived through it, nothing is so beautiful as a firm, plump healthy potato."

In between other tasks, a house was raised for Tam and Molly, double-walled stone with rubble in between, corners rounded so as not to catch the wind, thatch secured with fishing nets weighted down with rocks. Donald Gunn made the box bed and dresser-cupboard. Since she had been making towels and sheets and blankets for a long time, Molly had a well-filled chest, and family and friends contributed the other furnishings.

"I wish that Gran were here to build the first fire on your hearth," Mairi said to her brother and his affianced one night as they were checking stores of whisky, wine, and other drinks. "At least you'll have her heather wine at the wedding."

"We would like for you to kindle our first hearth fire, Mairi." Shyly, Molly turned to her future sister-in-law. "You will, and bless the house, won't you?"

"Indeed, I will be honored." Mairi smiled fondly at the younger woman but Christy thought it must startle her to realize that with Gran gone, Morag so dour, and the older women so unassuming, that she, Mairi, was now the principal woman of Clanna, the one to whom others would turn. From her youth, Mairi had led her folk, found a way for them to stay on the island,

and strengthened them with her harp. But there had always been Gran, wise and merry, even in the years of her delusion that her husband was not dead.

In the months since Gran's death, her specialties had been taken over by various women, though none pretended to her skill. Morag, with Sheila assisting, brewed heather ale that autumn from the thickest, finest blossoms. There was enough of Gran's ale for the bride and groom, but the guests would have to be content with Morag's.

Peggy MacPhail from Sollas had a knack for dyes learned from old Ishbel MacLean, whose nearly blind eyes could still see the colors and advise on whether more roots or leaves or lichen were needed. Una MacFarlane, Katie Gunn, and Marta MacAskill were all expert midwives. Barbara and Rose Nicolson, from plenty of experience with their own broods, were good with croupy or fevered children. Flora Ferguson brewed teas that eased cramps, headaches, or loosened bowels.

Clanna managed. But there was no one with Gran's cheeky grin, earthy wisdom, and sometimes ribald humor.

"I hope Magnus gets here in time," Tam said anxiously. Iain had taught him the pipes and Tam had admired him to idolization, but Magnus was Tam's model, a crofter lad whose hard work had made him owner of his own fine ship. And it was Magnus who sixteen years ago rescued a terrified boy from a sadistic captain.

"Och, if he isn't here when the chaplain comes, he can drink a toast later," Molly said. "You've dallied long enough, gavallachan. No more kisses until we're wed!"

Beautiful, young, and strong they looked together, Tam's bleached hair even brighter against his browned skin, Molly with raven's wing hair and deep blue eyes. The prospect of their marriage had given the villagers something happy and hopeful to think about. Christy felt the loss of Gran every hour of the day and even more at night in the big lonesome bed, but she knew Gran was with her beloved Fearchar and Iain and Mairi's daughter, that all was well with her. Besides, Gran would snort at grieving more than one must, and she had ever loved a wedding.

The wedding day dawned golden as the last brave irises defying winter from their ranks across the moors. Three waulking tables covered with snowy linen sheets anchored with branches of rowan thick with scarlet berries set in a row outside Mairi's house. Delicious odors drifted from every house except the new one of Tam and Molly. Tonight Mairi would bring peats from her hearth to kindle their first fire, and with Molly's mother, ask a blessing on their hearth and all who would be warmed by it.

Mairi wore her arisaid, her own wedding dress, and the brooch her husband had given her one birthday, a sprig of whortleberry set with amethysts. He had liked her hair uncovered by a cap, and Mairi's wavy hair was coaxed into a ribboned snood and tied back with a bow.

Molly prinked at the mirror in the hearth room with most of the younger women lined up behind her. Their mothers and older and younger sisters were carrying food to the tables. Christy helped Mairi take out bowls of crowdie, fresh butter, and other good things, dodging bustling women, lounging men, and frolicking children.

Mairi put down the dishes and stood looking about her with such a bemused expression that Christy asked a question she would not have dared put before the closeness that had grown between them ever since Greenyards.

"Mairi Mór—how has Clanna changed since your wedding?"

Mairi smiled as if she had been thinking on that herself. "There's Iain's mill and Kelpie to haul seaweed, peats, and grain we once toted in creels. We have all the cattle and sheep we've grazing for and Chul to guard them. There's the quay and curing shed and school for the children. Look at them, Christy! Aren't they like moving flowers?''

"Or weeds!'' Christy, one of the tenders of the younger children, sometimes had problems keeping them in order, but they were a pleasing sight, rosy and strong, with hair of every hue, mostly auburn or yellow and every shade of blue eyes, some green, gray, and hazel, only a few brown.

"They'll grow up at Clanna,'' Mairi said like a vow. "With any luck, none should have to leave Clanna unless they wish it.''

Christy felt someone loom behind them. Someone tall and broad of shoulder, someone whose strong wind-burned hands closed over Mairi's.

"So here you are, lass.'' Magnus's deep voice boomed. "Tam just told me about—about Iain and Rosanna. Och, m'eudail! To lose both without a breath between! And after your Davie lost the use of his legs! Cruel it is and sorry I am I wasn't here to do whatever could be done.''

"Oh, Magnus!'' Mairi's lips trembled. "David has faced his crippling better than I have—he wants no pity. He'll have a good life yet. Iain and Gran—'' Her voice choked off a moment. "There—there was nothing to be done. Nothing but to bury and mourn them.''

"Still, lass, I wish I had been with you.''

She lifted her head. "You're here now. Tam will be proud as a king with two crowns that you came to his wedding.''

"And you, Mairi?''

"You know well, gavallachan, I'm always glad to see you.''

His eyes searched hers and evidently did not find what they hoped for. With the smallest squaring of great shoulders, he said, "I am sorry to tell you, lass, that two Greenyards people were brought to trial at Inverness. Ann Ross was sentenced to a year in prison, Peter Ross to eighteen months with hard labor.''

Mairi bowed her head. "Iain was going to speak in their behalf,'' she said huskily.

"I doubt it would help, m'eudail. The justice told the jury it was absolutely necessary to crush what he called a 'perverted feeling of insubordination' against legal evictions."

"Legal!"

"Several journalists wrote strongly against the verdict."

"That does not change it."

"No. But exposing the truth is swinging public mood against clearances. When that happens, laws change."

Mairi's laugh was bitter. "I used to hope I would live to see it. Now, I am not so sure." Neither was Christy, remembering Greenyards.

Magnus said in a positive tone, "It will come, Mairi."

They stood a moment in silence. Then Magnus looked over Mairi's head and smiled to see the bride run to meet the chaplain, who was just riding up on a shaggy little pony. "Molly means to make sure of Tam," Magnus chuckled.

"Small wonder!" sniffed Mairi. "Tam has held back till it would have served him right had she taken Rob MacRae or one of the others who asked her! It's been plain as the nose on your face that they'd marry—been plain for years!"

Magnus shot her a look of lightning. "So, Mairi, when something's sure to happen, you see no use in putting it off?"

Mairi's color brightened. "That depends on what it is. By your leave, Magnus, we'll talk later. I must greet the chaplain and bring him a glass of cold buttermilk."

She fled. Magnus and Christy were left staring at each other. He grinned and said, "Well, Christy, I've been patient all these years. A few more—or a dozen—won't hurt me." He turned to watch Mairi welcome the chaplain. His tone rang with quiet determination. "I stood aside for a living man even though Iain was gentry and I did not dream he could ever wed her. But I will not let her wed herself to the grave of Iain also!"

"Captain Ericson, she loved him so—"

"Aye. She will mourn him—and he is a man to mourn. I will

not ask what she cannot give, but whether we wait one year, or two or three, or five, we will share a hearth, and we'll be happy."

"I hope you are right," said Christy. Her heart lightened. Magnus was not Iain but he was very much his winning, vigorous self. More important, he could, for Mairi, fill some of the void left by Gran. He was ten years older than Mairi, worldly wise, and best of all, though he worshiped her, he wasn't afraid to laugh at her or treat her like a woman.

The service began. The Reverend Robert MacMillan kept them on their feet for over an hour while he instructed the young couple on their duties in the state of matrimony, but the pledges themselves were quickly over.

Magnus was the first to kiss the bride. Then he kissed all the women within his reach, Katie, Sheila, Una, even Morag. He didn't approach Mairi.

The bridal pair were first to serve themselves from kettles of barley broth and potato soup, potato scones and raisin scones, cream scones and spiced scones, blackberry scones and ginger scones and every kind of bannock, mealie pudding, and fish served many ways, from smoked haddock to fresh-caught broiled cod and turbot. Clootie dumplings, rich with currants and cinnamon, were smothered in custard, and there were Dundee cakes, cream cakes, Madeira cakes and sponge cakes, fruit buns, and baskets of crisp shortbread and oatmeal-gingerbread or broonie, an Orkney treat Magnus had taught Mairi to bake. Mairi had also made a great bowl of crannachan, Tam's favorite, and though she would never have Gran's knack for the dish, she was liberal with whisky and whipped cream, so there were no complaints.

The minister allowed himself two glasses of French wine with his meal before he went his way. He seemed human, not dour and doom prophesying. Still, the kirk frowned on music and dancing and there was a relaxing of constraint when he departed. The young couple was toasted with Morag's ale while they sipped the last of Gran's.

Mairi, Morag, and the children were the only ones who drank oatmeal whisked with water or buttermilk instead of ale, wine, or whisky, so as time passed along with jugs and decanters, there was much teasing of the newlyweds and more laughter than the jokes really deserved.

Lucas got his fiddle. "You'll play, too, Mairi?" he invited. "And Christy, will you bring your little harp? Tam can't skirl his pipes and dance as a bridegroom should."

Christy and Mairi fetched their harps, blended their notes with Lucas's lively reels and strathspeys though it must have been bittersweet for Mairi to play tunes to which she had danced at her own wedding. Magnus hunkered down by Mairi.

"You will not be dancing, lass?"

"Magnus! You gave me a start!"

"Small wonder. You were far away—or was it far back?" He sang, softly, the words to the tune they were playing, "The Lewis Bridal Dance."

> *Red her lips as rowans are, bright her eyes as any star.*
> *Fairest of them all by far is our darling Mairi."*

Smiling, he added, "That's true, lass. Clanna is blessed with fair maids and women, but none holds a candle to you."

"You've been eating honeycomb! I know what I look like, lines at my mouth and eyes, a few gray hairs—"

"You will be beautiful and even more queenly when your hair is white as snow. The lines only show that you have lived."

"Deep in the whisky already!"

"Devil a bit! One cup of Morag's ale I drank to toast the young ones."

"You'd best go dance, then, while you're still sober."

"You will not dance? Just once, to honor your brother?"

"I will honor him by playing."

"Then I will dance with the bride."

He danced with everyone, of course, from budding, shy little Janet MacPhail to Ishbel MacLean of Sollas, who had drunk enough to oil her old bones and said she didn't need her vision to dance if her partner had a good strong arm. Magnus liked women and they liked him. A throwback to the Vikings he was, descended from a seal woman or selchie, as were many islanders. Coming to Clanna as he did once or twice in the year it was easy to fancy that at other times, on far skerries, he wore his seal shape and lived more in the waves than out.

But where in all of this was David? He had stood patiently on his crutches through the long sermon, congratulated his Uncle Tam and bashfully pecked his new aunt's cheek. Refusing Christy's help, he'd supported himself on one crutch while he chose his food. Christy hadn't seen him since.

He couldn't be among the dancers and he wasn't among the few who preferred to watch. Christy couldn't bear to think of him off alone somewhere. Cridhe and the fiddle made music enough for the dancers. Maybe she and her little harp could make some for David.

He wasn't in the house or barn or on the hill with Chul. Nor was he on the rocks where he sometimes went to watch the seals and birds and probably be alone. Chieftain and Kelpie both grazed along the slope, so he hadn't gone riding. Christy could think of only one other place.

Of course! He would be in the hollow of the cliff with those who could not, at least in their mortal shape, dance at the wedding. Well, they—and David—should have their music, too. With her harp, Christy stole away.

David sat with his dog between Gran's grave and his father's. The creamy white burnet roses Christy and Mairi had planted there were so fragrant Christy could smell them a good way off, mingled with the scent of wild thyme. Larks and peewits turned melodious somersaults and the sound of the waves came from below.

Chul raised his head at her approach. So did David. She was glad to see that he had not been crying. "This is a beautiful place, Davie."

"Aye."

"I wonder if—if the captain and Gran can see the wedding."

A faint smile touched David's lips. "If Gran were there, she'd dance."

"She would. And sample all the whisky and only drink the best."

"Go back to the wedding." David's voice roughened. "No need to miss the fun."

"I'd rather be with you."

He scowled and looked away. "That's a daft thing to say!"

Christy blinked at the sting in her eyes. "Daft indeed when you're so grouchy!"

He looked ashamed but said fiercely, "Get one thing through your curly head! I won't have you feel sorry for me. You should be down there dancing."

"Get one thing through your head, David MacLeod! I'd rather be with you than anywhere, with anyone!" They glared at each other. Then Christy added softly, "Besides, I loved Gran as much as you did—maybe more, since you had your mother. I came to play for her—and the captain—and your sister."

He looked at the tiny grave. The edge of a frayed blue ribbon was just visible where rain had washed away the shells and pebbles. "I don't know how mother stands it."

"She has you."

His lip curled. "Oh, aye! Who couldn't go with her to Greenyards—"

"You helped row over to fetch us. Davie, Davie! You must think on what you can do, not on what you can't!"

He crimsoned. For a moment she thought he'd strike her. Then the tautness eased from his neck and shoulders. "What a funny, wise little body you are, lass! I could almost believe a fairy left you with us. But if 'twas Old Nick himself, may the fire singe him a bit the less.'' He patted the purple-pink wild thyme beside him and grinned. ''Why did you bring that harp if you didn't mean to play?''

They stayed in the hollow till twilight. Neither Gran nor her great-granddaughter nor the captain appeared but Christy felt their presence. She could almost hear them laugh, see Gran whirl with the captain while a blue-ribboned girl clapped.

As they started down the slope together, David said, ''Thank you for coming, lass. Thanks for your music.''

Her heart filled with gratitude. She *had* helped him. He had let her share his watch with the beloved dead. She felt something of what Mairi must when her harp eased sorrows. Christy would have given her own legs to restore David's, but all the same, as they returned to the wedding, she knew it was in some ways the best day of her life.

IX

The wedding dispelled the sadness that had weighted the village since the deaths of Iain and Gran. Women laughed and chatted at the mill or kaleyards and merriment floated up from the shore as the men cleaned and repaired *The North Sea* before hauling it high on the shore where it would be safe from the greediest high tide. Through the winter, fishing would be done from the two smaller boats in coastal waters.

Mairi's appetite improved. Her eyes were seldom red in the morning but she went about her work like a sleepwalker and often had to be asked a question several times before she heard and responded. At meals Bruce Urquhart and David carried most of the conversation, but neighbors began to come by again in the evening and Mairi seemed glad to undrape Cridhe and play. Those were the times she seemed most alive.

She put the captain's bagpipe in his chest and said to Tam, "He would want you to have it, and you shall. But for a while, I cannot bear to see or hear his pipes."

Tam nodded and awkwardly patted her shoulder. "To be sure, I would not for anything grieve you more."

She gave her brother a wavering smile. "Gran used to say we missed our loved ones terribly for several years. All we can think is how much we miss them. But gradually the happy, good times start coming to mind and begin to overweigh the grief. When that happens, laddie, I shall be glad to hear you play Iain's tunes on his pipes.''

David, too, seemed often lost in pondering. It was as if he were strongly tugged in two directions. When he was not in class, he was usually on the hill with Chul. They were in Christy's view one afternoon when she was cutting kale.

She cried a warning when the deer, three of them, jumped the stone wall that had taken the folk of Clanna so many toilsome hours to build. Bending their graceful necks like aristocrats, the deer browsed at the stubble which the cattle needed to fatten on before they were brought into the byres.

''Chu-u-u-lah!'' ordered David, his intonation of the command telling Chul exactly what was wanted.

Chul never barked. He ruled Clanna's sheep and cattle with his watchful stare, but these wild trespassers needed chastisement. He dashed around them, nipping their fleet heels, and sent them bounding over the wall as a blast resounded.

The dog lurched backward. His shoulder crimsoned with blood. He struggled to crawl toward David. David crawled, too, forgetting his crutches. Christy, screaming, dropped her basket and ran for the field.

As she panted up, David and Chul reached each other. ''Chul! Chul, laddie!'' David gathered the small spotted dog in his arms. The shot, when it came out on the other side, had torn away half the shoulder.

Christy yanked off her petticoat and tried to staunch the pumping blood, but the cloth was quickly soaked. Chul licked David's cheek and tried to wag his tail. It gave two feeble waves and drooped. The loving tongue was stilled.

David rocked his dog, sobbing his name. Christy looked toward the wall. A red-haired, sparse-bearded man in a billed tweed cap was watching them. He was no crofter, no gentleman, either, and she suspected at once he was the gamekeeper, Dugald Craigie, who had stalked Mairi for Chellis Tarleton.

"You—you killer!" she shouted at him, springing up. "May the devil drag you to hell and quickly! You—"

He smiled, showing small pointed teeth. "Yon brute chased the laird's deer. It was my right to shoot him—indeed, my duty."

"You never shot him in all the years Captain MacDonald was alive!"

Green eyes flickered. "To be sure, he is dead, isn't he? As dead as Mrs. Tarleton, that poor sweet lady."

David, smeared with blood, looked up from his dog. "I'm not dead," he said in a queer, brittle voice. "I'll see you paid for this, Dugald Craigie."

"You're just another crofter, now your father's gone." Craigie showed more teeth. "A crippled one at that. Good day to you, I'm sure." He gave them a mocking smile and disappeared.

David's face set. He brought his sleeve across his face to wipe off blood and tears. "I'll carry Chul," Christy said. "Where shall we bury him, Davie?"

"On the slope where he liked to lie in the sun." David's face twisted. "I'll crawl back to my crutches."

"No! I'll bring them."

The sound of the shot had roused the village. Mairi ran foremost. "David's all right," Christy shouted. "But Chul—" She held the limp body closer. How could it end so quickly? All that love, all that faithfulness and skill, all those years as David's companion?

She laid Chul on the slope and ran to take David's crutches to him. By then the villagers had gathered. David and Christy told what had happened, one taking over when the other's voice broke.

Tam said angrily, clenching his fists, "Who'll go with me, to catch yon gamekeeper and give him a drubbing?"

"No one will go." Mairi straightened, arms around her son, eyes glistening with tears. "Craigie acted within the rules and regulations of the Estate. All you men have signed an agreement to abide by them."

"But—" began Tam.

"If you set on the gamekeeper, Sir James could not pardon it. You'd get fines and the tolbooth and—depend on it—although he and I are friends of a sort, Sir James would evict every soul from Clanna."

Molly caught Tam's arm. "Mairi is right, lad. 'Tis a shame for dear Chul and for Davie but Chul is dead. Thumping Craigie will not bring him back."

The men glowered and muttered but their wives and mothers clung to them. The truth of Mairi's words was all too evident. David stood away from his mother and said, "Mother speaks truth. It will not do to destroy Clanna. Uncle Tam, if you would make Chul's grave, I would be mightily obliged."

Relief flooded Christy. He was going to be reasonable, then. She had been afraid he wouldn't. A crofter's dog has few treasures to take into his grave but she hurried to find Chul's raggedy leather ball. It would go under the turf with Chul and much of David's heart, all that was left of his boyhood.

Next morning was Saturday and no school. It seemed strange at the hearth without Chul. David ate only half a bannock, almost curtly refused Mr. Urquhart's offer of a chess game, and went off to the schoolroom where he usually studied. Mairi had been called away before breakfast to help bring Barbara Nicolson's fourth baby. The schoolmaster, as if respecting David's obvious wish for solitude, took himself off to Tam's. Christy was peeling potatoes, wondering if she should seek out David or leave him be, when he came out of the passage.

He wore his cloak but Christy glimpsed the pistol belted at his waist. He must have got it out of his father's chest. "Davie! You can't!"

"I can. Father taught me how to shoot."

"You'll never get away!"

"I won't try." His tone was hard, too hard for a lad of four-teen. "I shall kill the gamekeeper and then go straight to Sir James. I will tell him no one knew what I planned—that it was my doing altogether and he must not punish Clanna."

"Why should he," Christy demanded, "when you'll do it so well, especially your mother?"

David stared. Christy stormed on. "I don't know if they'll hang you but you'll surely go to prison! Won't that be fine for your mother?"

His jaw thrust out. "I can't bear it, Christy! That misbegot Craigie strutting the earth while Chul lies underneath—"

Christy drew a deep breath. "Show me how to shoot the pis-tol, then."

"What do you mean?"

"If you must have Craigie dead, I—I'll do it."

"Christy! You daft little—"

"It's not daft to face facts," she threw at him. "Your mother has lost too many that she loves! Don't you see she goes around like a body without a soul?" Christy swallowed hard. "She—she likes me better than she did but it won't break her heart if I go to jail. I don't have kin to mourn me. So, David MacLeod Mac-Donald, if you are set on vengeance, give me that pistol."

He let out a long shuddering breath. "You know I cannot do that." In a burst he added, "I'd mourn you, Christy. You and Chul—I couldn't have managed without you after I fell. Mother and father were so worried I couldn't let them know how bad I felt. So—don't you be a daftie!"

"I won't if you won't." She felt as if her legs would go out from under her, so relieved she was.

"Somehow, someway, sometime," he said slowly, "I will be quits with Dugald Craigie."

"God grant it, laddie. But for now, put away that pistol before your mother comes home. Go over to your Uncle Tam's, why don't you?"

He didn't. He spent most of the day on the slope beside Chul. As Christy ached for him, her outrage grew. It wasn't fair, it wasn't right! She was going to Stornoway Castle and tell Sir James so, right to his face. He couldn't blame Mairi Mór or Clanna for what a twelve-year-old girl did. Surely, there'd be dogs at the castle. Sir James wasn't a wicked man. She would ask him to give David a puppy.

She carried food to Barbara Nicolson's house as the women were congratulating the mother and cooing over the new baby—ugly red little mite, Christy thought. Lucky that a few months greatly improved babies! She promised to make supper for David and Mr. Urquhart, since Mairi intended to stay the night and next day. Then Sheila would take over, and then another woman, cooking and looking after the family while Barbara cuddled her wee son and regained her strength.

Ah! thought Christy as she walked home. There's a fine full moon tonight. What's to keep me from creeping out as soon as David is asleep? I can rest when I'm fagged and still be early at Stornoway Castle. I'll make chowder and bannocks for tomorrow and leave David a note—

That would say what? Nothing, for sure, that would bring him riding after her! I'll say I'm not doing anything wild or dangerous— Well, it wasn't! Sir James wouldn't beat her or throw her in jail. I'll say it's a secret and I'll tell him all about it when I get home.

What a long way it was to Stornoway! As far as to Callanish. It was a year since she had prayed among the Stones. *You said David would be a great man,* she silently told Fearchar. *Right now he's still a boy, a boy who mourns his dog. If you can, help him—and help me, too!*

She felt a little braver, less as if water horses and water bulls lurked in the bogs. Frost silvered the moor. Lochs and lochans reflected the chill moon. Twice she stopped in old shieling huts and drowsed in her shawl.

The light of the moon mingled with that of dawn to shimmer on the waves of the great inner and outer harbors that made the hulking Beasts of Holm loom even darker. Many ships and boats had wrecked on those treacherous rocks, including Fearchar's. A number of vessels lay at anchor and the quays and connecting drive that ran along the shore were crowded even at this early hour with carts, wagons, and people.

From across the inner harbor, the square-towered, turreted castle looked over the town. The stronghold of the island's previous lairds had been destroyed by Cromwell, but Sir James had begun building this massive dwelling in 1847, three years after he bought the island. The trees planted at Lady Matheson's behest, Corsican pines, sycamores, and willows, did not yet shield the castle from view, but they were already much taller than the dwarfed rowans and alders and hazel trees that tried hard to grow where there was a little shelter from the wind.

Christy's stomach twisted as she took the way to the castle. How would she dare speak to the laird? Would she even be able to see him? It had seemed simple, back in the snug hearth room, to march up to the laird and tell him of Craigie's iniquity. It didn't seem easy now, or even possible, for here was a small house in the way and a grouchy-looking man coming out to glare at her.

"What do you want?" he snapped.

"I have come to see Sir James."

"Have you indeed, bratling? He won't want to see you. Take yourself off."

Christy dodged around him and ran up the drive fast as her legs could pump. The man shouted and came after her but he was fat and heavy on his feet. She was almost to the great heavy door when a man stepped out. He had a squarish body, thick shoulders, rough red hair, and little black eyes. He grabbed Christy by her hair as she almost pelted into him.

"What's this?" He gave her a shake and glared past her to the gasping watchman. "MacBride, what do you mean by letting urchins slip by you?"

"Och, Mr. Munro, sir—"

It was Red Donald, the laird's factor! Of all the evil luck! Christy's knees threatened to collapse and her teeth chattered. Mr. Munro gave her hair a final yank and shoved her toward the other man. "Get her off the grounds and don't let her or any like her get by you again if you value your position."

"Aye, Mr. Munro." The watchman gave her arm a brutal twist. "I'll watch her like a hawk, sir."

"Sir James!" Christy shouted. "Sir James! Please help me—" A thick hand closed over her mouth and nose, almost stifling her. Her captor gave her a vicious shake and dragged her along the drive.

"You little slut! Getting me in trouble with Mr. Munro! Stop kicking and walk or I'll—"

"Let the child go, MacBride." The big gray-haired man with the ruddy face and piercing eyes made Christy feel small and insignificant as he stepped outside. "Well, lass, why were you calling on my name and who may you be? I think I have seen you before."

She thought of Chul and did her best to stand boldly though her knees knocked together. "Don't let the impudent brat trouble you, sir," began the factor. The laird raised a finger. Mr. Munro hushed.

"I am Christy MacLeod from Clanna, Sir James." She had no true last name but had assumed Gran's. "You may have seen me at Iain MacDonald's funeral. Your keeper has shot David's dog."

"David? The son of Major MacDonald?"

Christy nodded. "You must see that was wicked, sir! The deer jumped the wall and were eating the stubble our beasts must have to fatten for the winter when they get so little food. Chul chased the deer away. He didn't hurt them." She swallowed hard and blinked back tears. Dear, funny Chul, with whom she had cuddled ever since she could remember—Chul, to whom Davie told things he wouldn't say even to her!

"A dog must not chase deer, my lass."

"Are we to starve then?"

"You brazen chit!" A scowl tugged Munro's brows together. "My lord, let me—"

Sir James ignored his agent. "I recognize the sentiments, girl," he said in a dry tone. "You must be the orphan reared by Mistress Mairi MacLeod MacDonald. But it is a shame that the great-nephew of my old friend, Sir Roderick, has lost his dog. I mind the lad is crippled."

"Sir James!" choked Munro.

"Be good enough, Munro, to find a likely pup for this lass to carry home. And tell Craigie not to shoot a dog of Clanna without my express permission."

"But, sir—"

"See to it." As the factor scuttled away with a furious glance at Christy, the laird steered her to the castle and into a vast hall lined with paintings, weapons, and stags' antlered heads. He tugged a rope that sent a distant bell tinkling. A rosy young woman in a crisp cap and apron appeared. Sir James told her to take Christy to the kitchen for tea and scones and to be sure the puppy located by Mr. Munro was healthy and intelligent.

"Good day to you, Christy MacLeod," the laird said. "Greet your foster mother for me." He paused. "Tell your young friend that I know the new pup can't take the place of his old companion but I hope he can like him."

The little black-and-white creature was full of love and wriggles. When his stubby legs failed, Christy carried him. "David will have to love you," she crooned. "How could he help it? Next summer you'll be herding the cows and sheep and sleeping on his bed at night, just like Chul."

David wouldn't have the pup. "It's Chul I want—not just a dog." He glared at Christy.

Stunned, hugging the puppy to her as if to shield him from David's rejection, she bit her quivering lip and tried not to cry. She had thought to make him happy and instead he was furious.

He said more gently, "Christy, you were brave, marching to the castle like that. I am obliged, indeed I am."

Wordlessly, she held the puppy out. David wouldn't look at it and she knew why. If he did, his heart would melt. "I don't want to forget Chul!" he said. "I'm going to remember him. I'm going to bring the day when keepers can't shoot our dogs."

"But Davie, how will you be doing that?"

His fine, flashing anger changed to glumness. "I'll have to go study on the mainland so I can be a lawyer or journalist or something of that ilk that makes a lot of uproar. But I'll do it, whatever it takes. I can't go while mother's still mourning father and Gran, but when she's not so sad, I must make a start." His jaw hardened. Each day, he looked more like his father. "It's not the life I would have chosen," he said with a grim laugh. "But it's the one I've got."

Christy was desolate at the thought of his going but she couldn't argue. As he grew older, it was ever harder for him to watch Alai and the other boys slipping into men's work, moving light and swiftly, while he was hampered by his crutches.

"Forbye, Davie, you're not leaving tomorrow. It wouldn't hurt to take this bit dog. See how he wants to come to you—"

David turned away. "If I got to love him, I wouldn't want to leave. It's hard enough to leave mother and Tam and all—"

Was she included in the "all?" Christy wondered with a stab of hurt. "Give the dog to the Gunns," David said gruffly. "When Alai's off fishing, his little brother and sisters can use the dog to keep cows and sheep out of the crops."

So the pup, christened Laddie, was ecstatically welcomed into the Gunn household, sharing the box bed sometimes of the girls, sometimes that of the boys. He had the same markings as Chul, the same spot over one eye, but David never stroked or spoke to him, though he did ask Christy to give the pup Chul's old sheepskin.

There was plenty of food, fodder for the beasts, and peats for the hearth, yet it was the saddest, loneliest winter Christy could remember. The captain had not been home enough for her to truly miss him but at every turn she expected to see Gran and felt a wave of loss. The ceilidhs helped—neighbors came almost every evening—but it was strange not to see Chul curled by David's feet. If it was so for her, what must it be for David?

It was as if he were somewhere else, with only the husk of him at Clanna, though he studied harder than ever. Christy was sure he was trying to summon up the resolution to leave and when he did, she didn't know how she could bear it.

Spring came at last, whooper swans and geese calling as they winged northward to their breeding grounds, larks caroling, sea pinks a fragrant carpet wherever they found a bit of soil. The cows lowed their pleasure at being outside again and many ewes bulged with the lambs they would soon be dropping.

Spring always comes, thought Christy. Life moves along and takes us with it and that's how people go on after their loved ones die. It was almost a year since the captain died and Gran followed him along the low road. Mairi smiled now, even laughed, and seemed as delighted with her new wee niece, Tam's and Molly's baby, as if she had been her own.

All the Clanna folk had set out that morning to walk the seven miles to the church for the christening and then return to prepare a grand feast. David said, though, that he would not be going. Mairi gave him a searching look, sighed, and kissed his cheek before she joined her brother's family.

"You can always come if you change your mind," she told him. "You as well, Christy."

"If I don't come, I'll make the crannachan and start the barley broth," Christy said. She and her foster mother exchanged glances, Christy silently assuring Mairi that she wouldn't leave David alone.

As the procession moved over the slope, Christy pleaded, "Davie, you could ride to the kirk."

"While my mother and the old ones walk?" He turned away, stared toward the sea and the rock where he'd fallen a year and a half ago. Christy would never forget how he had seemed to fly. Still, in her dreams, she saw him running as he used to, fleeter than all the others, even Alai.

"You go to the christening," David said. "I don't want you fussing after me."

Christy's tears welled up at the harshness. She knew it came from David's misery but she couldn't keep from retorting, "I won't fuss after you, gavallachan, but I'm not going to the kirk, either!"

She picked up her creel and set off for the shore. Tam and Molly would understand why she didn't come to the christening of their baby. It was an unspoken rule at Clanna that David should never be left by himself for more than a few hours. It was usually Christy who stayed, finding an occupation so he wouldn't guess why she hadn't gone with the others to the peat cutting or heather gathering or whatever the occasion was.

While David got over his temper, Christy decided to soothe hers down by the sea, gather eelgrass—the mattresses needed new stuffing—and lichens for dye.

Why did Davie have to be so mean, bite off her head, when she only wanted to help? That was it, of course. He hated sympathy. All the same, he'd be glad enough to have fresh, hot bannocks that day instead of cold, hard ones. The tide was out and Christy wandered along the shore, gathering crotal and other lichens from the rocks, watching the play of dolphins.

The cliffs were alive with noisy tribes of nesting birds.

Christy's feelings calmed as she watched a score of young and old seals sunning on the rock or easing into the protected sea loch.

If Davie was looking that way with the fine spyglass Magnus had given him, he'd have to smile at the seals. Better allow him plenty of time, though, to get back in a good humor. Gray-green beard-of-the-rock covered a ledge of the cliff where spray splashed it at high tide. Wedging her creel in a crevice below the ledge, Christy climbed up, avoiding barnacles, and collected the hairy lichen, which would make a lovely yellow-brown.

Warmed by the sun, the ledge was pleasant and the rhythmic sound of the waves made her sleepy. Goodness knew there was no rush to get home and be snapped at by David. She'd just lie here a little while, soaking up the sun . . .

🐱 It was raining. What was she doing out in it? Christy sat up and remembered where she was just in time to keep from falling off the ledge. Mary and Brigid save her, the tide was surging in, hurtling against rocks and cliffs! The sun was still bright, but she saw it through foaming spray.

Christy looked frantically about but there was no way to reach the higher shore, even when the breakers retreated before the next assault. How much higher would the waves dash? She'd heard of other people stranded like this and had always wondered how they could be so daft as not to keep an eye on the tide. Some had been swept away and drowned. Others managed to keep a hazardous perch till the tide turned.

That was her only hope. The sea gushed over the ledge, tugged at her with greedy hunger. She gripped a rift in the rock wall with straining fingers, held till the waters made a sucking, disappointed sound as they swirled back. If they came much higher . . .

Gran! Oh Gran! Help me! The next swelling whitecap foamed around her, tugged as it receded. It drenched the rock cranny she held to, turning it slick. Her numbed fingers almost lost their grip. Sodden skirts dragged at her as the water pulled them with it in grudging retreat.

Gasping, Christy wondered if her body would wash ashore. If she had to die, she wanted to be near Gran in the hollow beneath the cliff. But she didn't want to die! No one could hear her but she cried out with all her might. "Davie! Davie!"

If she must drown it would be with his name on her lips, with his image locked inside her darkening eyes. But she'd hold on as long as she could. Mairi Mór had taught her that.

Through the roar of the sea and the shriek of birds, she thought she was imagining the voice, snatched by the wind, that shouted her name.

"Christy!" it came again. "Grab the rope!"

A heather rope with knots tied in it dangled down the cliff. Far above, David leaned over, gripping the other end of the rope, which must be anchored around the rocks beside him. "Climb up!" he yelled. "Set your hands above the knots and climb! Hurry!"

Indeed the sea was flooding in, breaker after breaker. "My creel!"

"Leave it!" The rope gave an imperative jerk. "And leave your skirts! They'll cumber you!"

The cliff reared almost straight up, but there were niches and small ledges. Christy shed her wet skirt, gripped above the first knots, and found purchase on the cliff with her bare toes. The wave dashed against her knees, hauled at her, swept her feet from the rock. She clung to the rope, so panicked that she scarcely knew the water had ebbed till David's command pierced her terror.

"Climb, Christy! Climb!"

She did, sometimes slipping, losing many a precarious foothold, but always saved by the rope. The spray blinded her each time the breakers crashed against the cliff, higher with each onslaught. Her hands and fingers were tough from work but they were raw and bleeding from the heather. If Davie hadn't been there, she might have given up. But he was.

"Climb, lass! Come along now! Reach for the next knot, up you go!"

Sustained by his voice as much as by the lifeline, Christy finally neared the top. It was sheer, no cracks or footholds. She was too exhausted for that last effort, to scramble above the edge. But Davie reached over.

"Take my hand! I'll haul you up!"

His other hand must grip the rope at the anchoring rock. Could his one hand hold her? If it couldn't Christy's worst fear was that she'd drag him over.

He commanded her again. Christy shut her eyes, put one hand in his, then the other, as she let go the rope. Somehow, her toes found tiny roughnesses that let them push upward. David's strength drew her up. She was over the brink with her upper body. David caught her under the arms, dragged her to safety. She saw that the anchor for the rope was Chieftain. David had rigged a rough harness to ease the tug at the horse's neck. She lay spent beside David while the thwarted waves howled below.

"Davie," she said when she could speak. "How did you know?"

"The tide was turning and you were still gone. I used my spyglass—and there was the blue drogad of your skirt like a flag on that ledge, and you either asleep or fallen, I couldn't tell which. Against that tide, I couldn't get a boat to you."

If he hadn't seen her, thought of a way to save her—Christy began to tremble and went all weak again. Her shift and blouse were soaked and the wind chilled her.

"Here." David made her put on his shirt. He chafed her feet and legs, making the blood tingle. "Let's go home and get some hot tea and broth into you."

She helped him undo the makeshift harness. Using the

strength of his arms, he mounted and offered her a hand. "Chieftain can carry double this short way."

"I'll walk. 'Twill warm me." Her lips quivered. "My creel! My skirt! Mairi Mór will think I'm stupid!"

David tugged her plait. "So you are, having a doze on a cliff ledge!"

"I didn't mean to go to sleep! I was just going to rest for a minute where it was so nice and warm—"

"And where I wouldn't growl at you." David gave a brief laugh and said nothing more till Christy was in dry clothes, her only others, snug on the settle. David brought her a bowl of hot broth that warmed Christy to the core. Luxuriating in sips of steaming tea while David rubbed salve into her scraped fingers, she sighed with bliss and gratitude.

"No use putting it off." His blurted words shattered her peace. "I'm going to the university at Inverness as soon as I can."

"Davie!"

"It's time. I've known I had to go ever since Chul was shot but—well, it's main hard to leave."

"But Mr. Urquhart's teaching you your Latin and Greek and physics—" She had absorbed some of those subjects herself, just from listening.

"Yes. That's so I can go directly into university." He stared at the glowing peats. "When I get my degree, then maybe I'll be some use."

"You were plenty of use today!"

He brushed away her protest. "You'd have gone to the christening if you hadn't stayed for me. Then I was snarly so you kept away till I'd be in better humor—*that's* why you went to sleep on the ledge. I'm a worry to mother, too. You'll both be better off without me to fret over."

He stuck to that resolve. In three weeks, with Sir Roderick's help, it was all arranged. David rode Chieftain to Stornoway and took the old horse with him to Inverness where he could graze in

Sir Roderick's pastures. Mr. Urquhart rode along to Stornoway on Kelpie to see David embarked on the steamer.

Except for Mr. Urquhart, who slept in the schoolroom, Mairi Mór and Christy were now alone in the chieftain's house Clanna folk had built for Mairi and her captain.

Fortunately the house filled often with ceilidhs, and even in summer, Mr. Urquhart held classes a few hours a day when the children weren't needed to work. Still, Christy felt so lonely and deserted that one night after Mairi had gone to bed, she left the storeroom bed she'd shared with Gran and crept into David's box bed facing the hearth room. She cuddled into his blankets and pillow. They seemed to still hold his scent. *Davie, you'll be back, won't you, when you've got your grand education?*

She sat up abruptly. Maybe he wouldn't! A lawyer or a newspaper writer or any of the other mysterious things the university might make him would likely have to live on the mainland, or at least in Stornoway.

Whatever he became, it wouldn't be a crofter. He was lost to Clanna. Christy smothered a wail in her pillow. She could endure his being away if he'd come back sometime. If he never did—

Well, then, she'd have to get an education, too, so she could follow him, live where she could see him. She'd talk to Mr. Urquhart. He wouldn't laugh.

The bed curtains parted. Mairi Mór stood there, looming in the faint light of the banked peats. Christy smothered a squeak, hastily scrambled down. "I—I'm sorry. I was just—"

"Missing David?" To Christy's surprise, Mairi gave her a hug and Christy felt a rush of gladness that even if Mairi Mór might not ever be able to love her, she seemed to like her now.

"You must sore miss Davie," Christy said.

"Yes. But this is what his father wanted. No doubt 'tis the best road for David. So, lass, we must be glad he's set out bravely."

Christy nodded. She started for the storeroom. Mairi caught

her hand. "I should have thought of it before. This bed is snugger by the hearth. Sleep here if you've a mind to, m'eudail."

Darling. The endearment Christy almost never heard from this woman she idolized. Before she could stammer her thanks, Mairi spoke as if making a sudden decision. "You'll soon be thirteen." Christy's true birthdate was unknown, so Gran had declared it would be marked by Midsummer, June 24. "It's time I took you to the Stones."

Christy's breath seemed to harden in her chest. "That— that's only for the women of your blood, Mairi Mór."

"It comes through Gran. She thought the Stones would accept you as Cridhe has."

"Oh, Mairi Mór—"

"I intend to play many years yet," Mairi said with the flash of a smile. "But after me, you will sing the old songs of the island— make new ones, too. We don't know who your parents were. You belong to the islands, not any particular clan. That makes you more than ever a daughter of the Stones."

"What if the Stones don't like me? They didn't say anything to me when I was there before."

Mairi's hand brushed Christy's cheek. The smile in Mairi's voice warmed and loosened the tight chill in Christy. "The Stones don't 'like' mortals. Callanish is a place to feel the centuries and know our folk will endure as the Stones have."

Something in Mairi Mór was like the Stones. She might not love Christy but she had taught her the harp—and now she was willing to present her to the Stones.

Cold filled Christy again, crushing her lungs. How could she follow David if she was pledged to the island? But she owed her life to Mairi Mór, who was offering the inheritance meant for her own daughter.

Christy knew Mairi's proposal was partly to comfort her for David's absence, to make her feel she belonged. It seemed flagrantly ungrateful, but Christy realized she dare not go to the

Stones. Not when she meant to follow wherever David would live.

And she did intend that. Life without David was like life without the sun. She couldn't say all this to Mairi Mór. She hung her head and tried not to squirm. "Mairi Mór, forgive me but—but I am not fit to go to the Stones."

Mairi was silent a long time. At last she said, "I will not ask what you mean or beg you. When you are ready, tell me."

She went back to her chamber. Christy felt as if the Powers of the hearth reproached her, as if Brigid, Mary, and Christ himself condemned her ingratitude. Worst of all, she had given Mairi Mór good reason to believe she was indeed a changeling, a cuckoo in the nest.

But what else could she do when she meant to follow David?

X

That December of 1862, six months after David left the island, five boats were lost in a wild storm off Port of Ness on Lewis's northeastern shore. That wind-scourged coast, exposed to the Atlantic's fury, was known for its disasters but this was the worst. Thirty-one men were drowned, from several small villages in the parish of Ness. They left twenty-four widows and seventy orphans as well as aged fathers and mothers who depended on them. And this was winter, the cruelest, hardest time of year.

Magnus Ericson had been in the Clanna harbor when the news came. Daring winter gales, he carried supplies from Clanna, everything from butter and salt fish to clothing. "The villages have scarcely an able-bodied man left," Magnus said when he returned. "It'll be years before the lads can take their fathers' places. I talked to one woman who lost her husband, son, and son-in-law a few years ago in another storm. This time she lost her remaining son and son-in-law. So that leaves three widows and five bairns in one house, and no man at all."

"Oh, Magnus," cried Mairi, "you gave her some money?"

"I did. And a relief fund is being started. Ness folk will feel this loss for a generation. But they've food for the winter, at any rate."

Clanna had been wondrous lucky. In eighteen years, the township had lost only Gavin MacKinnon to the sea. Everyone well knew, though, that should a fierce storm catch the boats out in the

Minch, Clanna women and children could weep like those of Ness. "I'll go to see the families at Whitsuntide when I pay Clanna's rents," Mairi said.

But at Whitsuntide, Mairi had a wracking cough and had to admit she was in no condition for the long tramp to Stornoway.

"You go along with Sheila to pay the rents," Mairi said to Christy. "It'll be more than a day's walk from Stornoway to the Ness villages, but your young long legs can manage it and any crofter will give you a place to sleep. See how the people fare. Bide there a night or two and then come home."

Christy smothered a disappointed sound. She'd only been to Stornoway once, when she went to see Sir James, but usually whoever paid the rents got to visit the shops and see all the things that came from far away. They brought home indigo and tea and raisins, nuts, and spices and sweeties for the children—and grownups, too.

As if guessing Christy's dismay, Mairi said, "Before you go to Ness, go in the shop and trade butter for a nice lot of sweeties and some tea to take along. And choose a penny's worth of whatever you may fancy." Mairi hesitated. "Why don't you take your little harp with you? It's not very heavy. You can tuck it into your creel. It may be the widows of Ness need a merry tune as much as anything."

Sheila was a few years older than Mairi, and bearing four children had softened and plumped her contours. Where her hair escaped the fluted mutch, though, it still shone bright gold. Knitting as she walked, she carried her creel with the ease of long experience. Most of the Clanna rents would be paid with silver coin, but for trading in the shops, Sheila and Christy carried butter, carefully wrapped eggs, and some woolens.

Purple-brown moor and twisted gray rocks greened with deer's hair grass and blue moor grass wherever the roots found a bit of soil. Bees and other insects buzzed their delight over feathery pink and white blooms of bogbean that grew in marshes gilded also by marsh marigolds. Red as wine, five-pointed stars of marsh cinque-foil jeweled shallow bogs where moorhens and coots swam.

A white-rumped brown curlew winged from the marsh, bubbling its "Quee-e-ee!" A redshank stalked on, legs and orange-red bill the only gay touches to its sober gray-brown summer plumage. Christy heard the grunting cluck of a water rail but could not spy the elusive bird as it complained among the sedges.

A tune began to form in Christy's mind and she hummed it softly. She had never dared sing the songs she made to anyone but David. David. Her heart twisted painfully. There was little way of telling how his life on the mainland truly was. His letters were brief and mostly full of questions about his friends and family. Mairi could write but it was laborious for her so she usually wrote a few sentences in her large, childish hand and asked Christy to finish with news of Clanna.

Between letters, Christy noted down events and funny happenings on an old envelope so that she wouldn't forget anything that would amuse or interest David. She was afraid of seeming ignorant, now that he was getting his grand education, so she labored hard with spelling and grammar and asked Mr. Urquhart's help when she needed it.

"You make me see the new calves and lambs," David wrote. *"And how Seana can't decide between Alai and Geordie MacPhail. You make me smell the peat smoke and hear mother playing Cridhe."* That rewarded all Christy's effort, but how she longed to see him! It was a long, difficult trip from Inverness, especially for a crippled lad, but she hoped he'd come home this summer.

"Let's rest our creels and munch our bannocks." Sheila halted at a grassy knoll and gave a chuckle of relief as she leaned her creel on a rock. "I'm not as young as I was, or the road's longer."

It was noon when they reached the castle. The same fat watchman was in the porter's lodge and let them enter the grounds. He didn't seem to remember Christy. Outside the factor's office, crofters, men and women, waited to pay their rents.

Inside, Mr. Munro sat at a desk with a big ledger and a cash box. Christy didn't want to give him a chance to remember her and intended to stay outside while Sheila paid the rents.

A frazzled young woman with a child in her arms, plainly scared of the thickset red-haired man, stood there as he examined the accounts.

"You go to the shop and on to Ness," Sheila told Christy. "It's a long way, twenty-eight miles. Don't try to get there tonight."

Just then the woman with the child came out. She was sobbing. "Didn't Mr. Munro give you your share of that relief money we've been hearing about?" asked a wrinkled older woman.

"He kept it all!"

"What?" demanded an aged man who leaned heavily on a blackthorn stick. "Why, the English queen herself gave money to that fund for the Ness widows! There should be a grand lot of coin for each family."

"We were behind on rent." The mother rubbed her eyes on her shawl and swallowed hard before she could go on. "We still owed for meal we bought those years the 'taties rotted. 'Twas fair enough to keep some of the money, maybe, but little Colin's so poorly I wanted to take him to the doctor and get some medicine."

"Shame on that big-gut chamberlain!" growled the old man. "Well, the worms know he fattens himself for their delight! Not to give you a shilling of the money kind people meant for Ness!"

"Och, 'tis wicked," agreed Sheila. She put her hand on the other woman's arm. They might have been of an age, but the widow's gaunt body and despairing face made her seem years the elder. "Listen, my dear," Sheila said. "Go to the doctor with Christy here. She'll pay him in butter and eggs and trade for whatever else you need. Christy, take more butter from my creel so you can take sweeties and tea along with you."

Christy scarcely heard. She was already making her way

through the line toward the open door. There he sat, Donald Munro, procurator fiscal; commander of the local volunteer force; justice of the peace; legal advisor to the four parochial boards; vice-chairman of the harbor trustees; director of the Stornoway Gas Company; director of the Stornoway Water Company; deputy-chairman of the Road Trust and heaven only knew what else— there he sat, the man who'd upheld the gamekeeper in shooting Chul, and now he was robbing widows!

Ducking past an astonished crofter with a murmur of apology, she still had enough sense to close the door and pitch her voice low. "Does Sir James know, Mr. Munro, how you're sharing out the relief fund?"

Startled, he half-rose, then settled back. A grim smile spread across his broad features. Like a great bull he was, knobs on his forehead and heavy shoulders and chest. Small dark eyes glittered with malicious amusement.

"So the gawky waif of Clanna has grown longer legs but little brain! You can't whine to the laird. He and his lady are on the mainland. I am the manager of the estate. Get out of here—and your village had better have every penny of its rents."

Indeed, with Sir James gone, there was no appeal. This man was all-powerful. He knew the laird's regard for Mairi, so Christy thought he wouldn't dare evict folk from Clanna, but there was nothing to gain by argument.

"May God judge you," she said with a long look before she went out. He laughed scornfully and called in the next tenant.

"What did you do?" whispered Sheila, aghast, while those around them stared. "Running in the Shah's office like that—" He'd won that nickname, as well as that of Red Donald, for his overbearing ways.

"I did no good. Sir James isn't here."

"Sir James!"

"Aye. If he knew it, he wouldn't let Mr. Munro take the Ness folks' money."

"Well, he doesn't know and now you've made Red Donald angry! He'll be as mean as he can with me!"

"You've got the rents. That's what he cares about."

Sheila heaved an exasperated sigh. "A hot tongue boils broth too hot for other folk to sip! Never mind, child. You meant well though how you had the brass——" She shuddered at the thought of confronting the chamberlain. "Go your ways now or you'll not reach Ness before dark."

Doctor Miller, the same who'd come when David fell, was visiting with a gentleman in well-cut clothes, but he excused himself, asking his friend to wait while he examined the tyke who cried fretfully at leaving his mother's arms. The boy's legs bowed and seemed to have no strength to hold him up. "Does he get milk, Mrs. MacNeil?" the doctor asked.

"A bit of skim from my neighbors. We had a cow but she was old and died the year Colin was born."

"But you nursed him?"

Peggy MacNeil flushed as if caught in a grave fault. "I could not, sir. My breasts caked and I was long abed with fever. We fed the babe with gruel and as I said, what skim the neighbors could spare. That was little enough with all their bairns." The woman lulled her child against her sunken breast. "Is there a medicine, sir?"

"The medicine he needs is milk, food to build his bones strong and straight. Skim is very well, and crowdie, but he needs plenty of them."

Peggy's face crumpled. "Och, if the chamberlain hadn't held back my share of the relief money! I could have bought two good cows!"

The waiting gentleman sat up at that. "What's this about a relief fund, my good woman?" he asked in Gaelic. He had a Lewis accent for all his fine clothes. Taking a small notepad from his pocket, he scribbled away as Mrs. MacNeil explained.

"I gave to the Ness fund myself," the gentleman said. "I think I'll stroll over and have a word with Mr. Munro."

"Och, sir, don't stir him up!" pleaded the widow. "He'll do you an ill turn."

"He'll do nothing to me, Mrs. MacNeil." Dark eyes laughed and strong teeth flashed in a grin. "I was born in Stornoway but I live in London. The papers there would be interested in how the chamberlain of Lewis took back rents out of the money collected to relieve widows and orphans. Good day to you, and good fortune."

He bowed as if they were ladies and took himself off. The doctor shook his head but his tone was proud. "Robert MacKenzie's gone far since I brought him into the world thirty years ago. Made a fortune in the China trade and now he owns publishing houses in Edinburgh, London, and Glasgow. He comes back every year or so to visit his old mother, whom he's set up in as fine a house as she'd let him build her over by the Female Seminary."

"I'm sure the gentleman means well, bless his kind heart." Peggy MacNeil looked woeful. "But I hope he won't put Mr. Munro in a fury and make an ill matter worse."

"Perhaps your neighbors can spare you a little more milk if they know the laddie's health depends on it." The doctor gave the child a sweetie and patted his lank fair hair. "For now, don't pay me, Mrs. MacNeil, but buy the child a mug of milk and some crowdie for the trudge home."

Wee Colin drank his milk thirstily and munched contentedly at a fruit bun while his mother helped Christy select treats and necessities for the bereaved Ness families. When the shopkeepers knew who the provisions were for, they piled more food in the creels till both were full and Christy was compelled to carry her small harp.

"Good souls for sure though they dwell in town," said

Peggy as they set off northward. "But how I'm to find milk for my little one—"

"Mairi Mór will send you a cow." Until she spoke the words, Christy hadn't realized how grand it was to *know* that Mairi would do that. "Let me carry your laddie for a while."

Christy had held all the Clanna babies, helping Gran and Morag tend them while their mothers gutted and packed fish or did other tasks where tykes were in the way. Never had she hefted such a pitiful mite.

Bag of bones, she thought, shocked as she helped Colin find a perch on her hip. Hollow bones they seemed, like those of a bird—only the bairn couldn't fly. Christy held him tighter during that terrible flash that still haunted her dreams—of that heart-stopped moment when David seemed to fly—and then fell.

Heavily laden as Peggy and Christy were, they stopped now and again to rest and handed wee Colin back and forth as their arms tired. "Not only my husband drowned in that storm," said Peggy, "but our eldest son, the only one strong enough to cut peats and delve with the cas-chrom. He'd have wed his lass this summer." Peggy dashed away her tears and went on as if it were a relief to talk.

"It's the same tale in most households around Port of Ness. No men to fish or plow or cut peats and several years before lads your age and younger can do such work. We eat seaweed and shellfish but how will we warm our houses?" She sighed and answered her own question. "Instead of fine, proper-cut peats, we'll have to dig chunks out of the bank as best we can. But if we'd got even half the relief money, we could have bought more cows, chickens and sheep—traded butter, eggs, cheese, and woolens for our needs and had enough for ourselves."

Devil roast Red Donald! Christy thought. If David were grown up, a journalist or a lawyer, he'd know something to do about this! For the first time she was glad he was away, getting his education so he could battle Munro and Dugald Craigie and all that ilk that oppressed the crofters.

Later that day, she and Peggy were overtaken by some other Ness women who had gone to the factor's office for their part of the relief fund. All had been more or less in arrears but several got a few coins after rents were deducted.

"That ledger of the Shah's!" snorted a sturdy freckle-faced young woman named Barbara Morison. "Why, he went back through all his slippery, squiggly figures, pried out six pounds my husband's poor old father owed, and charged it to me!"

An older woman patted her hand. "Don't fash yourself, m'eudail. God keeps a ledger, too."

"That butters no bannocks for us now," sniffed Barbara and jabbed her needles vengefully into the sock she was knitting.

Since creels carried hopefully to Stornoway were still empty or nearly so, the women offered to help with Peggy's and Christy's loads and take turns with Colin. Except for two young mothers who were nursing babies, the others had left their bairns at home. Christy divided up the tea, sweeties, and food so that some went to each village. As they walked on, Christy managed to sort out conditions in the townships as disappointment and bitter humor salted the women's talk.

How comparatively well-off Clanna was! Christy couldn't remember being hungry after a meal or having to be careful of peats or not having warm clothes and a snug bed. She had gathered plenty of shellfish, of course, which made excellent stew, and carageen, dulse, and laver were valued foods. But every Clanna household had at least two cows, chickens, and half-a-dozen sheep. Stouthearted little Kelpie had gone to greener pastures that winter, but the township had bought two ponies to help with the heavy work. All the children got schooling without a long tramp in foul weather. To keep them safe and seaworthy, boats were replaced every five years or oftener as needed. White-maned Malcolm Ferguson and Murdo MacKinnon no longer fished except in small boats offshore, but they mended nets, repaired boats, cut peats, and had everything they needed.

Yes, but if most of the able-bodied men were lost at one time, it would go hard even with Clanna. Christy shivered at the very notion and wondered again if her father had been lost at sea or if he'd been a soldier, or been torn away from her mother and sent across the ocean against his will.

Had the beleaguered folk of Sollas not pitied the unknown woman and her babe—had Mairi Mór not taken her to Clanna— *Oh, I might be dead of the smallpox that carried off so many of the Sollas folk below decks on the frigate. I might have died that year they tried to wring a living from the barren inland acres given them by the Perth Destitution Committee. There are a score of ways I might have perished against one chance to live.*

Dusk and weariness made the party halt for the night, sheltering in the ruins of a cleared village now grazed by sheep. They had no way to make a fire but they made a good supper of bannocks and cheese. Shielded by the remains of a double house wall, they huddled together in their plaids for warmth, the bairns tucked in amongst them.

It was an adventure, sleeping in the sweet brisk air beneath the stars, but Christy thought of those countless families that had lacked even this much shelter. She thought of her mother, wandering homeless on the shore of Uist. And what of the family that had lived here? Where were they now? The wind lamented and Christy was glad when it was light enough to see and the first larks burst out singing.

It was midafternoon when the party reached Peggy's village, Siadar, which lay farther south of Port of Ness than the other stricken communities. Since it was so late, the other women declined Peggy's proud offer of tea—this was perhaps the first time in her life she'd been able to supply it—bade Christy thank Mairi Mór and Clanna for their kindness, and hurried on.

Huddled on the moor above a deep, narrow sea loch, Siadar

was a dozen eyeless houses, not a window in the storm-flailed scrabble of them. In the gloaming, the lazybeds looked like walled graves. Calves tugged so avidly at the udders of a few skinny cows that Christy guessed the cows had been milked almost to the last dribble. Sheep drifted together in a hollow as if to keep each other warm.

Several other Siadar women, including Barbara Morison, went off to their homes. Peggy called after them, "Bring your families tonight and we'll have real tea and listen to Christy play her little harp."

"Och, a ceilidh!" Barbara Morison laughed in anticipation. "The good God knows it's been a long time since we sang and had music at the hearth."

Christy had never played her harp alone except for David or when she was by herself. Panic gripped her. How would she play for a mort of strangers? Ah, but they were strangers who craved music, some melodies to ease their woes. And they were not truly strangers. They were people like those who had taken her in, at Sollas, and again at Clanna.

Peggy's oldest daughter, Bella, all arms, legs, and fair hair, looked to be a few years younger than Christy. She had soup cooking over the small peat fire that was the house's only light. Donnie, perhaps eight, stared with great blue eyes at Christy, but he took Colin piggyback and trotted around the room while the soup was ladled out, shellfish stewed with silverweed and nettles. Little Colin had crowdie as well, and there were cold bannocks left from morning. However, there was gingerbread from town to savor to the last crumb, and the fragrance of the brewing tea mingled with peat smoke in a rich odor of hospitality.

Except for the empty byre, the house had only the single room. A box bed was along one side and a sleeping shelf was built into another thick wall. The settle was of turf covered with an old blanket. There were several wicker stools and a wicker cupboard.

Even before the father drowned, this family had a meager existence.

Still, the hearth room filled with an air of hopeful festivity. Peggy added several peat chunks, blowing up a cheery blaze as her neighbors began to gather, bringing stools and sheepskins and their own cups.

"A ceilidh, forbye!" crooned one withered old woman who was bent almost double. "Och, ochone, my dears, I thought to be in my grave before we had songs again."

Bella led her to the settle where she was joined by three other women of advanced age. Amongst a flurry of children endowed with her red hair and freckles, Barbara Morison helped an ancient man locate his stool near the fire and wrapped a plaid around his frail shoulders.

"Grandfather," the buxom young woman said, "this is Christy MacLeod come from far south of Stornoway to play the harp for us. Christy, this is Adam Morison, my husband's grandfather." His filmed eyes peered sightlessly.

"Now how'd she lay hands on my father's harp? Hid away it's been under the box bed ever since he died—and before that, too, when the parson made a great fire for all the fiddles and harps and bagpipes of Ness. Parson claimed that was why my father drowned." The aged man cackled. "So did the rest of the crew, though, and none of them had harps."

"It's not great-granddaddy's harp the lassie has," soothed Barbara. " 'Tis her own small one."

Finlay MacNeil, Peggy's husband's great-uncle, was the only other man. He was not as frail and bent as Adam but he was much older than any man at Clanna. Five half-grown boys of twelve or thirteen would have to fill men's places before their strength and bodies matched the work. Three girls were Bella's age. Between them and several babes-in-arms, there were ten children.

Peggy poured out tea, watering it for the children. Everyone looked expectantly at Christy. She wanted to sink through the floor. If she had Cridhe, she'd be brave. The harp almost sang of itself. But her little harp had such a soft and plaintive voice——

You don't have to play salutes to the chief or battle tunes or funeral marches. You don't need to do the grand great music. Christy could almost hear Gran's voice. *Your small harp is just right for lullabies and gentle songs and frolics. What of that tune the bees and curlew and water rail put in your head this morning?*

Christy tuned the harp and closed her eyes to see the moor again. She began with the liquid "quee-e-ee!" of the curlew, the moorhen's "curruc," the redshank's melodious "tu-u-u." Then Christy's fingers flew into ecstatic trills of peewits and golden plovers with the hum of bees and murmur of beetles constant in the background.

"Och," murmured old Adam when she finished. "I saw lochs and lochans light with the sun. And the peewits, didn't they tumble and somersault and sing to burst their throats? You've a God-gift, lassie."

Wee Colin had crept to her and pulled up to lean on her knees, big-eyed with wonder. Just so she must have watched Mairi Mór. "Here's one for you, m'eudail," Christy told him. She sang of the cat who maintained his innocence of stealing the cream, the butter, the pullets of the exciseman, the black cock, and the white cock. By the end, Colin and almost everyone joined in the chorus. "Och, och, och, och, och! Alas for my condition . . ."

When Christy's fingers tired, she took Colin in her lap while old Adam and Finlay told stories. Poor laddie, with his bowed legs that could hardly bear the pitiful weight of him! But Mairi Mór would send a cow.

Indeed. But what would happen to this village without men? Christy looked at the lads, none older than she, and imagined them bent and stunted from working too soon at tasks too hard for them. The lasses, too, would do the work that would normally fall to the boys.

Christy's last song was a lullaby Gran had sung her. Colin

smiled sleepily and nestled his fair head deeper in the curve of Christy's arm. At last, reluctantly, brisk, birdlike Sarah MacNeil picked up her stool and helped her father-in-law, Finlay, wince to his feet to be assisted by his great-grandson, auburn-haired Johnny. In this disaster and the last, Sarah had lost all the other men of her family.

"Bless you for your music," she told Christy. "That ice-hearted Donald Munro may take what kind folk sent to help us, but he can't steal our songs." Her eyes misted. "We've not had a ceilidh since—since our laddies drowned, but now you've got us started."

"Och," muttered old Adam. "If only someone had the skill to play my father's harp! But there it bides, under the box bed." He groped to pat Christy's cheek. "Twas a grand ceilidh, lass."

After the neighbors took their leave, Peggy tucked Colin into the box bed. Donnie was already asleep in his wall niche. A yawning Bella helped Peggy make a bed for Christy on the settle and swiftly retired.

Peggy smoored the fire. Then, in the near-darkness, she said to Christy, "You've put heart in us, lass, in spite of the Shah's knavery. You mustn't fash yourself if your township can't spare a cow. Somehow we'll manage." She sighed. "It's heavy on my heart, though, that our bairns will get no more school. There's none here at Siadar, and with their labor needed, the young ones can't walk the four miles to Fivepenny Ness. Donnie's that quick, I'd hoped he could get an education and not be a fisherman."

"Maybe he can. When Mairi Mór sends the cow, I'll bring some books from our schoolmaster. I know he'll give you some."

"That's rare kind, lass. But none of us can do more than read scripture in Gaelic, write, and cipher a bit. No one has the English except the bairns who've learned to mouth it in school without really understanding what it means." She stroked Christy's hair. "There, m'eudail, you're good to care. If your dominie can spare a book or two, I know Donnie and the few others who love learning will treasure them like gold.''

A few books. A cow. So little against what the people needed. From practicing with David, Christy could read and write English almost as well as Gaelic. She had some Latin and Greek, mathematics, history, and geography, and had devoured every book on the captain's shelves and others Mr. Urquhart had added. Once he had said to her, "You'd make a fine teacher, Christy.''

That echoed in her ears though she tried to smother it. Her dream and determination was that when David was settled she'd find employment nearby. I don't want to come here! she thought. I want to be near David!

The earthen settle was hard beneath the blanket but that was not the reason it took her long to fall asleep.

XI

Morning did little to improve Siadar. Thatch had caved in on several abandoned houses. Peat stacks beside the seven inhabited dwellings had dwindled low in spite of some households moving in together to save fuel. None of three scrawny cows looked as if they'd calve that summer and there weren't enough sheep to supply more wool than needed for clothing.

Who would cut the peats? Put on the new layer of thatch and take off the smoky bottom layer to work into the lazybeds? Who'd bring in the fish the families needed for food? As she walked over the moor toward Stornoway and home Christy told herself she wasn't a man, she couldn't do those things.

But she could bring music. She could teach. And she knew herbs from Gran. Meadow rue might help Adam and Finlay's rheumatics, ease the gnarled hands of the old women. Hart's-tongue fern tea could soothe that cough of Anne MacEnnis. Hadn't Christy just that morning used a warm poultice of crowfoot and plantain to draw out the thorn broken off and stubbornly lodged for weeks in Bella's toe?

As she walked along knitting, she was so vexed and nagged by these thoughts that she didn't hear the horseman till he thundered into sight over a grassy knoll. No crofter would ride like that or have such a horse. Christy got well off the road. In astonishment, she recognized the square ruddy face of Mr. Munro. In more astonishment and some fright, she froze in her tracks as he jerked on the reins, veering toward her.

Did he mean to ride her down? If he did, there was no use dodging, but she shrank as the horse stopped so close that she felt the heat of his breath. "Limb of Satan!" Munro's eyes burned. "Setting Robert MacKenzie on me for doing my duty by Sir James! Have me in the London papers, MacKenzie will, if I don't turn over every penny of the relief fund!" He shifted in the saddle. Christy heard the chink of coins.

Oh, what hope and help that money would bring! Christy was shocked into joyful laughter. Munro raised his whip, then lowered it. "You need the flesh lashed from your bones but the laird's soft where Mairi Mór's concerned. My memory's long though, Christy MacLeod. I'll settle with you soon or late."

He jerked the horse around and was off at a reckless gallop. The most powerful man on the island barring Sir James, and she had him hating her! But he must give back the coin! Christy's feet fairly danced along the road and her heart sang clear and glad as Cridhe.

Mairi sent eight young ewes and two red heifers with their calves, descendants of her gentle Sholma with the same white helmets and faces. "Stay the summer at Siadar, lass, and help if you're of that notion."

"But Mairi Mór, I should be helping you—"

Mairi laughed and Christy could only marvel at the difference between her healthy bloom of full womanhood now that she was eating and sleeping better and the worn pinched look of Peggy and most Siadar women.

"We've plenty of hands to help, God be praised. Magnus plans to take his crew and go cut peats for the villages that lost their men and change the thatch as well. The women need to buy sheep and cows with the relief fund and save for the boats they'll need when their lads grow old enough to fish. 'Twould be a shame to pay out the coin for workers.''

''What would you do, Mairi Mór, were you in the widows' place? How can a village live without men?''

Mairi thought this over and chuckled. ''Men are like ponies, forbye. Strong backs but they eat a lot. For a start, Siadar won't have to feed them. The canny way is to put coin and effort into things women and children do well. They can work lazybeds and grow potatoes, peas, turnips, kale, and some barley and oats. They can gather seaweed to eat and build the soil, fish off the rocks, and gather shellfish.''

Sheila nodded. ''Butter and cheese and woolens pay the rent as handily as smoked fish or coin. After they've bought all the sheep and cattle they have grazing for, the women might buy a mill like ours for each village. The hours they save grinding meal can be used to weave and knit. If the relief fund and grazing stretch to a pony, he could pull a plow and carry more seaweed in a load than four creels.''

''Since there's some money,'' concluded Mairi, ''it should be used in ways that earn the most, not saved against the rent.''

Christy had one more question. Gazing off at the sea, she felt her face heat as she tried to sound ordinary. ''Mairi Mór, do you think David will come home this summer?''

''I wish he would.'' Mairi's eyes glistened. ''I've written there's money to pay his way but he must do what he thinks best. It may be he won't come the first few years because he's afraid he won't go back.''

Mr. Urquhart made up a pack of books from primers to Robert Burns and put in paper and a supply of quills. ''I've always thought you should be a teacher, Christy.'' He gave her his slow sweet-natured smile. ''Mairi agrees that you should attend the Female Seminary in Stornoway this autumn. You already know more than many teachers, I suspect, but you're young yet and a certificate would help if you want a position on the mainland.''

Christy gasped. To be able to follow her course with Mairi's blessing! Luck indeed.

With Seana and Jamie Nicolson, she set out at dawning for Siadar. They carried creels of provisions, but Christy's creel was almost filled with books, her clothing, comb, and harp. Jamie had taken over the care and training of Laddie when Alai Gunn was old enough to go on the summer fishing. The cows and sheep were not eager to leave their companions and Jamie was so busy directing Laddie that he had little time to tease his older sister about which of her suitors she was going to choose.

The gold of Seana's hair had not darkened and her skin was smooth as the richest cream. The oldest of the Clanna children, she had ever looked after the young ones, especially motherless Christy. Now the older lass looked at the younger one in concern.

"It might be well not to say you're staying first off," she counseled. "Then there won't be a moil if you decide to come home with us."

"I'll bide the summer." Christy felt she had to do that to ease her guilt over not staying longer.

It was a long day's walk, past peat-colored lochans, gnarled gray rock, and grassy knolls rising above the dark peat moors. They munched bannocks and crowdie at midday and as afternoon deepened to evening, they chewed dried dulse to fool their stomachs. When at last they came in sight of the blind houses, the women and young ones came running out, joyfully calling the ancient Gaelic greeting, "Failte duibh!" Welcome to you.

From his mother's arms, laughing, Colin leaned out. With stinging eyes, Christy took him and kissed his pale little cheek. "Peace be here," she answered, and prayed it would be so.

Midsummer night, she dreamed of the Stones. They stood like a company of cloaked elders on the promontory thrusting into the loch that opened into the boundless ocean. Christy breathed in the sweetness of sea pinks and the warm honey scent of the machair. A voice that was not a voice sounded in her mind and heart. *Why have you not come to us, daughter?* Gran spoke clearly though Christy looked around for her in vain. "You live in place of Mairi's child who sleeps by the sea. It's her place in life you must be taking. The harp and these Stones have called you."

"Mairi will play her harp for many years and I would not let her present me to the Stones."

A great fog swirled up, obscuring the Stones, shrouding the moor and sea. "Gran! Gran!" Christy moaned in panic. She woke with Bella shaking her. It had been so real, as if she were standing there, the Stones beautifully majestic yet familiar as Mairi's hearth.

She hardened her heart. A great deal had been done in the six weeks since she'd come to Siadar. It wasn't that she was that much extra physical help, but she wasn't stunned by grief and despair and could put hope into their efforts and lead the familiar songs for different tasks, clipping and smearing the sheep, hoeing potatoes, carding, spinning, weaving, and waulking the wool. Most important of all, perhaps, several evenings a week the village gathered for ceilidhs. She played her small harp, told some of Mairi's stories, and listened eagerly to those of old Adam, Finlay, and Granny Nicolson. Other evenings, books and slates were shared out according to reading and writing abilities and Christy moved from pupil to pupil, including most of the younger women.

Magnus and most of his crew had come in early June and cut a year's supply of peats, which the women and children spread to dry. At the Siadar folk's request, Magnus had undertaken to buy four more cows and eight sheep, which used up the village's grazing allowance. He did the same for the other bereaved Ness villages. All of them wanted to have money for boats as their lads grew old enough to form crews, so Magnus offered to invest some of the relief fund in merchandise he could sell in mainland ports so the money would increase till it was needed.

Three of his crew fell in love with young Ness widows while

cutting peats and decided to forsake the seagoing life. With the help of one well-grown fourteen-year-old lad from Fivepenny Ness, they could crew a small boat to fish coastal waters. The stricken townships agreed to share in the cost of the boat and provisions. The catch would be divided according to need. There'd be no fish for sale but families wouldn't be deprived of one of their main foods.

The seamen were marrying into three villages at a triple wedding planned at Lammas, the first of August. At Siadar, fair, willowy Marian Beattie had found a father for her three children in wiry, dark-haired Ewan Gilroy. Not even her drowned husband's sister and mother, who lived with her after being widowed in the storm, objected to the marriage. Long stints of mourning were for gentry who could afford them. The shipmates agreed to band together to do the heaviest work of the villages like next year's peat cutting so the future promised better than anyone could have dreamed at Whitsuntide when the chamberlain held back the relief monies.

Wee Colin was stronger, happier, and had more color in his cheeks. After plenty of milk and crowdie, it seemed to Christy that his legs were growing straighter. He climbed into her lap every chance he got, and often fell asleep while she was singing.

"A rare fancy he's taken to you," Peggy said. "He'll miss you sorely—but so will all of us."

"With the new cows and sheep and the mill and a share in the boat's fish, you should do finely. I've shown Rachel how to make the coltsfoot infusion for Granny Nicolson's breathing trouble and Barbara and Sarah how to brew meadow rue for Finlay and Adam's rheumatism—"

"And Millie MacEnnis how to use bog myrtle to rid her bairns of worms and Grace Beattie's stomach's been calmed with your bogbean infusion and didn't you save that sickly calf by pouring nettle tea down her? You're a better hand with dyes than even old Connie MacCaulay."

"Gran taught me."

"To be sure. 'Tis a grand way to live on, just as Fearchar MacLeod does in the songs you've sung us." Peggy sighed. "You've helped us in many ways, m'eudail, but it's your music we'll miss most of all. Puts heart into us, it does. Forbye, you must get on with your life. A notable teacher you'll make after you've been to the seminary."

Christy's heart smote her. "I'll leave the books and slates. Polly and Bella can teach the younger ones at least a little."

"Aye. They'll do their best, doubtless."

Neither lass nor the older lads had much aptitude for arithmetic. They needed to be able to reckon sums and not be cheated by Donald Munro's ledgers or the curers' figures. And they needed English so they could understand what was being said by officials and so they could speak for themselves and not be treated like ignorant savages.

Maybe Siadar could hire a teacher in four or five years when the lads grew old enough to crew a boat. But that would be too late for their education. And for Polly and Bella and Rosie, who might be mothers by then.

I can't help it. I'll teach them all I can before I leave and get Mr. Urquhart to send more books. I'll come back summer holidays to help and teach. But I have to get ready to go where David will be. I can't bear never seeing him!

It wasn't as if she couldn't find villages on the mainland where a teacher was needed as badly as one was here. Like the islands, the mainland had been scourged with famine and clearances. She wouldn't look for an easy place, she promised her conscience, Gran, and Mairi Mór. She'd find the poorest, neediest, most demoralized township that she could—just so it was situated where she could now and again hear David's voice, behold his face, sometimes touch his hand. Beyond that she did not plan or hope, but *that* she must have.

Ebb tide during summer was the best time to collect tangle or kelp, the tawny seaweed that, burned into alkali, had created fortunes during the Napoleonic wars and before 1821. Vast amounts were needed to fertilize the lazybeds, kale planticrues, and grain plots. When the stronger women, lads, and lasses weren't busy with other tasks, they took sickles and creels down to the sea loch and cut the tangle from the rocks. Christy was trudging up the bank to the village, weighed down by heavy wet tangle, when a horseman came in sight. He paused on the slope.

The proud tilt of his head—the erect set of his shoulders. No crofter held himself like that. Even the lads had a stubborn bent to their shoulders from hard work and battling gales. No, the rider sat his small island pony as if it were Chieftain and he Captain MacDonald himself . . .

David! Shedding her creel, Christy gave a glad cry, caught up her skirts, and ran. He lifted a hand and rode toward her, black hair blown by the wind. His laughter mixed with hers. So strong and fit and well he looked that as he reined in, she had a wild hope that he'd been healed somehow, that he had his good legs back. Then she saw the crutches tied with the bundle behind his father's saddle.

He dismounted, steadying himself with a hand on the pommel, hugging her with his free arm. "Christy! I wouldn't know you but for those yellow cat eyes!"

"Gavallachan! You could say they were gold or the color of honey!" She drew back to study him. "You're near as tall as the captain but you've some filling out to do! Rascallion! You never wrote you were coming home!"

He grimaced in the old way and tugged her plait. "What a welcome! All you do is call me names." His voice had been changing when he left. Now it was deep and vibrant. "I didn't intend to come. The journey costs a lot. I didn't want to borrow my fare from Uncle Roderick or ask mother. But Magnus sent the money and said I was to get myself to the island this holiday. His letter came on a morning when I woke up thinking I heard the waves and thought I couldn't stand another day away from home.''

He'd gone off a boy and come back almost a man, yet still, always, her laddie. He wore town clothes—he'd have outgrown his old ones. His wavy black hair was cut in what she supposed was the mainland fashion. The cleft in his chin had deepened and his cheekbones ridged on either side of his long straight nose. Very like the captain he would look. That must be to Mairi Mór both pleasure and pain.

''How long can you stay?'' she asked.

''A few days. I only have a fortnight because the trip takes so long.''

A few days! She stifled a protest. ''Oh, but David, it's good of you to come all this way—and for your mother to spare you. How is she?''

Some kind of struggle went on in him before he shrugged and laughed. ''Magnus is stopping longer and longer at Clanna. He makes mother smile. It's over two years since father died, Christy. Before I leave, I'm going to tell her that if she wishes to wed Magnus, she must not hold back on my account.''

''It would seem strange—''

''I'm glad for mother's sake she has a good man who loves her. I can't be company for her any time soon—probably never. She doesn't even have a child at home.'' He smiled at Christy and her heart turned over. ''I never missed a sister or brother, having you.''

''The first thing I remember is trotting after you, David.''

''You were my little shadow.'' His smile faded. ''I took you for granted till I couldn't run. What a good lass you were not to desert me.''

''Nothing good about it, lad. I never wanted anything better than to be with you.'' *That is still my wish.* ''Come on to the house and we'll fix you a bite and make you acquainted.'' She got her creel while he mounted Gillie, one of the young ponies that had replaced dear old Kelpie.

"I can't carry the creel for you," David said, scowling. "But I can cut tangle while I'm here and Gillie can haul it."

Christy swallowed a protest. David hated the thought of being a burden. As he had his bannock and buttermilk, he spoke courteously to Peggy and the others who came to greet him and accepted the loan of Peggy's husband's clothes. He rode Gillie to the shore but then agilely moved from rock to rock with his crutches. Christy collected the tangle he cut and asked countless questions between the times she led Gillie up to the village, laden with two creels slung like panniers. She grudged those short times away from David but was so joyful he had come that she seemed to float rather than walk. The sturdy little garron spared many aching backs and got praise, pats, and nibbles of dulse.

After supper, everyone gathered at Peggy's. They had never before had a visitor from the mainland and were much pleased when David said a pamphlet had been circulated about Donald Munro's attempt to charge most of the Ness relief fund against rents and arrears. David answered questions but was more interested in hearing about olden times from Adam, Finlay, Connie, and Granny Nicolson.

"A blessing and a curse they are, the 'taties," Granny Nicolson said. "Easy to grow, and a small plot can feed a family. Back in the kelping years, the laird—he was a Seaforth then—wanted all the workers he could get to gather the seaweed, dry it, and burn it to ash. Och, the laird made a fortune from kelp whilst the wars were on and England couldn't get its soda ash from Spain and France and Italy."

"Aye, but Lord Seaforth was set on raising men for his Seventy-eighth Highlanders." Adam grimaced. "Came recruiting himself, he did, and when that wouldn't serve, for we all hid out in the hills, he sent a press gang. I lived in Knockaird then. They marched off every able-bodied man 'twixt sixteen and thirty—and I was twenty, just married. My wife was screaming and weeping and trying to get me free, and the other wives and mothers did the same till the gang held them off with bayonets. Over the moors to Stornoway they marched us, and shipped us straightaway to the mainland. We fought in Holland and then in India under Sir Arthur Wellesley, him who would be the Duke of Wellington. Only a few of the Knockaird lads lived to come home again and cut Lord Seaforth's tangle.''

"Your wife was my cousin," said Connie MacCaulay. "How she wept for you! But all the time we must be burning kelp or get evicted, and she lost the bairn she was carrying."

All were silent, thinking back. "Lewis kelp sold for eleven thousand pounds in its two best years, 1819 and 1820," remembered Finlay. "Hard work it was and no letting up from early June till late July. We cut the tangle and tossed it on a round of heather rope twined with seaweed. This raft floated till we were ready to haul it in."

"Then every soul who could tote a creel loaded the weed and carried it to dry on the grass," put in Connie. She and Finlay MacNeil had been born at Siadar eighty years ago, but Adam Morison never let them forget he was ten years their elder. Her skin was fluted as deeply as her cap but her green eyes still held a sparkle. "When the tangle was dry, we lugged it to the kilns—ten to twenty-four feet long they were, two feet deep, and about two-and-a-half feet wide."

Granny Nicolson huddled deeper into her plaid. "I'd grown up kelping but it broke my heart to see my bairns fagged with fetching heather to keep the kelp burning day and night, night and day, till it was about the thickness of moist clay. Forty creels of weed it took to make a hundredweight of ash."

"We were told how much kelp we had to make," quavered Adam. "If we fell behind, the amount was added to our rent."

"June and July," frowned David. Like a handsome young

laird he looked to Christy though he sat on a pile of nets. "Surely, Mr. Morison, that's when you should have been tilling your fields and hoeing potatoes."

"Aye," growled Adam. "Forbye, that's when the past year's crops are used up and before the new are ready—when folk scavenge nettles and silverweed, dulse and shellfish. Kelping left little time to hunt food."

"But I've heard the wage was good," said David. "Perhaps eight pounds for the year, which is about what a fisherman clears if his crew follows the herring into the North Sea and owns their own boat. Wouldn't the laird's local officials sell you meal?"

"He would!" snorted Finlay. "But the *min bhan,* the white meal he wanted to sell us, cost so dear that it used up our earnings if we ate much of it."

"Our rents were raised," lamented old Connie. "Though we'd little time to tend our crops and animals. That's when we almost stopped growing oats and barley and got to depending on 'taties."

"Curse and blessing they've been," said Granny Nicolson. "My grandmother never laid eyes on a 'tatie till after she was married. She said they weren't grown on the islands till the MacDonald who was laird of North Uist brought them from Ireland and made his tenants grow them."

"Folk grew the 'taties but left them at his door, saying they wouldn't eat them," Adam chuckled. "That was well over a hundred years ago, about 1735 it must have been. So kelping made us live on 'taties and because the lairds needed more workers, they encouraged folk to marry young and have bairns."

"It must have been grand to live in a time when lairds wanted more tenants, not fewer," young Rory MacCaulay said bitterly.

"Trouble in the long run, laddie. Boys not much older than you married and started families because they could work at the kelp and needed only a patch of 'taties."

David nodded. "During the kelping boom, the folk of the islands doubled. Kelp brought twenty-two pounds a ton during the war with the American colonists and even after Napoleon was defeated, the price stayed at ten pounds. Then cheap potash was found in Germany in 1822. That was the end of the lairds' kelp fortunes."

"And their tenants' wages," Adam said. "So now the lairds say there be too many people and ship us across the waters." He laughed so hard he coughed and his grandson's widow, Barbara, thumped him on the back while Peggy brought a cup of water. "I cannot help but laugh," he sputtered. "When I finally came home from the wars, I had a great wish to go to America where there were no lairds or press gangs. Fares were cheap but by the time I saved our fare and wheedled my wife into the notion, didn't they pass a law—the Passenger Vessels Act it was in 1803—I remember it fine for it wrecked my dream?"

Startled, David said, "But, Mr. Morison, that was a good law. It made ships carry enough water and food for passengers."

"Aye. But it tripled fares. That's what the lairds wanted. To keep us burning kelp. When the bubble burst, it left twice as many folk to scratch a living from less land."

"Our rents have stayed as high as they were in the kelp years," Finlay nodded. "But our best grazings and croplands were given to sheep. Och, 'tis a tale we know all too well and you didn't ride all this way to hear it, laddie."

"In a way I did," returned David. "I need to learn all I can because this isn't in my textbooks. Mr. Morison, with your name you must be kin to the brieves of Lewis, the hereditary judges of the isles. What do you know about them?"

Adam's skull-like face seemed to plump out a bit. "Why, lad, when the Irish came long before the Norse, they brought their law and judges or brieves to mete it out. There was no proper law in Norse times except the sword but when Norway gave over the islands to Scotland, the brieves returned to power. There were judges on most islands as well as the mainland, but there was something special about the brieve of Lewis, who was always the Morison chief and had his seat at Habost here in Ness. The law wasn't written down. The brieves had to know it. It was their duty to deal out justice between man and man 'as evenly as the backbone divides the two sides of a herring.' "

Finlay MacNeil doubled over and clapped his knee. "Hear the man! As if the only brieve of Lewis who's well-remembered, Hugh Morison, wasn't a fornicating, plundering, deceiving, murdering, swindling rascallion who seduced the MacLeod chief's own wife!"

"I doubt she took much seducing," retorted Adam, "since yon giddy wanton later ran off with John MacCallum of Raasay."

Finlay reared back so hard his stool almost went out from under him. "You won't deny that Hugh Morison captured MacLeod's son by treachery and gave him to the MacKenzies to execute."

"No more than I'd deny that a MacLeod killed Hugh Morison whose guts were buried on Brieve's Island out in the Minch when his friends couldn't bring his body all the way to Lewis because of contrary winds."

The two ancients glared at each other as if these perfidies had happened yesterday instead of well nigh three hundred years ago. "Och, dear men," soothed old Connie, "my kin were in it, too, the MacCaulays helping the MacLeods. The breaking of the clans was a sad thing entirely but at least we're not warring with each other."

After a moment, Adam nodded. " 'Twas Hugh's son, Alan, who left us the most beautiful boat song mortal ever sang. He was killed in a sea fight with the MacLeods, but my great-uncle used to play the tune on his harp. Christy, lass, would you know that *iorram?*"

She did, and then there were more songs and stories and David's tales of Inverness till yawning but reluctant, the villagers went off to their beds. Christy and David talked on softly long after Peggy's gentle snores came from the box bed.

"A barrister friend of Uncle Roderick talked with my professors and invited me to read law with him in Edinburgh after I graduate," said David with some pride. "Duncan Stewart has a big house and only a daughter to share it since his wife died. He suggests I live there till I'm earning a living."

"How old is this daughter?" Christy couldn't keep from asking. David looked at her in surprise.

"I didn't ask. Still in the nursery, I should think. But her name is Alison and Mr. Stewart smiles when he speaks it."

Christy writhed inwardly. That another lass should live in the same house as David, see him every day, talk with him whenever she wished! It seemed unbearable. Even if Alison Stewart were a child now, she'd be growing up by the time David was ready to join her father's firm.

"Indeed, your Mr. Stewart must be a man of broad vision to invite a crofter lad into his home and practice."

"He is that." David flushed but didn't raise his voice. "He listened to me—as Uncle Roderick will not—when I told him why I must learn law. He was a poor lad from Sutherland—his family and their village was cleared and he grew up in the Glasgow streets."

Doubly shamed, Christy blurted, "Then how—"

"A minister took him in and saw that he went on to the university. The Latin teacher commended him to an old bachelor schoolmate who needed a bright young law clerk. The barrister became so fond of Mr. Stewart that he left him all he had."

"It would seem Duncan Stewart had a grand run of luck."

"Aye, after the bad. The important thing is that he, too, wants the laws changed."

"Does Sir Roderick know that?"

"Oh yes. They argue for hours about voting reform, trade unions, and workers thrown out of employment because of machines, like handloom weavers and nail makers.'' David grinned. ''Uncle Roderick foams at the mouth when Mr. Stewart quotes Friedrich Engel's *The Condition of the Working Class in England,* though he hasn't read it and never will.''

''Have you?''

''I borrowed Mr. Stewart's copy.''

''Gavallachan!''

''Not a bit. I'll take my degree but the university's not where I'm getting the most important part of my education.''

She tilted her head in puzzlement. He gave a harsh laugh. ''When Dugald Craigie shot Chul, that taught me more than ten years at school.''

''Does Sir Roderick know how you feel?''

''He doesn't think anyone younger than thirty is worth listening to, and not many of them.''

''It must be difficult to live in his house.''

''I seldom see him. He's in Edinburgh a lot. But Aunt Bea is jolly and little Becky dances in and out like a sunbeam.''

''How do you get on with the boys?''

''Roddy can think of nothing but being in a crack regiment when he grows up—he's my age and a good-natured sort. Alex is always in a scrape. He detests school and did so poorly that he studies at home with a tutor. All he really likes is riding and hunting. He says as soon as he's of age he's going over to live in Texas and hunt buffalo every day.''

''Och ochone! What would your Uncle Calum say to that?''

''He could surely manage Alex better than Uncle Roderick does,'' grinned David. ''That is, he might not try to manage him at all but give him something to do on his land.''

Christy laughed. ''That has a fine ring! *His land!* It's hard to believe that a onetime island crofter truly owns two square miles of land—that his horses and cattle can graze wherever they will.''

''If the Comanches don't run them off.'' His voice turned gently chiding. ''I heard something that pleased me and that you've kept out of your letters—that you'll be going to the Female Seminary in Stornoway this autumn.''

"Yes. Your mother and Mr. Urquhart are fixing it.''

"You'll make a good teacher, lass. Look at the start you've made here with just an hour or so snatched out of the day.''

Her conscience smote her. "It's little I've done at Siadar.''

"That's not what the people say. And when you come back—''

"I'm not coming back!''

He stared at her. "I—I want to find a school on the mainland,'' she said. "They must need teachers, too.''

"They do. The Highlanders have fared like us with clearances and famine.'' He brightened. "It would be grand, Christy, to have you close by. I must do my lawing on the mainland but it would be rare fine to see my best friend sometimes.''

"That's why I want to come,'' she dared to say. "When I can't see you, Davie, I feel half of me is lost—the best half by far.''

He took her hands and smiled so that her heart melted and warmed her whole body. "Well, then, I'll work for justice and you'll teach bairns so they can have a choice of work and look after their affairs—not be so much at the mercy of factors and lairds. It's work we have before us, lass.''

"Aye.'' But though she gloried in his pleasure at having her near, her heart felt heavy and reproached because she was leaving Siadar.

The triple wedding of Ness widows to seamen was more than the union of men and women. It was hope for the future, a sign of faith, and the three townships concerned joined in making the occasion as festive as possible. To wish his former crew members well in their new lives, Magnus came with a boatload of provisions and news of his own.

"Mairi has promised to wed me after harvest," he said to Christy with joyful pride. "You'll come for the wedding, lass?"

"Indeed I will!" The big seafaring man had always been kind to Christy and in the years since Iain's death, she had often hoped he would reap the reward of his faithful loving. She gave him a heartfelt hug and kiss. "I wish you happy, Magnus, for many, many years! But we had better hurry now or we'll miss your men's wedding."

After the minister of the parish performed the ceremony, the food was spread on waulking tables covered with linen sheets. Dundee cake; iced French sponge cake; cream cookies; spicy, treacle-sweetened parkin; scones of many kinds; Selkirk bannock rich with fruit; Atholl brose made with so much of Magnus's choice whisky that a few spoonfuls sent Christy's head whirling; cheeses from the villages' cows; fresh butter and heather honey to spread on oat bannocks; mutton from a ram that had fallen from a sea cliff; salmon taken when no keeper was near; herring fetched home by the combined new crew of the Ness folk; Scotch broth flavored by leeks and the ram's hock, thick with barley and peas and carrots. Christy had made a great bowl of crannachan, smiling through tears to remember how Gran concocted Iain and David's favorite dessert, stirring mounds of whipped cream into crunchy toasted oats.

And of course, there were the special Lammas bannocks, made with the first new grain. A small harvest it would be this year, but with Ewan to plow with the cas-chrom and the lads a year stronger and older, next season should be better. Oh, it would be! And maybe wee ones in the newlywed couples' cradles.

An ancient from Five Penny Ness had brought his fiddle. After the minister departed, the blind old man began to play. A cry went up from the Siadar folk for Christy to get her little harp. "Wait!" croaked Adam Morison, poking his skull-like head from his plaid. He commanded his great-nephew's widow, "Barbara, lass, bring Shenachie."

A *seanachaidh* was a teller of age-old Gaelic epics and stories. What could Adam be talking about? Christy's bewilderment changed to awe as Barbara returned from her house.

She carried a harp of the size and gracious curving arch of Cridhe and stood before Adam. The descendant of the brieves of Lewis tapped the soundboard, which gave forth a mellow note. "Black willow from Ireland," boasted Adam. "The soundboard's cut all from one piece. My grandfather had to sell the gold harp key and use one of brass and Shenachie's lost his rubies and emeralds but the crystals still make a brave show."

"Indeed," said Christy with reverence, " 'Tis a lordly harp." The string-shoes on the soundboard were brass, intricately wrought into beasts and birds. The three highest strings in the treble were of steel and the others of brass as were the tuning pins. This harp was a little bigger than Cridhe but was otherwise so like that it might have been shaped by the same maker.

"Wheesht, lass, take the harp and play it," said Adam crankily. "Is this not a wedding and you a harpist?"

"But the strings—"

"They're new," said Magnus with a grin. "Mr. Morison showed me what was needed last time I was here, and Mairi sorted them out of the store she keeps and sent some extras, too."

From infancy, Christy had marveled at Chridhe's songs and the harp had called her to it. Mairi had taught her that her fingers must be very clean before she touched the strings and Christy grew up cherishing the harp as if it were kin to her beloved Gran. But Cridhe belonged to Mairi and Christy had never thought to inherit it.

"Shenachie's weary of sleeping in my box bed," grumped Adam. "Forbye, lass, let him sing!"

So Christy handed her small harp to Bella, who had a natural gift and loved to pick out tunes, and she herself perched on a rock with another in front of it where she could rest Shenachie. Receiving the plectrum and brass key from Barbara, she tuned the strings.

The harp awoke, humming first, then voicing pure jubilant notes. They greeted Christy, seemed to cry, *I have waited for you. All these years, mute and blind in the dark of a box bed in a black house. Why did it take you so long? Ah, but it's a wedding! Touch me. Let me sing!*

Shenachie played almost of himself the gladsome notes of "The Lewis Bridal Song" while the newly married couples and their attendants danced a reel. Then they were joined by everyone able to point a toe, women dancing with women or the three seamen who had helped Magnus sail his small boat, and lads and lasses joining in.

Sometimes with the fiddle, sometimes alone, the old harp gloried in singing after generations of forced silence. Vibrating through the strings, Shenachie made himself known to Christy, murmured of the battles he had led, of the brieve's judgment hall where ancient Celtic law ruled even turbulent chiefs. He told her of triumphs and defeats, heartbreak and glory, christenings and funerals and weddings like this one.

All night the people danced. When Christy and the fiddler had to rest, folk danced to mouth-music, rhythmic sounds that took the place of instruments.

After a festive breakfast of leftovers, the wedding guests departed for their villages, still singing and laughing. With as much regret as if saying farewell to a marvelous new friend who had become closer than most do in a lifetime, Christy took Shenachie to the Morison house. It seemed a crime, like imprisoning a human singer, to shut that sweet voice back in the darkness.

"Now why are you here with the harp?" demanded Adam.

"It's yours."

"When I cannot play it, nor any of these Morison bairns have a trill of the music in them? Nay, you keep Shenachie, lass."

There were few harps left after the ministers condemned them as wicked and made bonfires of them in marketplaces through all the islands and Highlands. Shenachie, even stripped of his precious stones, was priceless. As if reading Christy's mind, Adam said, "I would no more sell Shenachie than the bones of my grandfather. Nor can I keep him hid away when you can free him."

"But I'm not staying at Siadar, dear man. In a few weeks, I'll go to the seminary in Stornoway."

Christy rested the harp beside him. It seemed to cry out at her, to plead and reproach. *How can you still me when I sang for you? How can you lock me away in the dark?*

"You will leave us?" the old man asked heavily. "Even with your wee harp, you cheered our hearts."

Barbara, too, looked stricken, but she rested her hand on Adam's shoulder in a hushing manner. "Och, Christy, we will miss you sore. But our legs are under us again." She stroked little Ailis's unruly red hair. "We'll do our best to keep the bairns at their reading and writing. The seminary! That will be a grand thing."

She gave Christy a kiss. Feeling like a traitor, Christy turned to go out. Old Adam stopped her. "Take the harp," he said gruffly. "It's no matter of use without someone to play."

"I can't—"

"You can. It's your duty to make music because you have the gift. I'd liefer Shenachie sung to other people than that he bided mute."

If the old man could give up his hoarded treasure—if Barbara could wish her well though they both knew the children's schooling would not get much further without direction—Christy thought of David, of when she finished seminary being near enough to see him. But the gift, the free gift, of Shenachie bound her.

She could not refuse such an offering. That would be a sin against something rooted even more deeply in her nature than her love for David. But she could not carry the harp away, either, not when its songs were so much needed here.

She knelt by Adam and put her face on his knee in order to hide her tears. "I will stay," she said. "Of course I am going to stay."

XII

The fragrance of wild thyme blended with that of heather at its deepest purple in mid-August, swarming with purposeful bees and hovering butterflies. Drifts of yellow iris edged the bogs, harebells swayed in drier places, and Christy caught her breath at a solitary snowy white five-petaled flower of grass-of-Parnassus. As sun glinted off a lochan with an islet of small silver-trunked rowans, she thought she had never seen a more beautiful day.

She came in sight of the shining waters of the sea, glimpsed the distant rearing of the broch that guarded Clanna and began to sing for joy though she had left Siadar the day before at dawn and her creel weighed heavy, the creel fashioned especially to hold Shenachie. Her few belongings were stuffed around the harp.

Home! She was coming home, with her work at Siadar done! After a visit, she could at last go to the mainland to find a school near David. Each of the past five winters, she had made her way through bitter weather to visit at Clanna for a week or so, but except for Mairi's wedding to Magnus, she hadn't been back in the summer or autumn when every hand was needed.

She had even missed the wedding of Seana and Alai, her old playmates. Strange to think they had two bairns now, but even stranger to think of Mairi's twins. Wee Cat—Catriona Jean—and Calum Tammas Olav were right Vikings, blue-eyed and blond. Mairi's hearth was again a scramble of children and she seemed herself like a girl again. Christy was glad, though to see her foster mother start a second family made her feel as if she were standing still while the current of life flowed around her.

Shenachie had sung at Mairi's wedding and the old harp of the brieves had played at a dozen Ness weddings these past five years, and crooned old Adam's favorite songs as he slipped away. Adam had confirmed his gift of the ancient harp, pressing Christy's hand and saying, "I kept him for you, lass. You've freed him. He is yours."

The harp lamented at Connie MacCaulay's funeral a week after it lilted at the wedding of Bella MacNeil and Jem MacCaulay. A month later, it played at the christenings of Marian Beattie and Ewan Gilroy's second child and Polly Nicolson's first. Yes, the lads had grown to take their father's places at peat cutting, plowing, and fishing, except for Alan Beattie, who was so quick and clever at his books that his stepfather, Ewan, was willing to spare him so the youth could live with a relative on Skye and study to be a minister.

Most of the Ness widows would sleep in cold beds the rest of their lives, but they had their children and a livelihood in their cows and sheep. Rosie MacCaulay was teaching the younger children now and Polly Nicolson had married a lad from Five Penny Ness and taught a school there. Christy had left them all her books and maps and slates David had brought the two times he had visited since that first occasion.

Christy had wept at parting with the folk of Siadar, especially the bairns and Peggy MacNeil and Barbara Morison, but they didn't need her now. She had taught them all she knew of Gran's dyes and medicines and she left her small harp with Ailis Morison, who had learned many songs and stories. Siadar was where she had grown from a girl to a woman, where she and her songs and knowledge had somehow put heart into beaten, grief-numbed people, where she had won Shenachie.

It frightened her to own such a harp, almost as fabled and rare as Cridhe. No matter what old Adam said, she wasn't worthy. Never could she be like Mairi Mór. Her conscience had compelled her to stay at Siadar till the village was doing well, but she had still not given her allegiance to the Stones, though every Midsummer they haunted her dreams.

Five years she'd been at Siadar. David had finished at the university and had been reading law for three years with Duncan Stewart. He hadn't been to the island for three years and his letters, for which Christy lived, had become infrequent. She hadn't heard from him, in fact, since April, almost four months ago. Her heart shriveled to think he might be gradually forgetting her. But he had written, hadn't he, in that last letter: "When are you coming to teach on the mainland, Christy? Mr. Stewart's on the parish school board and says that three schools need teachers next term and would employ you even if you haven't gone to seminary."

She'd replied that she should be able to take one of the schools and sent a letter of recommendation Bruce Urquhart had written for her. She'd heard nothing since, but letters to and from the mainland could take a considerable time.

Just in the few hours it took her to walk from where she could first see the broch to where she could make out every house of Clanna, the weather had changed from sparkling to stormy. Dark clouds roiled from the sea. Even from this distance, she saw the wild white manes of the waves as they dashed on the rocks and shore. Flocks of seabirds lifted off the rocks, screeching as they sought shelter. Cattle and sheep huddled in the most protected hollows.

The Clanna men would be off at the herring fishing in the township's two large boats. The small ones were beached beyond the reach of the highest tide. But—that was a boat out in the waves! Christy remembered all too many times when boats had spent the night maneuvering in the open sea, avoiding the breakers, till the gale abated enough for the skipper to make a run for the shore. But this boat was too close to the beach to escape.

The sail and mast had been packed away to keep it as much as possible on an even keel. Surely ballast had been placed in the stern to keep it low. If it reared up out of the water, the boat would be out of control and probably be dashed broadside on the shore. Clanna women had seen the danger and were bent low as they fought the wind to make their way to the harbor.

Christy put off her creel, stowing it in the shelter of a rock, and battled her way into the hollow where she could run till the blasting wind gusted at her as she passed the curing shed. She crouched to descend to where Mairi and all but the older Clanna women took such shelter as they could behind rocks while waiting for the boat to either be hurled ashore or, through a miracle and the mastery of the skipper and oarsmen, to ride a wave in and be pulled to safety.

"Who is it?" Christy shouted to Mairi.

Mairi shook her head. Through the foam and spray, it was impossible to make out the faces of the men. But there was something about the shoulders of one of the oarsmen—and there was a cloaked passenger—

Here it came! The bowman leaped out and struggled to shore with the painter. Some of the women took it from him and hauled while others beat through the water to help the crew push the boat onto the strand. One of the oarsmen didn't get out, nor the passenger. Christy, panting as she set her back to the boat and pushed, started to shout angrily at the oarsman. Then she saw his face.

"David!" She couldn't tell whether her voice echoed Mairi's or if it was the other way around.

"Aye." The boat was out of the reach of the worst surge of the breakers now. Gasping, the crew and women heaved out the ballast rocks and the men staggered to the shelter of the curing shed with the mast and sail. David shouted into the wind and laughed though Christy saw the angry pain in his eyes. "A good thing my crutches didn't wash away or you'd have to push me as well as the boat!"

He planted one crutch in the sand and got out of the boat at the same time that he braced the other crutch and held out his hand to the cloaked person. "It's all right, Alison," he soothed. "We're safe."

The hood fell back, exposing a childlike face with a snub nose and wide, tearful blue eyes, framed by ringlets yellow as a buttercup. "Oh, David!" she wailed. "I thought we'd drown!"

"We didn't," he said tersely.

Christy's head teemed with questions—and fear. Alison? That was the name of the daughter of Duncan Stewart, David's benefactor. A butterfly, David called her fondly when he mentioned her in his letters. No wonder she looked like a child! She couldn't be more than sixteen. Why had David brought her here? From what Christy knew of the gentry, it was scandalous for a young woman to travel with an unrelated man.

David swung along on his crutches with Alison clutching his arm. He had lost his hat, if he'd had one, and the wind whipped his wet black hair back from his forehead. His smoke gray eyes met Christy's, then veered away. A deep, dull flush colored his face, which was taking on the angular length of his father's. "Mother," he called. "Alison and I— We've just been married."

Christy stumbled. It gave her an excuse not to look at him. She felt as if a weapon, sharp on all sides, drove through her and twisted. She couldn't speak and scarcely heard Mairi saying kind, welcoming things in her best English to this unexpected daughter-in-law.

Till now, Christy had not quite allowed herself to understand her love for David. Raised together as they had been, it seemed almost forbidden to think of him except as a brother. But he wasn't her kin! No blood relation at all. These past five years she had looked no further ahead than being where she could see him often. Now the deep-rooted waif child's love had turned into the longing of a woman.

And he was married! *Did you wed her because she'll be an advantage to you?* From some strength and pride she hadn't known she possessed, Christy managed to say, "Alison, David, I wish you happy."

Then they were in the fasgalan of Mairi's house where the travelers took off their wet cloaks and spread them over the stanchions of the byre. Mairi's three-year-old twins, golden as their father, Magnus, hurled themselves on Christy and asked if she had brought them sour plum drops. She had, of course. The children settled down to enjoy a sweetie each. Soon they got over their shyness of David and the pretty lady and began to clamber over their half-brother with joyful hugs and questions.

"Olav! Catriona!" Mairi called from the hearth where she was building up the fire and setting water to boil. "Let your brother and his wife get into dry clothes and warm themselves before you plague him!"

Molly ran to fetch some of Tam's clothes. Mairi brought linen towels for the soaked couple and took Alison off to change. When they had on dry things and were settled with cups of steaming tea, David explained that Alison had only a few words of Gaelic and looked at his mother as if pleading for her not to be hurt or angry.

"Mother, Alison and I were married two weeks ago. I—I'm sorry there was no time to ask if you could be there."

What Mairi must be feeling! Weddings were the great happy festivals of life. To hold one without inviting kindred— Of course, it had been on the mainland, but had she known in time, Mairi would certainly have journeyed to the celebration. Christy forgot her own misery in sympathy for the mother who had borne this son out of wedlock—who, in an attempt to have him christened, had stood humiliated outside the kirk while the parishioners passed by. Mairi had been younger than Christy when she endured great shame for David's sake. He was the child of her youth, the child of a love that had swept aside every rule and custom. He was the son who had fallen from the cliff, for whom Mairi must have shed more tears of grief and regret than anyone could know, and he was the image of Mairi's captain, who had died so tragically.

So it seemed to Christy that Mairi proved herself Great Mairi indeed when she embraced the shivering girl and kissed her on both cheeks. "A hundred thousand welcomes, wife of my son," she said in English. "It was sweet of you to make the journey here so we could become acquainted. And now let's see what we can find for you to eat! After that crossing, you must be hungry indeed."

The skipper and crew of the boat hired in Stornoway had been taken into various houses. With all Clanna, they came to the ceilidh that night in Mairi's house. Christy had fetched Shenachie and the harp of the Morisons played with that of its ancient clan enemy's, the harp of the MacLeods.

The storm had blown itself away almost as swiftly as it had come so the dancing was outside. Magnus was at sea and the Clanna men were at the summer fishing. Bruce Urquhart and the boatmen were far outnumbered by the women, but that did nothing to quell the merriment.

Christy's age-mates, Rona Nicolson and Brigid Gunn, had married two of Magnus's seamen and were both too big with child to dance. That, and seeing Seana cuddle her two bairns, made Christy feel old—old, especially now that the goal she had lived for was suddenly destroyed.

She couldn't bear to live near David now, couldn't bear to see him with Alison, or watch her have his children. Nor could Christy live at Clanna, though Mairi seemed to take it for granted that she would.

Just as there should not for long be two fabled harps at Clanna, Christy knew she could not live in Mairi Mór's village. At Siadar, she had grown into the place Mairi held here, but Siadar did finely without her now. She must find a place that needed her— needed a teacher and the knowledge she had gained from Gran and Mairi, a place that had no music. Bruce Urquhart would know.

"Will you dance?" asked the Stornoway skipper, a husky fair-haired man. "There's music enough without your harp."

"Lasses enough, too," she said, smiling. The lads of Siadar, several of them near her own age, had mooned after her enough to give her practice in good-natured but firm refusals.

Good heavens! she realized with horror. Twenty years old and she had not even been kissed except by David in an all too brotherly way. He sat with Alison, watching the dancers. His feelings might have changed toward Alison, but Christy strongly resisted the notion that he could fall deep in love with a girl he had referred to as "a happy little butterfly without a thought in her head beyond what ribbon's most becoming."

Nor, after the first instinctive urge to think ill of him since he had wounded her, could Christy believe he'd married his employer's daughter in order to advance himself. But why had they married so hastily without sending for Mairi?

Sometimes a lad and lass didn't wait for the kirk's blessing but Christy couldn't believe that David would take advantage of a motherless girl whose father had welcomed him into their home.

Alison stayed by David the whole night except to fetch him Morag's heather ale. A small, shy, forlorn lassie she looked, not a joyful bride, the daughter of a famed well-to-do advocate. Christy tried hard to work up anger at her and think her a brazen hussy who'd enticed David, but she did not succeed.

Mairi must have noticed her daughter-in-law's drooping head. She played the last notes of "The Crooked-Horned Ewe" and rose to her feet. "Good dreams to all of you," she called. "It's time our travelers found their beds. Thank you for joining in the ceilidh for my son and bonnie daughter-in-law and for Christy, who's made such a difference at Siadar."

There was much cheering and many warm good nights. Bruce Urquhart retired to his bed in the schoolroom. That left David and his bride at the hearth with Mairi and Christy.

Alison looked pale and exhausted. No hint of the butterfly

about her except for her yellow hair. "My dear," said Mairi kindly, "you're quite worn out. Some nice frothed milk will help you sleep sound." Her English was not as ready as it had been when she practiced with Christy and David, but at least, mercifully, there was not that barrier between her and this frightened girl whose eyes opened even wider.

"Thank you, but I don't want to put you to any trouble—"

"No trouble." Mairi got a bowl of milk, poured a handful of oats into it, and whipped it to fluffiness. "Drink that and tuck in. We'll get acquainted tomorrow."

Alison took a cautious sip, liked the drink, and swallowed deeply. Color rushed into her cheeks. "You—you're so kind—"

"Why would I not be, to my own son's chosen?"

"But I'm not! Not his chosen—" She burst into sobs and buried her face against David's shoulder.

"Hush, Allie," he soothed, stroking her hair and producing a handkerchief. "No need for that, no need at all."

"But there is!" She straightened and looked straight at Mairi though pulses fluttered wildly in her slender throat. "I have to tell you, Mrs. Ericson, so you won't think David—so you'll understand why we couldn't wait for you to come before we had the wedding."

"Allie!" David warned.

She swept on. "I'm going to have a baby."

"I thought it might be." Mairi's tone was calm. "It happens, m'eudail."

"But it's not—not David's baby—"

The room went utterly still. Alison gulped and hurried on. "Please, Mrs. Ericson, I didn't know what was happening until—" She broke off and scrubbed at her face with David's handkerchief. "He's my uncle—married to my father's sister, and he was always so jolly and played games with me when they came to visit. My aunt has a weak heart. If she knew, it would kill her and she's such a dear lady . . ."

Again there was silence. "Does your father know?" asked Mairi.

"Y-yes."

David said quickly, "Mr. Stewart didn't ask me to marry Alison, Mother. But when I made her tell me why she was crying all the time—"

"My governess noticed that—that things were different," Alison said. "When I told her what my uncle did, she called me a wicked girl and packed her bag."

"Better she had taught you a little about your body," Mairi said with a pitying sigh. "But that evil man! Is he to go on preying on young girls?"

"No. Father talked with him. He told Uncle he must have an operation or no matter what it did to Aunt, he'd have Uncle in prison." Alison colored. "The operation—it's something they do to cattle and sheep and horses. I don't exactly understand it, but if it happens to a man, he can't make a woman have babies. Uncle had the operation."

Castration. But there was still the shameful secret. How awful for David, to have to pretend to be the father of a child got by such an unscrupulous man! Yet fond of Alison as he was and under obligation to her father, there seemed little else that David could have done.

Mairi came to the settle where David and Alison sat and put her arms around them both. "Alison, love, this was hard for you to say. I thank you for refusing to let David take the blame—though, as he may have told you, when he was born, his father was far away and believed dead. We didn't marry till David was more than two."

"And then I told father to go back to Afghanistan," David chuckled. Awkwardly, he smoothed Alison's hair. "You mustn't fret anymore, sweetheart. Everything will be all right."

Not for me, Christy thought with an inner wail. *Never for me.* Yet David being David, what else could he have done?

"It's not all right!" Alison cried. "I don't want Uncle's baby! I——I'm afraid it'll look like him and I'll hate the poor little thing!"

"Allie——" David began. Christy suspected this was an argument they'd had before.

Mairi still held her son and his bride——yes, and the child of the gormless man who'd brought this woe on them all. "Daughter, I think you'll love your bairn when it lies in your arms and seeks the nourishment only you in all the world can give it. I think you will, and David, too."

Alison shook her head. "I can't love that awful man's baby!"

"If you cannot like the child, I promise you this," said Mairi. "I will care for it as if it were my own. We will say the air here is healthier for the wee one. So do not have that fear."

Alison pressed the crofter woman's toil-roughened hand to her lips. "You are so good to me! Can you let me call you mother?"

Mairi smiled. "That would make me glad, my dear. Now finish your milk and go to bed. All will be well, and very well."

"You almost make me believe that," Alison said with a wavery smile. She kissed Mairi fervently and rose, turning to Christy. "You are the same as David's sister, Christy. Thank you for making me welcome."

She gave Christy a hug and kiss. Fortunately, she either was too relieved or overwrought to notice that Christy received the embrace like a wooden image.

Alison and David went off to Mairi's chamber. Mairi would sleep in the storeroom Christy had shared with Gran while Christy had David's old bed. Feeling heavy and cold as stone, Christy stared at the glowing peats. Mairi knelt to smoor the fire and glanced up at her.

"I know you cannot be glad of this marriage, but it's done, lass. You were ever David's faithful friend. He needs to know you still are."

You called her—that stranger—daughter. A word you have never said to me in all our lives, a word you will never say though now you have two fine children. You will never quite forgive me, that I lived instead of the baby on the hill.

Yet tonight indeed Mairi had once more proved herself Mairi Mór, Great Mairi. At least I will not curse or cry, thought Christy. She spoke through stiff lips. "I will be David's friend while there is breath in my body. But I cannot go now to the mainland and take a school near him. Tomorrow I must talk to Mr. Urquhart."

Mairi invoked the kindly Powers before she got to her feet and looked into Christy's eyes. They were of a height now. For the first time, Christy saw the tiny lines at her foster mother's eyes and mouth, a very few gray hairs. Mairi still did not wear the married woman's cap, but her rich brown hair was braided and coiled up instead of in one plait over her shoulder.

"Will you go to the Stones now?"

"You should pass that trust to Catriona."

"I will. But as the harp called you, so have the Stones." Mairi paused. "Gran made me promise to take you. It would please her if you went."

"I can't go to them yet, Mairi Mór, even to please Gran. I'm angry, not glad, to be staying on the island. The Stones would know that. The sooner I get to my new school and get busy, the better."

"Work saves us. But you've won your own harp and will always have the songs." Mairi touched Christy's cheek. "Gran would be proud of what you did at Siadar. And I am very proud, my dear."

Christy's eyes stung at the praise. How much she longed for Mairi's approval! Bitter that it came when Christy's long dream of living near David was shattered and there was no dream to take its place. It was more than a dream. It had been Christy's resolve since childhood.

But Mairi had gone on when Iain died. The Ness widows had

held their crofts and raised their families. Christy told herself her own loss was nothing compared to many she'd seen. Her laddie was alive, started on the road of *his* resolve. She must find her own. Still, long after she pulled the curtains of David's box bed, Christy wept into her pillow.

XIII

Sure enough, Bruce Urquhart did know of a place that sorely needed a teacher, Ardan, a village on Great Bernera, the island off the west coast that could be seen from Callanish. A friend of Mr. Urquhart was the schoolmaster at Tobson, another Bernera village, and he had written to see if Mr. Urquhart knew of a teacher for Ardan. If he did, wrote the Tobson dominie, he could send the person along with no formality.

David looked like he'd rejoice in battle when Mr. Urquhart said, "A hard time Bernera folk have had of it, and harder coming. For centuries, Bernera cattle and sheep had sufficient grazing between two lochs on the Lewis mainland. Around 1850 when Uig Deer Forest was put together, much of the pastureland was added to the forest. The crofters had to build a stone wall all along the boundary to keep their animals out of the forest, all at their own expense and had the responsibility to maintain it for twenty years. Now an American railroad millionaire, William Winans, is buying up shooting rights and has his eye on Scaliscro Forest, which adjoins the crofters' grazings. I've heard he wants even these pastures added to the deer forest."

Christy grimaced. "An American? Why doesn't he hunt in his own country?"

David snorted. "That wouldn't cost enough. And he couldn't get away with what he does here. I've heard of Winans.

He hires 'watchers' to guard his leases. If a local person takes one step off a road, he has them fined for trespass."

"Aye." A smile brightened the schoolmaster's serious face. "I heard tell that a naturalist from Glasgow was kneeling in the forest grass to study insects and didn't Winans rage at him till the Glasgow man got back on the road? They made a fine shouting match of it with folk marveling at what they call the Battle of the Midges."

Everyone laughed before Bruce Urquhart sobered. "Knowing the Shah, Red Donald of the Hens, I expect the millionaire will get his way." He looked straight at Christy. "Education could help the lads and lassies make their way if Bernera people lose their grazings and have to flit."

"Deer forests!" David spoke between his teeth. "To drive people away to make great sheep farms was ill enough but sheep do at least give wool and meat. To evict folk so rich men can invite their friends to hunt stags and have fine heads to hang in their halls—it's an evil that stinks to high heaven!"

"Spending fortunes on what one does not need is the crowning sign of wealth, lad." The schoolmaster peered through his spectacles at his former pupil. "Prince Albert made deer stalking fashionable. Landseer's paintings and Sir Walter Scott's novels have romanticized it. The railway to Inverness makes it easy for sportsmen to reach the Highlands and take steamers to the islands. Deer forest rents are enormous and increasing."

"So sheep are cleared for deer as crofters were cleared for sheep, and gamekeepers and foresters lord it more than ever." David made a sound of disgust and his voice rang as his father's must have when he commanded his men. "If God grants me one thing, may it be that I help bring the day when lairds can't turn people out of their homes and land."

"May God grant it." Mairi's voice was full of hope and pride and love. She kissed her son and for the first time, Christy was able to think that if it had compelled David to seek an education and accomplish with his mind what he could not with his body, then his laming was not entirely cruel waste.

David looked from his mother to Christy. "You'll go to Bernera?"

Since she couldn't be near him, she cared little where she went provided she could work so hard that she'd have little time to think about him being wed to Alison. "Yes. I'll go."

Something flickered in David's eyes. Was it regret? He hadn't asked her why she'd decided not to seek a school near him. She thought he knew. What she didn't know was whether she was to him more than a lifetime companion and ally.

If she were—if his love, too, had changed—that only made a cruel matter worse. He was married to a sweet, pretty lass he cared for. It wouldn't be amazing if love followed. Christy knew she should wish for that. Only she couldn't.

"I'll take you to Bernera," he said. "Mother wants to send all my Grandmother MacDonald's crystal, dishes, and silver with us. They can be packing them."

"Oh, I can't take your beautiful things, Mother Mairi," Alison protested.

"Haven't I been saving them for David's wife?" demanded Mairi. "Too fine they are for me. David, you know your father's and grandfather's swords are packed away till you want them, and your father's pistols."

"You gave me great-grandfather's travel desk when I went off to school and very handy it is," said David with a smile. "The weapons can hang on a wall some day—and it's my hope they stay there." One blessing at least about his lameness. He would not be called off to the queen's far-flung wars.

It was a misty day in late August when David clucked to the stout little ponies and they set off in a cart across the moor. A special creel held Shenachie, and the cart was heaped with books and slates, chalk, foolscap paper, ink and quills, bedding, cheese, meal, smoked fish, and wrapped in a heavy plaid were Christy's best dress and shoes, her extra skirt and blouse, stockings and undergarments. Because of the threatening weather, Mairi fetched oil skins to wrap around the baskets and boxes so all was secure.

This journey would only last the day but it promised to Christy more joy than she might have in the rest of her life and the almost equal pain of knowing it might well be the last time she would be alone with David. The cart couldn't cross to the island, of course. Christy would have to get a boat in some coastal village like Callanish or Earshader.

But first, there would be this one whole day with David. She had never wished for more than to be at his side. That wish could never be satisfied. When he entered her mind, she must pray for his good and yes, that of poor foolish Alison, and fix her will and thought on her own work. That was what Mairi had done when she believed Iain dead, or in any case, beyond her. *But I'm not Mairi! And she had David.*

No whining out of you! she scolded herself. If you can't be happy—and it's your duty to put on a bright face and be as happy as you can—you *will* be useful and prove to Mairi Mór she did right to bring you home.

Still, as Christy watched David's strong hands on the reins, she longed for the touch of them. It wouldn't do to ride along in silence. Wouldn't do at all. Like a tongue drawn to an aching tooth, she wanted to know more about his marriage, but it would be wicked to pull away what little remaining concealment Alison had. Besides, it didn't matter. David was married. That was an end to hope if not to yearnings.

Yearnings like wanting to touch his face, smooth away the grim lines at his mouth . . . Looking for a safe subject, she asked, "So how do you get on with your Uncle Roderick, Davie? He sounds a right fearsome gentleman."

"Oh, we had a wrangle when I wouldn't take charge of his

legal affairs." David shook his head and chuckled. "I've been telling him for years the only reason I took up law was to win some justice for crofters, but uncle never listened."

"He listened this time?"

"Not for long. He turned purple and shouted that trade unions and the notions of Karl Marx would destroy society—"

"And I daresay you told him it was high time!"

"Yes. I asked him if he had read *Das Kapital*. Uncle said he wouldn't read anything that wasn't published in English and that *The Spectator, The Scotsman,* and the *Inverness Courier* told him all and more than he cared to know about radicals and socialists."

Christy laughed with David, then sobered. "What do you think of the Reform Bill that passed this year?" she asked.

He shrugged. "It gives the vote to all tax-paying householders, lodgers who pay ten pounds annual rent for unfurnished rooms, and owners of five pound property or fourteen pound tenants in the countryside. That still leaves out most of the crofters and poorer town folk but it gives the vote to many who weren't included in the first Reform Act that brought the number of voters from five thousand to sixty thousand."

Christy sighed. "Things *are* getting better, but I don't see how women will ever get to vote since only men are elected to Parliament."

"They can nag their husbands and fathers, brothers and sons, as soon as the men can vote," teased David. "Good grief! We were stepping along smartly and here's another bog to go around!"

"Ah, but look at the rowans on the little isle, with their berries turning shiny red! A feast for the birds! And the last of the yellow iris! And here's bogbean and bell-leaf and common heather all in bloom."

"Yes. And it's starting to rain."

Indeed, the mist had thickened. Christy pulled her shawl

over her head. She wore her three skirts, including the top one of tight-woven wool that shed water. The oilskins protected her belongings. But David's town hat and clothes didn't look up to a drenching. He must have thought so, too, for he reined the ponies off the track.

"Let's duck into that shieling," he suggested. "I'm ready for the bannocks and crowdie Mother sent along."

"Why, this looks like the one I stopped in when I went to Callanish all those years ago," said Christy. Would David remember that was when she unsuccessfully pleaded with the ancient Powers to heal his spine? She added hastily as she scrambled down, "The ponies can at least poke their heads in out of the weather."

They shared bannocks with the ponies and savored the creamy white cheese. It was snug here out of the weather. Christy touched the crumbling heather in one of the two beds made low in the thick walls. She thought the heather still gave out a muted fragrance. If David weren't married—

She glanced up to find him watching her. He turned quickly away but not before she had seen that light deep in his eyes, a light that sent through her a wild, quivering sweetness.

If he reached for her— He didn't love Alison after all, he was shielding her from kindness. *And all I have of him is this one day.* Christy somehow knew if she turned into David's arms, if she raised her mouth to his, that he could not repulse her.

But he would suffer afterward. And so would she. She didn't want this one time they had to be tainted. Breathlessly, she asked, "Would you like to hear a song of the shielings?"

"What better time or place?" *To lie down with you. Lie down and be your love.*

"You must sing the chorus with me," she said in haste. "It's easy enough. 'Sing, o ho ro sing, sing o ho ro, sweetheart, sing, o ho ro, sing!' " He lifted his rich baritone and Christy went on with the old song.

> *In the shieling of merriment,*
> *our bed was of heather,*
> *our pillow of bog cotton.*
> *And thrushes sang.*
> *Lad of beguiling blue eyes,*
> *Although I should not tell it,*
> *I fell in love with you as a child . . ."*

As a child. Thus she had loved David. Now he was wed with a babe coming and a cause to pursue in the great world. Christy's throat ached as she wondered when she would see him again, if they would ever again in this world be able to talk and read each other's hearts and minds the way they had from her earliest memories.

Neither of them heard an approach till there was a surprised neigh from Gillie. The room darkened as the small door was blocked. They turned to confront a slight wiry man of medium height. He wore gray tweeds of the kind a gentleman might for a day's hunting, but this was no gentleman. He had a long-nosed narrow face, close-set pale eyes, and his grin revealed large discolored teeth.

"Trespassing, be you? Get back on the track at once or I'll have you before the judge!"

He spoke in Gaelic. David answered in his gentry English, with a hauteur Christy had never heard from him. "Who are you, my man, to take such a tone with people who are only sheltering from the rain?"

The intruder's manner changed. He took a step back and spoke civilly. "I be Jem Howard, gamekeeper to Mr. William Winans, young sir."

It was almost funny, the way the man's bearing had altered. David's accent alone proclaimed his class, and as the keeper's eyes adjusted to the dimness, he must see that David was not dressed like a crofter.

Christy was. Howard puzzled over her before he gave a nod of comprehension and a sly chuckle.

"I see you've found game of your own, young sir. Good sport to you, and good day."

"My sister is not sport." David spoke in his softest way.

"Sister, is it?" The keeper was thoroughly confused.

"What is it, Howard?" The raised voice was like no English one Christy had heard. "Have you caught a poacher?"

"God knows what they be, sir!" The keeper turned from the door. "A young gentleman, and a lass he claims as a sister but she's a crofter or I never saw one!"

"Whoever and whatever, they must know I'll tolerate no trespassing!" A tall black hat, dripping rain, thrust through the door followed by a man so solidly built that he seemed massive though he was by no means fat.

He scanned them in turn, frowning, but his slate dark eyes came to rest on Christy in a way that made her feel that three skirts and shoulder plaid or no, he saw her mother-naked. She liked his smile less than his scowl. "I suppose it's no great harm for a pretty maiden and her gallant to come in out of the rain," he said. "I'm William Winans and I own shooting rights to this property."

"Ah, yes." David's voice was smooth as cream. "I've heard of your shooting. It's famous on the mainland."

"Is it?" Winans seemed pleased.

"Apparently you prefer to hunt where the only danger is your own gun," David said. "The crofters whose lands are taken to make your deer forests would never dare shoot at you."

Winan's face, solid as his frame, went red. "You seem a true sprig off the branch of gentry. What would your father say to your rambling the moors with a crofter lass?"

"My father's dead but my uncle would have an apoplectic fit. In truth, sir, he gets even more exercised when he and his friends discuss your style of hunting."

"Oh, does he? Just what is his objection?"

"He says you use the old method that hasn't been practiced since firearms became reliable. Your gillies drive deer into one spot where you shoot them at your convenience. Uncle calls it butchery, not sport."

Winans swelled up. "Scots lordlings too poor to lease a forest dine daily on sour grapes."

"My uncle doesn't hunt but if he chose to, he wouldn't need to lease a forest. He owns several."

Christy could not keep from bursting out, "It has been a curse to the islands, sir, the coming of rich Americans."

"Your betters don't think that way, girl. Or will you claim your family owns these moors?"

Power flowed into Christy. She was one small wave swept forward by a mighty ocean. The Callanish of her dreams towered in her inner vision. "I am an orphan, sir, but indeed my people own these moors—own them whatever lairds and factors and shooting tenants do." She could not recognize her own voice and felt as if she blazed with spirit flame. "Our bodies have melted into the soil for centuries just as the shell sand sweetens the peat. We *are* the land. One day even folk like you will know that."

Winans stared at her, looking startled, even unwillingly impressed. David said, "You should be the advocate, Christy!" Very sweet to her was the admiration in his eyes.

Shrugging, Winans said, "Meanwhile you trespass. Get back on the track and stay there or I'll have the pair of you before the judge."

"My uncle is Sir James Matheson's friend," said David. "You could have us fined a few pounds but your lease might not be renewed."

The force that had so overwhelmingly possessed Christy slowly ebbed. She was again a crofter, fearful of what a man like Winans could do, if not to her, to others. Wasn't she going to Bernera in the first place because the people were being crowded from their grazings to the point where they might have to leave?

"We must be on our way," she said. "It's still far to Bernera and I must find a boat to take me over."

"Are you going to Bernera to infect the peasantry with your radical notions?" demanded Winans.

"I'm going there to teach school."

"The poor are better off without education. It only makes them discontented and rebellious."

"That's a strange sentiment for an American," said Christy.

"As to educating the poor, your lawmakers are more sensible," retorted Winans.

"Do you think so? Three hundred years ago, John Knox called for all children to be educated through parish schools. It's true there were few schools in the Highlands and islands till the Society for the Propagation of Christian Knowledge began its work in 1709. Many poor children still can't go to school but it would be a brave Scot, sir, who said they should not be educated."

David nodded. "Scots like to boast that any lad who does well at parish school can go on to a university."

"Most poor lads cannot be spared from work," added Christy. "But it gives the rich the excuse to say that poor ignorant people prefer to remain poor and ignorant."

She pulled her shawl over her head, stepped out into what was now more mist than rain, and climbed into the cart before David could make shift to try to help her. When they were out of earshot, David glanced back at the American and his keeper. "It's bad enough to have the Highlands overrun with Lowland and English cotton manufacturers, coal producers, and ironmongers. After all, Aunt Bea's father piled up his money from textile factories. He knows to the shilling what he's worth, goes to his office every day, and gives not a fig for society or fripperies like hunting leases. But these Americans—"

Even where crofters were allowed to stay, there were rules and regulations on every hand. Turf and peat could only be cut in certain places. Heather and rushes and bent grass and seaweed could be gathered only when and where allowed by estate officers. Fish and game belonged solely to the proprietor. People were not to venture off the tracks or roads. And so on and so forth, a rule at every bend and a regulation at every turn.

"Someday," she said, "if we outlast the Red Donalds and Winans, gamekeepers and lairds, the land will be ours again."

"Yes, and look how much better it is on this side of the island than on the east coast, where peat runs almost to the cliffs. Atlantic storms blow the sand inland where it's rooted down with grass and other plants to form machair or meadow. There's no machair on Clanna's side."

"Great flocks of barnacle geese winter on the machair and leave their dung," said Christy. "It's the best land on Lewis, both for grazing and crops, so it's been taken from crofters and given to sheep and deer as your mother's village was."

"Yes. Aosda is a sheep farm now."

"But your mother still smoors the fire on the hearthstone from Gran's house," Christy pointed out. "And look! There's Callanish!"

Shafts of sunlight illumined the distant Stones on the knoll above the sea loch, standing like a group of meditating elders. *I will not come to you, ancient Stones, while I am forced to stay on the island. I will only come when I stay gladly, of my own choice. Gran, forgive me, but I cannot lie to the Stones.* Down on the shore fishermen were baiting their round wicker lobster pots. Floating in mists like a fairy island was what must be Bernera.

A shroud of mist obscured the Stones. Guilt, regret, and anger took their turns with Christy as David drove the cart as far down the beach as possible without getting stuck. His silver coin assured more profit than the best catch of lobsters. The cart's load was quickly shifted to a boat.

The day was over, her single day with David.

Why did he take her hands when she was feeling frozen and

numb and hard enough to endure this last snatch of time with him? His touch blazed through her, paining like thaw from frostbite.

For a moment their fingers clung and their eyes locked. Transfixed as if by lightning, shaken to the depths, Christy gazed at her love and knew she was his love, too. What must never pass between them in words flowed with their blood, with quickening pulse, with inner trembling.

The time seemed forever though it could only have been a heartbeat. David released her as if her flesh was potent flame. He was learning to be a lawyer, learning to hide his feelings. His eyes were masked now; but his hands had spoken, and his voice was husky. "Well, Christy, you'll teach on Bernera and I'll go back to learning law."

"Learn it well." From somewhere, she summoned a laugh. "I'll need you if Red Donald or Winans hauls me into court."

David grinned back. For a minute, they were playmates again before his face took on such hard angles that she seemed to be looking at the captain. "I'd like right well to get the Shah in court. Here he is, the procurator fiscal, who makes charges, and next the judge who passes sentence. What offices he doesn't fill are assumed by his clerk. Sir James doesn't know the quarter of his chamberlain's cheats and feats."

Christy nodded. "Munro leaves Clanna alone because of Sir James's regard for your mother, but he has all the other crofters terrified with his favorite saying, 'I'll have your land!' "

"Aye. It's a long reckoning he's run up these past fifteen years."

With Chul's death probably the first tally David had made. A thrill of hope shot through Christy. Could it be that David might bring down Munro? All too well she remembered how the factor dealt with the orphans and widows of Ness, tried to use the relief fund to pay old rents and unreasonable levies.

"May you be the one to settle that reckoning, lad!" Christy smiled at David and he smiled back.

Oh yes, she thought with a rush of gladness. They were still companions. She would rather have that even with time and space between than to live wedded to any other man and lie in his arms at night. David's hands had told her that he loved her. She had that. If it had to be for all her life the only hint of man's love she could have, she'd still call herself blessed.

"Good-bye, Davie. Fare you well."

"And you." His lips brushed her forehead.

She couldn't bear to look at him as the skipper helped her into the boat. "Ardan's across East Loch Roag and a distance up the coast," the Viking-like fisherman said. "You take one look at the place and you may be coming straight back. Perched lorn and lonely above the water it is, a long way from other villages."

"That must be why they need a teacher."

"Oh, aye. A great thing for the bairns." But he still eyed her doubtfully as his crew pushed the boat off the strand and ran alongside to launch it.

Five years ago, only a girl, Christy had gone to Siadar. Now she was a woman, robbed of her love. What would she find at Ardan?

Book II

THE
HEIRESS

XIV

Whooper swans gave their hoarse call as they winged north from their wintering grounds at Islay. Terns, guillemots, kittiwakes, and puffins were rejoining shags and cormorants on the rugged cliffs. Shags drying on sandbanks with wings outstretched had not yet grown their dashing recurved crests of the breeding season. They glinted green-black rather than the bronze-black of cormorants. One dived from the surface of the water and stayed submerged for an amazing length of time before surfacing with a hapless fish in its long, hooked bill. The fish was expertly tossed down a sinuous throat, swelling the cormorant's neck in passage.

An oyster catcher waded in the muddy inlet where Ardan folk collected the shellfish they used for both food and bait. Stalking along on pink legs, the bird speared his bright orange bill down for a limpet or cockle. Ringed plovers searched along the shore for smaller shellfish and crabs. Since they ate different food from oyster catchers, plovers often hunted in the same rich mud and even nested close to oyster catchers along the shore.

The Flannans rested in the waves to the west like a flock of seabirds. Across the narrow channel gleamed the white shell strand of Little Bernera where long ago there been a temple. The daughter of the priest had been carried off to Norway by Sweyn the Viking, but she had so longed for her home that after seven long years he brought her back.

Seven years, thought Christy. It is nine years since I went

away from Clanna. Five at Siadar and I have been here almost four. The Merry Dancers had four times swirled their scarves among the winter stars and burnet roses had bloomed among the Stones on three Midsummers' morns. There was the awesome glory of God in the tempests that hurled frothing breakers against the rocks and sent seabirds winging inland. There was the singing of the seals and wee ones holding to their mothers' backs with their tiny flippers to be carried through the waves. Countless wonders for delight and worship, and Christy had worshiped and delighted and tried to live by Gran's counsel: *Weep at night if you must. But when day comes, put on your morning face.*

Still, looking back, those four years had one aching barrenness. She had not seen David, not a glimpse in four years. She had an occasional letter from him, full of his law work but with little to say about Alison and nothing at all of his feelings.

Alison's baby had died a few weeks after birth. Since then, Alison had been afflicted by severe headaches and other ills. There had been no more children. Christy refused to let herself speculate on the intimate side of their life but she couldn't keep from wishing that if Alison's child was fated to die it had done so before David was snared in a marriage that seemed to give him so little.

Shaking off dismal thoughts, Christy stooped to wee Elspeth Hardy, taking her piggyback while the older students followed them away from the sea cliffs and joined in Christy's chant.

> *Matthew, Mark, Luke, and John,*
> *Hold the pony till I leap on.*
> *Hold it fast and hold it sure*
> *Till I win over the misty moor!''*

Elspeth squealed with joy. As soon as Christy had brought her group far enough from the cliffs to be heard above the pounding of the surf, she set the child down. Elspeth at three was too young for school. She was allowed to come because her mother had died that winter and the bairn wept herself sick when her older sister, seven-year-old Marjorie, got out of her sight. Marjorie now took Elspeth's chubby hand and warned her to be quiet and listen to teacher. Christy ached for them both.

Their yellow hair needed combing and rebraiding, their faces were smudged, and their clothing had more holes than solid parts. With their father, Lachlan, they lived with his blind old mother, Honora. She still churned butter and ground meal by touch, mixed the bannocks and directed Marjorie in cooking. Neighbors helped and milked the Hardys' cows when Lachlan was fishing, but they all had more than enough to do for their own families. Besides, Lachlan was fiercely proud and after almost four years, he still seemed to mistrust Christy. She was an outsider, and educated, and he was among the villagers who feared education would lure their children away to Stornoway or even the mainland.

Still, the little girls looked so pitiful that Christy resolved to keep them after school and mend their clothing and comb their hair even if it did make Lachlan cross. More than likely he'd never notice, which was part of the trouble, since his poor blind mother couldn't.

Christy glanced around at her pupils, the family faces she had come to know, most linked with the ancient clan names of Lewis: MacLeod, MacKenzie, Morison, Nicolson, and MacDonald. It made her feel a great age to reflect that lads who'd been eleven or twelve or thirteen when she first taught them now did a man's work at the fishing or on the croft. Several girls had married and one had a baby.

That was the way of it for teachers. Bairns passed under their hands and voices like incoming waves and flowed back out again. A teacher could only hope they carried something with them and pour her hope and energy into the next wave. Thus far, thank goodness, the waves still swept up the same shore. Bernera crofters had been left in peace on their summer grazings on the mainland though throughout the Highlands and islands, pastures and even crofts were being turned into deer forests just as previously crofters had lost their land to sheep.

Christy's gaze came to rest on her quietest but perhaps brightest student, twelve-year-old Donald MacLeod, who took such interest in things of the deep sea that she intended to ask Magnus if the boy could sail with him in a few years.

"Long ago, three hundred years before Christ, a Greek named Pytheas sailed to the Baltic and what he called Thule which must have been Norway or Iceland," she explained. "He might even have landed and stood where we are now. The tides of the Mediterranean where Pytheas came from are trifling, since the swell has to squeeze through the Straits of Gibralter."

"Doesn't Great Britain own Gibralter?" asked Donald.

"Yes. Spain ceded it to Britain in the Treaty of Utrecht, along with the right to supply South America with African slaves. That was in 1713 when England, France, Holland, and Spain shared out a good bit of the world amongst them. Anyway, the tide at Gibralter scarce forces its way into the sea when it ebbs back. So when poor old Pytheas went home and told of the great tides he had seen along ocean coasts like ours, no one believed him."

"No one ever believes deep-sea sailors," scoffed red-headed Archie Nicolson with a wrinkle of his freckled snub nose. At thirteen, he was the oldest lad in school. Katie, his ten-year-old sister, ruddy of hair and gray-eyed like all the Ardan Nicolsons, vigorously nodded. She worshiped her elder brother. He ignored her unless another boy teased her, a sure way to pick a fight with Archie. He never lost so no one tried it often.

"Miss Christy, what makes tides?" asked Donald.

The rise and ebb of the tide twice every twenty-four hours had always seemed mystical to Christy, especially the way that spring tides, named that because they were high, not for the season, swept up rocks and shore to their farthest reach twice in each lunar month, at or near the time of the full and new moons. Mystical, too, that a woman's flow came each twenty-eight days, the length of the moon month, and that the highest tide of the whole year was the spring tide nearest the solstice. It seemed to Christy that if you knew what caused the tides, you would understand the workings of the universe, but she gave Donald the best answer she could.

"There was a great man at the ciphering, Sir Isaac Newton, who's been dead for well over a century. He thought tides depend on the gravitational pull of the moon, which changes as the earth turns and all its waters move with it."

"That makes me dizzy!" Fiona MacKenzie gave a small shudder. At twelve, the pretty fair-haired lassie's attention was already fixed more on the lads than lessons, but her plain, scrawny younger sister, nine-year-old Beth, devoured books and was so quick at her lessons that Christy thought she might become a teacher.

"Aye." Golden-haired Queenie Morison seemed to live more in daydreams than reality except when something caught her fancy and brought an interested sparkle to her green eyes.

She, her older brother, Francis, and younger sister, Nellie, lived such a far trudge from the school that Christy had turned over her snug room in the schoolhouse to them and Sally and Liam Mac-Donald who also had miles through the bogs to their home. Queenie was only eight, but she showed promise of beauty and was of such a sweet nature that not even mischievous Liam teased her much. Smiling at Donald, her hero, Queenie spoke softly. "It does make the head whirl, but isn't it wonderful, forbye, that the moon and sun in the heaven rule the tides of our own shore and all the earth?"

"It *is* wondrous, lass." Donald smiled back at her but flicked a warning glance toward Liam and Archie who sometimes hooted at Queenie's notions. "But all nature is wondrous, especially where the seas touch land. Look where the high tide cast up that bank of wrack. If the next spring tide covers it with sand, sea rocket and campion and all manner of plants may grow there as long as the waves don't sweep them away. In time, it might become meadow. Where the line of seaweed's thin, terns may find good nesting. But where wrack piles thick, it rots and breeds those flies that make misery on the beach.''

It was such knowledge that made Christy wonder how crofters could be called ignorant. Glancing at the sun, she said, ''That's lessons enough for the day. Study your spelling and sums. Liam, Archie, I've corrected your compositions so you can copy them out in a fair hand and put them into your folders.'' Every year, all pupils made folders to hold their special work. These were great treasures by term's end.

The girls walked along with Christy. This western coast had many more flowers than grew on the east side where peat usually stretched right down to the rocky cliffs. It would be another month or more before the machair was a profusion of varied blooms. Sea pinks braved April chill, though. Marsh marigold gilded damper spots, and Queenie cried out with delight and knelt to gently touch the exquisite lavender spring squill growing in a rock ledge. Christy kept a close eye on plants and gathered them, as Gran had taught her, for dyestuffs and medicines, practical knowledge that impressed the villagers more than all her book learning.

''Here, Miss Christy!'' Liam's grubby hand opened to let a mass of tiny black things fall into her palm. ''I found a berried hen under that big rock waiting for the tide to come in.''

''You didn't hurt her?''

''Och, no! Just plucked some of her thousands of eggs off her legs. She's still got plenty. She had several big acorn barnacles stuck to her shell and a great black conger eel was alongside of her under that rock!''

He ran off after the boys. Christy shared the spoonful of lobster eggs so that each girl who liked them got a taste of the delicacy. In order to replenish their kind, lobster hens with eggs glued to their legs were supposed to be released if they were caught. But greedy or hard-pressed fishermen added them to the catch sold to the entrepreneur who owned rights to the oyster and mussel beds in Loch Roag and shipped these delicacies to London.

"Marjorie, m'eudail," said Christy. "Stop off with me a little while. You and Queenie and Sally can practice your spelling together while I take a needle to your clothes."

"Father—"

"Father can't bend his fingers to a wee needle. Come along in. Liam, be a good lad and pour cups of milk for all you bairns." He and Francis Morison bolted their milk and ran out to play. The girls sipped more daintily. Queenie took the speller and began to pronounce words to Marjorie and Sally.

Glancing at Shenachie, who stood in the corner, plaided and seeming to welcome her, Christy unbraided Marjorie's hair and brushed and combed it carefully to avoid jerking. She plaited it into a plump yellow braid and tied it with a bit of yarn and blue ribbon. "There, love. How nice you look! If you comb it every day, it won't get tangled. And remember to wash your face and neck and ears, Elspeth's, too, before you go to bed."

Queenie was a kind-hearted lassie. She'd never tease Marjorie about needing the teacher to tend to her. Besides, it was only this past few months that Queenie did her own hair and her sister, Nellie's, and began to mend their clothing. Christy still braided Sally MacDonald's hair. The MacDonald and Morison children walked to their homes on weekends if the weather wasn't too foul and returned with their school fees in the form of eggs, crowdie, meal, and smoked fish.

Ardan folk kept Christy in food and peats and paid her five pounds a year. She spent most of this on school supplies and things needed by the children. This was no hardship. When Mairi visited the Stones at Midsummer, she always brought Christy clothes and books. Christy felt guilty and somewhat resentful at Mairi's unspoken hope that she would one Midsummer join her foster mother there. Deeper than her conscious mind, Christy felt as if the powers represented by the Stones had prevented her being with David, had forced her to duty, since she had not chosen it. In a way, the Stones were her conscience. She couldn't go to those ancient guardians till she was at peace within herself—until her heart united wholly with her will.

Early in Christy's first term at Ardan, Magnus had sailed through the Sound of Harris and up to Bernera with a real desk and chair, planks for children's desks, a globe, household plenishings, and a chest of warm blankets. *Almost a dowry. A dowry for an old maid.*

When Christy turned her living quarters over to the Mac-Donald and Morison children, their fathers ranged far and wide to collect and borrow driftwood sound enough to construct another box bed for the boys. The girls had Christy's and she slept on the settle in the hearth room, which was also the school. This again was no great hardship. She'd slept on the settle at Clanna after David's accident and she only needed a narrow bed. Maybe that was all she would ever have.

Neither was it hard to cook for her five "boarders." She could simmer kale or soup or fish or potatoes while teaching and she had no chores like milking, churning, or grinding grain. Still, she was exhausted by the time she went to bed at night. Ten months of the year, school began at seven in the morning, let out for an hour at ten, commenced again at eleven and ran till about four. Three nights a week in the winter, from six to nine, Christy taught adults who had a thirst for learning.

Ceilidhs filled the house on the other nights because people were used to coming there, it had the largest hearth room in the village, and there were two benches and the settle. Donald Mac-Leod's father, Hugh, played the pipes, and Lachlan Hardy had a lovely tenor when he could be persuaded to sing.

This was a ceilidh night. Christy wrapped Marjorie in a shawl while she mended her clothes, combed Elspeth's fine hair, and put the bairn down for a nap while her dress was patched. By then the boys came rioting in and Christy hastened to make bannocks and ladle out big bowls of steaming chowder.

The ceilidh was in full swing that night, Hugh skirling away on tunes he'd learned as a piper in the queen's army and Christy blending in with Shenachie, when there was a hail at the door. Now what stranger would be coming at that hour? Anyone from Ardan would have simply entered and called a greeting. Christy put her harp aside and opened the door.

A burly dark-bearded man stepped in without waiting for an invitation. "The ground officer!" someone whispered. "James MacRae!"

Christy's heart sank. Ground officers were the underlings of Red Donald, located in each parish to make sure the factor's bidding was done. A ground officer's visit never meant anything good for crofters.

"I've come to bring you Mr. Munro's orders," said MacRae, thrusting out his heavy jaw in an unpleasant grin. "Your Cuallin grazings are needed to enlarge Scaliscro Forest."

Into the stunned silence, old Diarmid MacLeod, Hugh's father, said, "But Mr. MacRae, you will mind that when Uig Deer Forest was made in 1850, we were deprived of much of our grazing and had to build a great long wall and maintain it. How can Mr. Munro take more of our pastures?"

"Och, he can, and you know it. He can take them all, even your crofts, so you'd best keep a civil tongue." MacRae waited, relaxed and easy, for what could they do?

Dismay and anger were on every face but no one protested further. The officer went on in a magnanimous tone, "Mr. Munro will give other grazings, between the Uig road and the sea at Earshader. However, you must build a wall between your pastures and the deer forest before you put a single beast to graze. The fine for an animal trespassing the forest will be three shillings a head, so I advise you to build that wall stoutly and well."

"But Mr. MacRae, we need to be soon at the fishing," said

Lachlan. "The herring shoals will be in our waters. We must catch them while they're here."

The officer shrugged. "That's no concern of mine. Will you accept the Earshader grazings in place of your old ones?"

"What else can we do?" rumbled Hugh with the muffled fury of a strong man beaten by words and laws.

"And you agree to build the wall?"

The men glanced around at one another. Hugh said, "What it is, lads, is we and the other Bernera folk must agree that none of us will fish till the wall is built. 'Twould not be fair for some to fish while others toil at the wall."

There was a chorus of assent. MacRae nodded. "Well and good. I'm glad you're showing sense." He reached inside his coat and brought out a paper. "This is an agreement between Bernera crofters and the estate in the person of Mr. Munro. It says if you accept the Earshader grazings and build and maintain the wall then you shall possess those pastures so long as your rents are paid and you obey the rules and regulations. Sign your names or your marks and I'll tell Mr. Munro you accept his offer."

"But not with thanks," muttered Lachlan. "Miss Christy, will you read yon paper and say if it assures us the new grazings?"

The ground officer gave him a sharp glance but shrugged and handed Christy the paper. She read it aloud. MacRae had summarized it truthfully enough. She set out quills and ink. Each man wrote his name or made an *X* and she wrote his name beside it.

The ground officer watched. When the last man's name was on the agreement, he folded it and thrust it inside his coat. "I'll bid you good night," he said. "I must be on to Tobson where I trust folk will be as sensible as you."

When the door closed behind him, a clamor broke out, angry and helpless, but indeed there was no recourse. It was take the new grazings or lose pastures altogether, and perhaps their small crofts as well.

But someday—someday the laws David was working for

would surely be passed. Someday an outrage like this couldn't happen. Christy took Shenachie and the harp found its own tune, the one Mairi had sung at Stornoway Castle when she thought it was Cridhe's last song and the last song of Fearchar, dear Gran's husband.

> *Some will endure between the rocks and the sea.*
> *If you would be rid of us, you must sink the stones,*
> *You must sink the islands beneath the oceans.*
> *One day will come justice.*

The wall must go up as quickly as possible, the whole six miles of it, or the crofters would lose most of their income from the herring, an important part of their livelihood. All able-bodied Bernera men, from Tobson, Kirkibost, Bolsta, and Breasclete joined those of Ardan to carry rocks and lay them up in a wall that would stand against the ocean gales. Christy turned school over to Meg MacClennan, a young mother who had been one of her first pupils. The older boys were helping and so were the stronger women who, like Christy, had no young children. While they worked on the wall, the women left in the villages took care of the workers' families and chores, and Christy's five housemates, of course.

Folk had been cleared from this region thirty years before to make a sheep farm. The crofters had carried away their precious roof beams and the fallen thatch had rotted away, but sails stretched over the sturdier walls gave some shelter and privacy to the wall builders. Christy shared a ruin with five other young women. They carried rocks till their backs ached, cooked for the men, and made innumerable bannocks.

"This wall's the length of Bernera itself," growled Hugh MacLeod. "Six miserable miles! When Red Donald's in hell, may the devil set him to building walls of scorching brimstone that are pushed down every night!"

"You know what they say about a wall," said Lachlan. "It

must be high enough to keep a crofter's beasts inside but not so high that it can't be jumped by the laird's deer!''

A fair-haired young man from Tobson, Angus MacDonald, lit his clay pipe. "Thank God we have no deer forest on Bernera! Folk with fields near a forest often lose their whole crop to the beasties and not a thing can they do about it.''

Lachlan said bitterly, "Yet a crofter can be fined up to ten pounds—nigh two years' earnings—if a witness claims he trespassed in a deer forest in order to take a deer to feed his family.''

"And guess who the witness is?" grated Hugh. "The same gamekeeper who can arrest a man who won't give his name and where he lives.''

"This Dugald Craigie is a grummilie sort," said a man from Breasclete. "He runs his cows and sheep on pastures we pay rent for but yon ground officer MacRae winks at that, since he does the same.''

"Gamekeeping's a dangerous profession." Angus MacDonald tossed back his yellow hair and his hazel eyes glinted. He had been in the army. It was not easy for soldiers to stay meek and mild under persecution. "A man who prowls the deer forest may slip among the rocks and break his neck, or drown in a bog if he's a trifle bosky. Forbye, his gun might go off and shatter what heart or brains he has.''

"Nay, lad, don't talk so," cautioned his father. "In the end, Craigie, MacRae, and Red Donald must stand before God.''

"That's not soon enough," retorted Angus.

"Still we must wait for it," said old Diarmid in a warning voice. "Look crosswise at ground officer, gamekeeper, or factor, and we're as good as off our land.''

"I'll do whatever I must to stay," his son Hugh reassured him. He stroked the dark head of young Donald who, twelve-year-old body exhausted, had gone to sleep against his father's side as they sat on the turf. "But my lad here—if things don't get better for crofters instead of worse, I'm going to counsel him to go to America, miss him though we will."

"I can give him the name of kinsmen in Texas," said Christy. "But let's pray it won't come to that. Let's sing a song or two before we seek our beds."

"To sweeten our tempers?" Angus laughed. But he led into a rowing song that celebrated Bernera, "green gem in the ocean's bosom, girdled with white shell sand . . ." A few more songs and they went off to their shelters or simply wrapped up in plaids.

Half of the detested wall was built. In several weeks, they could get back to their real lives and hope to be secure in these grazings for at least a generation. Oh, David! Christy thought as she lay down among the rushes and drew her shawl around her. Work hard, laddie! Change these wicked laws.

The wall was done at last. Gray miles of it stretched from sea edge to sea edge, laid in place stone by stone, uphill and down, along the Uig road. The men hastily cut peats, transported livestock to the new grazings except for cows that had to be milked, and went off to fish for herring, which they would sell to the curers in Stornoway.

That left the women, youngsters, and elderly men to cultivate the fields, hoe potatoes, and move kale from planticrues to kaleyards. A few people from each township went to stay at the grazings at lambing time to help ewes in distress, castrate the male lambs, and clip the sheep. These had to be smeared with tar and butter to protect the animals from parasites, a wearisome, smelly chore since the fleece must be parted and the mixture spread thinly all over on the hide. It was a good thing Ardan crofters had plenty of butter accumulated, for it took thirty pounds of butter and twelve pints of tar to smear the township's hundred sheep. Going back to Clanna made Christy miss David so much that she preferred to spend the two-month school recess at Ardan and help with the numerous summer tasks.

The men came home in time to harvest barley and oats. When the grain was gathered, it was time to bring home the cattle and winter them in the byres. The sheep would find such shelter as they might in valleys and hollows.

Where stones had shifted or the ground sunk, the wall needed repairing. At the weekend, Christy and some of the older children went over to help. From the occasional sound of guns from the deer forest, Mr. Winans and some friends must be enjoying a hunt.

"From the sound of it, the American has gillies driving the deer toward him," said Angus MacDonald. "Great sport that is!"

Since so many stones had been used in the wall, it was needful to search farther away for new ones. Christy was prying up some usefully shaped rocks from the bank of a stream when she heard a shout from the wall.

She looked up to see a stag leap over it, stagger, and run on, tripping from exhaustion or wounds. Blood pumped from his throat and side, stained the turf. He fell a few hundred feet from Christy. His magnificent antlers seemed to weigh down his head. It lay on the ground a moment. The stag forced himself up again. As if by sheer will and heart, he reached the water, plunged into it, as if to refuge before he collapsed. The water ran wide and not very deep where he lay just above a waterfall, where the stream narrowed and dashed down to flow through a steep chasm. Below, the water looked deep and the current churned whitely.

If you had just made it to the waterfall, my brave beauty! Winans would not have got your splendid antlers, the whole reason he has killed you. Christy heard the distant shouts of men. As stalkers, the hunters wouldn't be mounted. It would take them a little while to follow their quarry's blood trail.

She blinked back tears at a sudden thought. If she dug away at the stream bottom beneath the stag—if she shoved and tugged, maybe, just maybe, she could launch him over the waterfall where he might be carried out of reach of the huntsmen or snared in water deep enough he couldn't be found.

The deer had tried so valiantly! Besides, she hated hunting, hated the cruel sport that had driven countless numbers of her people out of their homes. She couldn't keep Winans from amassing the heads of most deer he slaughtered, but if she could keep him from claiming this one, it would be a triumph for her and the gallant stag.

Christy slipped out of her outer skirts and fastened her bottom one around her waist. She was already barefoot to keep from soaking her shoes in the bogs. The water pushed at her legs as she bent to scoop at the silty bottom with a flat stone. Blood from the stag's wounds mingled with water. The current channeled the new track her stone made, slanting toward the waterfall. The stag's body began to move.

The shouts were closer now. Men were scrambling over the wall. Christy sat down in the chilling stream, braced her feet against the deer's shoulder, and shoved with all her might. The haunches hung at the ledge a moment. She thrust again. The stag went over.

Gasping, she crawled up the bank, caught a last glimpse of the stag's antlers as they disappeared beneath another cataract. The stag didn't surface again. Most likely, the pronged antlers had caught in a rock crevice that held the carcass to the bottom.

Christy pulled on her dry skirts, slipped off her wet one, kicked it under a thick clump of gorse, and began prying at a rock. In her pity and admiration for the stag, in her loathing for men who would kill just for a trophy, Christy had forgotten everything else. Now, as the hunters advanced with their rifles, four gentlemen, Craigie, and a dozen gillies, her pounding heart sledged oppressively.

All Bernera folk could suffer for her impulsive act. They might be fined or even, God forbid, lose their pastures after the tedious back-breaking labor of building the wall. Whatever happened to her, she must try to protect the crofters. Still, though she prayed they wouldn't interfere, she was inwardly warmed that Angus and Lachlan had come down along with her pupils, Donald MacLeod, Archie Nicolson, and Liam MacDonald.

Craigie reached her first. As he scanned the water and banks, his narrow face twisted with disappointment and wrath. "What went with that stag, woman? His blood leads right into the burn but doesn't go out on the other side. What went with him?"

"He went over the waterfall," she said, truthfully enough. Relief made her head whirl. Could it be they hadn't seen her?

All the men except Winans hurried to look over the gorge. His flat-angled face was impassive but with inner shriveling, she knew from the expression in his dark eyes that he had seen.

Why didn't he accuse her, then? Why did he let Craigie order the gillies to search up and down both sides of the stream? As if he must vent his rage on someone, the keeper swung back to her.

"The water's not deep enough to float a stag of that size, you daft woman! A royal stag he was of twelve points, brow, bay, tray tines and a three-point top on each beam."

"He would have been a brilliant trophy for my business associate from Chicago," said Winans. "Since the walls in all my dwellings have become trophy-cluttered, I only keep twenty pointers." He shrugged. "If the beast does wash up on a bank below, no doubt his antlers will be ruined from striking against the rocks. Take the gillies over the wall to the forest, Craigie, and see what new sport you can find for my guests."

The crofter men and laddies picked up stones and carried them back to the wall as the gillies boosted the gentlemen over and scrambled across themselves. Christy was left with the foreign millionaire.

"Now," he said in a careless way, "let's have the truth. I remember you. Several years ago, you trespassed with a young gentleman in a shieling hut and I'll confess I've had an eye out for you ever since when I come shooting. I was first on the wall today, my lass. In time to see you shove that stag over the waterfall——at considerable risk to yourself from the look of it." He tilted his head. "Why?"

What did he intend? Christy summoned her courage and looked directly into his eyes. "If you saw me, sir, then you know the others had no part in it. I doubt if any of them even saw me, the way the wall runs there."

"Why did you do it?"

"You will not punish anyone else?"

"You're in poor case to bargain."

"The deer had awful wounds. He fell once but dragged himself up again."

"They often do that."

"Then how——" She bit off the rest. *How do you find the heart to hunt them, creatures who love life as you do?* "The stag was brave and proud," she said. "It didn't seem fair that his beautiful head should hang in some gentleman's hall."

She waited for anger, for scorn, for him to say she'd be accused and tried in Red Donald's court. Instead Winans said, "You wasted a lot of venison. Too bad, since I would have given most of that beast to your people. Hunting's not all vainglory, you should know. Most sportsmen I know give such venison as they can't use to crofters."

She *had* to say it if the skies fell. Did the man have the slightest notion of what his pleasure had done to hundreds of people? "If sheep and deer hadn't taken our lands, we'd have food enough without charity."

He shrugged. "The simple truth is that there are many more crofters than the land can feed. You're fools to starve on here when you could go to America and homestead many times the acreage of your pitiful little crofts, own it outright for a sum that pays a few years' rent here."

"You forget one thing, sir."

"Do I?"

"This is our home."

He gave her a look of disgust tinged with grudging admiration. "Control your sympathy for deer next time, young woman, or I'll have you up for theft, and do not brag of this to your people. I'll let you off this once. I myself do not kill roe deer. I shot one once. It was pretty and cried like a child. I've never hunted them again." He started away, then turned with a crooked smile. "You should go to America, my dear. Your spirit will get you in trouble here but it would serve you well across the ocean."

Chuckling, he sketched a salute and made for the wall where gillies waited to help him over. Christy picked up the loosened stone and trudged to the wall where Angus took it from her.

"The American had a word with you, Mistress MacLeod. He was not discourteous?"

Christy shook her head. Angus grunted. "If it had been us charging over the wall and chasing across his forest, he'd have us fined for trespass but there's naught we can do to him!"

"He's not as bad as some," said Diarmid MacDonald. "Once he gets crofters cleared from his deer forests—and Scaliscro's only one of them—they say he's generous. Pays his men eighteen to thirty shillings a week, a lot more than they'd earn even working for the railroad on the mainland."

"Pays them to watch the roads so no one steps off on his Mightiness's land," jeered Lachlan. "I'd rather live on shellfish and seaweed than eat high on money earned like that!" His blue eyes searched Christy's. "How did that stag, that royal twelve-point stag, slip over the waterfall?"

"The current took him, daftie." Christy went off for another rock. She kept away from the glistening trail of blood.

XV

The pungency of fresh-turned earth filled Christy's lungs as she mounded it over a bit of seed potato. On Saturdays, she always helped with crofting work. Compositions had to be graded and lessons planned but she would have felt lazy to sit snug by the hearth while there was much to do outside. Oats must be planted soon, and when the weather warmed enough, the cows would be brought out of their byres and taken to the Earshader summer grazings.

It had been dreary toil, building that wall, but this would make Bernera livestock's third summer on the pastures. If raising the wall insured longtime secure use of the grazings, the crofters were minded to consider it as good a bargain as they could make.

Two boats were heading for the shore. They seemed laden with what looked like long poles and other timbers. The men bent with their oars to come in with a wave, the bowmen sprang out and splashed through the surf with painters while the crews jumped out and pushed the boats as far as they could up the strand.

These were not Ardan men. They were off after lobsters. Christy, the other women, and a few elderly men hurried down to greet the strangers, most of whom waited by the boats. A few came to meet the Ardan folk.

"Cousin Meg!" The foremost man, broad-shouldered and slim-flanked, shoved back red-brown hair dripping with spray and heartily kissed the cheek of Meg Nicolson, Archie's mother. "I haven't seen you since our grandfather's funeral. Eight years, it must be, but you're bonnier than ever!"

"You had ever a flattering tongue, Alisdair. But what brings you here with what look like roof timbers?"

The big man sobered. "What you might think. Our little township, just four households of us left, is being added to Scaliscro Forest. We must flit, twenty souls, from babes to ancients." He spread his sinewy calloused hands. "It's much to ask, that you let us live at Ardan, but we own and crew our two boats and win most of our living from the sea. We can pay a fair share of the rents. If we can plant 'taties and kale, we'll buy meal if there's no bit of land to spare for our grain."

"But your beasties——" said Meg with a troubled frown.

"Mr. Winans, who seems to think he needs even our wee crofts for his hunting, has offered a good price for our sheep and cattle. We would only keep what you folk agree can be allowed on your grazings without stinting your own creatures."

"From me, cousin, you're welcome with all my heart, and I'm sure from my husband, too. But you'll understand 'tis a matter the whole township must agree to."

Alasdair nodded. "To be sure. We know it is much to ask, but we have already been to other townships and none have room. They all have taken in evicted relations and lack space for even one more kaleyard." His chin lifted. "We have our boats, though. We can make a living. If you can't spare land for barley or grazing, we'll just eat more fish."

A wiry gray-haired man behind him said, "Have we leave to unload our roof timbers and carry them and our boats out of the reach of the tide till you can take council with your menfolk?"

"Och, aye, do that, dear men," said Meg. "And then come up, all of you, and have bannocks and soup."

Three of the roof ridges, the central, most important timbers, were safely carried well above the high-water line. The fourth, though, cracked rottenly as it was lifted and splintered in half.

A groan went up from everyone, including Ardan folk. They knew what a disaster this was in a treeless land where even battered driftwood was hoarded for building. The most cruel and final act of forced eviction was to break or burn the roof timbers because they were so hard to replace. The gray-haired man fell on his knees by the shattered roof ridge. When he saw it was past mending, he buried his face in his hands and began to sob.

"Och, ochone, Bart, lad," mumbled Alisdair. "A stout log is bound to wash ashore soon or late. Till then, if I have a roof, you'll share it."

"Ours, too, Bart," vowed the oldest man of all. The three lusty yellow-haired men who'd helped move his roof ridge were his sons by the look of them, and nodded agreement at their elder's words.

The owner of the third sound timber put his hand on the kneeling man's shoulder. "Your grandparents are my wife's as well, Bart. They can bide with us. If we do well with the herring this summer, maybe we can all help a bit and buy a fine new fir timber for you in Stornoway."

"Come on to your soup," Meg urged.

"Aye." Old Diarmid cleared his throat gruffly. "I've been saving some good uisge-beatha. It's time for a sip, I'm thinking. Come your ways in, lads, and a hundred thousand welcomes!"

There was never any argument over accepting the evicted crofters. Such dispute as there was hinged on how many cows and sheep could be allowed without running over Ardan's prescribed share of the Bernera grazings, and how much cropland could be spared. Part of Christy's wage was grazing for one cow and a kale-yard. She'd never claimed these but now she yielded the rights to the homeless.

One cow had plunged to her death from the cliffs last summer. One had died during the winter and Ardan was allowed two cows more than the villagers possessed, and ten more sheep. "I think the Tobson folks, too, have fewer beasts than their share," said Lachlan. "They should be glad to grant the grazing to you if you pay part of their rent."

In two days, it was settled. The incomers could have two large kaleyards, build sufficient lazybeds for their potatoes on the stonier ground that was presently uncultivated, and they would share in the work and harvest of grain crops. They would bring their six best cows and twenty ewes, sharing the Ardan ram.

" 'Tis a good bargain for us, too," said Hugh MacLeod at the ceilidh held the night before the new villagers went back for their livestock, gear, and families. "Your sharing the rents helps forbye and we can fine use twelve more husky men at the peats and plowing and other work."

"Aye, but you'll first be helping us build our houses," Alisdair reminded him. "It will take us a while to catch up——not that we ever can!"

"Wheesht, man," said Diarmid. "Don't we know too well that we could stand in your brogues? While you're gone, we can get a start at laying up your walls."

Somehow, the people of Ardan did, though it was a busy time for them. Stone by stone the double walls of the first house rose, the core filled in with earth and rubble. The incomers returned in time to link rafters with tie beams, place the roof ridge, and cover the timbers with chunks of heathery sod that overlapped like fish scales. The thatch of marram grass and rushes was secured by fishing nets weighted at the sides with stones. Before next winter a byre and barn would be added but for now longtime Ardan crofters and incomers labored hard to build two other dwellings while sowing oats and planting potatoes.

Christy had six more pupils. None could read or write, so she turned teaching the younger bairns over to Donald while she worked hard with the older newcomers. Fortunately, they wanted to catch up with their friends and studied relentlessly till noon, when she dismissed the older children to help with the building. After school, she carried stones or thatch till dark.

She had her arms full of marram grass one afternoon when a strange boat landed. While the crew waited, James MacRae, the ground officer, came up the shore to Ardan, his burly shoulders hunched as if he dreaded his errand.

"Building houses for landless folk, be you?" he demanded, halting by the last of the new houses, which was just getting its thatch. "You may not be so ready to share when you hear Mr. Munro's instructions."

"Instructions?" echoed Lachlan. "Now what would he be instructing us about? The wall is sound all along our mainland grazings."

MacRae grimaced. "Aye. You built a good wall. I'll not deny that, nor that you've maintained it. But—och, it butters no bannocks to make a long story of it though I wish I didn't have the telling."

"What, man?" asked old Diarmid.

Macrae sighed and looked miserable. "Mr. Munro is taking the Earshader grazing from Bernera. You may have Haclete Farm instead, here on the island."

Stunned, the villagers gazed at each other before they advanced on the ground officer. "Say you're jesting, Mr. MacRae," said Hugh MacLeod.

"I wish I could."

"But we signed a paper!" Lachlan knotted his fists and his eyes blazed. "It said we would have those grazings if we built the wall so long as we paid our rents! And you know well they are paid."

"Aye." MacRae lifted a helpless shoulder. "I told Mr. Munro this was not fair, not after you built that wall only two years ago. But he will have the land for deer forest."

"He won't!" cried Lachlan. "There was a paper signed!"

"And we lost a month's fishing to build that infernal wall!" growled Murdo Nicolson, Meg's husband.

"What can you do?" asked the ground officer. "Listen, Haclete's a grassy big farm. Better take it."

"It's not big enough for Bernera's livestock," protested Diarmid. "You know that, Mr. MacRae."

"I know that. But if you refuse to take Haclete in place of Earshader, Mr. Munro may evict you completely."

A roar went up at that. MacRae retreated a few steps but said doggedly, "The factor is set on this. I'm main sorry, but if you cause trouble, you'll suffer for it. Take a few days to think it over."

The crofters looked at one another. Finally Lachlan said, "I think I speak for all. We will not trade our grazings."

"I fear it will be the worse for you." MacRae waited. When no one spoke, he went back to the boat, head bowed.

"What shall we do?" wailed Meg Nicolson, catching her husband by the shoulders.

He gave her a hug and kissed her cheek. "Why, right now, lass, we'll finish thatching your cousin's roof. And then we'll visit Tobson and Breasclete and Kirkibost and see if they agree with us."

"Red Donald may send constables!"

"He might. But there's that paper we signed. It says we have a right to those grazings." Murdo looked hopefully at Christy. "What do you think, Miss Christy?"

"With luck, we'll make noise loud enough to reach Sir James's ears. Times have changed since those clearances at Sollas and Greenyards when constables broke women's heads." A blinding hope flashed into her mind. "I'll write a letter to David Mac-Leod MacDonald in Inverness, the lawyer, Mairi Mór's son. If he can, he'll help us. And so will she."

"That will be grand," said Alasdair MacAulay. "Unless I

greatly miss my guess, we're going to need all the help there is, God's above all.''

''Meanwhile,'' said Diarmid, ''let's fasten down your roof.''

That night, Christy wrote to David and to Mairi. Next morning, Lachlan and his crew took the letters to the nearest post office at Callanish, a village not far from the Stones. When Lachlan returned, he handed Christy a letter from David that had been at Callanish for several weeks. To her great surprise, there was also a letter from Alison. Meg Nicolson had a letter from her aunt in Canada and Lachlan, frowning, managed to spell out his letter from a cousin who had emigrated to Australia a few years before.

Christy's hand trembled as she opened David's letter. She trembled all over when she read the first words.

> Alison has killed herself. Poor little lass, she has never been right since the baby died. I tried to comfort her but I fear I didn't do enough. The doctor had prescribed laudanum for her nerves—she could not sleep—and she used it to end her life. There must have been a way I could have prevented this. I can never forgive myself. Her poor father is heartbroken. I feel I've repaid him ill for all his kindness.

Numbly, chilled as if her blood had turned to ice, Christy opened the other letter. Alison's handwriting was large and childish, looped with curlicues and exaggerated capitals.

> I can't go to God with this on my conscience but I can't tell David or Daddy. It would kill Daddy. I've brought him enough sorrow. But if David thinks he's somehow to blame for what I'm going to do, then tell him the truth, Christy. Tell him why I can't go on. David's helped all he could. It's not his fault. I hope he will be happy someday.
>
> I killed my baby. Even as I write this, I can't believe it, but I did. He looked like Uncle. Every time the poor mite laughed, he looked even more like that awful old man. One

day, he kept laughing. I screamed at him to stop but he didn't. I pulled the covers over his head and held him while he kicked. Then he was quiet, so quiet. When I looked, I knew he was dead.

The terrible thing is that I wasn't sorry. I was glad, glad I had killed that much of Uncle. I still am. But I dream about the baby. He laughs and laughs and grows till he's big as Uncle and then he starts after me. Wherever I run, he's right behind. I can't bear it any longer. I have some sleeping medicine. I'm going to take a lot of it and lie down. I know I can't go to heaven but pray for me, pray I will sleep and sleep and somehow be in my mother's arms and never have bad dreams again.

Christy left Donald in charge of the school and hurried to walk along the shore. Poor little butterfly with maimed crushed wings! What a nightmare her life had become, hating her own baby—yet how could she love it? She must have been almost insane.

No wonder David hadn't written about their life. It must have been terrible, but at least he'd had his work. His body had not been violated and forced to bear the result of that shame. And he was alive. He was free now. Even in her horrified grief, Christy couldn't keep from thinking that. He blamed himself now but that was nonsense. In time—

Guilt flooded Christy. She couldn't keep from hoping that she and David could finally have a life together, that their long-suppressed love could come to full flower, but if she could bring Alison back to a comfortable life by renouncing David absolutely and forever, she would do that. She owed the sad little ghost its due of mourning and regret and David must heal.

If Christy could possibly avoid it, she didn't want anyone else to know what Alison had admitted. It would seem a betrayal of the poor girl's confidence and could only add to her father's and David's horror and grief. For now, Christy would be David's friend as she had been all their lives, especially since he fell. The future must work itself out.

What answer would David send to her message about Munro's flouting of his agreement with the crofters? It would be weeks before she could expect an answer. Mairi's response might take even longer, since Stornoway was the nearest post office to Clanna and months often passed before letters were sent or collected.

Red Donald himself came to Bernera that week. He summoned all the crofters to meet him at Haclete Farm. His red hair was grayer and his paunch and jowls sagged more heavily than when Christy had last seen him, riding fast to scatter the relief fund he'd stolen from them to the astonished widows of Ness.

Eleven years ago! She had only been thirteen then. Would he recognize her? She hoped not. He was famed for his grudges and detested Mairi Mór because Sir James had bid him leave Clanna in peace so long as the rent was punctual. Now he sat on a stone bench outside the farmhouse and put on a benevolent smile for the crofters who filled the yard. Save for the Ardan newcomers who thought it best not to draw the factor's attention, the able-bodied men of the fifty-six families of Bernera were there, and many of the women.

Munro waved an expansive hand at the greening fields that stretched on all sides. "Look, I am offering you this fine farm in place of grazings that require you to cross your beasts back and forth to the mainland. It is a favor I am doing you."

"We thank you, sir," said Angus MacDonald respectfully. "Haclete is a good farm. But it cannot supply grazing to all Bernera's animals."

"Then you would be wise to reduce your cows and sheep to what Haclete can pasture."

"What of the paper, sir?" asked Hugh MacLeod. "What of the paper granting us Earshader grazings if we would build the wall?"

"What paper?" Munro glared at the piper. "I remember no paper."

"We signed it, sir." The other crofters nodded and murmured approval of Hugh's words. "Mr. James MacRae, the ground officer, said he would give it to you."

Munro reddened. "There is no paper!"

Angus threw back his head. "There is, Mr. Munro—or was."

The factor slammed his fist on his knee. "Paper or no, like it or no, you must keep your animals on Bernera."

"It is less than two years since we had to give up our Cuallin pastures," protested a young man from Kirkibost. "They had been ours time out of mind. The Earshader grazings were not as good but we resolved to be content with them."

"Well, now you must be content with Haclete."

No one answered. Munro's black eyes raked over the stony faces. "This is your last opportunity to be sensible. Will you accept this farm and agree to keep your livestock on Bernera?"

No one answered. Red Donald rose angrily to his feet. "Since you're not content with your island, I'll have you off of it. You'll be served with writs of eviction within the week!"

Ever since she had fearfully encountered the factor about Chul's killing those many years ago, Munro loomed in Christy's mind as the embodiment of ruthless power. The laird, James Matheson, could be kind, as proved by his treatment of Mairi Mór and Clanna. He had poured a fortune into building roads, draining bogs, improving Stornoway harbor, supplying a regular steamship link to the mainland, building paraffin and brick factories, and otherwise attempting to bring prosperity to the island he had purchased thirty years ago. Aging, and disappointed in the results of his efforts, he spent less time on Lewis and left the management of the island almost entirely to Munro, whose tyranny had increased each year he had been factor, twenty of them.

Christy feared Munro with more than her own dread. She

shrank from him with the bred-in-the-bone trepidation of crofter folk oppressed by his like for generations, perhaps with the very fear of her own young mother cast out to wander and die on the Uist coast. As when she held Shenachie, she sometimes felt possessed by those who cherished and played the harp before, Christy now was almost overwhelmed with the sick horror of the countless islanders this man had abused and driven away.

She was gripped with their fear and despair, but she had to speak for them. Stepping forward on legs that tried to refuse to obey her, Christy swallowed and got no sound the first time she opened her mouth. When her voice did come, it sounded overloud.

"Mr. Munro, the tenants of Bernera do have a written agreement with the estate that secures to them the Earshader grazings. Mr. MacRae brought the document. Each man of our township signed it. For those who made a mark, I wrote their names beside it."

Red Donald swung toward her, his corpulent body seeming to swell even larger. His eyes bored into her, showed a sudden glint of recognition. "Och, the changeling of that riot-making troublous Mairi MacLeod MacDonald Ericson! I had hoped you gone over the ocean or at the bottom of it. So you're the root of this impudence!"

Angus moved as if to shield her. "Indeed, sir, Mistress MacLeod took no part in our decision to remind you of our agreement with the estate and beseech you to honor it."

"You may not think so. But like that bothersome Mairi Mór with her harp and singing, I'm bound this one infects those luckless enough to be around her."

Lachlan also drew protectively close. "Sir, Mistress MacLeod is a grand teacher and—"

"Aye! A teacher of rebellion and foolish clatter of ancient clan rights!" Munro glowered at all of them. "This island was bought by Sir James Matheson for one hundred and ninety thousand pounds. He has since spent upwards of two hundred and fifty thousand pounds improving it. He owns every stone, every shell, every grain of sand. You walk the land only by his sufferance. It is my duty to protect his interests. It is not to his interest to harbor seditionists.'' The factor pointed his walking stick at Christy. ''And you, you nameless meddler, you bit of human driftwood, give me the least excuse and I'll have you in the tolbooth!''

He stormed inside the farmhouse. The crofters glanced about at one another in stunned dismay. A white-haired man from Tobson shifted his feet and spoke almost beneath his breath. ''Where can we go if we're evicted? If we beg the Shah's pardon and accept this farm, perhaps he'll let us bide.''

A few nodded. Anything they might have argued was drowned out by a chorus of indignation. Angus spoke above it in a ringing voice. ''It will take constables or soldiers to put me off my croft and I will fight them as long as I can stand! This is past bearing, lads!''

''It is,'' cried Lachlan. ''Two long walls we have built to keep some mainland grazing. Now we are to be turned out again to add to that American's deer forest!''

''Sir James paid money for the island,'' quavered old Diarmid. ''But are the bones of his people here, has their flesh for centuries gone back into the soil?''

''We cannot win,'' said Hugh, standing close and comforting to his father. ''But we must fight for our rights so our sons will not be shamed by us.'' He was, Christy knew, thinking of bright young Donald.

Angus shrugged. ''Let's go our ways home, then, and see what the Shah will do. For my part, I intend to take my livestock to Earshader soon and, when the herring come, start with the fishing.''

Hugh managed to grin. ''I wish I'd brought my pipes. 'Tis a war tune we need!''

''No doubt you'll get to skirl it,'' said Lachlan. ''But for now let's tramp home and sow our oats.''

XVI

Red Donald was not slow in carrying out his threat. Late in March, Ardan folk were sowing oats and school had turned out for the ten o'clock break when two lads came running over the moor from Tobson with the news that Sheriff's Officer Colin MacLennan, Ground Officer James MacRae, and a customs official had landed their boat near Breasclete, served summonses of eviction on crofters there, and were now doing the same in Tobson. They would come to Ardan next. After milk and bannocks, the lads hurried on to warn the crofters at Kirkibost.

"Och, there we have it!" Hugh straightened. "What shall we do?"

"Tear up yon writs and tramp them in the mud!" Lachlan gritted.

"Nay, laddies." Diarmid shook his white head. "Mr. MacRae feels for us in this. No profit in making him wrathy."

"But, Father—" began Hugh.

Diarmid placed a soothing hand on his big son's arm. "Our rents are paid till Whitsun. Even Red Donald won't try to force us out until then. That's seven weeks."

"They'll pass," said Lachlan gloomily.

"Yes, but who knows what may happen by then?" coaxed Meg Nicolson. "Red Donald might burst a blood vessel or choke on one of those hens he steals from crofters."

"Heaven grant it," her cousin Alasdair said with a hardy

laugh. "The Shah's had some of us out of one township this year. That's enough."

"More than enough." Hugh the piper glanced around at his neighbors. "We'll take the writs, then, with no manner of fuss, but we will not flit."

"Not till we're dragged out," said Lachlan.

"I've written to a lawyer, David MacDonald, Mairi Mór's son," put in Christy. "He may know of some way to enforce that agreement you signed, though it seems to have disappeared. Still, I should hope that all of us swearing that the paper existed should carry some weight in court."

"Court?" frowned Hugh. "Forbye, lass, never has a court and the law been for us crofters. Law and lawyers serve the rich."

"Not David," said Christy. "Can you think that of a son of Mairi Mór?"

No one answered, but Christy could see the people were justifiably afraid of law, courts, and lawyers. It was wrong, so wrong, that the law did not shield the poor and powerless who most needed its protection. The law must change, but even now a dedicated and able lawyer should find a way to prevent such an outrage.

She called the children back to school just as the three officials came legging it over the slope. Later, she heard how they grumbled that three Tobson men were away and would have to be served writs next morning. It was dusky when they departed for Haclete Farm, where they would spend the night, and it was dusky on the following evening when Angus MacDonald and a dozen other Tobson men stopped in Ardan.

Invited into the schoolhouse, they were refreshed with food and drink brought by the Ardan women. It was quite a story they had to tell, some of them like Angus in rollicking high spirits, others considerably worried.

"We didn't put the young ones up to it," said Angus. "But some of the lads and lassies followed the officers. After the men

left here and were bound for Haclete, the gloaming let the youngsters get close enough to pelt the sheriff and his friends with bits of
turf—and perhaps a rock or two. The officers yelled at the imps,
of course—''

He was interrupted by muscular, brown-haired Neil Ramsey,
who was not laughing. ''Sheriff MacLennan shouted that if he had
his gun, many a mother would mourn her son that night. A fine
thing, threatening bairns, my ten-year-old Adam among them.''

''The sheriff's bellowing only made the clods fly faster and
thicker,'' shrugged Angus. ''The officers forgot their dignity. They
were running when they got to Haclete, the fastest they've moved
in years, I'll be bound.''

''They were in foul temper when they tramped back to Tobson to serve the three men they'd missed the day before.'' Rory
Nicolson was a cousin of Murdo Nicolson and had the same red
hair and freckles. ''The sheriff's deputy told one of the men he was
summonsing that next time he came to Bernera we could be sure
he'd bring his gun and it would be the worse for anyone, bairn or
grandsire, who gave him trouble.''

''Forbye, we came up from the fields and talked it over after
the officers were gone,'' said Angus. ''We decided to ask the sheriff if it was true he'd said he'd bring a gun against us. We caught up
with them near Breasclete where their boat was and stood in their
way. I asked the sheriff if he was the fellow who was threatening us
with a gun.''

''He turned white as shell sand and shouted at us to get out of
the road.'' Neil grinned at the memory. ''He was blustering about
what he and the law would do, but he had nothing to say about his
gun. Angus here tore his oilskin—''

'' 'Twas not my fault. It was over his arm and when I laid my
hand on him, he jerked the coat away so hard he ripped it.''

''Ground Officer MacRae advised us to go home,'' said
Rory. ''We told him our business was not with him, but with the
sheriff's deputy.''

"At the end," concluded Angus, "MacLennan promised he would never come back to Bernera to serve eviction summonses."

"You did finely," said Hugh MacLeod. "But be sure we'll hear more of this from Red Donald."

"He's already summonsed us out of Earshader and Bernera." Angus thrust back his yellow hair. "What more can he do?"

"There's prison," said Diarmid.

Rory gave a reckless laugh. "It's worth whatever comes to have seen MacLennan quake in his boots and vow to serve us no more writs."

"Sure as white milk comes from black cows, the Shah will hale some of you into court," predicted Hugh. "However, men, we'll stand behind you. What you dared today deserves a skirl of the pipes." He smiled at Christy. "Will you take the plaid off your harp, lass?"

"Indeed I will." She tuned the harp and the strings seemed to call their eagerness. It was a rare sight, one that sent her blood tingling, crofters elated because they'd faced down Red Donald's henchmen and were determined to hold out against eviction. How she wished Mairi Mór could see it!

Laughing proudly, Christy swept her fingers across the strings. "Dear friends and neighbors, let's make music for this day when crofters ran three officers out of Bernera!"

Shenachie rejoiced with the pipes. It was easy to fancy that hundreds of years rolled back, that this was the time of music in Highlands and islands before Culloden with the chief among his clanna, his kinfolk, who all had acknowledged rights to croplands and grazings.

Yes, there were bloody clan feuds then, and wicked doings, but the chief lived among his people and could not wrong them without losing their loyalty and service. His obligations were equal to his rewards. But since the breaking of the clans and England's unceasing efforts to destroy the ancient fabric of Gaelic society, there were few hereditary chieftains left, and most of them considered only how to wring the utmost farthing from their estates.

> *One day will come justice. Isle men will take deer*
> *from parks made of their fathers' fields. Their sheep*
> *and cattle will graze on the moorland and on the*
> *flowery machair . . ."*

Shenachie and Christy sang the song of Mairi Mór. Looking around at the faces, old, young, smooth, withered, lit by glowing peats, Christy felt a warm melting of some hard, lonely kernel in her heart. Mairi Mór might never love her because of the baby on the hill. David, after Alison, might not love her, either. But she was not a waif. These people were her clanna, her family won through faith and unremitting work.

If she could have in that moment, she would have knelt at the Stones.

On guard against reprisals, the crofters cut their peats. Several weeks passed and nothing was heard or seen from Red Donald. One night when the villagers were gathered in the school, Hugh said hopefully, "Maybe he's decided to leave us in peace because of the wall, the agreement and all."

"Not he!" Lachlan curled his lip. "Doubtless he thinks we'll flit at Whitsuntide the middle of May, so why should he bother with a pack of troublesome crofters?"

"We need to take the beasts to their summer grazings," said Murdo Nicolson.

His cousin by marriage, big, blond Alasdair nodded. "And we must go after the herring."

To her confused embarrassment, they all turned to Christy. "What do you think we should do, lass?" Hugh asked.

They wanted her advice because she had seen more of the

world than they, was educated, and Mairi Mór's fosterling. Christy turned the question back. "What do you think you should do?"

"Take our beasts to Earshader!" said Lachlan.

"And then follow the herring," proposed gray-haired Bart MacKenzie, he whose roof timbers had broken. His household were living with their old neighbors in the three houses raised that spring but he was eager to buy a new roof ridge and have his own hearth by winter.

"I think we should go on as if this eviction foolishness had never happened." Hugh nodded for emphasis.

"But what of the rents?" cried his wife, Ellen. Young Donald had his dark hair from her and eyebrows winging above blue eyes. She nursed her new baby under cover of her shoulder plaid. "If we don't pay them, we'll be evicted sure and certain!"

"The best thing might be to give the rents to the ground officer, James MacRae, at Whitsun," suggested Christy.

"But the Tobson lads and lassies threw clods at him!" protested Meg.

"Aye, but Mr. MacRae himself said it was a shame to take away the Earshader grazings. He won't do anything to lose his position, but would it be his fault if the rents were left in a bag at his door with a letter asking him to hand the money over to Red Donald if he will accept it, or hold it until the matter is settled? The factor might still push for eviction, but he couldn't say your rents were in arrears."

Amidst the nods and murmurs of approval, Hugh said, "If it's agreed then, when we take our beasts to Earshader, we'll also take the rents." He grinned. "It's the first time, I'll wager, that crofters ever paid their rents a whole month early!"

The cattle had been out of their byres long enough to regain their strength as they grazed on the fresh green herbage. Except for a few cows to supply milk, the cattle and sheep were taken across to the walled pastures, and Hugh deposited the rents for all Bernera with James MacRae.

The ground officer said he wanted no part in the trouble between Red Donald and the crofters but he said that when the rents were due, he would offer them to Munro. If the factor refused them, MacRae was finally persuaded to hold the money until the crofters asked for it. He warned them that reluctant as he would be, if Munro insisted on evictions, the ground officer would have to take part.

Herring were moving out of the coastal waters and the men followed them, staying in crude shelters along the shore. They gutted and headed the fish and took them to Stornoway to the curers. Bernera fishermen didn't have the large boats, as Clanna did, that would allow them to pursue the herring into the North Sea, so they would come home after the great shoals of herring moved north into deeper waters.

Hugh MacLeod spoke for all the men as he kissed his wife and baby farewell. "It pains me to leave you, lass. If the Shah tries to carry out his summons, I want to be here."

"Och, he'll make noise about it first." Small, slender Ellen patted her brawny husband's cheek. "It could drag on for months."

"Don't worry, Father." Donald stood straight as he could and managed to look as tall as his mother. "I'll take care of mama and the baby."

"I doubt Red Donald will risk putting women and bairns out on the moor while their men are gone," said Christy. "That was done in the old days. It was done to Mairi Mór. But just as what people on the mainland thought made the factor hand back the relief fund to the Ness widows, what they think will make him a bit more careful in what he does here."

"May you be right!" said Hugh. "Have you heard aught from Mairi Mór's lawyer son?"

"Not yet. But I'm sure to soon."

Indeed, Christy was troubled that no word had come from David. Was he so distressed about Alison that he could think of nothing else? She couldn't imagine David taking to drink, but grieved men often did.

Her worry grew in spite of the joyful soaring of larks, the cartwheels of ecstatic peewits, and green moors flowering with whortleberries, crowberries, orchids, and masses of bogbeans with petals rosy-hued on the outside and white within. The machair along the coast bloomed with daisies that closed and turned pink at a cool wind. This was where the remaining cows fed, and their milk and breath smelled of the flowers.

Late one shining blue evening, Christy was about to call her young lodgers to supper when she saw a man coming up from the shore. A man on crutches.

"David!" She flew to meet him, but when she came close, when she saw the rigid set of his lean face, the remoteness in his eyes, her outstretched arms fell to her sides.

He didn't look like David at all! A silver plume waved back from each temple. Grooves at the corners of his mouth seemed to draw his lips straighter and tighter. He looked ten years older than his twenty-eight years. *Oh my laddie! Why must these things happen to you? First the crippling, your father and Chul lost so cruelly, and now Alison . . .*

Christy's first memories were of trotting in David's careless, high-hearted wake. She had thought him all things wonderful, a belief fortified when he pulled her out of a bog or up a rock she couldn't conquer alone. Fleetest of all his band he had been, the best at shinty, the most agile on the cliffs. For a moment, she couldn't bear the sight of his crutches or the hurt lines of his face.

She closed her eyes. Again she saw him running along the cliffs. As he had over fifteen years ago, he seemed to fly for a moment. Then he fell, he lay among the rocks like a bird with broken wings. Rebellious grief overwhelmed her.

Why had it happened? Why? She saw him again on the slope with Chul, watching the beasts while Alai and Seana led the merry throng that chased from houses to sea to moor. And then Chul—

beloved funny Chul with his spotted face and frisking tail, who had followed David even before she had—Chul was shot. Now Alison—

Stop it! she commanded herself. Stop it at once! He didn't die in that fall, he wasn't paralyzed. He's become a handsome, distinguished lawyer and can move in the great world and speak for the crofters. But still her heart wept, Oh, my laddie!

"Davie, you've come!" She didn't embrace him but permitted herself to kiss his cheek. After all, she was his foster sister. "You got my letter?"

He nodded. "That's why I've come."

"I—I'm mortal sorry about Alison—"

"I can't talk about it." His tone was harsh. "What has been happening here? I see that at least the Ardan folk haven't been evicted."

"No, but Red Donald summonsed every crofter on Bernera out of the Earshader grazings and off the island as well." She told him all that had happened and that the crofters were determined to resist eviction. "Have you been to see your mother?"

"Aye. She asked me to tell you that she went to see Sir James about the Earshader grazings but he was away. If the Shah threatens forcible eviction, she wants to know, for she'll come then, with her harp."

"And be trampled by constables as she was at Sollas and Greenyards?"

"She thinks that cannot happen again. The minds and hearts of most people of all classes have turned against brutal evictions. If there's enough clamor, she thinks Munro will fear to proceed. Munro knows that Sir James is fond of my mother and held father in esteem."

"Well, that is good news! Most of the men are off fishing, but you must come up and tell our folk about it. First, though, you'll have your supper. What about your boatmen?"

"They'd welcome some bannocks, but they want to get back to Callanish tonight."

One of the husky young men brought David's bag to the school. They had their bannocks and buttermilk and took their leave, agreeing to return for David next day after they put out their lobster traps.

"You must leave so soon?" Christy asked.

Not only had it been nine years since she'd seen him, but she couldn't bear for him to leave before she found in him something of the old David, something of the blithe laddie she had tagged across the moors.

His smile was bleak, but at least it changed the frozen set of his features. "I have a deal of work before me, Christy."

"What?"

For the first time, his eyes lost that distant chill. His smile became less of a grimace. "I borrowed Gillie from mother. He's going to carry me about the townships to collect evidence about the Shah, and Dugald Craigie, and other gamekeepers while I'm at it."

"Evidence?" A fine, lawyerly word, that. "What will you do with it?"

At last his smile was genuine. "I'm going to bring charges against Red Donald Munro."

Dumbstruck at the notion, it was a moment before Christy could say, "You mean to have him in court?"

"Exactly."

"But——but he's the procurator fiscal! 'Tis *he* who brings charges!"

"Yes, and then tries them as baron baillie or justice of the peace. I know all about the seventeen offices he holds, with his clerk taking the less important ones. That's why he's been able to rule Lewis and grind the people for a score of years."

Christy said forlornly, "I don't see how you can bring him

into court since he controls the law. Why, he's even the commander of the island's volunteer force."

"My dear, I have been studying the law." Casual as the endearment was, Christy's devastated heart warmed and leaped at it. His deep well-modulated voice moved like sunlight through her blood. "Munro is guilty of a good deal more than compelling crofters to keep his kitchen in hens."

"He is indeed, but—"

"I know the sheriff of the shire of Inverness, which includes Lewis. If I can put together a firmly grounded indisputable case against Munro, the sheriff has promised to come to Stornoway and hear it."

"Oh, Davie!" She started to throw her arms around him, but his posture checked her. It was as if he braced himself to endure an unwelcome assault. Stricken, her first joy quenched, she said in as hearty a tone as she could manage, "That's grand news. But in your study of law, can you name a case where the court took the part of crofters against a laird or factor?"

"No. But I believe I can condemn Red Donald out of his own mouth. If we win this case, it will not be the last even with present laws, which give all protection to landlords and none to their tenants." His voice and eyes kindled. "But there will be a law for tenants, lass, a law made by Parliament. I would guess it will come in the next ten years, sooner if Gladstone can ward off Disraeli's attacks and stay prime minister."

It dizzied her to hear him speak so authoritatively of the most powerful men in Great Britain. "What makes you so sure?"

"I've talked several times with Gladstone. His mother is from this island, so he has feeling for it, and indeed, for the common people, the poor and oppressed. He's promised to send a commission to the Highlands and islands to question the crofters, see how they live, and prepare a report to Parliament along with recommendations."

"Do you know what these will be?"

"I've discussed reforms with the prime minister, his advisers, and several members of Parliament who will work for such legislation. The main points will be security in tenure so long as the rent is paid—and the rents, which are still set at the highs they reached during the kelp boom, will be examined by an independent board and set at a reasonable figure. A crofter will be able to leave the croft to a blood relative. If he decides to vacate, he shall be compensated for buildings and improvements made by him or his forebears."

Christy drew a deep breath. "It sounds too wonderful to be true! That a laird won't be able to make tenants flit at his will! That Red Donald and his ilk won't be able to terrorize folk by threatening to take their land! Why, Davie, 'tis a dream!"

"A dream that will be real, lass, before my hair's completely white."

"You've told your mother?"

"Of course."

"She must be so proud of you she can scarce contain it."

He laughed and Christy blessed the sound, though it was far from exuberant. "She hasn't tried to contain her hope and pleasure. God knows she's entitled. Look what she did with Clanna and the other townships she helped through the famines. But for her, there would be few crofters left to benefit from the justice that I know will become law."

"What does Magnus say to her coming to Bernera if there are evictions?"

"Magnus is off trading with the Russians. Anyway, you well know he'd never interfere with what she felt was her duty. He would interfere, mightily, with any man who raised a hand to her."

"You like Magnus?"

"Who could not? There was never a question of his trying to

fill my father's place—with me or my mother. I'm glad she has his worship and strength and I'm glad they have their twins.''

"The twins must be seven now.''

"Aye. Proper Vikings, the pair of them, bonnie lass and bold laddie.'' He smiled a bit regretfully and shrugged. "I hope Mother doesn't guess, but though I'm fond of the youngsters, I cannot feel a brother to them. An uncle, perhaps, not overly doting.''

"You were at school when they were born,'' she pointed out. "It's little you've seen of them, to be sure.''

"You were better than a sister, Christy. You were my dearest friend.''

Were? But of course he had many friends now, gentlemen he'd met through his Great-uncle Roderick and his mentor and father-in-law, Duncan Stewart. At least he hadn't said she was his sister. That was some comfort. "Now, Christy,'' he said into the deepening silence, "tell me more about this agreement that you witnessed, the one guaranteeing the Earshader grazings.''

When she finished, he said, "It's a pity we don't have a copy of that paper, but the testimony of thirty-four crofters should outweigh Munro's word before any fair judge. If Ground Officer Mac-Rae will testify that the document exists and that he gave it to the Shah, there can be no doubt that the factor broke a written contract. Still, I'll travel around collecting all the facts I can against Munro. I want this to be more than a case against one rapacious and arrogant petty tyrant. It must be a case against the whole wicked system that denies a crofter the right to work his land in peace and confidence that he and his heirs can enjoy the fruit of his labor.''

"Half the crofters are women,'' Christy reminded him.

Again, he smiled. If he smiled often enough, perhaps his face would lose that masklike rigidity. "The greatest crofter is Mairi Mór and well I know it. But have mercy, lass. One battle at a time.''

"This battle's enough for now, but I won't let you forget

that women deserve the law's protection, too. Why, even in America, women can't vote though former slaves can. And—''

"Please, may I have some dinner?" He spoke so plaintively that she had to laugh and ladled out his soup before she went to the door and called the children in.

XVII

Christy's heart swelled with pride as David explained to her neighbors what he intended to do. "Och," said old Diarmid MacLeod. "Wouldn't it be grand to put yon wicked Munro on trial, let the world know his misdeeds?" He shook his white head ruefully. " 'Tis hard to imagine it might come to pass, laddie."

"We'll pray it will." Blind Honora Hardy, Lachlan's mother, held wee Elspeth on her lap. "Och, it would seem like heaven to live without Red Donald over us!"

David got out a notebook and pencil. "Will you tell me all about this trouble with the Earshader grazings?"

"Aye," said Diarmid. "And Honora and I remember how, twenty years before we were fobbed off with Earshader, we were deprived of a big part of our Cuallin grazings and had to build a great long wall to keep our cattle out of their old pastures."

"My husband helped build that wall," quavered Honora. "He hurt his back moving stones. Never a step did he take after that without paining."

"When a sheep or cow somehow strayed around the wall, it was impounded and we had to pay dear to get the creature back," said Diarmid.

"All folk in Uig parish have to use the mill at Callanish," Meg Nicolson sighed. "It's far for many, and for us it means getting the crop across Loch Roag, so we use our querns. But we still have to pay the value of every twelfth peck to the mill."

"And we're charged for making and maintaining roads we never use," put in Ellen MacLeod, rocking her baby who was fretful with cutting teeth.

David filled his notebook with the Ardan folks' miseries. It was late before the litany ended. Diarmid covered a mighty yawn. "Could we have a song or two, Miss Christy?"

She was shy of playing before this different, much-changed David. When she hesitated, he glanced up from his notes. For just the flash of an instant, his gray-blue eyes had a sheen of gold, seemed really to behold her, but the warmth was gone so quickly that she thought it a trick of the flickering cruisies.

"If you're not too weary, lass, it would be good to hear you play." He didn't look at her as he said it but a hint from him was enough.

Out Shenachie came from beneath the plaid. Christy sang to David what she could never say. *"I would go between you and the rock, I would go between you and the wind, I would go between you and death where ravens would make a cry . . ."*

Diarmid and Honora sang of a terrible shipwreck on Bernera's shore. Young Donald recited from Robbie Burns. Ellen and Meg asked riddles. When it came David's turn, he gave several poems in Gaelic and ended with a ringing indictment of the chamberlain of Lewis, Donald Munro.

> Then shall the crawling maggot praise
> The bulkiness of your carcass . . .
> It will say, 'Here is a corpulent body
> Whom the crevice creatures shall enjoy
> Since he beggared hundreds
> To fatten himself for me.' "

"Now that be God's truth!" cried Diarmid. "Did you write those words, laddie?"

"I wish I had. They are the work of John Smith of Earshader.

He's a young man who was studying medicine when tuberculosis made him return to his village. He cannot have much time left, but his verse will live as long as there's a Gaelic language.''

"I must go to see him," Diarmid vowed. "I must shake the hand of the poet who dared tell Munro what his end will be. And I must take your hand, too, David MacLeod MacDonald, for what you are doing for us.''

The old man shook David's hand as he went out. The women did the same, Honora reaching up to kiss him and smooth his hair. "May I touch your face, dear man?" the blind woman asked. "I would like to know what you look like."

At his consent, she traced his features, slowly, carefully. "Och, laddie! 'Tis great sorrow draws your mouth tight and furrows your bonnie forehead and hardens your jaw. And so much bone! You stint your nourishment and sleep, too, belike. Have a care for yourself, m'eudail, as you have for us poor crofter folk."

"You're kind to worry, grandmother," he said. "But truly, I am in excellent health.''

She shook her head till the ruffles of her cap jounced. "You be in sore grief about something, laddie. That aye drags the body down. Better if you weep or rage and let it out.''

He smiled and kissed the withered cheek. "I'll rage at Red Donald, grandmother.''

Still murmuring her distress for him, Honora went out, led by her older granddaughter and carrying the younger. Lachlan had an eye for Grace, the sweet, pretty daughter of Bart MacKenzie. Perhaps the bairns would soon have a new mother.

As the others voiced their thanks and good nights to David, Christy wished she dared speak to him as Honora had—that she dared to touch his face, tenderly knead away the tightness at mouth and eyes and jaw.

Had he been only her foster brother, she could have attempted it. Since she loved him as a woman, she could not take such liberty.

Tormented, she made up his bed on the settle, softening it with extra blankets and her own pillow. How willingly, joyfully, she would have shared that narrow space! But his silence forbade her to try to breach the walls he had reared around his inner self. She smoored the fire, quickly told him good night, and retreated to the bedroom.

Sharing one box bed with her "boarding" lassies, Nellie and Queenie Morison and Sally MacDonald, she could not sleep. David, her love, her only love, was steps away through the door, but from the distance he imposed between them, he might as well have been in Inverness.

He seemed so *frozen*. When Alison killed herself, had she killed something in him, too? Had he, after all, come to love her? At the sudden thought, a searing blade seemed to pierce Christy deep and twist slowly. She tried to take comfort in that fraction of a moment when gold had warmed the chill of David's eyes, but that might have been a trick of the lamps.

She had thought nothing could be worse than his being married, but this would be much worse, if he were free, yet not free, bound to a dead woman whose clasp could never be broken.

If only she could ask him about his feelings! But he forbade that by his closed expression, the tone of his voice, the way he held himself, like one whose bones have been broken, who fears any motion may bring agony.

He'll be on Lewis for a while, Christy told herself. Maybe he'll change. But knowing David and his unswerving will, she had small hope for that. Several times, a nightmare grasped her, Alison coming toward her with a wild distraught look, holding out the pale corpse of a baby who grinned terribly. Christy was awake enough to shake off the horror, but it was little rest she got and no peace at all. She rose with the first larks and went out in the dim light to walk along the shore till women came to the machair to milk their cows.

Going back to the school, she found David building up the

fire. His bedding was neatly folded. She took a deep breath. "David—" she began. Then the lassies ran in, giggling at something Liam had said. The chance for quiet words was gone—if there had been one.

His boatmen arrived while he was finishing his porridge. They would sail around Bernera to Tobson and then to Breasclete before returning to the shore. With the Bernera crofters' testimony in his notebook, David would journey about the townships on Gillie and then return to Stornoway to compile his evidence.

It was hard to believe that he really might, after twenty years, bring Munro to justice, yet the women crowded around to wish him luck and thank him. "However it goes, laddie," said old Honora, "may you be blessed now and forever for having a care for us." She kissed him and spoke so softly that only those nearest could hear, "May the God of Life heal the pain that is in you and bring you to joy."

"If I bring Munro to an accounting, that will be enough." David's gaze veered past Christy. He got into the boat, and it wasn't long till it vanished around the headland.

It was July when the Ardan men returned. To their relief, they had not been molested when they took their fish to Stornoway. It was late one evening a week later when old Malcolm MacDonald and a crew from Tobson landed their boat and came up to the school where most of the village folk were gathered.

"They've taken my Angus!" Tears glinted in Malcolm's eyes. "We'd settled accounts with the curer and Angus went alone up Cromwell Street on an errand. Some rascallion pointed him out to the constables as one of those who sent the sheriff's officer packing."

"He put up such a fight that they tore the clothes off him," said a younger man. "He's in the tolbooth. We hunted for Mr.

David MacDonald, that canny young lawyer, but the innkeeper said he was gone on one of his jaunterings."

"The porter at the castle wouldn't let us in or even carry a message to Sir James," said Malcolm. "When my lad is brought before yon Red Donald——"

"This is enough and too much, forbye!" Lachlan jumped to his feet and glanced around at his neighbors. "I say we should march on Stornoway, all the men of Bernera! We should demand to see Sir James himself. And if he won't help us, let's take a ship's mast from the harbor and batter down the tolbooth door!"

"That be rioting, lad," warned Diarmid.

"If the Shah has his way, Father, we'll be evicted from our grazings and crofts," said Hugh MacLeod. "Indeed, let us go and make such a noise Sir James will have to hear us! I'll play the pipes to cheer us on the trudge." He turned sheepish and glanced toward his wife. "Ellen——"

"Go!" She cradled her sleeping baby to her heart and gave Hugh a look of great love and pride. "Should you be clapped in the tolbooth, Donald and I can manage as well as Angus MacDonald's wife and bairns."

"I want to march, too!" Donald's blue eyes, often dreamy, were ablaze. Archie Nicolson and the other older boys joined in the plea, but Hugh shook his head.

"Nay, laddies, you must be the men of your families. I'm thinking that even if we win through this moil, there'll be time enough for you to march, and maybe even your sons, before crofters have their rights."

Christy's heart pounded with fear overwhelmed by the sweet fierce taste of seeing these crofters, these oppressed and harassed folk, usually so docile, decide that they would endure no more, that they would fight for their comrade. "I will come, too," she said.

"Och, no, lass!" said Diarmid. "There may be broken heads before the end of this."

"It might help if I speak with Sir James. Long ago, when I was a child, he tried to right a wrong done by his keeper. And Shenachie belongs with you, singing with Hugh's pipes."

Hugh threw back his fair head and laughed. "Now that will make a fine sight and sound! Harps called our folk to battle in olden times before the racket of artillery and guns drowned out the music. Aye, lass. March with us and welcome, but if the constables start swinging their truncheons, you get out of the way. Your skull be no means so thick as ours."

"When David MacDonald returns, he'll defend anyone who needs it," said Christy.

"Belike we'll all need it," said Hugh. "Unless Sir James steps in, Red Donald may call for troops from the mainland to clear us off our lands. But it's time we stood up for one another and made such a clamor that we have to be heard, whatever happens after."

This was a far cry from what Christy knew of Sollas and Greenyards, where most of the men hid away while their women confronted the constables. True, the women had told them to vanish, because in the general way, constables were less likely to beat women than men. Now, in Bernera, fifteen years after Mairi was struck down at Greenyards, the men were determined to defy the chamberlain of Lewis, who held their fate in his hands.

Christy herself could not have urged the Bernera men to risk long prison terms. That they were willing, even eager, to challenge Red Donald proclaimed their desperation louder than any words.

Would it move Sir James or anger him? She brought food and drink for the Tobson men while the expedition was planned with the long-suppressed almost joyful vigor of those who have decided on a course from which they cannot retreat.

Donald and Archie were sent off to tell the folk at Breasclete and Kirkibost what had happened and ask them to join the march. It was agreed that next morning, the Bernera men would rendezvous on the beach near Callanish. The Tobson men would stop at Earshader on their way to see if anyone from there would dare to join them.

"The more the merrier," said Hugh, who, because of his pipes, was becoming the leader of the foray. "We'll have to depend on stones and our fists if the constables and militia come at us, but whatever happens to us afterward, we Bernera men are fifty, and we'll have Angus out of jail."

"That we will," pledged Lachlan.

"There be no words to thank you," gulped Malcolm.

Hugh put a bracing hand on the old man's shoulder. "Your son went to jail because, for all of us, he warned off Sheriff's Officer MacLennan and Ground Officer MacRae. It's for ourselves we do this, dear man, as much as for your laddie."

The Tobson men departed. Hugh grinned at Christy. "Well, lass, shall I bring my pipes so we can practice some warlike tunes?"

"Aye," said Christy. She called on Mairi's spirit as she drew the plaid from Shenachie and began to tune the harp. The first notes of "The MacLeod Salute" coursed through her in a calling that made her tremble, that made the Stones loom in her mind.

It was time. Tomorrow, she would go to them.

The men of Callanish shouted their desires to join the force. While the unlikely little army waited for the Tobson group in the village, Christy took Shenachie and walked toward the shrouded promontory where the Stones seemed to move as mists thickened and lightened around them. The plaintive trill of the whimbrel blended with the musical song of its larger relative, the curlew. A cuckoo coughed from a clump of blue moor grass, and Christy remembered that the earliest returning cuckoo of spring was supposed to fly first to Callanish and call among the Stones. As she entered the mists, they seemed to swirl and coalesce into almost palpable forms, shadowy beings thronged about the pillars, surrounding, enclosing her.

Christy was only a little way from the village but the fog muted its sounds. When she turned to look, she could not see the houses, or anything beyond the haze-wreathed aisle stones on either hand. The air was so thick with moisture that her lungs strained to breathe. Were the Stones angry that she had denied them so long, that she, who was not of the blood of those women of the ancient shrine, had come without Mairi's support?

Overwhelmed by panic, Christy embraced her harp protectively. "Gran!" she cried before she could think it was futile to call on one dead so many years. "Gran, help me!"

She heard Gran's unforgettable laughter. "Wheesht, lass! You've taken your time!" For an instant, one of the twining vapors gave a flash of Gran's merry blue eyes, just the hint of her smile. "But you are welcome, a hundred thousand times."

Rays of golden light colored the mists. Christy moved down the aisle to the circle of pillars, which looked like cloaked elders facing the great squared central stone that had a flowing bend to it, as if graceful vapor had hardened to rock.

In the diaphanous haze, Christy caught an image of Mairi and her captain. The mists grew dense. Christy smothered a cry. A young woman, great with child, with Christy's own face, her same tawny eyes and hair, stumbled along a rocky shore. Beyond her, almost obscured by shifting haze, Christy glimpsed the same lass in the strong arms of a brown-haired young man, saw him fight off constables while his sweetheart fled, watched him dragged away and bound, thrown into a ship . . .

Her father. Was he alive across an ocean? Had he even known his darling was with child? Poor lad, poor lassie! Blinded by tears, Christy sank to the earth. Her fingers moved of themselves. Shenachie lamented her parents, and with them, all who had perished of hunger or cold, suffered in the stinking alleys of Glasgow, or died in the pestilential holds of crowded ships. In her playing, Christy vowed never to forget them. Whatever happened with David, she would teach crofter children, work with the people for a better life.

The pipes called to her through the lifting haze. The Tobson men must have arrived. She pressed her forehead to the ancient stone. "Well done, m'eudail," Gran seemed to say. "And now it's time you marched!" Christy rose and went down to the village.

She could scarce believe her eyes. The marchers had swelled to what seemed several hundred and small groups were arriving at every minute. The men from Earshader and other coastal villages must have come by water, for dozens of boats were pulled up on the shore, with more coming.

"It's an army, forbye!" Hugh told her, eyes glowing. "Is not it a wonderful sight, lass? Old men on canes, young ones whose voices still squeak and who lack a hair to their chins!"

A lump rose in Christy's throat. Tears stung her eyelids. Everyone here knew they risked eviction and imprisonment but it might have been a holiday. Those who didn't know one another shook hands. There were many clapped shoulders and even hugs. That many who didn't even know him would take up Angus MacDonald's cause was a marvelous show of comradeship, especially from those who were presently in Red Donald's good graces and in no danger of being summonsed off their crofts so long as they kept to their own business.

This was what Mairi had hoped and worked for, a feeling of unity, of kinship and concern, of being *clanna* in the broader sense, feeling like one people rather than members of one clan.

"There'll be more," Lachlan exulted. "Callanish bairns and women have run to other villages with the word. Give us a tune, Hugh, Miss Christy, and let's be off."

Hugh settled the bag under his arm and set the blow tube to his mouth. The tune of the chanter sprang from beneath his nimble fingers as he launched into "The Flowers of the Forest" and strode forward. Christy, beside him, wove Shenachie's notes around the pipes as Mairi used to do when she played with her Iain. The morning mists vanished as the sun rose higher, sparkling off lochans where yellow iris were in their fullest bloom. Bees and green and blue butterflies swarmed the bell heather. Christy was so exhilarated by the glorious day and the exuberance of the marchers that she played until Hugh stopped.

"I need my breath for tramping," he chuckled. "But, lass, look around you. Here be the old island names, MacLeod, Nicolson, Morison, MacAulay, all descended from the Norse who settled here a thousand years ago and married or buried the Gaels as the Gaels had buried or married the Pictish folk. Here be folk of the old clans alongside those brought in by the Kintail MacKenzies when King Jamie, he that was son to Mary, Queen of Scots, and heired the English throne from the woman who'd had his mother's head struck off—that Jamie Stuart made the chief of the Kintail MacKenzies his justice and commissioner for Lewis—sent him here with fire and sword to hunt down Neil MacLeod, my own far ancestor, who was hanged, you ken, at the Market Cross in Edinburgh and his head stuck on a pike above the Nether Bow Port where his brother Murdo's head had been twelve years before. Year of Our Lord 1613, that was. Anyway, here be MacIvers, MacLennans, MacRaes, and MacKenzies descended from those who helped King Jamie's commissioner take over the island. But here we are with one cause, marching to Stornoway."

"Aye," said Lachlan. " 'Tis something never seen before. But I think it may be seen again—and again—until we have our rights." He said to Christy, "Let me carry your harp till you play again. It's a long tramp over the moors."

It was indeed, and all the way, more crofters hurried to join till the band spread over hillocks and moor like an army, an army in fishermen's jerseys and homemade brogans, drinking from burns and munching on bannocks.

High spirits never flagged. Now and again, Hugh and Christy

played, sometimes together, sometimes singly. When they stopped, someone would start a rowing song or some merry ditty or martial chorus.

The sun had reached its height and was slanting west when old Malcolm MacDonald caught Christy's sleeve. "Wheesht! Lass, use your keen young eyes and tell me! Is that my laddie coming there?"

Christy shielded her eyes, but before she could be sure, Hugh shouted, "Aye, man, 'tis your Angus! Not beaten or in tatters, forbye, but walking along proud as a king with two crowns!"

Malcolm hurried ahead. His son saw him and came running. They embraced as the expedition gathered around, cheering and laughing, full of wonder. Malcolm spoke for them all. "Now how came you out of the tolbooth, laddie, and in new clothes? Did you attack the jailer and strip him bare?"

Angus laughed, glancing at the throng in wonder. "So the word was true! A rumor's run like wildfire through the town that hundreds of crofters were on the way to break me out of yon jail. I thought the Tobson lads, maybe, but—" He shook his head and ducked it as tears sparkled in his eyes before he raised his voice to carry to the most distant man. "Some of you I know from the curers or fairs, but many I never saw before. I thank you, lads, from the roots of my heart, and if ever any of you be clamped in jail, I swear I will aid you if it costs my life!"

He told them how the jailer, on hearing of the marchers, let him wash off the blood and dirt of his struggle with the constables, gave him new clothes to replace his torn ones, and sent him off with the urgent plea to persuade his friends not to mob the tolbooth.

"No need of doing that now you're free," said Hugh. "But we still have some words to speak to Sir James concerning yon Red Donald." He raised his hand for silence and shouted, "What do you say, lads? Shall we tramp on to the castle and lay our wrongs before the laird?"

There was a thunder of "Aye!" and "To the castle!" Angus walked beside his beaming old father. No question of weariness now. Christy and Hugh played till Stornoway came in view, the shining harbor with its crouching Beasts of Holm, and they played to the very porter's lodge of the castle.

A man in constable's garb came to meet them, none too eagerly. Facing three hundred men, even unarmed ones, was far different from bullying the dozen or so men of a village. True, if the marchers completely lost their reason and assaulted the constabulary, they would win that day through sheer numbers but would pay a terrible price. However, they had clearly lost their wits or they wouldn't be here, with a piper and harpist at their head. As if addressing lunatics, the constable cleared his throat and addressed Hugh.

"Why have you come here with such a racket, right to the laird's gate? MacDonald's out of prison. What more can you want?"

"We wish to see Sir James," said Hugh. "Would you do us the favor, sir, of taking him that message?"

"It's Mr. Munro, the chamberlain, who's in charge of all estate dealings. I'll see if he will come."

"No, man!" Lachlan barred the constable's way. "Indeed, that will not serve. It's about the chamberlain that we've come."

Christy stepped forward. "Be so kind as to tell Sir James that the foster daughter of Mairi Mór is with Sir James's tenants. We wish to speak to him of matters he should know about."

The constable, reassured by their civility, took a bolder tone. "You can't suppose the laird will speak with the lot of you!"

"No," said Hugh. "But we think he would receive, surely, some spokesmen from Bernera and Mistress MacLeod."

"I will ask, that's all I can do," growled the officer, turning sharply on his heel.

To Christy's amazement, people from Stornoway crowded

up to them in welcoming glee, many of the men with bottles, the women with baskets and jugs of milk.

"So you've come to tell the laird how his chamberlain rules us!" cried a buxom middle-aged woman, offering bannocks and crowdie. "Weary you must be after such a march! Rest on the hillside and have a bite and a sip."

Crofters felt that Stornoway people looked down on them as ignorant rustics, but there was no hint of that this day. Not only fisherfolk but workers and tradespeople vied in sharing their drams with the marchers while their women carried around smoked fish, scones, cheese and bannocks, even some precious hard-boiled eggs.

"Soon as a lad ran in with the news you were coming, we started baking," a pretty blond young woman told Christy as she offered her a cooling draught of buttermilk. "The Shah has his foot on our necks, too. On top of making the charges that he later judges, he's chairman of the school boards of each of the parishes, runs the harbor and the gas and water companies and road trust— och, there's no end to the ways he can grind poor folk!"

"He had my son in prison because he couldn't pay the fine for a lamb that strayed onto a deer forest," said an older woman.

"He banished my uncle for seven years because in the famine times, he stole a loaf of bread to feed his bairns," put in a brown-haired lass who had not yet assumed the married woman's cap.

Others added their grievances. In the twenty years he had literally ruled the island, Red Donald had run up a long reckoning. But the hate and fear he evoked made it all the stranger that these town folk would openly come to the aid of crofters from the other side of the island.

"Aren't you afraid Munro will have revenge on you for befriending us?" Christy asked.

The winsome blond woman laughed and spread her hand toward the Stornoway people. "I think our case is like yours. There are too many of us to punish without a great uproar."

"Besides," added the brown-haired lass, "there's been a young lawyer in town—handsome he is and a real gentleman though 'tis pity he's crippled—and he's been taking down complaints against the Shah. The whisper is that he intends to bring the chamberlain to accounts."

"A fine man, that David MacDonald." The blond woman smiled appreciatively, and Christy glowed to know that other women thought her lad was bonny. "A son he is to Mairi of the Isles, the lass who wed one of the gentry. It's too much to dream we could be rid of Munro, but perhaps Sir James will curb him when he's compelled to see what his factor's been doing."

The constable returned. Giving Christy a curious glance, he said to Hugh, "Sir James will receive three of you Bernera men. He wishes also to see this young woman."

Hugh left his pipes with his father, who also took charge of Shenachie. Angus MacDonald was urged forward, and Lachlan agreed to go. The constable escorted them past the porter's lodge, up through the trees Lady Matheson had planted and her rosy blaze of rhododendrons, to the entrance of the castle, where a uniformed servant brought them through a great hall into a book-lined room where a ruddy-faced, strong-featured man with gray hair sat reading before a cheerful fire. Sir James Matheson, laird of Lewis, who held their fates in his hand. The men bobbed their heads and Christy made a curtsey, awkward since she had only read of the maneuver in books.

"Good day to you." Sir James put aside the book. At least he didn't seem angry. His dark eyes scrutinized the men and came to rest on Christy. "We met before, I recollect, when you were only a bairn. Your foster brother's dog, wasn't it, that the keeper shot?"

"Yes, Sir James." Christy's throat was tight.

"And did the dog I sent him comfort the lad?"

"That was kind of you, Sir James, but David would not have another dog. He left soon after to go to school on the mainland."

"Mairi Mór's son," mused the laird and sighed as he seemed to look back through the years. "He must be well into manhood now."

"He is, sir." This did not seem the time to say that he was on this island gathering evidence against the laird's chamberlain.

Sir James turned to the men. "You have, I believe, a complaint to lay before me."

Diffident at first, Hugh soon warmed to his story, going back over twenty years to tell how as a lad he had helped build the first wall at their reduced Cuallin grazings. Sir James was frowning by the time Hugh told how they had built the long Earshader wall only two years ago and how, that spring, those grazings, too, had been taken away.

"And there was a writing, sir!" cried Lachlan, unable to keep silent. "A paper the ground officer brought us to sign." He looked to Christy for confirmation.

"There was an agreement that if the Bernera folk built the wall, they would be secure in the grazing and their crofts so long as they paid their rents and abided by the regulations."

"And that's not so easy!" said Angus. "Begging your pardon, my lord, but my old father says that God himself expects us to keep only ten commandments in order to hope for heaven, but no one could keep all the rules and regulations ordained by the Shah."

"The Shah?" Sir James raised a heavy eyebrow.

Angus crimsoned. "Begging your pardon, again, sir! That's what everyone calls Mr. Munro."

There was no telling from his expression how that struck the laird. "So," he said judiciously, "because you resisted Mr. Munro's command that you give up the Earshader grazings, he has summonsed you out of your crofts as well, in spite of what you maintain was a written agreement?"

"That be the sum of it, sir." Angus went on with how the sheriff's officer and Ground Officer MacRae had served the writs, the children had thrown clods, and the sheriff's man had threatened them. "The bairns should not have pelted the officers," Angus admitted. "But they were frightened to think we would lose our homes, and wrathy to see their mothers weep. Some of us did not care to have our young ones threatened with a rifle and so we told the officers. I was put in jail for this, but as God will judge me, my lord, we did not hurt the men."

A hint of a smile flitted across the laird's face. "You are not in jail, I see."

Angus blushed again. None of the deputation knew how much the constable had told Sir James, if he were aware of how many crofters were resting on Goat Hill, or if he'd heard of why and how Angus had been set free. If he didn't know, he would, after this encounter, certainly inquire. Fear of riot and revolution flared up in many a well-disposed gentleman at any hint of popular protest. Christy prayed Sir James would not decide that he must preserve his authority by supporting his chamberlain.

"Angus was put in jail for warning the officers not to bring a gun against the crofters," she said. "Since that was the opinion of everyone on Bernera, and since Mr. Munro had brought on the trouble by breaking his word, we didn't think it just that Angus should be imprisoned."

Again that flicker of a smile. "You are nothing like Mairi Mór in looks, lass, but you have her way of speaking." He studied the men. "I confess I did not know of these matters. I will discuss them with Mr. Munro and see what can be arranged."

"You——you might leave us our crofts, my lord?" ventured Angus.

"That will depend. But I will look into your leases and try to come by that agreement you signed." He rang a bell. "Lady Matheson desires that you have tea in her conservatory, of which she is inordinately proud. For myself, I will wish you good day."

The same manservant led the way to a wonder that made Christy and her companions catch in their breath. The room was huge and walled and roofed with glass. Panes and panes of it! Most dwellers in black houses counted themselves lucky if they possessed one small windowpane. Many had none at all. There must be enough glass here, Christy thought, to put a window in the home of every crofter on Lewis.

Flowers and plants of every hue and shape luxuriated in the sun streaming through the glass. It was the warmest place Christy had ever been. A small woman in a braid-trimmed maroon dress welcomed them graciously. Her graying brown hair was topped with a lace cap, and she had a sweet face and kind manner.

Bidding them be seated, she poured steaming tea into china cups as delicate as those Mairi Mór had inherited from Iain's mother and given to David and Alison, since she had always felt they were too fine for her to use. There were cream scones and blackberry preserves, fruit tarts, various cakes, and thin-sliced ham, chicken and cheese.

"No fish to be seen," muttered Lachlan into Christy's ear before, at Lady Matheson's urging, he filled his plate again and had more tea.

Grand tea it was, brewed with plenty of leaves. In crofter homes, when tea could be had at all, it was used sparingly, more as flavoring than a brew. Lady Matheson spoke of the fine weather, of the plants in the conservatory, and how she hoped that more lassies from the countryside would attend the Female Seminary she had endowed.

"I wanted to attend the seminary, Lady Matheson," said Christy. "I never quite got there myself, but I'm a teacher and I've encouraged a number of my students to study there."

Lady Matheson beamed at that and poured another round of tea. As they were taking their leave and thanking her for the refreshment, Lady Matheson looked appealingly from Hugh to Lachlan and Angus. "I hope you and your companions will not visit the taverns or dram shops. Drinking is a vice that leads to misery and robs families not only of coin needed for food and clothing but of a husband and father's kindness.''

"Bless your heart, my lady," said Hugh. "We can promise we won't run amuck. We'll have just a sip with our friends from the town and be quickly on our way."

The manservant ushered them out. Hugh drew a deep breath and dropped a hand on Angus's shoulder. "Wheesht, lad! It could scarce have gone better!"

"Aye." Angus chuckled. "When I tell my wife Lady Matheson herself poured us tea—"

"In that great glass room!" Lachlan shook his head. "I doubt the queen of England has anything to match it." He added wistfully, "I wonder if there'll come a day when crofters will have a proper glass window or two in their houses."

"I can do without the glass if I have the house and land with it," Hugh said.

They started up Goat Hill and were sighted by marchers who jumped up and came eagerly toward them. "What says Sir James?" called Diarmid.

Before they could answer, the constable overtook them. "You, Angus MacDonald," he said, "you are accused of wickedly and feloniously assaulting Colin MacLennan, sheriff's officer, in the discharge of his duties. Your trial will begin the eighteenth of July." He sneered slightly. "That's only a few days hence. Will you lodge in the jail till then or give your word to appear?"

"Wicked and felonious, is it?" Hugh set his brawny form between the constable and Angus. "Wasn't it wicked to send men with firearms amongst us? And evict us after we had a promise in writing?"

"Aye!" Old Diarmid joined his son and the other crofters grouped around them protectively. "Put the lot of us on trial! We all be guilty as Angus—or wish we were!"

The constable backed up a few steps. He was not used to resistance from crofters. But he said doggedly, "Is it jail now or later, Angus MacDonald?"

"Give your word, Angus." Christy laid her hand on the big man's arm and gave the constable her coolest smile. "We have a grand lawyer for you—David MacDonald."

XVIII

The jubilance of the marchers over Sir James's promise to look into Munro's injustices was somewhat dimmed by the upcoming trial. Neil Ramsay of Tobson and Tam MacIver of Breasclete had been summoned to court at the same time as Angus for their part in the warning away of the officers. Still, there was a hopeful feeling that this trial might not turn out like all the others where crofters had been severely punished for resisting authority. Wasn't Sir James himself sympathetic, and wasn't David Mac-Donald, son of Mairi Mór and raised on a croft though he was a mainland lawyer—wasn't he to defend the men?

But he had to be found. Volunteers left the expedition to go north to the Ness villages, south down the coast to Clanna and to the borders of Harris. As they neared the west coast, messengers would fan out north and south. Wherever David was, the search should surely find him.

As it turned out, he met them on the road from Callanish. Folk there had told him the news, and he had set off at once for Stornoway. Christy's heart swelled with pride and love as he listened to the marchers' story. He sat the saddle of the island pony with a grace that made tough little Gillie look a high-bred gentleman's mount.

Hugh finished with, " 'Twas the best tea I ever drank, sir, and those cream scones—" He smacked his lips and grinned.

"Och, it's something to tell my grandchildren, having tea in Lady Matheson's glass room!"

"If I can manage it, you'll have a better tale for your grandchildren," said David. Ah, thought Christy with a burst of gladness, the gold warmed his eyes again. "As soon as I get to Stornoway, I'll send for the sheriff. He'll ask to hear this case." David paused and gazed around at the men's faces, old and young and in between, before he looked at Angus. "Through you, we'll try Red Donald."

A shout went up. Caps waved in the air. David touched his saddlebag. "I've testimony here from every township in Lewis, and the stories of those whose townships were taken from them. Twenty years of Munro's wickedness are in my notebooks. If I can't turn the tables against him, then I'll give up law, for this evidence would convict him even before his mother."

Another cheer went up. David's eyes came for a moment to Christy. The gold in them vanished. The blue-gray turned bleak and hard, though his words were reluctantly approving. "It's a brave thing you have done. Mother would be proud of you." He reined Gillie onward, then said over his shoulder, "I'll send for her. She asked me to let her know when I brought charges against the chamberlain."

"Tell her I'm coming to the trial, too," called Christy. David, if he heard her, gave no sign.

What was the matter with him? Was his heart in the grave with Alison? When this case was over, would he return to Inverness, and would there be between them not only land and sea but the inviolable barrier of a dead beloved?

I won't just let him go, Christy vowed. If he can't love me, at least I want my friend back, the lad I've followed after ever since I could walk. Pride or no pride, we'll have that out between us. But, oh, she longed for him to be her lover with every fiber of her being, desired him with body, heart, and soul.

There were ceilidhs that night in many a village, and in

Ardan, Hugh, Lachlan, and Christy had to answer scores of questions about the meeting with Sir James, Lady Matheson's amazing hospitality, and the upcoming trial.

"We can't all go," said Hugh. "We've got to get back to our fishing. But on the way home, we agreed that to show support for Angus and his friends—and to get the word across the island faster—a few folk from each village will be there."

"You must go," said Ellen, smiling above their baby's head though she must have been afraid for her husband. "If they're freed, our lads must be piped home. If they're kept in jail, the pipes must lament."

"The pipes will do more than lament if Angus and his friends are sent to prison," said Hugh. "Christy must come. Either way, we'll need her harp."

"Mairi Mór will be there with her harp," Christy reminded him.

Hugh smiled. "Then let us have two harps forbye. Your foster mother's harp is far famed, justly. But it's your Shenachie that knows our Bernera folk, you who have played for our weddings and christenings and funerals, and you who marched along with us to the castle. Of course you'll bring your harp!"

"Aye, you must," Lachlan said.

He was echoed by everyone in the room. Overwhelmed at such trust, Christy drew a rippling note from Shenachie. "Whatever happens, we will sing."

🎵 Mairi Mór had brought her twins over the moors with a pony to carry her harp. At seven years, the golden pair were straight and tall with the misty blue eyes of their father. Magnus's cherishing had kept Mairi in bloom. At forty-seven, when many island women were bowed over from work and carrying burdens, there was little gray in Mairi's wealth of auburn hair. Mairi's step was light and springy as the girl's who'd been wed in that same arisaid a quarter of a century ago. Along with the wisdom and sorrow in her gray-green eyes, there was laughter and joy in life.

As she and Christy embraced, Christy murmured, "I have been to the Stones. Gran spoke to me. And I saw my mother."

Mairi took a deep breath. She kissed her foster child on both cheeks. "I am right glad to hear that, lass." She hesitated. "I want you to know that I—I have missed you since you left Clanna. But you have done bravely. It was a grand day for the island—and a good day for me—when I brought you home from Sollas."

The words released a flood of aching memories in Christy, the puzzled hurt of a child who couldn't understand why the woman who saw so carefully to her physical needs never touched her more than necessary, never hugged or held her as Gran did. It had helped a little to realize gradually that Mairi Mór grieved for her real daughter, but Christy had felt as guilty as if the baby's loss had indeed been her fault—as if, like a greedy cuckoo chick, she had shoved the true child out of the nest and stolen her nurturing. Mairi said softly, "Can you forgive me, lass, that my heart was so frozen it could not warm to you?"

Christy shook her head in protest and caught the older woman's hands. "I owe you my life. I owe you music. I owe you—and Gran—all that I am."

Tears glistened in Mairi's eyes. "You have come to be the child of my spirit. I can never tell you how grateful I was that you could comfort David when I could not."

Again, Christy shook her head. "He will not let me comfort him now. Oh, Mairi Mór, did he come to love Alison so much that now his heart is in her grave?"

"I do not know." They gazed at each other, troubled, and then made their way into the courtroom, settling their harps beside them as they took a bench at the rear.

David was at the front, conferring with Angus and his friends. The jurymen were dressed in town suits and Christy recognized several well-to-do Stornoway merchants. Mairi's face glowed as she looked at David, the child of her youth and her great, forbidden love, the son she bore without his father's name, without his father's even knowing.

"Whichever way this goes," she murmured to Christy, "I want Olav and Cat to remember."

Could it be that she also wanted the ebulliently healthy twins to watch their half-brother at his calling and understand that though his legs were crippled, he himself was not, that with his knowledge and training he could accomplish more for their people than if he had been the fleetest-footed man in all the Highlands and islands? In David, too, Mairi must see her Iain.

The room was packed and more kept crowding in, standing at the sides and at the back. Four strong young fellows beamed at Christy and leaned in from the center aisle to clasp her hand. "Don't you know us, Miss Christy?" asked one with dancing gray eyes whose face was strangely familiar.

"Jem MacCaulay!" Jolted back to Siadar, she now recognized the men her students had become. Dark Tom Nicolson; Jem's devilish younger brother, Rory; and rusty-haired Donnie MacNeil. "It's grand to see you lads! How are your families—and I suppose you've all started your own?"

They had, and Jem's wife, Bella, was still teaching school. Glancing around, Jem said, "Forbye, there are men here from every Ness township. We mean to let Red Donald see that we support the Bernera folk."

A lump rose in Christy's throat. "Bless you for coming."

"How could we not, after those songs about freedom and rights you used to sing?" demanded Rory with a grin. "Och, here comes the judge, Sheriff Spittal himself, from Inverness!"

The crowd parted to let the tall, stern-jawed sheriff through and then packed tight again, with the overflow peering through the door. There was a stir as a small man in a stalker's cap shoved his way through.

It was Dugald Craigie. "You'll be taught a lesson," he hissed in Christy's ear. "And that jumped-up Davie MacDonald, he'll leave here with his tail between his crippled legs!"

Thank heaven Mairi was busy with the twins and hadn't heard or seen the gamekeeper. A bailiff called the court to order. The judge, in a solemn voice, in English, read the charge of felonious assault on Sheriff's Officer Colin MacLennan.

"My clients plead not guilty, your honor," David said.

The prosecuting attorney, a gaunt red-haired Stornoway lawyer named Daniel Ross, called MacLennan to testify, which he did, in Gaelic. "In fear of our lives we were, just Ground Officer Mac-Rae and the customs officer and me, with this mob around us, swearing and threatening and acting as if they'd tear us to bits. Ripped my good oilskin, they did, and wouldn't let us go till we promised not to come back to Bernera with more writs of eviction."

"You were afraid the accused might actually kill you?" asked Ross sympathetically.

"Mortal afeard," nodded MacLennan.

He was turned over to David for cross-examination. "Now, Sheriff's Officer MacLennan," said David in a pleasant tone, relaxed and easy. "I can well imagine that you were frightened, but did my clients actually strike you?"

"No, but—"

"We already know what you feared, sir. Now we are trying to clarify what *happened*."

There was laughter at this. The judge frowned and a hush fell. "My clients say they spoke with you because you had told people in Tobson that if you'd had your gun the night before, when some children pelted you with clods, there would be mothers bewailing their sons. Is that true, Officer MacLennan?"

"What if it is? Those young devils might have killed us!"

"It seems you lead a parlous life, sir. The charge says you were interfered with in the discharge of your duty, but did you not deliver the summonses without any trouble?"

"Aye," admitted MacLennan unwillingly.

"And for all your fears of what *might* happen, when the Bernera men asked you if you meant to bring a gun against them, did they injure you in any way?"

"They tore my oilskin!"

"Mr. MacDonald says he put his hand on your arm, over the coat, and you jerked it away so hard that it tore."

"It would not have torn, would it, had he not grabbed hold of my arm?"

"Still, it was not deliberate damage. One might almost think the Bernera men conducted themselves with restraint, considering that you had been in Tobson telling their wives that you'd have used your gun on mere lads if you had it with you."

MacLennan scowled. "Those young rascallions—"

"Thank you, Sheriff's Officer," said David and sat down.

Loud enough for Christy to hear, though the muttering didn't carry far, Dugald Craigie said, "They know better than to try that kind of trick with me!"

This time Mairi heard him. She turned to stare at him in shock, this man who had spied on her for Chellis Forsyth and later shot Chul. David had seen him, too, from the sudden tightening of his lips. Years ago, a broken-hearted boy had wanted to kill the murderer of his dog. Now, if David could indeed break the power of the Shah, the power that supported Craigie in his oppressions, it would be a lasting vengeance.

Ross next tried to get the customs officer and MacRae to say they'd been in terror for their lives, but they were inclined to shrug it off. "One cannot much blame the lads for chunking turfs at us," said the burly, dark-bearded ground officer. "We had just summonsed their families out of their crofts. Officer MacLennan doesn't know the Bernera folk as well as I do. He should not have threatened to take a gun to them, but I was never afraid that they would hurt us."

Upon questioning, the customs officer said, "I've been jostled worse on Cromwell Street. The men said from the first they meant us no harm but the sheriff's officer must understand they would not bide his returning with his gun."

David, cross-examining MacRae, established that MacLennan had indeed blustered about what he would have done to the clod-throwing boys if he'd had his weapon. "Now, sir," David went on, with a glance at Red Donald, who sat in stony arrogance on the front row. "Did you bring an agreement to Bernera that promised the tenants security in their leases if they would accept the Earshader grazings?"

"I did."

"They signed it?"

"Aye. And those who could not sign made their mark and Mistress Christy MacLeod wrote their names."

"Always meddling!" came Craigie's whisper.

"What did you do with this agreement?" David pressed.

"I sent it to Mr. Donald Munro."

"There was no agreement!" snarled Munro.

A rumble of protest rose from the crofters. The judge rapped his gavel and called for order. Munro was called as a witness for the prosecution.

He said he had tried to help the Bernera folk by giving them Haclete Farm in place of Earshader. "They refused to take the farm," he said righteously, glaring at Angus and the others. "When I went myself to reason with them, they were so insolent and pig-headed that I had no choice but to be rid of the whole lot."

To David, he denied there had been an agreement. "Do you say then, Mr. Munro, that Ground Officer MacRae is lying?"

"I know naught of a paper," said Munro doggedly.

"You felt justified in forcing these men to build a six-mile long wall and then taking the enclosed grazing from them after less than two years?"

"It is my duty to manage the estate to benefit Sir James. The

Earshader grazings were needed to add to Scaliscro Forest, for which a very handsome rent is paid.''

"And though their rents were admittedly not so handsome, had not the Bernera tenantry faithfully paid them?"

"I never said they didn't.''

"You felt no concern at all for these tenants who would not have sufficient grazing for their beasts? No responsibility for the weeks of toil they spent making that wall?"

Munro shrugged. "If they do not like it here, they can go across the ocean, the sooner the better, the whole rioting, mobbing gang of them."

"They had never caused trouble before, had they, though they were turned out of their Cuallin grazings, where they built another long wall over twenty years ago? Did they not peaceably accept the smaller Earshader grazings and agree to build the wall, although they needed to be at the fishing?"

"Beggars can't be choosers."

"Beggars? Did you not say their rents were paid?"

"It was a manner of speaking."

"And thinking, too, I fear, sir." David paused and then asked abruptly, "What did Sir James say when you told him you were evicting fifty-six families from Bernera?"

"I did not tell him."

"What, sir? You did not ask his opinion?"

"Sir James employs me to take care of estate business. I do not bother him with details."

There was a swell of indignant murmuring. The judge rapped his gavel, but he himself looked startled, as did the jurymen. "So," said David in his silkiest voice, "you consider it a small matter, Mr. Munro, to leave fifty-six families homeless? A small matter for old folk to have no fire to warm their bones and bairns no roof above their heads?"

"The fools should have thought of that before they refused Haclete."

David studied some papers. "Mr. Munro, would you tell the court what offices you hold?"

Munro puffed up a bit. "Well, I am Sir James's chamberlain, of course. Baron baillie, justice of the peace, and notary public. Because of my public-spiritedness, I am legal advisor to the four parochial boards and chairman of the school boards of each parish."

"Are you not also procurator fiscal?"

"I am."

"And your duties as fiscal?"

"I prefer criminal charges when such are warranted."

"And then hear the cases as justice of the peace or baron baillie, and pass sentence?"

"That is my responsibility."

"Are you not also the commander of the local volunteer force?"

"Aye."

"Then are you not, in fact, the law on the island, both accuser and judge?"

" 'Tis no matter for shame."

"A matter for wonder, sir." David read from a paper as if each title were an indictment. "Director of the Stornoway Gas Company. Director of the Stornoway Water Company. Vice-chairman of the Harbor Trustees. Deputy chairman of the Road Trust. Commissioner of supply. Commissioner under the income tax. Is there any office on Lewis that you do *not* hold, Mr. Munro?"

"The island's affairs run much more smoothly this way."

"That, I believe, sir, was the argument for tyrants in ancient Greece. Rule by one all-powerful person is much more orderly than the untidiness of a republic or democracy."

Munro's lip curled. "I will remind you that my employment, young man, is to efficiently conduct Sir James's affairs. The island is his. He bought it. He has poured thousands of pounds into improving it. As his agent, it is fitting and necessary that I control the important commercial and civic posts.''

"And with them, the lives of every mortal on this island, saving the wealthy leasers of deer forests and Sir James and his lady?''

"How else could it be, man?'' The chamberlain was genuinely astonished. "Crofters are an ignorant lot and lazy to boot.''

"You can scarce expect them to improve their crofts when this will raise their rents or when they may be expelled on the whim of a man like you.''

"Sir James should have shipped them all away during the potato blight instead of feeding them. Look at their gratitude!''

"I'm sure it's a good thing for Lewis folk that you were not Sir James's agent during the famine.'' David put down his papers and looked at the chamberlain so steadily that, with a disgusted grunt, Red Donald fixed his stare on the ceiling. "By your own admission then, Mr. Munro, you wield a despot's power over law, education, commerce, transportation, and most of all, a crofter's land and livelihood. Probably every tenant in this court has heard your threat, 'I'll take your land from you!' ''

A mingled roar of affirmation came from the listeners. "Aye, we have!'' "He evicted our whole township!'' "He divided my croft among three tenants and charged us all the same rent!''

The judge quelled the uproar, but not before a woman behind Christy shouted, "You stole so many hens from us that 'tis a wonder you haven't sprouted pinfeathers. A common chicken thief you be, for all your airs!''

"Aye!'' called several others and clucked derisively. "Red Donald of the hens, Shah of Lewis!''

Munro jumped to his feet. "I mark you all!'' he screamed. "I'll have your land!''

"You will be seated, Mr. Munro,'' commanded the judge. He repeated the charges against Angus and his comrades and turned to the citizens of Stornoway. "Gentlemen of the jury, you will withdraw and reach a verdict.''

Mairi's eyes blazed with pride as she watched her son sit down to confer with the accused men. "It's not our lads on trial today. 'Tis Red Donald. And more than he, the cruel laws and wicked men like Craigie."

"David turned the Shah inside out for sure," said Christy. "But will this jury be different from the ones that sentenced crofters after Sollas and Greenyards and any other time poor folk resisted eviction?"

"Times have changed. Few lairds care to be written up in the papers for the kind of evictions that were common when I was your age. And there's more, Christy. The children you taught at Siadar and Ardan, a whole new generation, are now young people who are *not* the ignorant louts Munro likes to think they are. Look around! There are folk from all over the island, come to support the Bernera lads in spite of the woe it may bring them. This could not have happened thirty years ago."

"You gave them hope, Mairi Mór. You suffered with them."

Mairi shook her head. " 'Twas the harp. Our songs, our old stories, gave our folk faith and courage."

"What would the harp be without you to play it?"

Mairi smiled. "What would I be without the harp?"

When the jury foreman announced a verdict of not guilty, such a roar of jubilation sounded through the court, such a tossing of caps in the air, and crowding to shake hands with Angus and his friends, that the judge didn't even try to control the clamor. Dugald Craigie, narrow face livid, slunk toward the back as silence fell and the judge addressed Donald Munro.

"Mr. Munro, the evidence I have heard this day proves you unworthy to hold the offices you have abused. Whether Sir James retains you as his agent is his choice, but as sheriff of the County of Inverness, I hereby strip you of your governmental offices and powers."

Munro's face worked. He buried his face in his hands. No one cheered. Perhaps they couldn't believe that a few words could destroy a reign of twenty years. Perhaps, much as they hated him, it seemed indecent to exult at a man's ruin. Dugald Craigie, the gamekeeper, walked out like a man stunned. If this could happen to the Shah, how long would he keep his free grazing on crofters' land, how long could he shoot their dogs, levy fines, and lord it over them?

A new day had come for the crofters. Mairi had held on through the darkest night, between the rocks and the sea, heartening the people with Fearchar's songs. Christy, unwilling, had labored as a few faint streaks of light appeared. But it was David who had brought the dawn.

"Lass," said Mairi, "let's go out into the street and play our harps."

There was dancing in the streets of Stornoway, for all the parson might say. When Munro, walking feeble and suddenly old like a great fat insect with its back broken, slipped down an alley, no one followed or taunted him.

David, flushed, eyes shining, had come outside when he could escape his congratulators. He embraced his mother, kissed Cat, and tousled Olav's bright hair. Then, as he pressed Christy's hand and let it go as if it had burned him, the triumph faded from him, and Christy feared that it was for a far deeper reason than that he couldn't dance.

"I think I'll go to my lodgings, Mother," he said.

"But we've scarce had a chance to talk!"

"I've bespoke rooms at the inn—for you, too, Christy. We'll have the best supper our landlady can produce."

Mairi touched her son's lean cheek. "Run away, then, Davie. You must be tired. But you'll answer one question first."

"What is that?"

"When are you going to wed Christy?"

He turned pale and flinched, as if struck by an invisible hand. From his mother, he turned to Christy. "I—I cannot, lass."

At the look that must have filled her face, he added huskily, " 'Tis not your fault, love. Indeed, I would give my soul to be free to ask you."

"You *are* free!" she burst out.

He shook his head. "No. Alison despaired of her life because of me—because I could not love her. I'm as good as a murderer."

Christy caught his hands. "You are not!"

His face was stone. She had not wanted ever to tell anyone else of Alison's crime, but surely that poor little lass would not have let David go through life punishing himself—and even if she would have, Christy could not.

"Davie," she said. "I have a letter. I can show it to you."

When she had told the pitiful story, David's eyes were wet. "How terrible for her!"

Christy could only nod. Terrible indeed.

"I saw she never held the babe," David said as if to himself. "But people said she'd get over that. If I had known—"

"Wheesht, lad!" Mairi shook her finger at him. "No more of that! You did all for the girl that you could."

He shook his head. "If I had really loved her—"

Christy could bear no more. She grasped his shoulders and shook him. "David, I love you! I have loved you and only you all these years, all my life. Is that nothing to you?"

"It—it is everything."

She took his hand and pressed it to her face. "Well, then, laddie?"

The torment left his eyes and a radiance deep within them warmed Christy. A slow, sweet trembling went through her like the softest plucking of harp strings.

"Will you have me, Christy?"

"With all my heart," she whispered, lifting her lips to his. "With all my soul and all my strength for all my life."

Mairi made Cridhe sound like the "Incitement to Battle." The dancing stopped. She took Christy's hand in one of hers, David's in the other. "Friends," she called so the farthest away could hear. "You're bid to the wedding of my son and Christy MacLeod of Clanna, Siadar, and Bernera. In two week's time, at the Stones of Callanish."

The joy was as great as when the crofters were set free. Hugh skirled into the "Salute to the Chief" and the dancing began again.

"I—I can't play now," Christy blurted to Mairi. "I'm going with David."

"Of course you are." Mairi gave them each a kiss and picked up Hugh's tune.

Christy carried David's leather case of legal documents. They were clear of the crowd and nearing the inn when a man rose up from behind a cart. It was Dugald Craigie, pallid fox face twisted as he leveled a pistol at David.

"I shot your cur," he grated. "And now I'll do for you! That'll pay out your cursed mother for causing the death of the only woman I ever fancied!"

The gun went off in the same instant that David swung his crutch, knocking Craigie's arm up, sending the shot into the air. With his next swing, the crutch clubbed the keeper to the cobblestones. The constables, on hand for keeping order during the trial, were on him in a twinkling. He was dragged into the jail.

David, breathing hard, grinned at Christy. "That's the first time I've been glad of these damned crutches. They've helped me pay the debt for Chul."

"You've paid a lot of debts this day," she told him. "Oh, Davie, Davie! Am I dreaming? Is it really me you love instead of Alison?"

"It will be the sweetest case I've ever argued, trying to convince you. Since we're to marry in a fortnight, I'd better start now!''

Folk from all the island attended the wedding, with many from Ness and almost every soul from Clanna and Bernera. They were secure in their grazings and crofts. Sir James had discharged Munro and engaged an agent with a reputation for fair dealing. Dugald Craigie had been heavily fined and banished for life from the island. So, apart from the wedding, island folk congregated to celebrate new hope and freedom and hear the ancient harps sing together as Tam and Hugh played the pipes and Lucas and other fiddlers joined in the tunes.

The gift of Clanna to Christy had been an arisaid like Mairi's, with the big silver brooch and silver-plated belt. "It was Gran's notion that I should be wed in an arisaid like her grandmother's— the old island dress," said Mairi. "I know she'd want you to have one, too." Indeed, wearing the archaic costume while she played Shenachie made Christy feel part of the past as well as the present and future of Lewis.

David's partner and former father-in-law, Duncan Stewart, had come, hard as that must have been for him. "We'll have your husband in Parliament," the kindly gray-haired man promised Christy. "I won't grudge his setting up practice in Stornoway, so long as he'll come to help me when needed."

Sir James and his lady attended the service performed by his chaplain in the circle of timeless stones. Then parson, Alison's father, and the Mathesons wished the couple well, toasted them in heather ale, and departed.

A great feast, contributed to by all the guests, was spread on linen-covered waulking tables and barn doors brought up from the village of Callanish. Magnus had just returned from a voyage, and delicacies from the mainland added to the festivity.

Since David could not dance, Magnus, as a sort of foster father, partnered Christy in the first reel. " 'Tis a glad day, lass. I've ached for you all these years when you could not have David, for it was many a year that I could not have Mairi." His eyes shone like the twilight. "I'm not her Iain, but we have been happy. I wish you as happy, m'eudail, or even happier."

Rob MacRae, still more gold in his hair than gray though he was nearing fifty, swept Christy away. He had come from Sollas when Christy did, a live unwanted babe beside Mairi's dead beloved one.

"Who could have guessed this would happen when I found that poor lassie, your mother, along the shore?" His blue eyes had a glint of tears. "You had no name, no family. But you have made one! Just as Mairi is truly called Great Mairi, Mairi of the Isles, you are Christy of Siadar and Bernera, Christy of Lewis, Christy of——"

"Christy of David," said her bridegroom, coming up. He smiled into her eyes so that it seemed they were alone together in the midst of all that company, alone together after all their years apart. "It's late, my love. Do you think our guests will excuse us if we make shift to slip away?"

"I don't think they'll miss us at all, laddie. Not with Tam and Hugh skirling, a brace of fiddlers, and your mother with Cridhe."

They passed among the ancient Stones to a little hollow below the knoll where he had already brought plaids. "I was conceived and got my christening here," he said as she trembled beneath his hands. "Do you think our child will be so lucky?"

"We'll try our best," she said.

Mairi's harp sang with joy and thanksgiving. As Christy drew David down and closed her eyes, she caught a flash of Gran dancing like a girl, toasting them with a flask of uisge-beatha. And then there was only the soft sweet night and David. At last and always David.

AUTHOR'S NOTE

Magic as are all the Western Isles of Scotland, the one that touched me most was the Long Isle, Lewis and Harris. With a small group led by Sandy Mitchell of Strathpeffer, I walked moors and rocky cliffs, rested in flowery hollows out of the driving wind, smelled the peat smoke in an old black house of the kind lived in by Mairi and her folk, gazed in awe at the Callanish Stones grouped like hooded ancients, and visited weavers, including the only one still carding her own wool and using native dyes. There was a grand ceilidh with neighbors and harvest workers in to dance and sing till dawning. I wish I knew the names of the gentleman and ladies who joined our smaller ceilidh some nights later at the Harris Hotel. He played the Northumbrian pipes. One lady played her Celtic harp and the other sang "Over the Sea to Skye" and tried to teach us some Gaelic songs. And several years later, in Arizona, Ellen Zweifel James, who spent a year on the island of Mull, played lovely music on her Celtic harp and later sent me a song she collected about the Clearances.

In South Uist, I found the book that made me want to write the story of the crofters, John Prebble's powerful, graceful, passionate *The Highland Clearances,* Penguin, Middlesex, England, 1969. After that, I looked at the black-faced sheep with different eyes and wondered what stories were hidden in the crumbling walls of abandoned black houses, so called because they were laid up without mortar.

Most of us know of the Irish potato famine but few realize the potato blight had just as cruel an effect in the Highlands and islands of Scotland. Even fewer have heard of the brutal Clearances that scoured thousands of crofters from lands held by their families for centuries. Perhaps because these uprootings went on for a hundred years and were carried out at different times by different landlords, there's no accurate count of how many were forced to the slums of Glasgow and other Lowland cities or compelled to emigrate to Canada, the colonies that became the United States, and Australia. Three hundred here, two or three thousand there, these wretched folk were driven out of their homes to make room for sheep and for huge deer forests, which could be very profitably leased. Certainly, many islanders chose to seek new lives over the ocean, but hundreds of others had their roofs burned and their walls leveled.

The Clearances continued into the 1850s but gradually dwindled, partly because of public indignation, partly because the crofters had already been driven off most of the land that proprietors wanted for sheep farms or deer parks.

The clearances in this book happened as related, though of course Mairi was not there. The names of the sheriffs, officials, landlords, and principal crofters are genuine. Sollas is still a bitter memory. Greenyards was perhaps the most vicious of all attacks of police on resisting women. So that Christy would be old enough to be there, I moved Greenyards from 1854 to 1861 but except for the presence of my heroines, events happened as described.

The best thing about the happy ending of this book is that it's as true as the evictions. Red Donald Munro was indeed the hated tyrant of Lewis for twenty years and well-earned his nickname, the Shah. The Ness villages were bereft of their men in one terrible storm, as related, and Munro did attempt to keep the relief fund subscribed to by even Queen Victoria—and he gave it to the widows, when word of his trick was circulated in a mainland pamphlet.

All his dealings with the Bernera folk happened as described. Winans, the American millionaire, did want crofters evicted to enlarge his deer forest. And finally, exasperated past bearing, several hundred crofters marched on Stornoway to break Angus MacDonald out of jail, and they were led by a piper. Sir James did receive a delegation and promised to see what he could do about the Bernera grievances. And his lady did invite the delegation to tea in her conservatory.

The trial of Angus and his friends was turned into a trial of Munro by a clever young Inverness lawyer, Charles Innes. The crofters were acquitted and the sheriff stripped Munro of his many offices. Sir James discharged him and Munro died a poor man, taunted in the streets by Stornoway children with his old threat, "I'll have your land from you!"

The so-called Bernera riots led to the first victory of the crofters over their oppressors and set the tone for future demonstrations over their claims to land.

As David predicted, Gladstone did appoint the Napier Commission to investigate the abuses of landlords and agents. In 1886, the Crofters' Holdings Act was passed by Parliament. This provided for fair rents, security in tenure for crofters, and the right to transfer a holding to a son or near relative. So Mairi's long dream at last came true.

A good many of the books I needed to reconstruct the crofters' story aren't available in the States and were ordered through Tam Mac-Phail, who has an excellent bookshop in Stromness, Orkney. Mr. Mac-Phail was very helpful in tracking down and recommending useful works. I owe a great debt to Moris Farhi of London, who diligently searched for out-of-print books and also sent me volumes I wouldn't otherwise have had.

Published by John Donald Publishers, Edinburgh, are the following: *The Making of the Crofting Community* by James Hunter, 1976; *The Scottish Gael* by James Logan, vols. I and II, 1976 reprint of 1876 volumes; *The Native Horses of Scotland* by Andrew Fraser, 1987; *Discovering Lewis and Harris* by James Shaw Grant, 1991; *Deer Forests, Landlords and Crofters* by Willie Orr, 1982; and *Country Life in Scotland* by Alexander Fenton, 1987.

The History of the Highland Clearances by Alexander MacKenzie, first published in 1883 and reprinted in 1986 by Melven Press, London, was written by a man who watched the horror and tried to move the government and lairds to help the people. *The Western Islands of Scotland* by W. H. Murray, Eyre Methuen, London, 1973, is an excellent overview containing much natural history, which was supplemented by many specialized small publications bought locally in the islands, and F. Fraser Darling's classic *Natural History in the Highlands and Islands,* Collins, London, 1943. *The Clans of the Scottish Highlands,* with wonderful paintings by R. R. McIan and text by James Logan, was first published in 1845 and 1847 and is now available in a 1980 edition from Pan Books, London. *Queen Victoria's Little Wars* by Byron Farwell, Harper, New York, 1972, tells how Highland regiments fought all over the world to expand Great Britain's empire. *Folklore and Folksongs of South Uist* by Margaret Fay Shaw, Aberdeen University Press, 1986, is a treasure house of waulking songs, other songs, proverbs, and customs. I. F. Grant's *Highland Folkways,* Routledge and Kegan Paul, London, 1961, is a trove of lore and facts, delightfully told. *Living the Fishing* by Paul Thompson, Routledge and Kegan Paul, London, 1983, has a humanized picture of the industry. *Tales and Traditions of the Lews,* collected by Dr. MacDonald of Gisla, published by Mrs. MacDonald, Stornoway, Lewis, The Hebrides, 1967, is a treasury of history, economics, folklore, and memoirs. *Skye* by Derek Cooper, Routledge and Kegan Paul, London, 1977, has much of interest. *Lewis, A History of the Island* by Donald Macdonald, who grew up on Lewis, has extremely valuable insights into every facet of daily life and work. It was given me by Sandy Mitchell of Strathpeffer, who introduced to me the islands and who has graciously cleared up many perplexities.

Many islands remain unpopulated to this day. But Gaelic is still spoken and there are many island families that survived the evil days, fought for their ancient rights, and are proud of their heritage. Many times I've written of emigrants to the American West, but in these stories of Mairi, her Clanna, her son, David, and her fosterling, Christy, and their harps, I was called to tell the story of those who stayed, who lived on seaweed and shellfish between the rocks and the sea, and who finally triumphed.

—Jeanne Williams
Cave Creek Canyon
The Chiricahua Mountains
June 8, 1993

I'm delighted to learn the identities of the musicians who added such magic to the ceilidh at the Harris Hotel. Elizabeth Matthews, who played the Celtic harp, was longtime Convenor (chairman) of the Clarsach Society, which is based in Edinburgh, and her husband, who played the Northumbrian pipes, was for many years Honorary Piper to His Grace, the Duke of Northumberland. It's a deep pleasure to thank them by name for sharing their wonderful music.

December 29, 1993

GLOSSARY

Atholl Brose—Mix half-a-pound of oatmeal with half-a-pound of honey and enough water to make a thick paste. Then slowly add two pints of whisky and stir briskly till mixture foams. Bottle and cork tightly.

bannock—Flat bread cooked on a griddle.

Beasts of Holm—Treacherous rocks guarding Stornoway Harbor; caused many shipwrecks.

Beltane—May 1, the ancient Celtic festival that marked the coming of summer. Hearth fires were extinguished. Sacred fires were built to honor Bel, the sun god, and cattle were driven between them to protect them from disease. Hearth fires were then relit from this purifying flame.

blatherskate—Person with a loose, careless tongue.

blethering—What blatherskates do.

Brian Boru—(941–1014) King of Munster who united Ireland and made it so safe that a beautiful young woman, richly bejeweled, could travel without harm from one end of Ireland to the other. In his old age, the Norse dwelling in Ireland rose against him. He defeated them at Clontarf near Dublin but was killed shortly after in his tent.

Brigid, Brigit, Brid, Brighde—Ancient Celtic mother goddess who also was patroness of learning, art, and poetry. Her day was February 1, when she restored life to the dead winter and dipped her hand in the sea to warm it. Transformed into Saint Brigid and the nurse of Jesus, she was especially revered in Ireland and Scotland, and mothers besought her help in childbed.

broch—Defensive towers found throughout the Hebrides, built by Picts or earlier folk. People took shelter in brochs from raids but did not live within them on a regular basis.

brochan—Porridge, gruel.

Callanish—Bronze Age stones ranking with Stonehenge and Avebury in interest. A circle of megaliths has the tallest stone in the center; from the center, four aisles lead to the outer boundaries of the circle. Sir James Matheson had the peat cleared away from much of the site.

carrageen—Seaweed that when dried and powdered makes a nutritious pudding, especially good with fruit or jam.

carnaptious—Capricious, touchy.

cas-chrom—"Crooked foot," a foot plow. The six-foot shaft of oak or ash had a bent lower end or head about two-and-a-half-feet long with a six-inch metal tip. A wooden peg was fixed on the right side of the head. The ploughman set his foot on the peg and drove the head into the ground with two jerks. The cas-chrom could turn up boulders weighing two hundred pounds. Twelve men could dig an acre in a day. Because of the rocky soil, this implement worked better than a regular plow.

ceann-cinnidh—Head of the clan.

ceilidh—Informal party when neighbors gathered for an evening of music, stories, riddles, and dancing.

ceud mile failte—A hundred thousand welcomes; traditional welcome.

Cheviot—A breed of sheep that could withstand the island and Highland winters.

chiel—A youth.

clanna—Children; an extended family or clan.

cogg—Wooden bucket.

Conn of the Hundred Battles—Semilegendary high king of Ulster who ruled from Tara circa 125 A.D. Ancestor of the MacDonalds.

coof—Fool.

crannachan—Dessert of toasted oatmeal, honey, and whipped cream.

croft, crofter—A small individual holding of land, seldom more than seven acres, and the person who rents or owns it. Pasture was usually shared by a township.

crotal—Lichen that yields a rust-brown dye; not used for fishermen's clothing since it was believed crotal came from the rocks and would try to return to them.

croman—Hoe.

crowdie—Soft white cheese.

Cuchulain—Greatest of the Celtic heroes whose feats were celebrated in bardic poems called the Ulster Cycle.

Culloden—Battle in 1746 when Bonnie Prince Charlie, who, as a Stewart, had a claim to the English throne as well as that of Scotland, was defeated by the English. Many harsh laws were enacted to break the clans and insure that there would be no more uprisings against England.

dotterel—A plover, a shorebird with white eyestripes, chestnut lower breast, and black belly. Chief call is a sweet trill, *wit-a-wee, wit-a-wee-wit-a-wee.*

drogad—Dark blue cloth with cotton warp and wool weft, much used for petticoats.

drystone—Stone walls laid up without mortar.

dulse—Seaweed with flat brown leaves. Nutritious but must be simmered for five hours.

each-uisge—Water horse; malicious spirit that lures people to drown; a kelpie.

eelgrass—Used for bedding.

excise man—Tax collector, much hated by distillers and smugglers of whisky.

fasgalan—Entryway of hut that holds quern and bench with milking vessels.

fash—Worry, fret.

Finnan Haddie—Haddock smoked over a peat fire.

Fir-chlisne—The Merry Dancers or Men of the Tricks, the Northern Lights.

forbye—Anyway, besides, all the same.

gavallachan—Daredevil, happy-go-lucky; devil's boy.

gille—Follower or manservant.

gille Brighde—Follower of Brigid. The oyster catcher is a handsome bird with scarlet-rimmed eyes and is black except for white breast and wingtips. He earned the cross on his back by hiding the baby Jesus in seaweed to protect him from Herod.

gloaming—Twilight.

gormless—Brainless, lacking in initiative.

greenshank—Long-legged wading bird of moors and bogs that has slightly upcurved bill and olive green legs.

gruagach—Giant or giantess.

gruamach—Grouchy.

grummilie—Sour, sullen.

guillemot—A short-necked, short-tailed diving seabird. Commonest of the auks. Breeds in colonies in inaccessible cliff ledges.

iorram—Rowing song.

James I of England, James VI of Scotland—Son of Mary Stewart, the ill-fated Queen of Scots who was beheaded at the order of Queen Elizabeth I. Ironically, James inherited the English throne, since Elizabeth had no closer heirs.

kelp—Seaweed that could be dried and used for fertilizer; brought a brief prosperity to the islands.

kelpie—A water horse, a supernatural creature that would carry off and drown the unwary.

kittiwake—A white gull with gray wings tipped with black. Graceful, buoyant flight. At breeding time, cries *kitt-ee-wayke*.

lazybeds—Planting beds from three to eight feet wide, often built on rocks or steep hillsides. Soil may be dug to heap on the rocks, or, where there is no soil, sand is carried from the beach and layered with seaweed. Where necessary, rock walls hold the planting mixture in place.

lochan—Little lake.

Long Isle—The Outer Hebrides consisting of Lewis and Harris, North and South Uist and Barrá. These islands form an almost continuous chain; Lewis and Harris are actually the same land mass.

m'eudail—My darling.

machair—Flowery meadow on soil enriched with fine-ground shells that stretches between some beaches and other land, on west side of some islands. Rich pasture.

Mairi nighean Alasdair Ruaidh—Mairi of the Isles; a seventeenth-century bard who composed poems in the ancient manner. Because she sang of freedom, she was forbidden by the authorities to make her songs within or without the threshold. She therefore composed her poems while standing *on* the threshold.

marram grass—Coarse, deep green grass that binds the sand and shields the machair from the sea wind.

Minch—Water between the Long Island or Outer Hebrides and the Mainland and Inner Hebrides.

mo graidh—My dear.

Mór—Great, as in Mairi Mór.

mutch—Frilled cap worn by married women.

Niall of the Nine Hostages—Irish king of about 358 A.D. who invaded Wales and was killed on a raid into Gaul. He was the ancestor of the O'Neill kings of Ireland. During the reign of Niall's son, St. Patrick came to convert Ireland.

papish—Catholic.

peat—A fuel of partially carbonized plants that long ago decayed underwater. Still the common fuel of Ireland and the Hebrides.

Peerie—Pict or fairy. Picts were mysterious folk who inhabited and ruled the Highlands and islands, successfully repelling the Romans. When the Scots crossed from Ireland, after some fighting, the Scots married into the royal house of the Picts and the Picts were absorbed.

planticrue—Round stone-walled planting bed for kale filled with sand and decaying seaweed.

pound—Money measurement, for example £2, 5s, 6d means two pounds, six shillings, and six pence. The *d* standing for pence comes from the Latin *denarius,* a small coin brought to Britain by the Romans.

Procurator fiscal—Public prosecutor, official who brought charges against an alleged offender.

quern—Grinding stone.

rascallion—Rascal.

retting—Soaking flax plants till stem and stalks rot and can be separated from fiber, which is spun into linen thread.

rowan—A tree of the rose family with bright red small berries.

Saint Columba—Irish missionary who came to the Hebridean island of Iona in 560 A.D., where he founded a monastery. From this former stronghold of Druids, he launched his efforts to convert the Picts and Scots (Irish) on the mainland. The monastery has been restored and most of the island is now administered by the National Trust for Scotland. Many Scottish, Irish, and Norwegian kings were buried here, including the Duncan slain by Macbeth.

Samhain—November 1, when burial mounds opened and spirits roamed; marked the beginning of winter and was the Celtish New Year.

sea campion—Low-growing white-petaled flower that grows in patches along the coast.

selkie—Seal. Some island families claim descent from seals.

shag—A large dark diving seabird, a sort of cormorant with a stout yellow hooked bill. Breeds in colonies on rocky cliffs.

shieling—Summer pastures where cattle and sheep were taken in the spring. On Lewis, the huts were stone, shaped like beehives. Young women often had charge of the herds and milked and made cheese and butter.

Sidhe—Fairies; People of Peace.

silverweed—Yellow-flowered plant with edible root.

skerry—Rock island.

Slainte!—A toast: To your health! Here's to you!

smoor—To prepare the hearth for the night, covering coals with ashes and removing large peats to save for next day.

sowans—Husks of oats with some grain left, steeped in water till liquid thickens and sours.

sheriff substitute—Deputy sheriff; a sheriff, in Scotland, had a great deal of authority and sat as judge on some cases.

spearwort—Lesser spearwort can be poisonous to cattle; used as rennet in making cheese.

stapag—Refreshing drink of meal mixed with cream, milk, or water.

stook—A stack, also to stack sheaves, usually eight of them, in a conical stack.

strathspey—Slow dance in quadruple meter, named for a locality where it was popular.

taraisgear—Iron tool for cutting peat.

tigh dubh—Black house; these thatched, double-walled houses of drystone or turf with a core of rubble or peat mold did turn black inside from peat smoke, but the name simply meant the walls were not laid up with the lime mortar used in constructing the more modern single-walled "tigh geal" or white house, which began to be built on Lewis about the time of this story.

tohbta—Broad wall ledge of a house used for making roof repairs and as a seat for people.

tolbooth—Town hall, which also served as jail.

tormentil—Low-growing flower with yellow petals; from roots and leaves a brew was made that helped women give birth with less pain.

Torquil the Viking—First of the MacLeod chieftains of Lewis and son of Leod or Liotolf, who was a chief in Lewis in the mid–twelfth century.

uisga-beatha—Water of life, whisky.

waulk—The process of cleansing woven wool fabric of oil and thickening it. The washed, wet material was stretched across a ribbed board or a frame of wattles, which could be set on a table or outside on the grass. Indoors, working in rhythm with their songs, four to fourteen women rubbed, pushed, and stretched the web back and forth across the board. Outside, they sat on straw bundles and worked the cloth with their bare feet. There were many waulking songs.

wheatear—Thrushlike bird of the moors with black wings, white rump, creamy pale brown breast.

whin—A spiny evergreen shrub with yellow flowers.